# JOSEPHINE
# COX
## Outcast

First published in Great Britain in 1991 by
Macdonald & Co. (Publishers) Ltd

First published in paperback in 1991 by
Futura Publications

This edition published 2015 by
HEADLINE PUBLISHING GROUP

2

Cataloguing in Publication Data is available from the British Library

ISBN 978 1 4722 3024 9

Typeset in Times by Avon DataSet Ltd, Bidford-on-Avon, Warwickshire

Printed and bound in the UK by Clays Ltd, St Ives plc

Headline's policy is to use papers that are natural, renewable and recyclable
products and made from wood grown in well-managed forests and other
controlled sources. The logging and manufacturing processes are expected to
conform to the environmental regulations of the country of origin.

HEADLINE PUBLISHING GROUP
An Hachette UK Company
338 Euston Road
London NW1 3BH

www.headline.co.uk
www.hachette.co.uk

The story of Josephine Cox is as extraordinary as anything in her novels. Born in a cotton-mill house in Blackburn, she was one of ten children. Her parents, she says, brought out the worst in each other, and life was full of tragedy and hardship – but not without love and laughter. At the age of sixteen, Josephine met and married 'a caring and wonderful man', and had two sons. When the boys started school, she decided to go to college and eventually gained a place at Cambridge University, though was unable to take this up as it would have meant living away from home. However, she did go into teaching, while at the same time helping to renovate the derelict council house that was their home, coping with the problems caused by her mother's unhappy home life – and writing her first full-length novel. Not surprisingly, she then won the 'Superwoman of Great Britain' Award, for which her family had secretly entered her, and this coincided with the acceptance of her novel for publication.

Josephine gave up teaching in order to write full time. She says 'I love writing, both recreating scenes and characters from my past, together with new storylines which mingle naturally with the old. I could never imagine a single day without writing, and it's been that way since as far back as I can remember.' Her previous novels of North Country life are all available from Headline and are immensely popular.

'Bestselling author Josephine Cox has penned another winner' *Bookshelf*

'Guaranteed to tug at the heartstrings of all hopeless romantics' *Sunday Post*

'Another masterpiece . . .' *Best*

'Compelling and very powerful' *Daily Express*

# *Dedication*

Like all mothers everywhere, I have children who instil in me constant feelings of inadequacy, frustration, and helplessness – not to mention anger and utter despair at times! But overriding all of these are the rewarding emotions such as joy, gratitude and shameless, bursting pride in their every achievement.

I thank God for giving my husband Ken and me two wonderful sons, Spencer and Wayne, who I pray will always face with strength and courage whatever obstacles life may put in their way.

This book is also for Elsie May, who befriended and loved me when I lost my own dear mother. Goodbye, Elsie. We'll never forget you, sweetheart.

# Foreword

My apologies to those historians who are familiar with convict transportation to Australia in the 1880s. Although I am aware that most of those transported to Western Australia were male, for the purpose of this story I have introduced female convicts, bearing in mind that countless numbers of women were made to suffer the same fate as their male counterparts when being transported to other coasts during earlier days.

Many of these wretches had committed crimes no more offensive than being hungry and ragged. There were many who were branded ruffians and murderers although they were innocent. But in the hearts of each and every one, there was always hope. There must always be hope.

Such hope, and the memories of those who had loved or betrayed her, kept alive Emma's belief that the day must come when she would seek out those who had loved her, and she would come face to face once again with her betrayers.

# Part One

## 1860
## Bad Blood

'– These wretches, who ne're lived, went on in nakedness, and sorely stung by wasps and hornets, which bedew'd their cheeks with blood, that, mixed with tears, dropp'd to their feet...'

*(Vision of) HELL, Dante*

# Chapter One

'Emma Grady, you're on the road to damnation! You have it in you to become a woman of the streets. A harlot! And as God is my judge, I will not have such a low creature under my roof!' Here the woman paused and a man's voice intervened, addressing the bowed head of the girl in low and trembling tones.

'Your good aunt sees in you what I have always feared and you will do well to heed her words. I believe the day must surely come when you sink beneath the evil bred in you – unless, by God's hand, you mend your ways. If you do not, you will be banished from this house! Disowned! Struck from our lives as though you never existed!' Caleb Crowther was a man of enormous physique – tall, with large ungainly bones. His movements were slow and methodical and his tone of voice – honed by his duties in the Law Courts – was deliberate and authoritative.

That same unenviable office yielded Caleb Crowther considerable status both within the sizeable community of Blackburn and throughout Lancashire, in whose courtrooms he regularly presided over the trials and tribulations of hapless law-breakers. There was many a petty thief or villain who had been unfortunate enough to have Caleb Crowther scowl down upon them. One condemning look from those piercing blue eyes was enough to render strong men weak. His features were altogether fearsome, close-together blue eyes above wide high cheekbones, a broad pale expanse of forehead, and a dark tangled mass of beard and whiskers. He could shrink the spirit of a man, but he could not diminish that of Emma Grady, his niece and ward, and such knowledge only served to infuriate him. As he drew himself up to continue his onslaught, a more gentle voice spoke out.

'Please Caleb, don't be too harsh on the child.' This feeble-looking man had risen from his sick-bed and struggled down to the drawing-room where he now defended Emma – this beloved girl who had been raised wrongly believing herself to be his daughter. The truth of her parentage would go with him to the grave – leaving only one other holding the grim shameful secret. 'She's young,' he continued, leaning against the door-jamb for support, 'the lass is only fifteen, and can't help her high spirits.'

'Fifteen or fifty, the devil takes no mind!' thundered Caleb Crowther as he turned to glare at the intruder. Then, upon a sly warning glance from his wife Agnes, he tempered his tone with a little gentleness as he further addressed the other man. 'Thadius, I know how great your affection is for your only child. But, think man! Think to the child's mother, passed on these many years. Have you forgotten the anguish she caused you? Don't you see her bad blood rising in this daughter of hers?' Seeing the other man momentarily falter beneath his cruel words, he stepped forward gesturing for his wife to do the same. When, instinctively, Emma also ventured to assist her papa, Caleb Crowther lifted his

4

hand, and in a forbidding voice told her, 'Stay where you are!' Then, returning his attention to Thadius Grady, he said, 'Agnes will see you safely back to your room.'

The tall dark-haired woman allowed her fragile brother to lean his weight against her arm. Without reassurance or word of comfort, she led him out of the drawing-room and into the spacious wood-panelled hallway. On painful steps, he went with her reluctantly. Their destination was a large room at the rear of the great house, a room from which, even though it was flooded with sunshine on a summer's day such as this, Thadius Grady would never again emerge a fit and healthy man. The lung disease which had struck him down was relentlessly draining away his life.

In the distance, he could still hear the condemning voice of his brother-in-law, Caleb Crowther, and his heart went out to that dear affectionate girl, made to suffer such a biting tongue. It grieved him that he could do nothing to ease her burden. It grieved him deeper still knowing that it was his own misguided weakness and blind trust that had placed both Emma and himself at the mercy of these two pompous devils.

For a long time after her darling papa had gone, Emma stood before her uncle, his torrent of accusations crushing her ears, but never bruising her heart; for she believed, most fervently, that of the two of them, *he* was the sinner. His wickedness was inherent in his dark thoughts, in that relentless voice which spewed them out, and in the way he brought his narrow penetrating eyes to bear on her. She wondered if, in the whole of his being, there had ever been one kind or loving thought, one gentle inclination or a breath of compassion for those less fortunate than himself. She believed not. Yet, Emma pitied him, for she had never seen his serious eyes light up with joy; never heard his laughter – only his condemnation that laughter was frivolous and a sure example of a worthless character; she had never seen him raise his face indulgently to the sun or pause for a moment to enjoy a blossom-scented breeze against his skin; not once had she witnessed his fingers reaching out to touch another person in genuine love or friendship. To her, all of these things were heaven-sent and because she treasured them – because it lifted her own spirits to laugh, to sing and to join hands with another of her own age while they ran freely beneath God's blue sky – she was condemned to stand before him like a sinner, while he poured scorn and damnation down on her head. But he would not make her feel like a sinner. Never! For, she was not, and, even if only her darling papa and her own heart believed that innocence, it was enough.

'You are a disgrace! Your brazen behaviour brings shame to this family, and I will not have it! Do you hear me, Emma Grady? I will *not* have it!' As he continued to glower at her, Emma felt the temptation to protest that she had not meant any harm nor seen any shame in her actions. But it would have been to no avail, for her uncle was not a man to listen nor was he a man who forgave easily. She would be punished, she was sure, just as she had been time and time again just for being young, for daring to laugh out loud and for being so shameful as to talk to those who had the misfortune of being 'born beneath' her. And the crime was all the more wretched if that unfortunate happened to be a boy, for then she was branded a hussy of the worst order!

'Out of my sight!' came the instruction now. 'Go to your

room at once. Your aunt and I must consider this latest incident and see what must be done!' That said, he turned from her holding his back stiff and straight. With the slightest curtsy, Emma took her leave from the room, thinking that he must have read her mind when his voice sailed after her, 'You will *not* call in on your papa. Go straight to your room . . . at once!' She might well have disobeyed him and stolen into her papa's room for a forbidden kiss, but, as she hurried down the hall, with her gaze anxiously intent on the narrow corridor, which led to her papa's room, the tall upright figure of Agnes emerged, her boots kicking out the hem of her long taffeta skirt and creating an impressive echo as they tapped the ceramic floor tiles. At once, she swept towards Emma, coming to a halt only when they were face to face.

'You're a great heartache to your papa,' accused the older woman, her hand resting elegantly against her skirt for a moment and her dark eyes riveted to the strong youthful features. 'You'll be the death of him yet – mark my words!' If she expected the girl before her to flinch and cower in the wake of such vicious taunts, Agnes Crowther was disappointed. For when Emma brought her gaze to rest on that overbearing countenance, it was not fear or guilt that was reflected in her warm animated eyes, but strength – the kind of challenging strength which only served to infuriate those who tried to belittle her. She looked a moment longer at that stiff and forbidding figure, at the staunch manly face and the dark hair coiled like a snake above each ear. She noted the two most impressive characteristics of her papa's sour-faced sister: the manner in which she held her head back, as though something distasteful had just presented itself to her, causing her to look down her nose in a most uncomfortable fashion; and her peculiar habit of joining her hands together and pressing them close to her breast as if she were praying.

As Emma momentarily regarded the woman before her, Agnes simultaneously contemplated her. She actively disliked this blatantly defiant child of her own kith and kin, for the girl possessed such a rebellious spirit, was far too imaginative, too talented and too temptingly attractive and there was too much of a blossoming woman in the gentle round curves of her small winsome figure. Those exquisite oviform eyes, which always seemed to be secretly smiling, were a shade too grey, too striking and too bold, and her rich thick hair was too velvety, and abounding with deep, undisciplined waves.

Agnes Crowther found herself mentally comparing the attributes of this wayward girl to those of her own non-descript and friendless daughter, Martha. A tide of jealousy surged within her, and her tongue lashed out all the sharper to disguise her bitter feelings. 'Unless you need to feel the sting of my cane against your knuckles, you will remove that insolent expression from your face this instant.' She trembled to control her voice.

Painfully aware that they were not very far from her papa's room, Emma slowly lowered her gaze. The figure before her gave a long audible shudder, followed by the curt enquiry, 'I take it you have been ordered to your room, while your uncle and I decide on a suitable punishment?' She waited for Emma's nod. Upon its receipt, she issued the impatient instruction, 'You may go. Do *not* leave your room until you are sent for!' Agnes Crowther stood her ground, while her scornful eyes watched the girl move out of sight.

At the top of the staircase Emma turned left, passing beneath the endless array of impressive portraits depicting Caleb Crowther's ancestors. Each wore the same arrogant smile; each held a stance that spoke of self-importance; and each was encased in elaborate and magnificent golden frames of immense proportion. Emma recalled how, on the day of her arrival in this grand house some twelve long months before, there had been no portraits; only grey spaces on the wall, where they had once hung. Soon afterwards, they had reappeared – no doubt having been purchased back from the person who had secured them against a debt. But, these portraits – re-hung amid great fuss and ceremony – did *not* impress Emma. 'Sour-faced and comical,' she called them. Emma was not unaware of the circumstances under which her papa had brought her to this house for she had overheard the servants discussing it and she was of the same opinion as them – that her papa had been used. Like all of God's creatures he had a weak and vulnerable flaw in his character – his was that he could never see the greed in others. But this just caused Emma to love him even more. She knew deep in her heart that whatever he had done – however disastrous the consequences might be – he had done it for her with the best intentions and fondest love. Before his pained and watchful eyes, she was always careful to make him believe she was happy in this awful house, when, if the truth were to be told, she was far more content out of it. She would go on pretending for as long as necessary, for Emma didn't intend to be the cause of her papa leaving this world a sadder man.

When Agnes Crowther was satisfied that her niece was safely on her way, she resumed her steps. On entering the drawing-room she immediately crossed to the fireplace where, with a short impatient tug on the bell-pull, she summoned a maid. Presently a small round female of about forty years appeared. She was bedecked in dark attire, save for the frilly white cap resting on top of her greying brown hair and a little collar of the same sparkling white, fastened loosely at her neck.

'Yes, ma'am?' spoke the homely little figure, as it bent at the knee and brought its enquiring brown eyes to bear on the lady of the house.

'Miss Grady is confined to her room. She is to be denied all meals until dinner tomorrow evening.' When the eyes looking upon her grew wide with surprise, Agnes Crowther took a small step forward and, with her head high and her hands folded in that familiar pose of prayer, she added in an impatient voice, 'Do I make myself clear?'

'Very well, ma'am.'

'Good! . . . You may go.' She gave an impatient wave of her hand and was obviously pleased to see the figure depart in great haste. She would not have felt so satisfied if she had witnessed the scene which took place below stairs on the housekeeper's return. Mrs Manfred relayed the mistress's instructions, which were at once greeted by a barrage of protest.

'T'aint fair!' declared Amy, the little dark-haired scullery maid who, despite Mrs Manfred's efforts to cultivate her in knowing her place in the hierarchy of a gentleman's house, had never acquired the instinct to keep certain opinions to herself. 'Them two's allus picking on poor Miss Grady.'

'Hey!' remonstrated Cook, a large and squashy, domineering woman, with a rolled halo of iron-grey hair and bright hazel eyes which, at this very moment, were sending warning signals to the pouting Amy. 'You'd do better not to wag that busy little tongue of yours, my girl. If the master should set foot in that door and catch you being disrespectful, you'd be out on the streets and begging fer yer living.' Here, Mrs Manfred intervened.

'Amy, isn't it time you began preparing the vegetables for dinner? . . . Go on, child!' she urged when the girl showed hesitation. The look on the housekeeper's face told the young maid that she'd gone as far as was wise.

'All right . . . I'm going!' she declared indignantly.

When the scullery door was closed, it was Cook who spoke first, saying in hushed tones as she poured herself and Mrs Manfred a small measure of good dark port, 'That one's a cheeky little bugger! But the lass is right all the same. Poor Miss Grady does seem allus to be in their bad books.' Pointing a thumb upwards and rolling her eyes towards the ceiling, she carefully lowered herself into a stout chair. Laying her chubby arms across the pine table-top, she began rolling the glass of port between her hands to warm it. 'The Lord only knows what'll become of Miss Grady when Mr Grady goes.' She shook her head slowly from side to side and, lowering her voice, she leaned forward to face the housekeeper who was now seated at the opposite side of the table. 'They'll have a free hand ter to do as they likes then, won't they, eh?' By the fearful look in her bright wide eyes, and the quick manner in which she threw a great gulp of port into her mouth, it was clear that the thought horrified her.

Not being one to readily participate in gossip below stairs, the housekeeper sat quietly, taking intermittent dainty and careful sips from the port glass, all the while thoughtful, her eyes downcast and with a deeply troubled look in them. She had no liking for the master and mistress. Indeed, if the truth were to be told, she positively disliked them. It was extremely difficult for her to regard them as her employers, for it was Mr Grady who had taken her on as housekeeper when he had resided in the smart area of Blackburn, up by Corporation Park. Five years she'd been with him and Miss Grady, five satisfying and happy years during which she had been much more than just housekeeper. She'd grown close to Miss Grady, caring for her affectionately because the child had no mother to love her – Mrs Grady having lost her life some years before in scandalous and unfortunate circum-stances best forgotten. But what a sweet darling girl Miss Grady was. A little hot-headed and wayward at times, maybe, but that was all part of her charm. For all her obstinacy and exuberance she was a caring creature, gentle of spirit and warm of heart; it grieved Mrs Manfred to see how desperately unhappy the girl had become. The only light in her life was her father – and he was fading fast. Mrs Manfred wondered why it was that the good Lord had seen fit to weaken and cripple such a good man – so much so that, in appointing his sister and her husband as both executors of his affairs and wards to his only child, his judgment had been severely impaired.

'I've allus said what a wrench that must have been fer you to come and bide in this house. One minute living in town, and the next, being fotched ter the countryside of outer Breckleton, at the beck and call of them two.' Here, Cook jerked a thumb upwards again. 'They may *act* proud and superior,' she went on, 'but I'm telling yer, Mrs Manfred,

I've said it afore and I'll say it again, if it hadn't been fer Mr Grady and his money, well, them two would be no more than beggers! Y'remember the state o' this place when yer all arrived? I were the only one left ter mek the best of an impossible job. All the silver gone. Money owed everywhere. Y'know, m'dear, fer all ye've been here over a year now, there's *still* things I could tell yer. Things ter shame the pair of 'em!'

'Excuse me. I must go.' Mrs Manfred had no wish to hear yet again how Caleb Crowther was a womanizer and a gambler who had squandered the fortune his father had left him – a fortune built up in the City through sound business sense, for it was not his rector's pittance that had lined Crowther senior's pockets. Nor did she care for another long and detailed account of how Agnes Crowther was a woman of disgracefully extravagant tastes, having a most unhealthy appetite for expensive jewellery and fine parties. She had heard it all before – and it had sickened her.

Thadius Grady had worked ceaselessly to build up his holdings in the cotton mills hereabouts – an ailing heritage he'd received from his father but one which now, thanks to his persistent efforts, was a thriving industry. How unfortunate that the two mills were to be entrusted to the Crowthers.

There was one other viper in this nest, and that was Martha Crowther. She was the same age as Miss Grady, but as different in character from her as chalk from cheese. Mrs Manfred for one would not be sorry to see that spoilt young madam shortly depart for the grand expensive school for ladies somewhere down south. Good riddance to her, that's what *she* said!

\* \* \*

'I've been such a fool! Such a blind, stupid fool!' Thadius Grady looked up, his pale eyes glittering with tears. 'I've betrayed her . . . done her a terrible wrong that can't be put right. It's too late . . . too late, don't you see, Mrs Manfred?' As he struggled to pull himself upright in the bed, the effort proved to be too much and, after a severe bout of coughing, he allowed Mrs Manfred to make him more comfortable. 'I've let her down,' he murmured, as though to himself. 'I've let my darling daughter down!'

'No . . . no.' Mrs Manfred tucked the bedclothes about him for, despite this being a warm summer's day, she could see him visibly shivering. 'You did what you thought was best for the child. You always have.'

'But I've turned it all over to them, don't you see? There was no one else and Mrs Crowther is my sister after all. Half the inheritance would have been hers anyway if only she hadn't angered Father with her choice of husband.' His voice grew quieter, and he continued in a more intimate tone, as though he was afraid they might be overheard, 'There were *other* reasons also why I entrusted my daughter to Caleb Crowther . . . and to his wife.' His voice strengthened, as he pleaded, 'Oh, Mrs Manfred, if only they would show more understanding towards her, more tolerance. Will she be all right when I'm gone? Oh, I fear so!'

Mrs Manfred smiled encouragingly. 'Don't you fret now, Mr Grady,' she told him in a firm voice. 'Your daughter is of strong character and well you know it. She'll be fine . . . just fine.' But however much she wished that to be so, there was little belief of it in her heart and even less conviction in her voice.

A silence followed. Then, suddenly, Thadius Grady let

14

out a great heart-rending sigh, followed by the murmured question, 'What date is it?'

'Why, it's Sunday, August 16th.'

'What year?'

'Bless you, Mr Grady . . . it's the year of our Lord 1860.'

'Almost a year to the day we came to this house . . . you, me and Miss Grady. Oh, dear God! Would that I were strong again!'

There were tears in Mrs Manfred's eyes as she comforted him. 'Ssh now.' She was tempted to say how he *would* be strong again, but it was Sunday and such lies would be tantamount to blasphemy. Instead, she went to a drawer in the dark elaborately-carved sideboard, and took from it a bottle of medicine and a spoon. Returning to the big brass bed, she poured a measure of the brown liquid into the spoon, stood the bottle on the small circular table by the bed, and then eased one hand beneath Thadius Grady's thin bony neck, while with the other, she touched the spoon against the blueness of his lips. 'Come on now,' she coaxed him, 'sip it down.' That done, she crossed to the long casement window where she gently pulled the heavy tapestry curtains part-way together to shut out the bright sunlight. She took a final glance at the now-sleeping figure, before, on tiptoe, she left the room.

A few moments later, Mrs Manfred hurried along the dark corridor which led from Thadius Grady's room, and into the brighter hall. From there she climbed the broad impressive staircase, hurriedly, before peering eyes might see her and sharp tongues find questions to put to her.

Meanwhile, Emma gazed out of the window, her trim figure leaning against the window-frame, her small fingers playing with the curtain-tassel and with a pitifully forlorn expression on her face. Her thoughts wandered: first they were downstairs with her papa, then they were back at their old home in Blackburn town where, from the window of her bedroom she could see the rolling splendour of Corporation Park. How could she ever forget that wonderful day in October 1857, less than three years ago. It was her thirteenth birthday – the very same day on which Corporation Park was opened. What memories! The mayor and other dignitaries dressed up in the regalia of office and thousands of people from all over the borough assembled to see the park opened. After the opening ceremony, they all surged through the arcuated gateways, some of the women wearing clogs and shawls, others dressed in finer fashion and the men sporting an assortment of flat cloth caps and tall black hats. Oh, the excitement of it all!

Emma missed the old house, and her nostalgia was heightened by the fact that, in those early days, her papa had been well – always laughing and ready to play games with her, always enterprising at his work and filled with enthusiasm.

Making a weary little sigh, Emma leaned forward into the window, her attention drawn by the sight of a threshing machine in a nearby field. For a moment she was enthralled by it, her eager gaze following its trail of steam as it got underway. Such things had always held a fascination for Emma, and it was that same curiosity which had caused all the terrible fuss today – innocent though the little adventure had started out.

Now her thoughts came back to her papa and a wave of guilt swept over her. 'Oh, Papa!' she murmured, a tremble in her voice. 'I'm sorry.'

So engrossed in her thoughts was she that, when Mrs Manfred's voice murmured in her ear, 'Will you never learn, Miss Grady!' she gave a start, before realizing who it was, and threw herself into the little woman's arms.

'Did you see him, Manny?' she asked, addressing the woman by a familiar nickname. 'It was *my* fault that he got up from his bed. Oh, Manny, he looks so desperately ill – and I can't go to him! They won't *let* me go to him!' She was crying bitterly now, more from anger than from sorrow.

'I know, child . . . I know.' Mrs Manfred took Emma towards the settle, where she gently eased her away, to hold her at arm's length. 'Oh, child . . . child! What are we going to do with you? What on earth possessed you to go wandering away over the meadows? And then, to hob-nob with the river-people?' She raised her eyebrows sharply and shook her head from side to side as she chastised in a lower voice, 'You know how your Uncle Caleb – yes, and your papa – dislike those people!' She did not explain how Thadius Grady's animosity towards the river-folk had come about, how it had been common talk for some fifteen years back when Emma had been no more than a wee bairn in arms. She hoped Emma would never learn how her mama had taken one of the river-men for a lover, and how the cruel gossip had labelled Mrs Grady a 'loose and shameless woman' who thought so little of her husband and tiny daughter that she could blatantly 'flaunt herself at other men'. It was during one of her illicit visits to her lover's arms that there had been a terrible event which had had such tragic and far-reaching consequences.

'But *why* does he dislike the river-people so much, Manny? Why?'

'It isn't for you, nor me, to ask the reason. All you need to do is to respect his wishes. It's a good thing for you, my girl, that he thought fit to see this morning's escapade as an impulsive prank!' Mrs Manfred's tone of voice betrayed her absolute disapproval of Emma's behaviour.

'Oh, Manny, are you so shocked? Are you so ashamed of me?' Emma asked. What she had done must have been dreadful or Manny wouldn't have chided her like that. She had no business even talking to the river-people knowing how her papa felt towards them. Emma's heart shrank within her. Why was she always so disobedient?

'I have to say I *am* shocked, Miss Grady, though, after knowing you this long while, perhaps I shouldn't be. Oh, but to be found with a young bargee, boldly laughing together on the banks of the canal! You, with your bare legs dangling in the water and he stripped naked to the waist!' Mrs Manfred's expression reflected the utmost despair. 'But worse! Oh, my dear, much, much worse . . . today is the Sabbath! And you straight from church!'

Emma fully realized that it *was* a bad thing she had done, but, at the time, she hadn't seen it like that at all. After the stuffy confines of the church, the sun had struck warm against her face, the breeze had moved the fields of grass so that they looked like a rippling sea of green, and, drawn further and further into nature's splendid beauty, she'd wandered away from the familiar footpath, towards the cool flowing canal, where the colourful barges bobbed about on the water and the sound of laughter emanated from every one. Laughter of the kind she had not heard in such a long while; laughter which infected and brightened her heart with rare happiness; laughter which reminded her of a different world than the one which now held her securely bound and caged. In that special moment, she had felt unfettered; and when she had seen that dark head skimming the surface of the water, something deep within her had cried out to be free also. 'I did it without thinking, Manny,' she said now, although she had given no such explanation to her uncle. She had felt too much anger at how he had embedded his walking-stick in the young bargee's back again and again until the flesh split open and the blood covered his shoulders like a mantle. Emma was convinced that if the men from the barges hadn't heard her screaming and dashed out to pull the young man safely away, Caleb Crowther would have beaten every last breath from his body. The enraged barge-men might have done the very same to Caleb Crowther had it not been for the intervention of the men from the village, together with Caleb Crowther's threat to bring the authorities down on every man-jack of the river-people.

'Have you no idea of the trouble you caused, child? Frightening ordinary god-fearing villagers who answered the alarm that you were missing! You said *nothing*, child! . . . You told *no-one* of your intention to wander away from the path between the church and home!' Mrs Manfred's voice was unusually harsh, but, on seeing Emma's eyes brim with tears and her auburn head fall in despair, she wrapped her two arms around the girl's shoulders and drew her into a loving embrace. 'You're only a child,' she murmured. 'I know you meant no harm and thank the Lord you came to none!' Then, she gave Emma a little shake, saying, 'But soon, you won't be a child. You'll be a woman . . . in a few months, when you're sixteen. When your papa's taken from us, you'll find the need to be more disciplined of yourself, for, there'll be no allowances made. Not any more!' She eased Emma away from her and, still gripping the girl by the shoulders, she levelled an anxious gaze at those sorely troubled eyes. 'Miss Grady . . . do you understand what I'm saying?' she demanded in a serious voice.

'Yes, Manny,' Emma murmured, 'please don't worry about me. When it's time . . . when Papa has to leave me at last, I *will* be strong! I promise I will, for his sake. And I really will try so very hard not to give them cause to punish me.' She gave a sideways glance towards the door and, as she did so, she was startled to see the grim face of her aunt. The little cry that escaped Emma's throat alerted Mrs Manfred, who swiftly rose to her feet and took a step forward.

'Oh, Madam! I was just explaining to Miss Grady that she is forbidden all meals until tomorrow evening!' Her voice was somewhat shaky, and beneath Agnes Crowther's dark accusing eyes Mrs Manfred's homely features were suffused in a dark pink flush. 'Excuse me, Ma'am,' she added, 'I will be about my business, if I may.' She hesitated to move, although she was now eager to be gone since she felt most uncomfortable in Agnes Crowther's company.

'Pray do that, Mrs Manfred . . . *without delay*!' Agnes Crowther stood for a moment longer, barring the doorway, with her head held high and tilted back and her hands clasped tight at her breast in that familiar and peculiar posture. Then, she stepped aside and waved Mrs Manfred out of the room, saying in a sour voice, 'Be careful not to abuse your position in this household. One master's choice is not necessarily another's!'

The threat was veiled, but to Emma, who was now on her feet and waiting to be addressed, there was no mistaking its meaning. Manny had come to this house with her and her papa when his health had deteriorated so much that he had felt obliged to accept his sister's seemingly generous offer that he be cared for at Breckleton House. Later, when all legal documents were signed and sealed – transferring all holdings and business interests into the trusteeship of Agnes and Caleb, and affording them a just remuneration for their troubles – a number of conditions were incorporated. One of these was that, on Thadius Grady's demise, his daughter was to be brought up a Christian and afforded every opportunity to be made aware 'in matters of business'. On the occasion of her marriage – or on her twenty-first birthday, whichever came first – Emma was to receive the sum of six thousand pounds. When she reached the age of twenty-five, all remaining assets would be released to her. These presently amounted to the two working mills and the handsome sum of five thousand pounds, which represented working capital together with a sum acquired from the sale of the house in Blackburn. This figure would have been considerably more, but excess cash was rarely accumulated in the course of maintaining the mills – the on-going costs and immediate necessities of production saw to that. It was on heeding his doctor's warning to 'make final preparations', that Thadius Grady had adopted a much more careful and frugal approach to expenditure, his uppermost intention being to leave his beloved Emma duly cared for.

To this end, he had made a further stipulation that Mrs Manfred be retained by his sister Agnes as housekeeper at Breckleton House. Agnes Crowther had made no objection, being well aware of both her own and her daughter's short-comings in this area. Furthermore, she had a high regard for

Mrs Manfred's talents as a housekeeper – even though she took a very dim view of 'the woman's high-handed attitude to her betters!'

Emma's papa had given over to his sister and her husband absolute authority, and guardianship, with regards to all matters – including that of Emma's upbringing. It was as bearer of such responsibility that Agnes Crowther now addressed the watchful Emma.

'Your uncle and I have discussed the matter of your future and have come to a decision.' Her features moved although it was hard to distinguish whether the movement represented sneer or smile, as she half turned towards the door. 'Your papa will be spared the details, at least until he has recovered from the consequences of your sinful behaviour this day.' That said, she brought down one of her hands to pluck at her skirt, looked down on Emma along the length of her nose and, with a small hissing noise emanating through her small straight teeth, she swung around and departed, leaving the door wide open.

Emma closed the door and returned to her place at the window, where she scanned the surrounding fields reminiscently. It was impossible to see the canal from here because it wound away behind the spinney, and from there it veered out of sight altogether. But, in her mind, she could still see the handsome young barge-man. He was tall and deeply tanned. She hadn't seen him swimming in the water until after she had stripped off her shoes and stockings so that she could feel the cool wet splashes against her bare legs. When he rose to climb out of the water, his naked muscles golden and glistening wet, and his shoulder-length hair, wet and shimmering blue-black like a raven's wing, he looked like a young god. For a startling moment he had taken her breath away. But how quickly he'd made her feel at ease, with his black laughing eyes and infectious smile. He had a low gentle voice, which trembled slightly when he spoke and filled her heart with joy when it was raised in laughter. They had laughed at simple things of beauty and wonder – the squirrel that peeped at them from the spinney and would not be persuaded to come closer; the fish skilfully swimming just below the surface of the water, now and then blowing bubbles at them; and the mallard which played hide and seek in and out of the willow branches that dipped deep into the water.

Emma thought long and hard about the young bargee, and her heart beat faster as it had done when they had sat close together on the warm grass, and a ripple of deep pleasure surged through her. She prayed he had not been too badly injured by her uncle's vicious attack. She hoped that, one day, they might meet again. Emma recalled his name, Marlow – such an arresting name. Emma knew she would not forget it.

Not far from where Emma gazed out of the window at Breckleton House, the sun beat down on the waters of the canal as it lapped and splashed against the colourful barge. The other barges had long since gone to ferry their cargoes of coal and cotton up and down the Leeds and Liverpool waterways. Presently, the Tanner barge would follow in their wake. But, first of all, there was an unpleasant task to be done.

Inside the cosy living-area of the moored barge, Marlow Tanner winced as the raw salt was rubbed into the open gashes across his back. In his dark eyes there was pain – but it was not simply pain of a physical kind, for the life of a bargee was hard and demanding and a man was used to the pain inflicted on his body. No, Marlow Tanner's pain emanated from his heart. It came from the all-too-brief memory of a young girl with laughing eyes and sun-burnished hair, a girl whose alluring smile had touched something deep within him; a girl who would never be for the likes of him, for she was of a gentler, more privileged stock. His instincts warned him that this girl, whom he knew to be called Emma, would only bring a heap of trouble down on his head; but he could not deny the murmurings of his heart which told him of his love for her. When the cane was brought down on his back, again and again, it was not the impact of it tearing into his bare flesh that hurt him most, but rather the helpless, compassionate look in her tearful eyes. Now, not for the first time since meeting her, Marlow wondered whether he would ever see this exquisite young girl again.

'Still dreamin' o' the lass, are ye?' Sally Tanner was barely past thirty, but, with her thin, wispy fair hair, coarse sun-weathered skin and long-lasting friendship with the beer-jug, she looked some ten years older. Her violet eyes twinkled merrily as she threw back her head, opened her cavernous, almost toothless mouth and gave out a raucous belly-laugh. 'Bugger me if I ain't never seen a lad o' sixteen look so cow-eyed an' smitten!' she roared, leaning forward once again to slap more salt into the wounds.

'*Seventeen* . . . the week after next!' her brother indignantly reminded her. Then he fell into a deep and thoughtful mood. Sal was right. He *was* smitten! It had never been this way with other lasses, for they had not touched him so deep inside; they had never lasted in his heart for more than the passing of a day or a week. The image of this girl, Emma, would not leave him. Nor did he want it to – whatever the consequences.

# Chapter Two

'No, Papa!' Emma reeled back from the bed as though she had been slapped in the face. 'Uncle Caleb could never take your place. *Never!*' The horror of such a prospect was painfully apparent on her face – the colour had completely drained from it and her eyes, which now stared disbelievingly at her papa, were totally panic-stricken. 'Caleb Crowther! Do you really think I could ever look on him as my p-a-p-a-?' Emma's pretty mouth shaped the final word as though the taste of it on her tongue was bitterness itself.

'Emma, please hear me out.' Thadius Grady was sorely pained to see that tears had sprung to her eyes. His heart ached for her and he knew now that he couldn't tell her what weighed most heavy in his heart. Hour after hour he had lain in this bed, his frail body wasting, but his mind active with thoughts of his darling Emma – thoughts which tormented his every waking moment, as he feverishly wrestled with his conscience. At long last, after all these years, he had found it within himself to forgive Emma's mama, who had been taken from them by her own thoughtless actions and their cruel consequences. He had made his peace with God and he had arranged as best he could that Emma be taken care of when he was gone. He had thought this was enough and had continued to carry the other matter which tormented him so, silently close to his heart, believing this to be for the best. But now, the closer he came to the Lord, the heavier the burden he and Caleb Crowther had kept between them became. Their secret was a part of the past which they had vowed never to divulge to another soul. It had all happened so long ago, yet, at times, when the memories played havoc with him, it seemed like only yesterday.

Only a few moments ago, he had been ready to confess everything to Emma. But his courage had failed him. He couldn't do it. Instead, he reached his tired hand out and wrapped it about Emma's fingers. 'Sit beside me, child,' he murmured. As she did, she leaned forward to stroke his forehead with her free hand.

'I'm sorry, Papa,' she said with a loving smile, 'but I couldn't ever do what you're asking.'

'I know that now,' he replied, his soft eyes searching her face, as though he might find in it the strength to leave her behind in this merciless world, for it took more strength to die than it did to live.

'I know you mean well, Papa, and I love you for it,' she told him, fondly lifting his hand and touching it against her face, 'and I admit that Aunt Agnes and Uncle Caleb are sorely tried by my behaviour at times. They do their best to cope with my wilful ways. But . . . look upon Caleb Crowther as my papa?' She shook her head from side to side. 'I'd as soon live in the workhouse!' There was no smile on her face as she said it, no mischievous twinkle in those serious grey eyes and Thadius now realized, to have made such a comment about an institution which struck dread in folks' hearts, indicated just how strongly Emma felt.

Thadius came as close as he dared to the truth when he told her, 'Caleb will be *like* your papa in that he will control your heritage. He will command your obedience and respect – on *my* explicit wishes, you understand. He will advise and guide you. You must trust his decisions, Emma, for in all truth he has good reason to see you prosper.' He hoped in his heart that Emma would bring out whatever good there was in his brother-in-law. He had to believe that there was some affection in Caleb Crowther towards Emma – such a thing would only be natural after all, would it not? Yet, the man was often unduly harsh and many had been the time of late when Thadius had bitterly regretted having signed over so much power and authority to Caleb Crowther; yet, Thadius had now found it in his heart to forgive Caleb, and he realized that there was no one else to care for Emma, no one with such good reason to hold dear her welfare than his sister's husband. That Caleb meant well and would cause Emma no harm had been Thadius's fervent belief. Now, it was not *quite* so fervent, but he clung to it nevertheless – he must, or his soul would find no eternal rest. 'He isn't a bad man, Emma – nor do I think him totally without compassion. But, please, try not to rile him nor to incur your aunt's wrath, for she sees in you your mama's failings.'

With this he touched upon a great longing in Emma's heart – a deep need to know more about her mama. She had long believed there were things her papa deliberately kept from her. Caleb Crowther's recent remarks intimating that Thadius's wife, Mary, had been a woman of 'bad blood' and that Emma showed signs of having inherited the same blood, had both hurt and intrigued Emma. Now, in a soft, persuasive voice she dared to ask, 'Will you tell me about my mama?' When her papa's response was to gaze on her with saddened eyes, which seemed to look far beyond her, into the distant past, Emma ventured, 'Please, Papa . . . you've told me *nothing* of her. All I know is that her name was Mary . . . she was very beautiful and was lost in some unfortunate accident. Would it pain you so to talk to me about her?' She pleaded with such hope and passion that on seeing it, Thadius was deeply moved.

'Oh, Emma!' There was a depth of anguish in his voice as, lifting his hand to touch her face, he went on, 'Your Uncle Caleb meant nothing by his thoughtless remarks . . . please believe that. There is no "bad blood" in you, my darling. There never could be. You're everything I hold dear, and that couldn't be if you were not the good, loyal creature you are. Your mama . . . well, she was never meant to be tied to one man, and *that* is the only regret I have about her – the only one!'

'You mean, she left you?' Emma was horrified that anyone could leave her papa. 'She left you for another man?'

'No, Emma. Your mama did not leave me. Like you, she was so full of life . . . always searching for some adventure or other. There is nothing "bad" in that. It was just that I was so very different – I was content to live the quiet life. I suppose that, compared to her, I was very serious.' He gave a small laugh. 'Not much fun at all. Also, in the early days, there was very little money, and things were not always easy.'

'You loved her very much, didn't you, Papa?' Emma hated herself for having brought up such a painful subject, but it was so important to her to find out more about her mama.

'I *adored* her!' Thadius Grady ran his outstretched hand over his face, as though, in so doing, he might be touching his beautiful wife, now so long gone. 'It was a terrible thing, Emma. Your mama was . . . visiting friends, along the canal. Nobody really knows what happened because those who could have told it all made good their escape immediately afterwards. Your mama was caught up in some terrible violence – and she never came home again.' Suddenly it was all too much for Thadius. As though in a frenzy, he grabbed Emma by the shoulders. 'The barge people are little more than wild ruffians, Emma! They're a law unto themselves . . . a bad lot! I want you to promise me that you'll steer clear of them. Will you do that, Emma? For me . . . will you give me your word?'

Emma gave it gladly, for she had never seen her papa so frantic. But, in that same moment she saw something in his eyes she had not seen before: he was keeping something back, she was certain and she was sorely tempted to press him further. But he was deeply distressed and she couldn't bear to see him grieved further. The river-people had taken the woman he loved, and Thadius Grady hated them for it! Emma knew that he was not a man to hate without good reason, and knowing this only served to make the promise he demanded from her all the more profound.

'I've caused you a great deal of anguish as well, haven't I, Papa?' Emma wished she was of the same placid, submissive character as her cousin, Martha. *She* was so obedient, so ladylike, and Emma had never known her to do *anything* on impulse. She said as much to her papa now. In answer, he sighed softly and enveloped her face with a look of love. 'Oh, but your cousin will be shrivelled and old before her time, my darling. There is little joy or laughter in her soul. And you . . . you must *never* wish to be anything other than what you are. You have the very essence of life in you . . . a vitality that shines from your eyes and lights up the space around you!' He paused and squeezed her fingers in his own. 'But try to curb your impulses, just a little, eh? Show your aunt and uncle that you *can* be responsible.'

At this point, the door opened and in bustled the tall commanding figure of Agnes Crowther. Sweeping alongside the huge ornate dresser, she brought herself to the opposite side of the big brass bed where, adopting that familiar and unsettling posture, she raised her brows and, holding her head stiffly, she lowered her eyes to look upon the prostrate figure in the bed. 'You are comfortable, are you not, Thadius?' A great weariness took hold of him and, as he half nodded his head and closed his eyes, she turned her attention to Emma. 'Leave your papa now, child. Let him rest.' Her voice was severe and totally without warmth.

Easing her hand from his, Emma bent forward to place a gentle kiss on her papa's tightly closed lips. 'Don't worry so, Papa,' she murmured in his ear. 'I promise I *will* be good, and I'll stay away from the river-people. I'll *never* let you down again!' It was a promise given in love, written on her heart with honour, and, one which would cost Emma dearly.

Some twenty minutes later, at eight a.m., the entire household was assembled in the dining-room, for daily prayers. This morning, Emma would not be promptly dismissed to her room afterwards, as she had been yesterday, since today was Tuesday and her spell of banishment was over. She had been given permission to attend dinner the evening before, but, not wanting the company of the Crowther family, she had pleaded 'a feeling of nausea' and was consequently excused. She had now been without food for almost forty-eight hours – save for the buttered muffin secretly sent to her yesterday lunchtime by the ever-faithful Mrs Manfred. Thus, it was not surprising when, during a long and frightful passage read from the Bible by Caleb Crowther, Emma's stomach behaved in the most disobedient manner – gurgling and growling with such enthusiasm that it caused the reading of the passage to be temporarily suspended. Caleb Crowther positively glowered at her from beneath dark angry brows.

'Beg your pardon,' she murmured apologetically, where-upon, from the rear of the room where the maids were kneeling in their rustling starched print dresses, came the sound of muffled sniggering. This brought a caustic, shrivelling glance from Agnes Crowther and a look of sheer horror from her offspring, Martha, who, up until now had been sitting with her large brown head most piously bowed, depicting the absolute example of solemn and reverent devoutness. Now, with her prayers so rudely interrupted, she began a series of tutting noises, which only appeared to add to the confusion.

Plunged now into a deep and dour mood, Caleb Crowther declared in sombre voice, 'We shall proceed!' He resumed reading from the great book in trembling and resonant tones. Emma bowed her head and folded her hands obediently, but try as she might, she could not keep her attention on the proceedings. Her heart and her thoughts were down the corridor, in that large sunny room at the rear of the house, where the window lent a lovely view of the curved and spectacular lawns which ran right down to the brook and were interspersed with ancient oak trees and all manner of shrubs and greenery. Emma pictured herself and her papa seated by the window: he propped up in the wicker chair, the high-domed back of which gave support to his wasting limbs; and she perched on the window-seat with her legs tucked beneath her and her great love for her papa spilling over in her excited chatter. How she enjoyed bringing a smile to his face and how wonderful it would be if now and then he would give a small delighted chuckle. Suddenly, Emma found herself praying, confiding in God her innermost fears. 'Please don't let Papa suffer too much,' she asked, 'for he is such a good man.'

Meanwhile, Martha Crowther walked sedately across to the splendid piano which was beside the huge open fireplace, and, with much ceremony, she seated herself on the carved stool of the floral-tapestry seat. She immediately began fussing with the voluminous, cream-coloured, taffeta skirt which rubbed and squeaked as she moved about. Firstly she clutched two handfuls on either side and spread the material out with great deliberation, until it was most admirably draped either side of the stool. Then she began patting and smoothing it, with her ample figure threatening to pop open the seams of her tight-fitting bodice at any moment. When it seemed like she might finally be ready, she paused to bestow a complacent smile on one and all. Though the smile worked her mouth and caused her head to incline slightly, and in so doing highlighting the fact that one of her nostrils was somewhat larger than the other, her small speckley brown eyes remained hard and glittering like pebbles on a beach. As they moved with precision over the sea of heads, they met Emma's warm gaze and, for a brief moment, they were held reluctantly mesmerized until, alerted by the impatient cough of her father, she swung them stiffly away to examine the sheet of music on the piano-stand. She placed her stubby fingers in the correct position on the keyboard, ready to begin the morning hymn. In anticipation of the first note, everyone simultaneously took a deep breath, but were forced to let it out again as Martha Crowther lifted her two hands to ensure that the tight spirals of brown hair, which sat priggishly above each ear, were satisfactorily secure. This was her moment – the moment when the plain, otherwise untalented, daughter of Caleb and Agnes Crowther considered herself to be the star of the stage. As always, she intended to savour every second of it. Unfortunately, she had chosen the wrong occasion to play prima donna, for her papa was not in the mood to be entertained.

'We will forgo the hymn this morning,' he declared, slamming shut his prayer-book. 'Go about your business,' he instructed the servants, who were looking at each other with mouths aghast. As for his wife and daughter, they appeared extremely exasperated: the latter rose from the piano and, pausing only to ask that she may be excused, flounced out of the room with an austere expression on her large, unattractive face. His wife, meanwhile, clapped her hands at the departing servants, with the order to 'serve breakfast at once!' Then she hurriedly followed her daughter out of the room, with not so much as a glance at Emma, who was now on her feet and quite taken aback by the speed of events.

'May I sit with Papa while he has his breakfast?' she asked her uncle, her heart sinking when he abruptly replied, 'You may not! . . . I expect you to be seated at the breakfast table in five minutes. After which, please remain behind!'

Emma felt an impending doom, knowing from experience that such an instruction could only mean one thing – she was to be given yet another lecture. But, for the life of her, she could not think what she had done since Sunday to evoke his wrath. On the contrary, she had made every effort to remain inconspicuous for her papa's sake.

In Emma's experience breakfast was always a trying occasion, but today it was unbearable. From the moment Emma entered the room, a heavy, forbidding atmosphere descended over the table. Even the maids, who might normally be seen to occasionally lift up the corners of their mouths in a secret shared smile with Emma, went scurrying about their business with sorry faces and deliberately averted eyes.

Emma was not the slightest bit hungry although, in an effort to keep the peace, she did manage to swallow a mouthful or two of the scrambled eggs and, surprisingly, she enjoyed her cup of tea so much that she indulged in a second one. For the most part, however, she picked at her food, skilfully pushing it about her plate, until it appeared that she had eaten more than she actually had. But her mind was preoccupied with what her uncle had in store for her and, throughout the meal, her attention constantly wandered. At present, it was captured by the monstrous sideboard which spanned almost the length of one wall, its twisted decorative pillars reaching up beyond the picture-rail and supporting numerous small oval-and square-shaped mirrors. On some of its many shelves stood large, black, prancing horses, and in the various arched cubicles all manner of bric-a-brac were displayed: heavily-decorated Chinese vases; assorted small glass containers, and little silver candlesticks. All along the top there were plates of every description; some depicting floral sprays, and others boasting hunting scenes. The accumulated impression was one of clutter and chaos. Emma also contemplated the idea that a small forest must have been sacrificed to provide the wealth of timber from which the huge ornate sideboard was constructed. The same could be said of the table at which the family sat, which was some five feet wide and twice as long, with bulbous legs of enormous dimension.

Emma's gaze went quietly about the room, going from place to place and seeing little there to give her pleasure – apart from the magnificent piano. It was a beautiful object in highly polished walnut, displaying two exquisite candelabras positioned at either end, with a selection of silver-framed photographs between them. This piano had been Emma's salvation since her arrival at Crowther House. She had enjoyed so many hours of pleasure at its keyboard, particularly in the early days when her papa had had the strength to sit close by and watch her play. Strangely enough, her uncle had not thought fit to punish her by forbidding her access to the piano. On the occasions when she had played for the family gathering, Emma had actually witnessed expressions of pleasure on her uncle's face – though *not* on the faces of her cousin and aunt, who remained po-faced throughout and showed little appreciation afterwards.

Emma sneaked a look at them now. As usual, there was little joy on either of their countenances, although, to Emma's left, Martha had a look of absolute bliss on her face as she stuffed great helpings of food into her rather large mouth. So intent was she not to miss a mouthful, that she took her own breath away, causing her odd-sized nostrils to flare open in their frantic gasp for air. When Caleb Crowther impatiently tapped his teaspoon against the side of his cup, Martha lifted her eyes to him. Upon seeing that he was not pleased with her table-manners, she gave a sheepish half-smile, straightened her back and dabbed at her mouth with a napkin. Then she proceeded with her usual irritating habit of picking at the deep pleats of her dress, lifting up great handfuls of her abundant skirt and arranging it about her with painfully laborious deliberation. When her mother let out a tight gasp of irritation, Martha immediately switched her attention to the muffin on her side-plate, collecting it daintily between finger and thumb in preparation for spreading it with butter. Unfortunately, Martha Crowther's thick, clumsy fingers were not designed for dainty behaviour, so when the muffin flicked out of them and somersaulted into the centre of the table, Emma was not at all surprised. Seeing the expressions of exasperation on the faces of her Aunt Agnes and Uncle Caleb, Emma desperately tried to restrain herself from laughing out loud.

'Really, Martha!' Agnes Crowther shook her head in disapproval, her dark green eyes virtually closed into angry slits. However much Emma thought of her aunt as being a sour-faced individual, she could still appreciate that she was a very attractive woman. She had the darkest of hair, drawn back from her high forehead and parted in the middle with exact precision, before being gathered up above each ear, where it was plaited and wound into thick, tight circles which nestled over her perfectly shaped ears – like sleeping snakes, Emma thought, not for the first time. Her dresses were always high at the neck, buttoned from there down to the tight-fitting waist. At the rear was a bustle as large and grand as Emma had ever seen and the skirt, as always, was extravagantly folded in layered pleats, culminating in a beautifully embroidered hem which swept out at the back in an exaggerated train. Her dresses were of the finest taffeta, always exceptionally handsome, yet never glamorous. The one she wore today was burgundy.

As Emma's mind wandered, Agnes Crowther secretly compared her own daughter and her brother's daughter. The former appeared much older than her sixteen years; she was coarse and ungainly, and Agnes Crowther held out little hope that finishing-school would do much to improve her. Her attention then turned to Emma, born a few months after Martha, and already showing the promise of great beauty. Indeed, she was wilful, and she cared little for material things, but even if she were dressed in rags Agnes knew she could command the eye of every man, for she had that elusive beauty which emanated from within and a God-given talent for making the most out of all things. There was a light in those magnificent eyes that shone from a pure and joyous soul – and Agnes Crowther resented her for it.

She glanced at Emma and saw how her longing gaze had sought out the door which would take her from this room, down the corridor and to her papa. She knew how Emma yearned to go to him. She knew also that, long after Thadius had been laid to rest, Emma's love for him would continue to live on. She envied her brother such steadfast devotion. She let her eyes follow the strong, classic lines of Emma's lovely face – the small neat nose, the delicate chin, that laughing full mouth. She noted how her sun-kissed hair fell naturally in deep tumbling waves. Her young figure was perfect – small and dainty, adding to the overall picture of everything a young girl growing to womanhood should be. Agnes Crowther saw all this in Emma, and envied her. She also begrudged the fact that, without her brother's intervention, there would be no finishing-school for Martha, no Breckleton House or comfortable way of life. She ought to feel grateful but all she felt was deep bitterness, since half of the business left by their father should rightly have been hers. It did not matter that the business was already ailing when Thadius took it on, nor that she herself might never have rescued it in the same way as Thadius had done. The fact remained that she had been cheated of her share, so whatever came her way now was no more than her rightful due.

When, presently, breakfast was over, Emma thought it not a moment too soon. Whatever it was her uncle had to say, it was better said sooner than later. When he dismissed all but her, telling the maids to 'Leave the table . . . You may return when I'm finished,' Emma's stomach felt as if it were going to jump out of her mouth. Yet, despite her inner anxiety, she felt that she was ready to hear whatever it was he had to say. However, even she was not prepared for the news he gave her. Her astonishment was clearly written on her face when it became evident that her uncle's intentions were to put her out to work.

'How do you mean, Uncle Caleb?' she enquired as politely as she could. She was not afraid to have to work – indeed, if anything, she welcomed it – but she was anxious to learn exactly what he had in store for her.

'It is, of course, your papa's wish that you be made wise in the matters of business, and as his business has always concerned the cotton mills, as did his father's . . . your grandfather's . . . before him, it is my belief that you will learn much from being involved in the day-to-day running of such a concern.'

'I'm not being sent away to school, then . . . like Martha?' asked Emma, with wide, relieved eyes. She had been dreading such a prospect these past weeks, ever since the dismissal of the woman who had tutored both her and Martha in the rudiments of education – of which embroidery, music and religion and the necessities of keeping house, were given paramount importance. When Martha's finishing-school was chosen, Emma believed it would be only a matter of weeks, once the holidays were over, before she herself would be packed off. She had respectfully raised the matter with her papa, who was under no illusion regarding her reluctance to leave him. But the issue was always side-stepped and Emma had to finally concede that it was her papa's wish for her to be sent away. Such a consideration had been painful for her to accept, but as a dutiful daughter it was not for her to question. At her Uncle Caleb's revelation, she was at first shocked, then delighted, but now she had become apprehensive. Would she have more time for her papa . . . or would she have less?

'May I ask *how* I am to be made knowledgeable in the family business?'

'It surprises me that you ask so politely, Emma Grady, for you have shown no such respect in the past.' Emma felt his piercing eyes bearing down on her, seeking as always to shrivel her spirit. But she stood straight and proud, her gaze defiantly meeting his. As he continued to look down on her, Caleb Crowther's thoughts were abruptly transported back over the years, to Emma's exquisite and beautiful mother, Mary, who had bewitched him beyond belief, and whose fiery, magnificent character was so painfully evident in this young girl who so often dared to challenge him. But she would not get the better of him – not this side of Hell she wouldn't. A pang of regret touched his bitter heart. If only he had been blessed with a son. If he had had a son to carry on his name, he might well have altered the course of things, the consequences be damned. As it was, despite his efforts to escape them, he had been shouldered with certain responsibilities towards this girl and Thadius which he would rather not have had thrust upon him. However, these same responsibilities had afforded him salvation from the debtor's prison and, because of Thadius Grady's impending departure from this world, had bestowed upon him a fortune and a great deal of power. That much, at least, he liked.

'Uncle Caleb?' Emma felt the need to catch his attention, for he appeared to be so deep in thought it seemed he had forgotten she was there.

'Hhm? . . . yes!' He cleared his throat and, taken by surprise at the sound of Emma's voice invading his secret thoughts, he cast down his gaze for a brief moment to quickly compose himself. 'Leave me now. All will be explained in good time once your papa has been acquainted with my intentions.' He straightened both his arms outwards, before placing one behind his back and dipping the long sinewy fingers of the other into the pocket of his waistcoat to draw out a silver watch. As he did so, something else came out with it and tumbled to the floor. It was the tiniest, most delicate, finely chiselled lady's pocket time-piece, enriched by the most intricate figuring. With a furtive movement, Caleb Crowther bent to scoop it up, but not before Emma had seen it. She was furious, for she knew the watch to be a precious gift from her own papa to her mama. It was a thing he had always treasured and she could not let the matter pass.

'That pocket-watch doesn't belong to *you!*' she accused, stepping forward a pace. 'It belongs to Papa!'

'The devil you say!' The self-indulgent smile had disappeared from Caleb Crowther's bearded features, and had been replaced by a look as evil as any Emma had ever seen. But she was not intimidated by him, and where lesser mortals might have fled, she stood her ground and repeated the accusation, this time with more vehemence.

'It's my *papa's* watch, I tell you,' she confronted him boldly as he began trembling from head to toe.

'Go to your room!' he insisted, his voice now hardly more than a whisper. But Emma made no move until, the next moment, Mrs Manfred appeared at the door. Her original intention had been to enquire when the master intended to allow the maids in for the purpose of cleaning away the breakfast things, but when she sensed the impending terrible scene, her enquiry was of a very different nature. She had heard Caleb Crowther order Emma to her room and had witnessed with horror how Emma displayed no such intention. Quickly now, she stepped forward in a bold attempt to diffuse the situation.

'Excuse me, sir . . . shall *I* escort Miss Grady to her room?' Her anxious eyes swept with relief as he threw out his arms in a gesture of helplessness, telling her in an impatient voice, 'Please do so; and quickly, or I will not be responsible for my actions.' He then swung round to face the fireplace. Meanwhile Mrs Manfred swiftly came to Emma's side where, casting a sideways warning look at her, she pleaded, 'Please, Miss Grady.' Emma's heart fell like a stone inside her as she thought, I've done it again. However, she did not regret having spoken up about the pocket-watch, but rather that the entire incident would be reported to her papa in a way that would put her in the wrong.

As Emma followed Mrs Manfred from the room, Caleb Crowther's angry voice called after them, 'See that she stays in her room until I send for her.' He did not look up, but remained poised with one foot planted on the brass fender, one hand clutching the mantelpiece above, and the weight of his body bent tautly over the fireplace.

It was now two o'clock. Emma had spent over four hours pacing the blue-patterned carpet in her room, asking herself again and again why it was that, without fail, she always managed to get on the wrong side of her Uncle Caleb. Then she would defend her actions by reminding herself that it was not entirely her fault. It was *he* who was the thief, not she: it was *he* who instilled in her the need to be ever on her guard; and it was *he* who saw wickedness in every innocent thing she did.

At ten minutes past two, Mrs Manfred came to fetch her. 'Oh, Miss Grady!' she chided. 'When will you ever learn to curb that impetuous tongue of yours? Lunch is finished and you arc to go without . . . *again*.' She made a clicking noise with her tongue and shook her head, a sad expression on her loving face. 'Here,' she said in a soft voice, sneaking her fingers into the pocket of her dark dress and taking from it a white lace handkerchief. Thrusting it into Emma's hand, she explained how it contained one of Cook's gingerbreads. 'Oh, but there's no time to eat it now, child!' she cautioned, as Emma began to unwrap it. 'Master is back from dispensing harsh justice with his own kind in the courts, so now, no doubt, he seeks to do the same with you.' At this, Mrs Manfred drew herself up sharply, as she suddenly thought of what the sweep had said when he'd come to clean the chimneys. It seemed the whole of Blackburn was deep in talk of how this very morning Caleb Crowther, along with other Justices of the Peace, must have been in a mood more foul than usual. A harmless rascal had been brought before them, whose misfortune it was to be crippled, and whose greater misfortune it was to have been apprehended in the act of unlawfully acquiring a loaf of bread from a baker's basket, during the process of which the portly baker suffered a slight seizure. The Court took a very serious view of the whole business and, as a result, the offender was sentenced to transportation on a convict-ship to the other side of the world.

'Quickly, child!' Mrs Manfred was quite suddenly overcome with a deep sense of urgency and panic. 'Don't keep him waiting. You'll only make matters worse.' Seeing Emma start towards her, she turned about and hurried out of the room, adding, 'They're all in your papa's room. You're to join them there.' She gave no answer when Emma demanded to know why they should congregate in her papa's sick-room, 'disturbing him so.'

When Emma was ushered into the downstairs room, it was to find not only her papa – who appeared to be somewhat uncomfortable in the dome-backed chair, supported in a half-sitting position by the use of several feather bolsters – but also her Uncle Caleb, her Aunt Agnes and a small nervous man with a mop of sandy-coloured hair and eyes of almost the same hue. Emma knew him at once to be Mr Gregory

Denton, manager at one of the two mills owned by the family. Her papa had a great deal of respect for Mr Denton, for he was an amiable and forthright character, a good son to his elderly, cantankerous mother and a first-rate mill-manager. His sense of fairness, his business acumen, and his utter devotion to his work, went without question. Even Caleb Crowther had been obliged to recognize the worthiness of Gregory Denton – talents made even more remarkable because of his age, which was not yet twenty-eight.

'Come in . . . Come in, child!' Agnes Crowther dislodged one of her hands from the other – thus abandoning her customary posture of prayer – and waving her left hand in a dismissive gesture to Mrs Manfred, she instructed her, 'Be good enough to close the door behind you on your way out.' However, she appeared somewhat exasperated when her husband in turn addressed her.

'You will not be required either, thank you, Agnes. I'm quite certain your brother and I can conclude whatever business is at hand without you. Would you be so kind as to escort Mr Denton to the drawing-room, where I'll join him later.' He glanced at the inconspicuous little fellow, telling him, 'I shall be obliged if you would wait a while longer. There is a further matter to be discussed which you will possibly need to be made aware of at some point.'

'Of course, Mr Crowther, sir . . . I shall be pleased to wait.' Pausing only to respectfully acknowledge the man he came to see, he wished Thadius Grady well, adding, 'It's been an excellent month, sir . . . I hope the figures cheered you.'

'They did indeed, Gregory. I'm most grateful for your constant loyalty . . . as I know is Mr Crowther here.' Thadius

Grady's weakened voice betrayed his sapping health as he abandoned his effort to lift his hand to point at his brother-in-law.

'Indeed. Indeed,' rejoined Caleb Crowther, growing impatient and whereupon, both his wife and their visitor left the room.

'Now then, Thadius.' Satisfied that the door was securely closed, Caleb Crowther shifted his piercing gaze from it to the gentler face of his brother-in-law, as he continued, 'To the business of . . . your daughter.' For the briefest of moments, he seemed almost embarrassed and to Emma, whose eyes were fixed intently upon him, his hesitation on referring to her as her papa's daughter seemed strange. Yet, she gave it little thought, for in truth, she considered her uncle to be altogether a curious man.

The next moment Emma found herself the centre of attention and concern on her face must have betrayed itself because her papa immediately attempted to put her at ease. 'Emma . . . there is nothing for you to be afraid of,' he assured her. But Emma sensed little conviction in his voice. What she did sense, however, was that her papa was slipping away from her. She took a step forward and would have come to his side were it not for his telling her at that point, 'Be still, child, and listen to what your Uncle Caleb has suggested. When you have given me your views on what he has to say . . . then, I will gladly give you mine. I know no more of your uncle's plans for you than you do, as I prefer we are told them at one and the same time.'

Although Emma was prepared for the worst, what Caleb Crowther had to say still came as a shock to her. It appeared that her uncle and aunt did not consider her worthy enough to be given the same opportunities as Martha. In Caleb Crowther's words, 'To send Emma to school would be a futile and expensive gesture, for, in no time at all, she will have found a way to bring shame and scandal down on our heads.' He also explained how much more embarrassing such a thing would be for *him*, being 'an upholder of the Law, and consequently a very eminent figure, expected at all times to set an example.' What he proposed instead was that Emma should be sent to work in the Wharf Mill, where she would no doubt be of some use in a clerical position, assisting the manager, Mr Denton, and 'where she might learn discipline and respect.'

If the plans for her future had come as a shock to Emma, they appeared to have left her papa totally horrified. All the time his brother-in-law had been talking, Thadius Grady had made no comment. But, Emma had noticed how grim his expression had become and how his eyes had darkened with anger. She was sure this anger must have been caused by her behaviour and she had let him down so badly. She was mortified when he looked directly into her shamed face and, in a trembling voice, instructed her, 'Leave us, Emma.' Then, seeing her hesitate, he raised his voice, 'At once!' Even when he was taken by a fit of coughing and she started to approach him, he waved his hand in a dismissive gesture and ordered, 'Go!' Reluctantly, Emma left the room. She sat dejectedly on the stairs outside, her head in her hands and her heart an unbearable weight within her.

It was here that Mrs Manfred found her. 'Aw, child . . . don't take on so,' she said, not really aware of what had taken place in Thadius Grady's room. She comforted Emma and would have led her away, but all of a sudden, there was a burst of activity. First, Caleb Crowther emerged from the room and swept past Emma and Mrs Manfred with a black and furious expression on his face. Within minutes of him disappearing into the drawing-room, Gregory Denton rushed out from it, cap in hand and looking eager to depart. Seeing this, Emma broke away from Mrs Manfred's consoling embrace, to return to her papa.

Shaking her head in exasperation, Mrs Manfred quickly closed the front door behind Mr Denton, after which she rushed after Emma, her intention being to ensure that all was well.

Emma was shocked to find her papa in a state of great anxiety. In his hand was the tiny watch that she had seen earlier in Caleb Crowther's pocket. Emma made no mention of that particular fact, but, somehow, she guessed her papa already knew, for, when she was settled on her knees before him, he told her in an urgent voice, 'This watch is *yours* . . . it was your mama's before you and now it's yours. I recently entrusted it to Caleb, in order that he would get it inscribed. I feared it lost. No matter . . . I have it now.' He paused a moment, before gazing down on her with great tenderness.

'Emma.'

'Yes, Papa?'

'Come closer . . . I have something very precious to give into your keeping.' He took the watch out of its case and held it up between his finger and thumb. 'Read the inscription, child,' he urged, placing it in her hands, with the back of it facing her. Inscribed at the top, in gilded lettering, were the words: *For Mary, Christmas, 1840*. Beneath that was a new inscription reading, *To Emma, 1860*.

'Oh, Papa!' She could hardly believe her eyes.

'Open the back,' he now told her. 'Press the button at the base.' As she did this, she saw, nestled into the tiny cavity, a lock of hair, still golden as the brightest ray of sunshine and so small that the softest breath of wind might blow it away forever. 'You see that, Emma? . . . That's a part of your mama. Her hair was so lovely.' He smiled at the memory and Emma thought the smile almost ethereal. He continued, 'Golden, it was, like a summer's day. You have a touch of it in your hair, Emma, now and then when the light plays tricks with it, and you have the same deep, undisciplined curls.'

Emma continued to gaze on that tiny piece of her mama . . . of *herself* . . . and all kinds of emotions took hold of her. 'Am I to keep this, Papa?' she asked, thinking that she had never been given anything more precious.

'I hope you will, Emma,' came the reply, 'because, small as it is, it holds a precious memory of a day shortly after we were married. It was a beautiful day in the month of June, and everything was smelling sweet and fresh after a week of rain.' After a long, thoughtful pause, he continued, 'I pray you will find a love of your own one day, child, for love is a wonderful thing . . . though it can often bring its own heartache.' The years rolled away in his mind and the tears brimmed in his eyes. Mary had been his only love, yet she had brought him so much pain with the joy. It hurt him to recall how, even when Emma was only a few months old, her mama had felt compelled to seek the company of other men. It was the flaw in her nature and a sad thing.

'Enough, Papa.' Emma could see he was emotionally exhausted. 'You must rest.'

'You'll take care of the watch, Emma? You'll cherish it?'

'Of course, Papa . . . always.'

'Good.' Taking a deep sigh, he touched her hand with his own. 'Fetch Mrs Manfred to me. I must speak with her.' No sooner had the words left his lips, than Mrs Manfred stepped forward. 'Forgive me, sir,' she said, her voice subdued by the emotional scene she had just witnessed, 'I came to see if you and Miss Grady were all right.'

'*I* will be safe from harm's reach, when the good Lord sees fit to call me,' he murmured, obviously relieved at her presence, 'but Miss Grady must be protected.' He began to grow agitated. 'I must see Holford, before it is altogether too late!'

'Mr Holford? The solicitor, sir?'

'Yes, yes. Send Thomas on a fast horse! *Quickly* . . . he must be fetched at once!'

'What is it, Papa?' Emma asked, when Mrs Manfred had departed with haste. '*Why* must I be protected? From what?'

'From *them*!' Emma could hardly hear his whisper. 'I've given too much into their keeping . . . too trusting. Have to make amends.'

'Please don't fret yourself, Papa.' Emma wasn't really listening, as she was too troubled by his cadaverous appearance and his erratic breathing. Suddenly, she sensed someone behind her. On turning, she saw that it was Caleb Crowther and, standing beside him, white-faced and fidgeting, was Mrs Manfred. 'Oh, Manny . . . did you do as Papa asked? He seems so agitated!'

Before Mrs Manfred could reply, Caleb Crowther stepped forward. 'No, she did not!' he said. 'It was just as well that I discovered her errand, for it would only serve to aggravate your papa's health even further. Whatever business he wishes to discuss with Mr Holford must wait, at least until he is stronger.'

Emma was obliged to agree with him. 'Quickly, Manny. Help me get him into bed,' she pleaded, beginning to link her arm beneath that of her papa's.

'Of course!' rejoined Caleb Crowther, as Mrs Manfred hurried to help. 'You two see to that, while I summon Mrs Crowther.' At this, without any further regard for their efforts, he went swiftly from the room.

Only once in those desperate few moments did Thadius Grady open his eyes, and that was to beg of Mrs Manfred, 'I *must* speak with Holford! My daughter's future depends on it!'

'We have to appease him, Manny,' Emma told her. 'For whatever reason, you must send Thomas to fetch Mr Holford straightaway.'

Mrs Manfred went at once, careful to avoid crossing Caleb Crowther's path. Within a few minutes, Thomas had departed on one of the hunting horses. 'I'll have the fellow back here in no time at all!' he had assured the concerned housekeeper. 'Mrs Crowther's sendin' me in the same direction . . . I'm ter tell the doctor to make his way along.'

In the meantime, Agnes Crowther despatched Emma from the sick-room. 'The doctor will be here shortly,' she told the protesting Emma. 'You're only disturbing your papa by being here.' Instructed to 'run and fetch Mrs Manfred. Tell her to bring more blankets and fresh hot tea,' Emma went at once. But wild horses would not have torn her away had she known that never again was she to see her papa alive!

\* \* \*

The next half an hour was one of the worst nightmares Emma would ever suffer in her eventful life. Time and again she begged to be allowed in to see her papa so that she could comfort him and give him strength. She knew that he was in pain for, every once in a while, he would cry out. Then he would call out her name in a fitful voice – wanting her, needing her.

'Let me go to him!' she pleaded to Agnes Crowther. 'I must be with him.'

'No, child! . . . you'll do more harm than good!' retorted her aunt.

At one moment, the grim face of Caleb Crowther appeared from the door of the sick-room. 'Be sensible, Emma Grady! Your papa needs to be kept calm until the doctor arrives,' he remonstrated, shutting the door in her face and turning the key from the inside. At this, Emma made such a commotion by throwing herself at the door and crying out for her papa, that Agnes Crowther, who was always nearby, grasped her by the arm and dragged her upstairs.

'You're hysterical,' she snapped, 'and better in your room, until the doctor has gone!' That said, she locked the door and hurried away, leaving Emma banging her fist on the door and pleading to be allowed down.

'I promise I'll be still and quiet,' she cried, 'only, don't keep us apart. Please! Don't keep me from him!' She was fearful for her papa. Some deep instinct warned her that she should be with him, for he was helpless and needed her now more than ever.

Emma's cries echoed throughout the house. The servants heard her and cried with her; Mrs Manfred silently cursed all the devils that had delivered Emma and her papa into the clutches of people such as these; even Agnes Crowther was made nervous by the pitiful cries coming from Emma's room. However, they made no impact at all on Caleb Crowther, as he stared down on Thadius Grady.

'Caleb . . . please.' Thadius knew that he was sinking fast. 'Bring her to me, I beg you!' Emma's desperate cries were tearing him apart. 'Have you no heart, man?' he pleaded. If only his limbs had an ounce of strength in them, he would crawl from this bed and go to his darling child. But, God help him, he was as helpless as a new-born babe!

'No, Thadius!' Caleb Crowther's face was a picture of dark and evil cunning as his eyes bore into the poor sick man before him, whose only dying prayer was that he could hold his beloved child close once more and make amends before he left this world. 'I can't let you talk to Emma, for I'm of the mind that you want to confess to her who her real papa is.' He shook his head slowly, as Thadius protested that this was not the case. Even when Thadius began to cry like a child, there was not an ounce of compassion in Caleb Crowther's body. 'Nor can I allow you to talk to Holford. Have you the intention to change your will, Thadius? Do you regret the terms already laid down?' The sneering smile on his face was terrifying to witness, and Mrs Manfred, who had been stocking a supply of blankets in the large walk-in cupboard and was, as yet, unseen, was so horror-struck that she began to tremble uncontrollably and retreated deeper into the safety of the cupboard.

The next moment there came a flurry of movement from outside, and a low drone of conversation which grew louder as the sound of footsteps came ever nearer. Thadius, his voice now weakened to a whisper, began calling, 'Emma!

Emma!' He would have dragged himself from the bed, with every ounce of strength left in him, but, although his mind was strong, his poor wasted limbs were not.

From her hiding-place within the cupboard, Mrs Manfred heard Thadius Grady's desperate cries, and her heart bled. When he suddenly grew silent and an eerie quietness ensued, she feared the worst. Her feet felt as though they were pinned to the floor; her legs were like water; and her heart was beating so fast within her breast that she thought Caleb Crowther must surely hear it. Gradually she crept to the door and dared to peep round. What she saw was the body of Thadius Grady hanging lifeless across the bed and Caleb Crowther standing over it, a pillow still clutched in his hands so tightly that the knuckles on his fists were sharp and white.

Quickly, Caleb Crowther swung the lifeless form of Thadius Grady back into the bed, placing the pillow beneath his head and arranging him in a natural position. Then, with an equally swift movement, he went to the door and unlocked it, only just having time to get to the window before the door opened and Agnes Crowther entered with the doctor, who at once hurried to the bed.

From his position at the window, Caleb Crowther followed the doctor's movements, a contrived look of deep concern on his face. When the doctor turned to declare, 'I'm afraid I was too late. We can do nothing for Thadius now,' the look of concern deepened, and, passing his hand wearily over his face, he gave a painful groan. 'Poor Thadius, but at least his sufferings are over now.' When, out of the corner of his eye he saw Mrs Manfred emerging from the cupboard and hurrying out of the room, a suspicious look crossed his face.

But he could not be sure of what she had seen . . . he would never be sure.

It was into this sombre scene that Mr Holford, the solicitor, came, but he quickly realized what had happened and left the room. Caleb Crowther followed him into the hallway, where he answered the solicitor's immediate question with regret, 'No, I'm afraid I know nothing of why Mr Grady should want to speak to you.' He secured an appointment at which time Thadius Grady's legal arrangements would be confirmed. Then, with a show of compassion for that same departed soul, he bade Mr Holford good day.

When Agnes Crowther made her way upstairs to break the news to Emma, Mrs Manfred found a quiet place to consider what had taken place. She could not be certain of what had happened. Already, she was trying to wipe from her mind all memory of what she had seen. After all, it was possible that Thadius Grady had passed away naturally as he tried, in his fevered state, to see Emma. It was possible that Caleb Crowther had simply recovered the pillow from the floor where it had fallen. It was also possible that she had too vivid and dangerous an imagination. Yes, all of these things *were* possible, but she was not convinced! All the same, she resolved that she would put everything that had transpired out of her mind. To *know* something was often a burden; but to suspect something was usually dangerous! She was just a housekeeper, after all. But she had a particular love of Mr Grady and young Miss Grady. Yet, what was she to do without proof of her suspicions? She would have given *anything* not to have been in that room – but she *had* been there, God help her! And, even if she was wrong in her suspicions regarding the death of Thadius Grady, she knew she was not wrong about the evil nature of Caleb Crowther: a man with no compassion; a man who had deliberately denied his own brother-in-law his last dying wish of the comfort of his daughter by his side; a man who had cruelly kept Miss Grady from her dying papa. What sort of creature could hear a father and daughter crying out for each other yet wilfully keep them from one another's arms? The composition of such a man was beyond comprehension. However, of one thing she was certain. He was a man with the power to completely discredit any accusation a mere housekeeper might bring against him! But what of the comment she had heard regarding Emma's real papa? No, it *was* her imagination! It had to be!

Later, when Mrs Manfred found a desperate need to confide her thoughts to Cook, they were greeted with scorn and given short shrift.

'I've never heard such foolishness from a growed woman! It's a dangerous thing to let your imagination run riot, and you'd do best to put such dreadful thoughts from your mind!'

Mrs Manfred reluctantly agreed. She immediately reproached herself for having broken her self-imposed rule of not indulging in gossip below stairs.

Emma was devastated! All through the service when the rector spoke in respectful and glowing terms of 'the good man, Thadius Grady', she gazed at that long wooden box beneath the altar. There, within its cold and silent darkness, lay her darling papa – denied in his last moments the words she would have uttered to him. Oh, there was so much she had wanted to tell him! She would have held his frail familiar hand in her own, and murmured of her deep and grateful love. She would have told him of her heartfelt intention to become the daughter she suspected he had always wanted – not wild or wilful, not bold and adventurous, but more sedate and ladylike. She would have given her word that, with all her heart, she would try always to be a sophisticated and genteel young lady, who, one day, would marry a man much like her own papa. She would be a good, respectful wife to that man, and a fine mama to the children she bore him. All of these things, Emma would have said. Instead, her papa had died without hearing any of them. So, she said them now in her heart, strengthening also her promise to steer clear of the river-people. But, even as she made this silent resolve, the dark, laughing image of Marlow taunted her memory and touched her heart.

Outside, in the churchyard, with the sun beating down on her bowed head, Emma waited until the last mourner had moved away. Then, hardly able to see for the tears burning and swimming in her eyes, she went on her knees. 'I love you so, Papa,' she whispered into the ground. 'I pray you know how much I'll miss you, my darling.' In her heart, there was such great sorrow that it felt like a physical weight pulling her down – down, into that place where her papa was sleeping his final sleep. But mingled with this pain there was a strange, inexplicable feeling of another loss besides that of her papa. Although Emma was aware of this, she did not realize its implications: this other loss was that of her youth, her girlhood, all the lightness and irresponsibility of laughter and innocence. But there was also something else. In the fullness of time, her joy of life would return and the laughter would once again light up her eyes, but this other feeling – so deeply etched into her very being – was destined to stay with her forever. Emma knew that no passing of years nor easing of grief could ever ease it, for, never would she forget how Caleb Crowther had so vindictively kept her from the one person she loved, thus denying him the touch of her hand in his last moments. It was vindictive! It was inhuman. Thadius Grady had always taught Emma to forgive and for his sake she would try – but not yet, for she truly believed it would be the hardest thing she would ever be called on to do.

Emma had been unkindly forced into womanhood by her suffering, and this now betrayed itself in the shadows of her lovely but sad face. These shadows carried away her youth and brought in its place the strong, resolute lines of womanhood. Not once during the service inside the church nor in the churchyard outside, had Emma moved her eyes to look upon Caleb Crowther. Thus she had not witnessed the terrible bitterness on his face as he stared at where her papa lay; she did not hear the secretly whispered words, 'Mary was mine, Thadius . . . she was *always* mine!' If only Emma had been aware of the black hatred eating at Caleb Crowther's heart at that moment, she might have been better prepared for the terrible injustice he would one day inflict upon her.

# Chapter Three

'Poor Mr Grady would turn over in his grave at the way they treat Miss Grady.' Gladys, the parlourmaid, joined Mrs Manfred at the casement window. From there they watched the dog-cart carry the master and young Emma out of sight. ''Twere a different kettle o' fish a week ago, when Martha Crowther left fer that fancy school!' declared the maid, in a scornful tone. ''Tis a great pity the solicitor didn't get here in time, don't yer think, Mrs Manfred? For I can't help thinkin' as Miss Grady's papa had begun ter see through the master an' that wife of his!'

For a moment, it seemed as though Mrs Manfred might engage in small conversation with the chubby, likeable maid, but, thinking it unwise to endorse such comments with a reply, Mrs Manfred instead gave a weary sigh and pointed out to the young woman that there was 'still much work to be done'. With this, the maid shrugged her shoulders, realizing she'd already said too much, and hurried about her business.

Mrs Manfred lingered for a moment longer at the window, her eyes fixed on the upward spiral of dust that marked the progress of the dog-cart along the sandy lanes, which, because of the lack of rain these past weeks – almost the whole of September – were unusually dry underfoot. Presently, she turned away, her thoughts with Emma on her first day as clerk at the Wharf Mill. She hoped it would not be too bad, for, in spite of Emma's deepening maturity resulting from the painful loss of her beloved papa, she was nevertheless untutored in the ways of the world. But, Mrs Manfred was not altogether despairing, for Emma had always had a deep and precious gift for accepting most things with a wisdom way beyond her years. Somehow, she was always ready to make the best of things, however daunting they might seem to another, and these traumatic past four weeks had only served to strengthen this precious quality in her. Mrs Manfred's thoughts reflected briefly on the dreadful thing which Caleb Crowther had done in keeping father and daughter apart at a time when they had needed each other more than ever before in their lives. She had convinced herself that Caleb Crowther must have thought it for the best, but it was still a terrible thing; it had swept Emma's childhood away seemingly overnight, taking with it a tender innocence and a certain softness from her eyes, which once had seemed to smile all the time.

Still, Mrs Manfred was most confident that Emma would not let this business of working in the mill get her down. Indeed, if she knew Emma, and she did better than most, the lass would seek to do well – if only for her papa's sake.

Certainly, as Caleb Crowther urged the horse onwards, out of Breckleton and into Blackburn via Preston New Road, Emma's thoughts were of a similar nature. After her initial reservations regarding her clerical assignment to Mr Gregory Denton, Emma had begun to look upon it as a test, and she vowed to herself she would show Caleb Crowther that she was her papa's child – made of the same stirling quality! It would take more than being incarcerated in one of the Grady mills to break *her* spirit.

There was no lasting envy in Emma's heart towards her cousin, Martha, who, only a week ago, had also departed to begin a new adventure. But how very different Martha's departure had been from her own, she mused with a wry smile. Such fuss and ceremony! From the moment the pampered creature was risen from her bed to the moment she clambered into that fine, luggage-laden carriage – when her doting mama had thrust into the grasping gloved hands yet *more* refreshments for the journey – Martha Crowther had utilized a whole range of emotions. She had panicked, whimpered, wept, and indulged in every manner of tantrum!

Martha's departing words to Emma had merely been an attempt to raise herself above her cousin, with a cut to the heart. 'Of course, Emma,' she had started, mimicking her mama by peering down the length of her nose at Emma, 'you would gain *nothing* by going to a school for young ladies, having shown yourself to be at times unruly and vulgar. Oh dear me, no! But, I'm quite certain you will do well at the mill. Papa is an excellent judge of your limitations. Such work should suit you eminently.' With that, she allowed her mama to kiss her lightly on the cheek, but had seemed somewhat depleted when her papa merely gave her a curt instruction to 'attend well to your studies'. She had then swept out to embark upon her journey, which was some two hundred miles long and taking her to a grand school situated in the heart of Bedfordshire.

Now, here am I embarking on mine, thought Emma, with a strange feeling of satisfaction for, if the truth were told, she would not wish to change places with Martha – not for all of Queen Victoria's crown jewels!

These past weeks had been a hard and painful experience. She had known for a long time that her papa was desperately ill and had tried so hard to prepare herself for his leaving her on her own. Yet, when it happened she was *not* prepared; the manner of his death was such that now she missed him even more. And it was all the fault of the man seated beside her now – his very nearness caused her flesh to creep. Once or twice since Caleb Crowther had climbed into the dog-cart and taken up the reins, Emma had sent a caustic glance in his direction, thinking all the time what a foul and sorry creature he was. His sober and serious expression gave nothing away; the tails of his long black coat were ceremoniously laid out behind him – like the mantle of a devil, thought Emma bitterly; his stomach protruded grotesquely over his lap; his back was as straight and rigid as the look upon his stern, forbidding face; and perched on top of his mass of brown and iron-grey hair was that tall, upright hat which he was so seldom seen without.

'I would rather have found my own way to the mill,' Emma ventured. 'It would be no problem, because Papa took me there many times.' She had made the same observation on the previous evening when Caleb Crowther had told her of his intention to 'See you get there, on your first day.' The resentment at his accompanying her was easily evident in her voice as she raised the issue again. So Emma was not surprised when he turned his head sharply to glower down at her. Then, giving only a grunt to signify that he had heard her, he returned his full attention to the road ahead. 'Giddyup!' his voice boomed down on the bay mare, as he slapped the reins in the air until they made a cracking sound which spurred the animal on at an even faster trot. It was not often that Caleb Crowther took it upon himself to drive the dog-cart into town, but on the odd occasion when he did, it was to be both heavy-handed in his management of it, and to present a fearsome spectacle to the less law-abiding citizens, who at some point along the journey would recognize him as Caleb Crowther – a tyrant who infused his sweating horse with terror, just as he did the miscreants upon whom he legally dispensed justice. He was not a liked man, nor was he respected – only despised and feared.

'Thomas has instructions to bring you in future. I have far more pressing matters which demand my time!' spoke Caleb Crowther now. 'As for you . . . Mr Denton has instructions to keep you plied with work and kept busy for the four hours you will be there each day; with the exception of Saturday, when no doubt your aunt will instruct you in duties of a more domestic nature. Later, of course, you will be called upon to put in a very much longer day.'

Emma thought this idea must please him intensely, for he now turned his head slightly to bestow on her a stiff little smile. But she paid him no attention. The prospect of work was not one that worried her. True, the mill was a daunting place in which to be confined – as she had witnessed on the numerous occasions she had been in there with her papa. She had seen for herself how dark and grimy conditions there were. But she had also seen how, despite this, the work-hands applied themselves wholeheartedly to the task in hand. And that is exactly what *I* shall do, Emma told herself now, certain that her papa would be proud of her resolve. Then she softly began humming a tune, as she assiduously observed the bustling activity all around, which increased significantly the nearer they came to Blackburn town centre.

At this early hour of eight a.m., there was much coming and going in every direction. The muffin-man was busy pushing his wicker-trolley along, his cloth cap perched precariously over his forehead, his step a lively one, and his lips pursed together in the whistling of a jolly melody. The brewery-waggon ambled along across the street, loaded with hefty wooden barrels brimful of draught beer. As usual, the big black shires harnessed up front were magnificent in their polished brass and leather harness, with their long tails neatly plaited, and their manes gathered in rows of intricate decorated braids. So delighted was Emma by this scene, that she raised her hand in a friendly wave as the waggon rolled past them in the opposite direction.

'Mornin' to you,' called one of the two men from the drivers' bench, both of whom were dressed in dark coats and trim little bowlers, with light-coloured breeches tucked into their black knee-length boots. These boots were polished to such a deep mirror finish that they gave the impression of being shiny wet. Emma thought the whole ensemble to be a proud and dignified one – albeit for the purpose of carting ale!

As they passed the grander houses of Preston New Road, the ladies emerged in twos and threes. Some were dressed in flouncy crinoline style, while others favoured the newest bustle line; but all were bedecked in extravagant bonnets, and all were unquestionably elegant and resplendent. It amused Emma to see how her Uncle Caleb's countenance suddenly changed at the sight of all this female finery. At once, he was wearing the sickliest of smiles, and doffing his hat in exaggerated gentlemanly gestures – only to scowl and curse, in characteristic fashion, when a four-horse carriage immediately behind began showing signs of impatience at his dawdling.

Emma grew more and more engrossed in the hustle and bustle as their route carried them farther away from the open countryside and wide roads, into the heart of industrial Blackburn town, with its narrow cobbled streets of tightly packed back-to-back houses, overlooked by towering and monstrous mill chimneys – themselves alive as they pumped out long creeping trails of choking black smoke. On a day such as this – when the earth was parched and devoid of a breeze which might cool it or lift the billowing smoke higher into the air – the dark swirling clouds could only cling to the roofs and chimneys like a thick acrid blanket enveloping all beneath, and shutting out the brilliant sunlight from above. But, to the vast majority of Blackburn folk it was a natural and accepted thing which was as much a part of their daily lives as breathing itself. The cotton mills were the life-line of almost every man and his family, whether they were mill-workers, mill-owners, river-people, or others who benefited from this industry. They tolerated the smoke and the shrill scream of the mill whistle calling them from their beds at some ungodly hour, for cotton was the thread by which their very existence hung. It gave them work; it gave them a means by which they could raise their families in dignity; and, above all, it gave them a sense of pride and achievement.

Cotton mills were going up at an unprecedented rate all over Lancashire, but, here in Blackburn the programme of mill construction was staggering. Emma had inherited her papa's own pride in these great towering monstrosities, and she knew all their names – Bank Top Mill, Victoria Mill, Infirmary Mill – and, oh, so many more! Cotton was big business, keeping the town a hive of bustling activity. No hard-working mill-hand ever grew rich by it as his wages were too meagre; but, for the man with money to invest, the opportunities grew by the day. The Leeds to Liverpool Canal was a main artery from the Liverpool Docks to the various mills. Along this route the fuel and raw cotton which kept the mills alive was brought, thus affording a living to the many bargees who, with their families, dwelt in their colourful floating homes and spent most of their lives travelling to and fro with their cargoes. This consisted mainly of raw cotton, unloaded from the ships which carried it across the ocean from America.

Even Caleb Crowther's brooding mood, and her own feeling of bitterness towards him, couldn't quell Emma's enthusiasm as they clip-clopped towards the wharf. Oh, it brought back so many pleasant memories! Over Salford, along Railway Road, and into Eanam itself they went. Then, marked by tall cylindrical chimneys reaching high into the sky, the mill came into sight. It was a huge building of some several storeys high, with each level lined with dozens upon dozens of long narrow windows. Soon, they were passing through the oppressive big iron gates of Wharf Mill.

As they came into view of the open warehouse doors, Emma could see a group of cloth-capped men gathered just inside, exchanging conversation – which was evidently causing a great deal of fist-waving, finger-wagging and head-shaking. It all seemed very intense. Suddenly, one of the men caught sight of Caleb Crowther approaching, whereupon there was a flurry of activity and the group dispersed immediately – all except for one hump-backed little fellow, who came towards them at an urgent pace.

'What the devil's going on here?' Caleb Crowther demanded as he brought the horse and vehicle to a halt. He clambered down as the hump-backed fellow caught hold of the horse's halter. 'Why aren't those men at their work, eh? . . . What the hell do they think I pay them wages for, eh? . . . eh?' His neck stretched forward and his voice grew shriller.

The nervous explanation was offered that it was an accident the men had converged on that particular spot at that particular minute – being 'all good souls, an' grand workers doin' a regular job.' But that, 'findin' theirselves face to face, had stood a while to voice their fears o' the terrible unrest as seems ter be grippin' America – afeared fer their jobs an' their families, if owt should come a tumble wi' the shippin' in of our cotton from there.'

'Be that as it may . . . I don't give a damn for their reasons!' exploded Caleb Crowther. 'If I suspect it happening again, on *my* time, you can rest assured they'll all be out of work – and it won't be because of what's happening in America! Do I make myself clear, yardhand?'

As the little hump-backed fellow nodded most fervently, Caleb Crowther made a mental note to bring the matter to Gregory Denton's attention. But at the same time, he grudgingly admitted to himself that if there *were* any truth in what the papers would have them believe – that there really was the rumble of unease in America, between the North and the cotton-growing areas in the South – then, by God, there would indeed be cause for concern!

'See to it that Miss Grady is brought along to the office,'

he now instructed the little man, 'then busy yourself, man . . . *busy yourself*. I don't hold with a man being a minute idle!' Then, leaving Emma in the care of this fellow, he strode away in the direction of the stairs which led up to the office where, at that very moment, Gregory Denton was nervously pacing the floor in anticipation of Caleb Crowther's arrival. The whole place seemed so much darker when *his* shadow fell upon the step.

'Hello, yardhand.' Emma fondly addressed the hump-backed fellow who would answer to no other name; indeed, most folk had forgotten what his real name was. Now, as he extended a helping hand, Emma leaned upon it, to swing herself to the ground. 'Are you keeping well?' She had a special affection for this poor deformed creature both because of his deep loyalty to her papa and because, in spite of his cumbersome affliction, he never grumbled or complained, but was always ready with a cheerful grin. He wasn't capable of putting in a heavy day's work but was invaluable in keeping the place free of clutter, booking loads in and out and generally making himself available wherever and whenever he was needed.

'Oh, I'm well, Miss Grady . . . very well . . . yes, indeed,' he replied in a jolly manner, but his face suddenly became crestfallen as he commented, 'I was so sorry about your papa . . . we all were. Thadius Grady were a good man, that 'e were!' When Emma gave an encouraging smile, but made no comment, he went on in an excited voice, 'I'm telled as ye'll be keepin' the books here? Oh, that's grand . . . keep your mind occupied, so it will, eh? Oh, we're glad ter have yer with us, Miss Grady . . . yes, indeed, very glad.'

As Emma started towards the office with the little fellow

chatting alongside her, she did not see the tall, handsome young man, stripped to the waist, carrying bundles of raw cotton from his barge to the warehouse.

But, although Emma had not seen Marlow Tanner, he had seen her and he was overcome by what he saw. Emma looked beautiful in her best cornflower-blue dress with its pretty white fluted collar and scalloped hem, from beneath which peeped the toes of her dainty ankle-boots. Her rich chestnut hair hung loose down her back, framing her magnificent face perfectly. Yes, he had seen Emma – and was now smitten even more by her. But he had seen Caleb Crowther also, and in his heart he felt a deep conflict of emotions. He would never hesitate to go through Hell's fire for this lovely lass; but for the man, he felt only bitterness and disgust.

As he paused to watch Emma disappear into the interior of the mill, Marlow Tanner presented a splendid and formidable sight, with his lithe, muscular form upright and taut and his two strong fists clenched tight at his sides. His heart was torn in two.

''Ave yer gone on bloody strike or what?' The voice of Sal Tanner rang out across the yard to call her brother's attention. Her heart was deeply troubled for Marlow, whom she loved with the fierce protective instincts of a mother. Since the death of both their parents some fifteen years before – in a manner which had never been fully revealed – she had been to Marlow mother, father, sister and friend. In all truth, Sal revered only one thing above him, and that was her precious jug of ale. For, while Marlow had her to rely on, she could only fill the empty void in her life by losing herself in the comforting dregs of that cherished jug.

As Marlow made his way back, Sal Tanner murmured to him, 'Don't ever look above yer station, darlin', else ye'll surely fotch a heap o' pain down on yerself!'

Her mind was drawn back over the years to the time when she was just a child, and Marlow was barely two years old. Their name was *not* Tanner then, but Royston; circumstances had forced them to change it. There had been the most dreadful scandal – the truth of which she had never learned, because, as was always the case when a boat-family was threatened, the others would close ranks to the outside world and closely guard their own. All she had learned over the years was that her dah had been seeing some fancy-born lady. There had been talk of it all up and down the river. So, when he began making plans to leave his wife and two youngsters, one of the bargees made it his business to warn the wife.

Sal Tanner remembered that very night like it was only yesterday. The awful way her mammy had looked when she left to follow her husband along the towpath. The fear within her when neither her mammy nor dah returned. Then, the following morning, both she and Marlow were snatched by the river-folk and hidden away for many a long month. It was then that their names were changed from Royston to Tanner. It was years later before Sal discovered why it was that her mammy and dah had never come back. It was rumoured that Eve Royston had found her husband Bill with his fancy lady, and, with the help of loyal friends, had murdered them both. Soon after, she was hanged. Sal never did learn more than that, and, she was so disheartened and ashamed that she had no desire to learn any more. Her only thought then, as now, was to protect Marlow from the truth.

Now, here he was, burning with the very same fever that got his dah murdered and his mammy hanged.

Her troubled violet eyes watched Marlow's downcast expression, and, for a moment, she made no move. Sal Tanner was a familiar sight hereabouts, with her long calico skirt flowing about her dark heavy clogs, her brown crocheted shawl flung haphazardly over her shoulders, and that unmistakable chequered cloth cap tilted at a jaunty angle on her wispy fair hair. She could generally be heard roaring with laughter long before one might catch sight of her, and straightaway one could picture her with two sturdy hands spread-eagled, one over each hip, head thrown back and mouth wide open, revealing more gaps than teeth.

Today, however, Sal Tanner was in an unusually quiet mood. She was afraid – afraid for both Marlow and for herself. She knew Marlow was in love – had known that since the day he'd been carried through the door, flayed and bleeding. Her instincts had told her then that her young, reckless brother had become a man. Her deeper instincts now told her that it was a blessing the Lord had seen fit to give Marlow a strong broad back and an iron will together with the stoutest heart, for, God help them both, she could sense a dark and troublesome time ahead. It was most frightening how history had a nasty habit of repeating itself.

'Bloody fancy folk,' Sal Tanner snorted, at the same time grabbing a small flask of gin from within the folds of her skirt. 'Ye'd best keep yer soddin' distance from me an' mine!' she grumbled, taking a long gulp from the flask and glowering after Emma's disappearing form. However, Sal had to grudgingly admit to herself that this particular young girl was maybe not so fancy as some she'd come across. In fact, the smile she gave that little hump-backed bugger was a genuine, warm one, and there was nothing posh nor dandy about the lass's voice. 'If anything, she seemed a deal outta place aside o' that sour-faced whiskered feller as fotched 'er 'ere,' Sal told the empty air, grunting and then helping herself to another mouthful of the fiery liquid. 'But I'll keep me bloody eyes peeled all the same, 'acause me bones tell me there's trouble brewing . . . Gawd 'elp us all!'

Brimming with an equal measure of gin and foreboding, Sal Tanner sought out one of the loaders from the warehouse, a brash, brawny fellow by the name of William. 'What d'yer know o' that there lass?' she demanded to know. 'That pretty little thing as come 'ere with the whiskered bugger!' When William explained how the lass was none other than Miss Grady, the daughter of the late Thadius Grady, whose own dah came up from poor and common stock, to make himself known and respected amongst the workers, Sal Tanner threw back her head and roared with laughter. 'There!' she cried with delight. 'I *knew* it! . . . I bloody well knew it! That lass . . . the one yer call Emma . . . she don't come fro' no more fancy folk than *I* do!'

'That's as mebbe,' William told her, 'but, thanks to her dah, she'll come into a tidy little fortune one o' these fine days.' Here, he pursed his lips and clicked in serious manner, 'That is if she ain't cheated out of it by that conniving uncle of 'ers.'

'Oh?' Sal Tanner was intrigued. 'Got 'erself an enemy or two, 'as she?' There was no shifting Sal Tanner until she knew all there was to know about the lass who'd struck deep into Marlow's heart. As Emma's story unfolded, the barge-woman found herself sympathizing with this Emma. 'Poor little sod!' she exclaimed, taking another swig from the flask. 'Livin' in a big 'ouse an' belonging to fancy folk . . . well, it don't keep the troubles off yer back, do it, eh? Not if ye've med an enemy or two, it don't!' And, suspecting what a terrible misfit Emma was in Caleb Crowther's house, William had to agree.

'Aw, but you an' me ain't plagued wi' no such troubles, are we, Sal darlin',' he laughed, giving her a puff of his pipe and a knowing wink. He and Sal had an understanding . . .

'Why, yer randy bugger!' roared Sal Tanner, slapping him heartily on his shoulder and feigning a look of surprise. 'There ain't no 'olding yer, once yer teks a fancy!' Quickly now, she looked about and seeing there was nobody watching, she grabbed his arm. 'Come on then,' she laughed, tugging him round the back of the stacked bales, 'but it'll cost yer a wad o' that there baccy!' And, with both of them laughing, he carelessly knocked out his pipe and flung his arm about her.

'By! Yer a rum 'un, Sal Tanner,' he said, 'but I ain't complaining.'

'Bless me, if I've never seen that ledger so correct and neat! What an astonishing young lady you are, Miss Grady . . . if I may say so,' remarked Gregory Denton, collecting up the sheaf of invoices and scrutinizing the leather-bound ledger which lay open on Emma's desk. He had always suspected the daughter of Thadius Grady was a bright, intelligent lass – in spite of the stories that flew around town of her foolhardy escapades. Mind you, who could blame her? She was young and healthy with a particular thirst for life which, by its very nature, must drive her to seek a taste of adventure, away from the scrutiny of that dreadful Crowther lot. What a great pity the lass's papa had been taken. It was a sure fact that he was sorely missed here at the mill. That being the case, how much harder it must be for young Miss Grady, now securely in the clutches of her uncle, who was renowned for his lack of compassion!

Gregory Denton's admiration for Emma was two-fold. For all the heartache she must be suffering, the lass bore it well; indeed, when he compared Emma to other members of her sex, including his own ever-complaining, elderly mater, Emma was a female apart. Furthermore, she was exceptionally lovely, and had stirred in him long-forgotten cravings which he had accepted would never be satisfied. Like a fool, he had thrown away his few early opportunities. Now, he had only one great passion left, and that was his work. This mill was his pride, his joy . . . and his only reason for living! It was also his means of escape from a woman who believed that to be given a son was to be given absolute control over his very soul. Oh, what regrets he had! And how much deeper they seemed now that he was privileged to have such a delight as Emma Grady gracing his office. More than once in these past few hours he had averted his eyes from her because of the havoc she wreaked within him. Yet, to secretly gaze upon her was a deep, satisfying pleasure which he found impossible to deny himself. And, after all, he told himself, was it not so that a cat might look upon a queen?

Emma had sensed his eyes on her, but had paid no attention. Mr Denton was a pleasant enough fellow, and she had no wish to embarrass him in any way. Now, she looked up as he replaced the invoices on top of the ledger. 'I'm glad you're pleased with my work, Mr Denton,' she smiled. But, in all truth, she believed she had earned his praise, for she had checked and re-checked every detail on those invoices, before meticulously entering them on to the page. Now, she was ready to make a start on the warehouse dockets – starting with the one directly in front of her with the name 'Tanner' on top. 'If you'll just set me an example,' she asked.

Gregory Denton was so caught up in Emma's enthusiasm that he made a suggestion quite out of character. 'The ledgers can wait a while, Miss Grady,' he told her, 'and, if you've a mind, I'd like to take you on a tour of the mill . . . so you can see for yourself what procedure is followed.'

Emma had already toyed with the idea of asking this very favour, once her clerical duties were done. 'Oh, I'd like that, Mr Denton,' she said, quickly climbing from the stool in case he should change his mind.

Just over an hour later, with only ten minutes to spare before midday, at which time Thomas was due to collect her, Emma followed Mr Denton down the stairs and into the warehouse. 'Thank you for taking me round,' she told him, greatly impressed by what she had seen. On visits with her papa, the farthest she'd been allowed to go was the office enclosure. But today she'd seen virtually the whole process the raw cotton had to go through. She had seen the loose bales thrown into a machine that tore any knots or lumps from the cotton; then she was taken to the cardroom where it was combed; after this she saw how the twisted rovings were spun on machines which were some twelve feet wide and two hundred feet long. The cotton was then washed, bleached, dried, beaten, folded and pressed, before being considered suitably finished and ready for use. In the loom-weaving shed, Emma had wondered how the mill-hands could stand the relentless noise, day after day, without going totally deaf.

They were now on the lowest level, where the bales of raw cotton, after being unloaded from the barges, were stored ceiling-high before samples were taken to ascertain the different grades and quality.

'Do you think you'll enjoy your work here, Miss Grady?' Gregory Denton ventured, feeling pleased with himself.

When Emma assured him that she'd had an exciting morning and was looking forward to learning all there was to know about the business, his face beamed with joy. 'Oh, that's grand!' he declared, feverishly nodding his head and rubbing his two hands together in a nervous fashion. 'That's right grand!'

By the look on his face as he leaned towards her, Emma could see he had a great deal more to say. But, at that moment there came a loud and frantic cry from the mouth of the warehouse, where the bales were brought in from the barges. This was immediately followed by a series of alarming noises and the unmistakable smell of fire. Emma was taken aback by the swift change in Gregory Denton as, grasping her arm, he propelled her at running pace towards the side exit. 'Take yourself out of here! Quick as you can!' he ordered, sending her the last few steps with a thrust of his arm. He then hurried towards the black smoke which was already billowing up to the ceiling and blocking out the light of day. By now there were men coming from all quarters and rushing to the scene. Emma's ears rang with the noise and her nostrils were overwhelmed by the smell of burning as the blanket of thick black smoke continued to grow. When the cry went up that someone was hurt, it took her only a moment to decide to try and help. Quickly now, she changed direction and hurried after Gregory Denton, her long skirt lifted high, and her throat burning from the dry smoke.

'You'd best stay clear, miss,' came the suggestion from one of the men who had been hurrying past, and grabbing her arm, he would have escorted her out of there.

'No! . . . If someone's hurt, I can help!' Emma cried, shrugging him off and hastening her steps.

Emma was determined to be of use, and what she saw when she reached the scene only strengthened her resolve. The fire had got a hold amongst the newly off-loaded bales, and was in danger of rapidly spreading right into the heart of the warehouse. Darting about and doing the work of ten men, Gregory Denton had swiftly organized an army of workers who, on his orders, were tearing down the great bale-stacks nearest the fire and throwing them outside, where other men quickly doused them with water bucketed from the canal. Over by the far gantry, near the area which the men were clearing in order to stop the fire spreading, a lone man was making frantic efforts to reach two people trapped beneath. He had bravely spurned all offers of help, insisting that the other men get the bales outside 'or we'll *all* end up burning.'

Ignoring all warnings, Emma made straight for this solitary figure. It was only as she drew closer that she recognized the handsome features, the shoulder-length black hair, and that fine strong physique, the back and shoulders of which were interlaced with a complex lattice of scars. Her heart gave a skip as she spoke his name, 'Marlow!' For a brief moment she hesitated as she stared at the young bargee who, because of her, had been cruelly whipped, and who, no doubt, would never want to set eyes on her again. She felt ashamed and deeply pained. How could she *dare* face him?

In that moment she would have turned back, had it not been for the fact that people were hurt and every other pair of hands but her own was frantically working to beat the fire.

In a moment, Emma was by Marlow Tanner's side, down on her knees, scrabbling to reach the injured woman, who was by now almost free from the weight that pinned her down. When, totally astonished by her presence, Marlow called out Emma's name, she turned her head to glance up at him. In that all-too-brief moment when their eyes met, Emma's heart was aroused by such unfamiliar yet exhilarating emotions, that they left her visibly trembling. As his dark, passionate gaze absorbed her face with love and admiration, Emma's sparkling grey eyes reflected her wonder at these turbulent and exquisite feelings which possessed her. There was a blossoming of some deep, inner awareness within her, unlike anything she had ever known before. But with it came a murmuring fear, and the echo of a promise she had made.

Tearing away her gaze, she and Marlow set about the task in hand with renewed zest. When the two injured people were finally recovered, it was all too apparent that the man was beyond help.

'It's William!' cried Marlow. 'Poor bugger . . . there's nothing we can do for him, I'm afeared.' He straightened himself up, his bare flesh glistening with sweat in the fiery light, and his expression clearly reflecting his anger that a good man should die in such a way. 'Christ!' he moaned, wiping the back of his hand over his face, 'What the hell happened here?' Quickly he came to Emma's side, where she was cradling the unconscious woman in her arms.

'Is she . . . dead?' Emma asked softly.

Bending to collect the prostrate form into his arms,

Marlow saw that it was his sister, Sal. His heart sinking deeply within him, he gave no answer to Emma's question, other than to instruct her in a gruff voice, 'Quickly! Away from here!' As he spoke, two men rushed in to carry away the body of William.

They made their way outside, where the scene was one of great confusion. Weary, red-faced men were frantically dashing about in their efforts to contain the still-raging fire, which, thanks to the quick thinking of Gregory Denton, had not spread to cause the major catastrophe that could have ensued.

As they came to rest in a quieter place by the canal bank, Emma watched as, with great tenderness, Marlow Tanner laid his sister on the ground. At once, she began moaning. Quickly, Emma got to her knees and, taking the limp form into her arms, she told Marlow, 'Get Thomas . . . hurry! We must get her to the infirmary.' Whereupon, Sal Tanner stiffened and began struggling in Emma's arms.

'Jesus, Mary an' Joseph!' she called out, reaching up to grab Marlow as he stooped towards her. 'The buggers are after killin' me!' When Marlow laughed out loud and hugged her, she threw him off, shouting, 'I ain't goin' ter no bloody infirmary . . . so yer can piss off, the lot on yer!' But when she made an effort to get to her feet, she promptly fell back with a cry of pain.

'You'll do as you're told for once, Sal Tanner!' Marlow told her, raising her skirt up to her knee and seeing her already swollen, twisted leg. 'Looks to me like your leg's busted.'

Emma was surprised to find herself smiling at Sal Tanner's outspoken manner. What was more, she'd taken an instant liking to her. 'You ought to go to the infirmary,' she said. 'Thomas will get you there in no time at all.'

'He bloody *won't*, yer know!' came the swift retort, after which she gave Marlow an accusing glare. 'An' as fer you, yer bugger! . . . Yer oughta be ashamed tryin' ter put yer sister in such a place!'

'Yes, she *is* my sister,' Marlow explained to Emma, having seen the puzzled look on her face, 'so, you can imagine what a cross I have to bear, can't you, eh?'

'William!' Sal Tanner's concern suddenly shifted from herself to that of the man she'd been with. 'What about William?' When Marlow told her, in the gentlest way he could, that William had been beyond saving, she fell back in Emma's arms making a sign of the cross and saying in a quiet voice, 'Get me 'ome, lad. I'll mend all right, wi'out goin' to no infirmary.' When he hesitated, she turned to Emma, 'I'd be done fer sure, if I was shut up in a place like that. You'll 'elp me, won't yer, lass, eh?' When she began crying, Emma held her close, her only concern being for this poor, distressed woman.

'Of course I'll help you,' she promised. 'Don't fret yourself . . . we'll get you to your own bed.'

The Tanner barge was moored close by, so Marlow gently lifted his sister into his arms, while Emma caught hold of her hand and held it comfortingly, half-walking, half-running, as she tried to keep up with Marlow's long strides. He was deeply aware of Emma as she brushed against him, and at that moment Marlow knew he would never love any other woman – not for as long as he lived. As for Emma, just being close to him gave her a wonderful feeling of belonging – one that she had not experienced since her papa had died.

As the horses thundered by, drawing the fire engine behind them, Marlow and Emma were forced to one side. 'They'll have it safe now,' he told Emma, and as their eyes met, they shared an intimate smile which made Emma's heart somersault. But, his eyes grew serious as he told her, 'I'll have to set Sal's leg . . . it won't be a pleasant thing to see. Do you still want to help?'

Emma was undeterred. 'Of course I want to help,' she said. Then she ventured, 'Is there no one else but you and your sister?' When Marlow replied that no, there was just the two of them, Emma boldly asked after their parents. However, she soon wished that she had not mentioned it when she saw Marlow's face grow serious, and in a darker mood he told her, 'No, we've no parents, me and Sal . . . we were *robbed* of 'em, some many years back!'

In the ensuing silence, Emma felt awkward and angry with herself. Sal Tanner, meanwhile, was totally shocked when she heard Marlow's reply to Emma's questions, for there was so much bitterness in his voice, that it seemed as though he knew something of the terrible way in which both their parents had been taken. Their father murdered and their mother hanged.

Indeed, Marlow was deeply troubled by certain things which he had recently discovered regarding what had taken place in the past. But his fine features betrayed little of his worries as he continued on his way – with his sister in his arms, Emma by his side, and an overwhelming love in his heart for both of them.

Emma was also troubled, for she knew that in going to Marlow Tanner's barge she was going against both her papa's wish and Caleb Crowther's instructions. She didn't feel that she was breaking her promise by helping an injured person, but she knew she was in grave danger of doing so through the irrepressible feelings she had for the man beside her. She could never betray her beloved papa, so she determined that she would give her help, as one human being to another, but after that, she must never see either of the Tanners again.

On seeing Emma disappear along the wharf in the company of the Tanners, and seeing how contented she appeared to be, Gregory Denton was overcome with jealousy. Without thinking too deeply of the possible consequences of his actions, he quickly searched for Thomas amongst the men who were busy helping to clear up the mess. On finding him, he instructed him to make haste and report to Caleb Crowther.

'Tell him we've lost one man – the fellow as started it, I reckon! Make sure he knows how quickly we got the fire under control. But, tell him as there's another matter he should know about. The matter of his ward, Miss Grady, being enticed away by river-folk . . . not fit company at all for a young lady of Miss Grady's standing, as I'm sure Mr Crowther will agree.' In this unusually vindictive mood, Gregory Denton might well have given the name of these river-folk. But he was no fool! Marlow Tanner and his sister were that rare breed of worker who could always be relied on, and he didn't want to be deprived of their services. Added to which, the men who worked here wouldn't take too kindly to having one of their mates put out of work on account of what *he* said. No, thought Gregory Denton, it would be enough to have Marlow Tanner realize that Miss Grady was a young woman he must steer clear of. Yes, that would suffice.

'Go on!' he instructed Thomas. 'Tell Mr Crowther exactly as I've told you.' Then, with a feeling of satisfaction, he watched the dog-cart move out of sight at an urgent speed. And, even though he astonished himself with his own boldness, Gregory Denton was thinking that one day he might even ask for Miss Grady's hand in marriage!

Emma had watched with admiration as Marlow firstly straightened Sal Tanner's leg, and then skilfully strapped it between two stout canes. During this painful operation, Emma had comforted the woman. She had talked to her, bathed her other wounds, mopped the sweat from her face and, at both Marlow's and Sal's insistence, had kept her topped up with a good measure of gin.

'Yer a good lass, Emma Grady,' Sal kept telling her. 'Yer don't belong ter them there Crowther toffs. Oh! . . . I've 'eard all about the buggers, full o' their own importance an' lording it o'er other creatures. An' that bearded divil . . . well! That's *Justice* Crowther, ain't it? Now *there's* a laugh, eh? What fair justice has *that* bugger ever given out? None at all, that's what! Oh, aye . . . that slimy sod's well known, by name an' bloody nature!' Peering at Emma, she added, 'Ain't that right, Emma Grady? . . . Ain't every word I say the very truth?' She waited for an answer, as though she was willing Emma to give the right one – or be damned along with the rest of the Crowther brood.

Emma, however, would not be drawn into Sal Tanner's little game, although, deep inside her, she knew every word Sal spoke to be the very same as those emblazoned on her own heart. 'Why don't you rest, Sal?' she suggested tactfully. 'You've been through a lot today.' She leaned forward and drew up the blanket from the bottom of the bunk, where Sal had contemptuously flung it. 'You need to keep warm,' she chastised, 'and you might get better that much quicker if you did as you were told.'

'Be buggered!' Sal Tanner retorted. 'You're nowt but a snotty-nosed kid an' I ain't being ordered about by no lass young enough to be me bloody daughter!' She began snorting and cursing and searching for her flask of gin. 'Sod off!' she told Emma. 'Go on, piss off back ter them fancy buggers yer live with.' Taking the blanket in both hands, she flung it to the floor. 'I ain't no bloody babby!' she grumbled, folding her arms and lapsing into a fit of sulks.

'Is that right?' demanded Emma, equally determined. 'Then stop *behaving* like one!' With that, she collected up the blanket and flung it over the stiff, angry figure, 'And you're not likely to get your own way by throwing insults at *me*, Sal Tanner . . . because I've been insulted by past-masters at it! So you'll have to think again, won't you, eh?' Emma's eyes were twinkling as they met the other woman's defiant yet curious expression.

'Well, I'm buggered!' Sal Tanner roared, throwing herself back into the pillow and cackling with glee. 'Yer a little she-cat, ain't yer? A little she-cat wi' claws!' Then, calling out to the galley, where Marlow was brewing up a jug of tea, 'What the bloody 'ell 'ave yer fotched under our roof, Marlow, lad?' she chuckled. 'A right little madam, I'm thinking!' At the same time she affectionately slapped the back of Emma's hand, as the two of them laughed together.

'A right little *angel*,' corrected Marlow, as he squeezed his broad shoulders in through the narrow doorway. 'And one that's got the better of *your* temper, I see,' he laughed.

Setting down three pots of tea on the little dresser, he cautioned both women, 'Be careful, it's piping hot.'

Emma helped Sal Tanner to a more comfortable, semi-upright position, and after carefully placing a pot of tea in her hands, she picked up another one for herself and proceeded to sip it. All the while, Marlow's eyes followed her every move, his love for her emanating from them for all the world to see.

Being so close that she could feel the warmth of Marlow's breath against her face, it took all of Emma's will-power to stop herself from looking up at him. Knowing her eyes betrayed the love she felt for him, she merely nodded and gave the slightest murmur, 'It *is* hot.' In the short silence that followed – when all that could be heard was Sal Tanner noisily slurping her tea, the loud ticking of a large round clock which took up the whole of the polished wooden panel above the tiny dresser, and the gentle slapping of the water against the sides of the barge – Emma experienced a welcomed feeling of happiness and belonging here in this homely barge.

It was the first time Emma had ever been inside a barge, and it had been a great surprise. Not for a moment had she expected to see such a cosy and exceptionally pretty home as this. All the walls and ceiling were made of highly-polished panels. In the living-quarters the walls were decorated with lovely brass artefacts – plates, old bellows and the like; from the ceiling hung three oil-lamps of brass and wood, each sparkling and meticulously kept; there were two tiny dressers, both made of walnut and displaying small china ornaments – which, according to Sal, were 'put away when we're on the move', as were the china plates which were propped up on shelves beneath each porthole; the horse-hair chairs were free-standing, but the dressers were securely fixed to the floorboards. There was also a small cast-iron fire, and the narrow galley which was well-stocked and spotless. In one of the two bedrooms there was a tiny dresser with a tall cupboard beside it, and a deep narrow bunk beneath a porthole. Emma had been astonished that everything a person might need could be provided in such a limited space.

All the time Emma had been attending to Sal Tanner, she had encouraged her to talk at great length about the barge.

'She's been in the Tanner family fer a good few years now . . . ever since me mammy an' dah were wed. It's named Eve . . . after me mammy, d'yer see?' Judging by Sal's moist eyes when she spoke of the barge, and by the proud look on her face, Emma could see that the barge was greatly loved. Not only did she see this in Sal's face, but she could feel it all around her. There was a special kind of goodness and love in this little home, which she would have given everything for!

Emma's mind was overrun by a multitude of thoughts – of her papa, of what they had both been denied at his last moments, and now, of this young man sitting so close to her that all she had to do was reach out her hand and he would surely take it. Suddenly she felt afraid, and as the tears sprang to her eyes, warm and stinging, she told Marlow, 'I must go . . . Thomas will be concerned about my disappearance.' But it wasn't Thomas she was thinking of so much as the possibility that, in his anxiety, Gregory Denton might have alerted Caleb Crowther. A quick glance at the clock told her that over an hour had passed since she had made her way here with Marlow and Sal.

Quickly, Emma got to her feet, before astonishing Sal Tanner by leaning down to kiss her warmly on the forehead. 'Remember,' she told her, 'you do as you're told.' Then, deliberately averting her eyes from Marlow, she edged her way towards the door, through the living-area, and up the small flight of steps to the deck. Once there, she glanced along the wharf, feeling less anxious when she saw that it was unusually quiet, save for two little lads in floppy caps and knee-length breeches who were scrambling up a stack of coal and occasionally skimming the smaller pieces on the water. Up to mischief while everybody else is giving help and clearing away the mess at the warehouse, she thought with amusement.

'Must you go, Emma?' She turned, startled, as Marlow climbed out to stand beside her. As her gaze settled on his face, her heart felt suffocated. He looked so handsome and was staring at her now with such intensity and passion. Soon after they had come into the barge, Marlow had grabbed a grey chequered shirt, quickly shrugging himself into it and rolling the long sleeves up to the elbows. He had been too preoccupied with Sal to waste time doing up the many small buttons down its front. Now, as he stood tall and upright before her, Emma was conscious of the breeze which play-fully tugged at his shirt, occasionally whipping it backwards to display his sunburned and muscular chest. Emma was immediately reminded of the vicious scars that Caleb Crowther had etched into Marlow's back. She had made no mention of the incident, believing it to be one that was best forgotten. But, as it now reared its ugly head in her mind she suddenly became fearful. Thus, when Marlow suggested that if she really had to leave, he would walk her back to the Wharf Mill, Emma felt frantic.

'No, I don't want that!' she told him. 'Please . . . your sister needs you just now.'

'More than *you* need me, Emma?' he asked in a soft voice, which was little more than a whisper, and penetrating her trembling soul with his loving gaze.

Deliberately now, and with every ounce of strength she could muster, Emma looked him in the eye, and in a quiet, controlled voice said, 'I'm glad that your sister wasn't hurt more badly, and I'm pleased to have been of help. But . . . believe me, Marlow, I *must* go!' Lowering her eyes, she tried to turn from him, only to find her way barred as Marlow placed himself before her. In a minute he had one hand on her shoulder, and, with the other, he gently touched her chin, tilting her face to look up at him. For a long cherished moment, he held her like that, his dark eyes burning into her and his fingers tenderly caressing her face.

Emma was mesmerized. Try as she might, she couldn't tear her gaze away from his; and though every instinct told her to run from this place, she was unable to move. I do love him so, she thought, and I don't want to go. I would wish for nothing else but that I could stay by his side. As he lowered his face so that it almost touched hers, Emma's heart melted; and when he murmured, 'I love you, Emma,' a wonderful tide of emotion surged through her. She offered no resistance when, suddenly, he grabbed her in his arms and kissed her with such longing that he took her breath away. In that exquisite moment, their passionate and intimate embrace warned Emma that, because of the way the river-people had taken her mama and ruined her papa's life and because of the promise she herself had given her papa, there could be no future for her and Marlow. Emma also knew that any relationship which might have grown between them would be dangerous for Marlow – the scars on his back were a caution that must be heeded. So many things were against them, against their love, and Emma's instincts urged her that she and Marlow could ignore these only at their own peril!

As Emma wrenched herself from his embrace, Marlow made no move to restrain her because he already feared he'd gone too far. Instead, he reminded himself that Emma was of a different kind to the lasses he was used to. She had been brought up accustomed to the finer things in life, and was used to folk who might seek her affection in a more restrained fashion. He had also seen that, in spite of her outburst with Sal, Emma was quiet and deep-thinking, and might be overwhelmed by his forward display of emotion. Having her so close, yet still so far away from him, gave him a feeling of desperation. He wanted her so much. He meant to have her. But even now, when he was no more than a heartbeat away, Marlow Tanner sensed the barrier between them. For the first time in his life, he felt unsure and afraid.

Hating every step that took her further away from him, Emma hurried along the quayside. On reaching the corner before she turned off towards the mill, she paused to look back, and, seeing that Marlow had gone, her heart sank within her. For a brief moment she was tempted to go back, and, as she stood there watching the spot where he had stood, an overwhelming sensation of warmth and joy came over her – just as she had felt on the two memorable occasions when she had found herself in Marlow's company. However,

Emma painfully realized that both times had been over-shadowed by suffering and tragedy. The first meeting had culminated in the agonizing beating inflicted on Marlow by Caleb Crowther, as well as the distress she had unwittingly caused her dying papa through her foolhardy behaviour. Now, at their second encounter, a man had been killed and Sal Tanner badly hurt. For a moment, these thoughts haunted Emma and she prayed this was not some terrible omen for the future. 'No matter,' she murmured, still gazing towards the barge, 'for our paths won't likely cross again. They must not, Marlow Tanner. And I hope you can see that just as clearly as I can!' But even as she muttered these words aloud, her heart was disobediently murmuring something to the contrary, and filling her with trepidation.

Emma was so engrossed in her tortured thoughts of Marlow Tanner that she did not hear the stamp of swift and angry footsteps drawing ever closer to her. When a hand fell upon her shoulder and roughly swung her round, she gave out a cry of fright, her alarmed eyes coming to rest on the furious face of Caleb Crowther.

'Well?' he said, in a voice which warned Emma to be most careful. When she hesitated, he dug his fingers deeper into her shoulder. 'I'm given to understand that you've been with the river-people. What I want to know . . . right now . . . is who are these people? What are their names? Take me to them this instant.' His eyes grew even darker as they glared at her.

'You've been misinformed, Uncle Caleb,' replied Emma in a remarkably controlled voice, considering the turmoil within her. 'There was so much chaos and confusion when the fire started, that Mr Denton urged me to get out quickly.

I would have made my way straight home but . . . I couldn't find Thomas.' Thomas was standing slightly behind Caleb Crowther, to his left. Emma glanced at him and gave up two small prayers – one that Thomas would not betray her, and the other asking forgiveness for the blatant lie she had just told.

At that instant, something happened which struck the fear of God in Emma's heart, and for a brief moment she was convinced it was her just punishment for the sin she had just committed. For, loud and clear, Sal Tanner's voice sailed the length of the wharf. 'Sod an' bugger it, Marlow! 'Ow the 'ell am I supposed to get better if yer keeps depriving me o' me bloody booze! Best medicine in the world is a swig of booze, yer silly arse!'

At once, Caleb Crowther stretched his neck to see where the voice might be coming from. Thomas also glanced along the wharf, a fearful expression in his nervous eyes. As for Emma, she crossed her fingers behind her back and kept her serious gaze constantly on her uncle's face. For a long, nerve-wracking moment, it seemed as though Caleb Crowther would stride off to investigate. When he looked back into Emma's calm and seemingly innocent face, there was still the germ of suspicion lurking in his fiery eyes. Without taking either his hand or his probing gaze from Emma, he said in a quiet voice, 'Thomas . . . is what Miss Grady says the truth? Were you not at your station waiting to speed her home the minute her duties were done?' Still, he kept his eyes securely fixed on Emma.

Emma felt Thomas's gaze on her, but she dared not look at him. All she could do was to hope desperately that he would give credence to her lie. For, Thomas had indeed been

ready and eager to take her away the minute Gregory Denton
had thrust her towards that side door.

''Tain't Miss Grady's fault at all,' replied Thomas, and
Emma had to stop herself from visibly showing her heartfelt
relief. 'When that fire started, I saw Miss Grady making her
way towards me . . . but I could see the way of things right
enough, Mr Crowther, sir. If it hadn't been every man to the
helm . . . so to speak, well, the whole place could a' been
engulfed, don't yer see? I called out to Miss Grady to get
right away from there!'

'And that's what I did, Uncle Caleb,' Emma intervened
with a wide, innocent look. 'I've been wandering up and
down the wharf . . . staying out of harm's way, that's all.'

Now Caleb Crowther let go of Emma and swung himself
about to address Thomas. 'Why didn't you tell me that
before, you bloody fool?' he demanded.

''Cause yer never asked me, Mr Crowther, sir,' replied
Thomas, looking suitably sheepish.

Caleb Crowther gave out a groan, together with the
instruction, 'Get Miss Grady home this instant. Then come
back here. There's damage to be assessed and a certain fellow
to be spoken to.' As he strode away, neither Thomas nor
Emma had any doubts as to who that 'certain fellow' was.

'Poor Mr Denton,' said Emma with a little smile, hurrying
alongside Thomas as they made their way back to the
carriage. 'As if he hasn't had enough trouble for one day.'

To which Thomas gave a noisy snigger. 'Oh, he'll be all
right, Miss Grady. They do say as how Gregory Denton can
handle any occasion *most admirably*!' The last two words
were greatly exaggerated, causing Emma to lightly reprimand
him.

'All the same,' she said, 'I shouldn't think he's yet had to deal with such an occasion as Mr Crowther in full sail.' In all truth, Emma hoped poor Mr Denton wouldn't be subjected to too much condemnation on her account. She was certain that Mr Denton would be unable to get a word in against the fury of her uncle's explosive temper; which was just as well since he had after all seen her going off with the Tanners – and there was not the slightest doubt in her mind that it was *he* who had alerted her uncle.

As they left the wharf, the dry acrid smell of charred cotton bales followed them – clinging to their clothes, stinging their throats, and causing Emma to be gripped by a severe coughing spasm.

'Lord love us!' exclaimed Thomas, expertly manoeuvring the horse and carriage in and out of the numerous highly-stacked piles of merchandise, and skilfully avoiding the dockers who were by now filtering back from the fire to their posts, ready to work that much harder in order to catch up on their duties. 'It's to be hoped you ain't goin' down wi' sommat nasty. By! That Mrs Manfred would 'ave me swinging fro' the end of a rope if you've tekken badly on *my* account!' It was well-known that Mrs Manfred considered Miss Grady almost as her own lass. Look at the way she'd almost thrown a fit just now when it was reported that Miss Grady was suspected of going off with the river-folk. But then, Thomas didn't blame Mrs Manfred, because Miss Grady was a grand little lass, that she was. What's more, he hadn't minded saving her with a lie just now – though it would cost him a prayer or two come Sunday! But then he was sure the Lord would understand, and he said as much to Mrs Manfred on their return, adding with fervent belief, 'I'm sure if the good Lord were faced wi' Caleb Crowther on the one side, an' Miss Grady on the other, Himself would a done the very same thing!'

'Away with you!' Mrs Manfred had told him, with feigned horror. 'You'll not ease your conscience *that* way.' However, before he skulked away, she brought back the smile to his face by adding, 'All the same, Thomas lad . . . there are times when we're called on to go against our teaching, in order to see justice done!'

As Thomas made his way to the stables, Emma found herself being unceremoniously ushered into the house. 'I watched from the window for you, Miss Grady,' Mrs Manfred explained. 'I wanted to come out and stop you, before you were confronted by Mrs Crowther.' As they drew nearer to the front door, she lowered her voice, saying, 'She's in the drawing-room, waiting for an explanation. You just tell her what you told Mr Crowther . . . you did *not* go near the river-folk!' Here, she gave Emma a suspicious look. 'You can tell *me* the real story later!'

It was six p.m. when Emma answered the knock on her bedroom door, to find Mrs Manfred standing there. Her audience with Agnes Crowther had been brief and, much to Emma's surprise, less of an ordeal than she had anticipated. Her aunt seemed to have other things on her mind, not least of which appeared to be a letter that she continuously played with throughout her questioning of Emma. She appeared to Emma to be extremely agitated and unusually nervous and Emma mentioned this now, to Mrs Manfred. 'She hardly seemed to mind a word I said, Manny,' Emma concluded.

'Aye, well . . . she and the master had a deal of words

over that letter . . . the pair of 'em got so worked up, we could hear the heated exchange all over the house!' explained Mrs Manfred in a hushed tone. 'And well they might be worked up!' she went on, drawing Emma away from the bedroom door, fearing that they might be overheard. Now, in an even more subdued tone, she told Emma how the letter appeared to have been sent by the headmistress of 'that posh establishment' to which Martha Crowther had been despatched with such fuss some weeks ago. 'A right to-do, there is, Miss Grady,' continued Mrs Manfred, her hand on Emma's arm as she constantly watched the door. As she continued, Emma was horrified to hear how Martha had caused such trouble at the school that the headmistress had insisted on seeing both of her parents straightaway. There was even a possibility that she might be expelled!

'Expelled? . . . *Martha Crowther*?' Emma could hardly believe her ears.

'There is every chance that such a thing could happen,' said Mrs Manfred, afterwards shaking her head and drawing her lips into a tight little pucker.

'I'm not surprised Uncle Caleb was in a worse mood than usual,' exclaimed Emma, 'and that certainly explains why I was sent so swiftly from the drawing-room, earlier.'

'Hhm! For all her airs and graces . . . and for all that she never once passes an opportunity to slap you down . . . Mrs Crowther's precious daughter is not the blameless little soul she would have her be! From what I was able to gather, the peevish and spiteful side to Miss Crowther's nature has been given full rein since leaving this house. Apparently, she's caused a deal of mischief, and upset a number of the other girls at the school . . . also, there's a question of something going missing, which Miss Crowther insists has been stolen by a certain individual.'

All the while Mrs Manfred was relating her story, Emma's eyes were popping from her head. She just couldn't believe it. Martha Crowther – that arrogant and thoroughly spoiled girl, who could never do anything wrong! Well, it seemed now as though her true colours were flying at long last! Trying desperately hard not to laugh, Emma thought how *dreadful* the scandal hereabouts would be if the only child of Caleb Crowther, the Justice, and his wife Agnes, the proud peacock, was sent home in disgrace from the posh school. Oh, the very idea! Emma swung away from the homely housekeeper and, throwing herself on to the bed, collapsed into a fit of laughter, burying her head in the pillow to smother the sound.

'You stop that at once!' ordered Mrs Manfred, striding to the bed and shaking Emma by the shoulder. 'This is a very serious matter, I'll have you know . . . not one to be taken lightly by any standards.' Mrs Manfred had very firm principles regarding a young lady's behaviour, and, at the moment, neither Martha Crowther's, nor Emma's in making so light of the matter, was an example of good upbringing.

'Oh, I'm sorry, Manny,' said Emma in a contrite voice, as she leaned on one elbow and raised her mischievously smiling eyes. 'I shouldn't laugh, I know. It's a disgraceful thing for Martha to cause such mischief and bring shame on the Crowther name . . . but . . . well . . .' Then, in spite of her best efforts to contain herself, Emma's serious expression began to crumble, her eyes grew increasingly merry and she evaporated into a convulsion of giggling. 'Oh, Manny!' she cried, looking directly into the other woman's disapproving scowl. 'Can't you just see the funny side of it?' Whereupon, she fell against Mrs Manfred and hugged her fiercely. In a minute, Mrs Manfred was also chuckling.

'You're a naughty one!' she reprimanded Emma. 'But you're right. I can just see Mrs Crowther's expression when she opened that letter!' Still holding Emma fast, she too shook with laughter.

When they eventually composed themselves, the discussion turned to the other incident of the day – involving Emma and the river-folk. Mrs Manfred related to Emma how the letter had arrived not long before Thomas had brought the message from Gregory Denton. 'In fact, the two of them were still loudly arguing over it,' she explained, 'when the news came, that not only had there been a fire, but that you had been seen going away in the company of the river-folk!'

As she listened to what had taken place, Emma could easily see how such a series of events might send Caleb Crowther into an explosive mood. Suddenly, she felt sorry for Gregory Denton, who had no doubt borne the brunt of that temper. In all truth, Emma thought, he had probably acted in what he thought were her best interests. She made up her mind straightaway to make amends with the poor fellow at the first opportunity.

'And *did* you go off with the river-folk?' demanded Mrs Manfred now, a tremor of fear in her voice.

For a long moment, Emma gave no answer. Instead, her thoughts had wandered back to the wharf, to that colourful, welcoming, Tanner barge, and to Marlow Tanner himself. Whenever she thought of him, that same warm glow and wonderful feeling of contentment came into her heart. She was both afraid and possessive of the thoughts which now suffused her mind – that special way in which his dark, lustrous eyes murmured to her in the warmth of his smile; the way her foolish heart trembled when he spoke to her in that soft, caressing voice. But, most of all, Emma was held forever in his embrace, with the tender strength of his kiss still burning on her mouth, and that passionate look of longing in his eyes doing unexplainable things to her aching heart. All of these emotions were alien to Emma. They frightened her. But, for all that, she could not help but cherish them.

'I *will* have the truth, child!' Mrs Manfred interrupted Emma's thoughts. She had watched Emma closely, and was filled with apprehension when she saw Emma's face light up as she became lost in her thoughts. Her treasured memories of Marlow Tanner were clearly reflected on her lovely features as she raised her soft grey eyes to Mrs Manfred. In answer to the older woman's question, she replied simply, 'I love him, Manny.'

'No, no, child! You *don't* love him . . . What can you even know of love? With you a child not yet sixteen?' The desperation betrayed itself in her voice, as she lifted her two hands and tenderly placed one on each of Emma's small shoulders.

'You're right, Manny darling,' Emma conceded, her heart moved by the stricken look on the older woman's face. 'I don't know anything about love . . . or how it should feel. All I do know is that, whenever I think of him, every corner of my being lights up, and I want nothing more than to spend my whole life by his side!' Emma held nothing back now, as she poured her heart out to the only real friend she had. She whispered of her love and her fears . . . of the way Marlow beckoned to her and how she could see in him all of her dreams. And now, with her eyes downcast and her heart heavy, Emma told Mrs Manfred of the fervent promise she had given to her papa, and how it weighed on her shoulders 'like the end of the world'.

All the time Emma had been talking, Mrs Manfred had softly wept. If she had thought Emma to be still a child, she was sorely wrong. If she had believed Emma could know nothing of love, then she herself knew even less. If she had convinced herself that, in having lost first her mama, then her darling papa, and consequently having been placed at the mercy of the Crowthers, Emma had been dealt all the cruelties that life could deal her, then she was indeed an old fool. For, Mrs Manfred had never seen a person so in love, and so tormented because of it, as her darling Emma was now. Because she regarded Emma almost as her own flesh and blood, she must advise her for the best: and that meant persuading Emma to put the young bargee out of her mind and out of her heart.

Having confided her most secret thoughts to Mrs Manfred, Emma now looked up and, seeing the still-wet tears on that much-loved face, she was deeply touched. 'Oh, Manny,' she murmured, bringing her fingers to brush against the older woman's face, 'don't fret yourself. I can be strong, you know that. Papa told me how he felt about the river-folk . . . and *why*. He asked me to give him my word that they would find no place in my life, and I freely gave it.' Emma's firm, clear gaze met the sorry eyes that looked into hers, and in an unfaltering voice she went on, 'Papa was a fine man, with a deep sense of justice. If he had not believed it to be for the best, he would never have asked it of me. I trust his judgment in all things and I *must* keep my word!' In her heart, Emma prayed to God that he might help her.

'Aw, child . . . much as I loved your papa, I have to say that he had no right to ask such a thing of you,' said Mrs Manfred with a sigh.

'He had every right!' declared Emma, and, to all intents and purposes, she considered the discussion to be at an end. However, in spite of herself, somewhere deep inside her, Emma had much sympathy with Mrs Manfred's sentiment. Furthermore, her curiosity concerning the past was now aroused; what had happened between her mama and the river-people? 'Bad blood' Caleb Crowther had said of her mama, and, though she had later been given an explanation for this by her papa, there was still a murmuring of unease in Emma's soul. How had her mama *really* come to die? *Why* was Caleb Crowther so bitter towards Mary Grady? And why had she herself been kept in the dark, only to be told of it by her papa as he lay on his death bed? Emma despised herself for raising questions which, by their very nature, must cast doubt on her own papa's word. Quickly, she pushed the entire matter to the darker recesses of her mind. But not before she was filled with the earnest hope that, one day at some time in the distant future, she might know the full truth of what had happened all those years ago.

It was nearing dusk when Marlow Tanner accompanied the little man to the place where his faithful old cob-horse was tethered. Both men were silent, both deep in thought – one wondering whether he had been wise to pay a rare visit to these parts; the other, curiously considering a guarded remark made some time before by Gabe Drury, concerning Marlow's own dah.

'Gabe . . . you take care now,' Marlow told the little man as he climbed on to the bare back of the cob. As Gabe Drury looked down, to find Marlow's dark eyes intent upon him, there was a long heavy silence, interrupted only by the slapping of the canal water against the moored barges. It was Marlow who spoke first, and what he asked only served to agitate the little fellow. 'Can you tell me *anything* . . . anything at all, about the fellow you saw making good his escape that day?'

'No! . . . I've told you before, Marlow,' already Gabe Drury was hurriedly spurring his horse on, 'I saw nowt but a pair of legs just running, that's all! I were sleeping off a boozy night . . . found mesel' spread-eagled in the hedge, an' when I heard all the commotion, I just looked up . . . saw *nowt*, except for a pair o' legs. I can't tell you more than that!' With a wary look about him, he urged the horse on its way, but not before glancing over his shoulder to warn Marlow, 'Leave the past be, lad. It's done an' there's nowt to change it. Take good care of your sister, and God bless the pair of you.'

As he went into the gathering darkness, Gabe Drury thought himself a fool. What in God's name had ever made him mention seeing anybody on that terrible day when Sal and Marlow's dah was murdered, together with his fancy piece? All these years he'd kept to the backwaters, out of harm's way, but when Marlow had recently sought him out – the subject of his parents being his motive – the lad had somehow managed to persuade him to reveal how he'd seen a fellow running from that place. Now, Marlow wouldn't let it be! All the same, Gabe Drury hoped that tonight he'd laid that particular ghost to rest once and for all.

As he reflected on events, Gabe Drury thought what a pity it was that he had been brought back to this area by the news of Sal Tanner's accident, for he was very fond of her and her brother. But, he wouldn't be so bold as to make his way here again – not for *any* reason! Because, even though nigh on sixteen years had passed since the murders, Gabe Drury had suffered many a nightmare ever since. Try as he might, he couldn't forget that fancy fellow who had rushed past him, with the dark crimson stain of blood on his hands. As he fled past, the man had turned to see him lying there. In that moment, Gabe Drury was horrified to recognize the gentleman as being one who was seen to be an upright and prominent member of the community; and who was well-known hereabouts; one who would never in a million years be thought capable of committing such a heinous crime as that which was later discovered. At the moment his frantic stare plucked out Gabe Drury's half-hidden form, he seemed like a thing possessed! When those mad, savage eyes scoured his face, Gabe Drury found a strength he never knew he had. Like the wind he had fled from there – and he'd been running ever since, knowing in his heart that if a certain evil fellow ever caught him, he'd be dead for sure! Wild horses wouldn't have dragged him back to these parts, only for the long-lasting friendship he had enjoyed for many years with Sal and Marlow's dad, Bill Royston, and consequently his affection for the two young 'uns. Added to which was Gabe Drury's shame at being such a fearful coward that he daren't speak up when their mother, Eve Royston, was hanged for the murders. He had come to despise himself for being no better than that fancy fellow. After all, wasn't the blood of Eve Royston on *his* hands . . . just as surely as if he'd hanged her himself?

With a grim face, Marlow watched horse and rider out of sight. Gabe Drury knew more than he was letting on. He was frightened, Marlow was sure of it! Well, he would be patient, and for as long as it took; if he came to one dead-end, there'd be other roads he could take. But, for now, he was driven by an even greater tide of emotion – his abiding love for Emma Grady, and the burning desire to take her as his wife. It wouldn't be easy, he knew that. But then, nothing really worthwhile ever was!

# Chapter Four

'There's a war brewing in America, I tell you!' The portly fellow tipped the brandy glass to his lips and drained it dry. Then, taking a chunky cigar from his top pocket, he placed it between his teeth and began biting on it. 'It won't be long now before Lincoln's elected to office, and, with the Republicans so intent on this anti-slavery policy, there'll be fur flying in no time. You mark my words, there'll be war on the other side of the Atlantic!'

'I hope to God you're wrong, Harrison!' declared a small, square-looking fellow seated in the deep, leather armchair by the fire, his weasel-features bathed by the heat from the flames, and his eyes most anxious as they swept the eight figures seated around the room. 'Each of us here has all our money sunk in the Lancashire cotton industry. *Should* there be a war in America . . . and the issue is the slaves who pick the cotton which runs our mills . . . it could mean catastrophe for Lancashire. And for every one of us here!' The thought appeared to horrify him because he was suddenly on his feet and pacing anxiously up and down.

'You're exaggerating!' protested one man.

'It's a fact though,' said another, 'it was *May* when

Lincoln was nominated for the presidency – six months ago! And just look how the southern states have put up every obstacle to keep him from coming to office. There *is* strong feeling. There bloody well is! If you ask me, it's a situation which needs to be watched most carefully!'

'You're panicking, the lot of you!' intervened a bald-headed man. 'I'm telling you, there'll be no war. The cotton will be shipped in just as regularly as it's ever been and the mills of Lancashire will continue to thrive, just as they are now.' With that said, he leaned back in his chair, embracing one and all with a smug expression.

'Gentlemen.' All eyes turned to look at Caleb Crowther. So far, he had made no contribution to the debate which, since the men's departure from the dinner table to the sanctuary of the library, had become somewhat heated. Now, however, he strode to the centre of the room where he tactfully waited to ensure that he held their absolute attention. When satisfied, he continued in a sombre tone, 'The very reason you were all invited here tonight, was to discuss this matter. Of late, there has been too much talk of what's happening in America and it's time to put an end to it!' Here, his vivid eyes pausing, he oppressively scrutinized each of his guests in turn, and each was visibly affected. 'Isn't it enough that the *Blackburn Standard* puts out such articles that have our very mill-hands stopping their work to air their views and spread even *more* unrest? It's up to *us* . . . the owners . . . to set an example! If we show ourselves to be affected by unfounded gossip and troublesome rumours, then how the devil are we to expect any different from the fools we employ?' Though his expression was one of fury, his voice was remarkably calm. 'I say there will be no war in

America. The slaves will pick the cotton as they always have, and the people of Lancashire will go on processing it in our mills. There is no place here for scaremongers!' Now, his accusing glare sought out the portly fellow who was chewing on his cigar in a nervous manner.

For a long, silent moment, Caleb Crowther and the man called Harrison, continued to glower at each other. Until, taking the cigar from his mouth and lowering his eyes, Harrison asked, 'You're saying we have nothing to worry about then . . . in your opinion?'

When Caleb Crowther firmly replied, 'Nothing. Nothing at all,' a wave of sighs filled the air and at once the atmosphere became calmer.

'Crowther runs more mills than any of us here,' said one, 'and if he's not concerned, then I'm buggered if I don't go along with him!'

'Well, I tell you . . . I was seriously considering looking to India for my cotton supply . . . but I reckon Crowther's right,' agreed another. 'The ships will keep fetching their cargoes from America, just as they always have. The North and South will have their domestic squabbles . . . as we all do. But I'm convinced it'll come to nothing serious.'

With this, they all agreed unanimously, and there followed another round of brandy and cigars, and an otherwise congenial evening. It was not until some time after midnight that the men joined the women in the drawing-room. Shortly afterwards, the guests departed from Breckleton House to make their homeward journeys – their various horses and carriages making an impressive sight as they slowly made their way down the lamplit drive.

* * *

The next day was Saturday, and, much to Emma's dismay, Caleb Crowther's mood was little better than on the previous night. All through breakfast he could be heard muttering under his breath, 'Damned fools!' and occasionally he would lift his eyes from the food before him to glare at one and all who had the misfortune to be seated around the same table.

Emma carefully kept her gaze averted. She had no wish for her day to be tainted by his thunderous mood since today was the one day she considered to be truly her own. She felt extremely anxious, because as a rule on a Saturday, she was given permission to go off on her usual errand without being accompanied, but it would be just like her uncle to vent his spite on her by maliciously forbidding such a thing. Thus Emma was on her best behaviour, and, when breakfast was finished, she crossed her fingers behind her back before asking, 'Uncle, please may I be excused . . . I don't want to miss the tram.' In that desperately long moment when he held her gaze, his mouth set tight and his manner unyielding, Emma was sure her request was about to be denied. But then, with a grunt and a dismissive wave of his hand, he told her, 'Go, if you must.' And she did, pausing only to excuse herself from Agnes Crowther, who seemed not to care whether Emma went or stayed. It had been like this ever since the disgraceful business of Martha, which had finally been resolved with her remaining at the school. All the same, Emma reasoned, the suspicions that Martha had stolen from herself in order to implicate an innocent person, had left a smear on her character which might never go away. It was a hard and bitter pill for the Crowthers to swallow, and their relationship was greatly strained because of it.

It was a fine October day, made even warmer for Emma

by the fact that in just one week's time she would be sixteen years old. She was so excited! As she left the house, waved off by the ever-vigilant Mrs Manfred, Emma's heart felt curiously light and her step was decidedly jaunty. How she loved her Saturdays! Oh, she didn't mind her work in the company of Gregory Denton, for he was a nice enough fellow, and had readily accepted part of the blame for the nasty incident with Caleb Crowther regarding the river-people. To Emma's surprise, there were even times when, not only did she find herself enjoying a good deal of laughter with him, but she also had come to be very fond of him. Indeed, on the odd occasion, he seemed almost like a brother to her.

'Good morning, Miss Grady.' The tram-conductor held out his hand to ensure that Emma was safely aboard. 'Off to the churchyard, is it?' he asked, glancing down at the small bunch of snow-white chrysanthemums in her hand. Like most people hereabouts, he knew of Emma and her circumstances. She was a grand lass, he thought, smiling at her, but immediately correcting himself, for she wasn't a lass any more. Indeed she was a woman – a good-looking and most desirable woman. He'd noticed the change in her these past weeks when, every Saturday as regular as clockwork, she'd board this tram for the trip into Blackburn. She always got off at the church where her papa, Thadius Grady, lay. She always had a ready smile for folks, and never once made them feel that she was not exactly the same as them. Why, Emma Grady might be any one of the workers who filed into the mill every morning, so straightforward and natural was she. Her papa had been the very same, God rest his soul.

As always, Emma asked after the conductor's wife and

three bairns whom she had come to know through his incessant and cheery chatter. All the way to the church gates she was told, in the greatest detail, of how well or how poorly they all were. As she alighted from the tram, Emma gave the fellow a friendly wave which he gladly returned, as did a number of elderly passengers.

As Emma entered the churchyard the uniquely sharp, fresh after-smell of newly-cut grass filled the air. 'This is a lovely place, Papa,' Emma murmured, as she checked the water in the container and, seeing enough there, arranged the flowers inside. Then, dropping down to her knees, she began to absent-mindedly play with the coloured marble stones in the well beneath the black headpiece. This was simply inscribed with the words:

Thadius Grady
1820–1860
Rest In Peace

It had taken Emma a long, heartbreaking time to come to terms with the fact that here, in the dark silent ground, lay that darling man who had been by her side for as long as she could remember. He had always been there, unceasingly reliable, and loving her, strong and true – like a mighty tree that could never be hewn, and which even time itself could make no impression on. Now, Emma had come to accept that no one was immortal. When God called you to his side, there was no use protesting. During his long illness, Thadius had answered Emma's heartfelt question when she insisted on knowing why the Lord was taking her beloved papa. Emma could recall the moment as though it was only a heartbeat ago, when, cupping her small tearful face in his hands, he had told her, 'I expect he's short of angels.' Emma had softly cried at his words. She cried now, but the tears were tempered with a smile. 'I wonder if the good Lord made you an angel, after all,' she said, fondly touching his name upon the headstone, her silent thoughts indulged in times long gone.

Some moments later, Emma went into the Church of the Sacred Heart where she lit two candles – one for each of her parents. Afterwards, she knelt before the altar and gave up a heartfelt prayer. 'Keep them both safe in Heaven, dear Lord,' she asked, 'and let them find again the love they have for each other. Tell them not to worry about me because, with your help, I'll be just fine.' She betrayed nothing of the ache in her heart and of her great need for the young bargee, who filled her every waking thought. All the same, Emma was convinced that the good Lord probably knew already; and she couldn't help thinking that if this was the case, then *why* had he brought her and Marlow together in the first place? Surely he must have seen the heartache that would follow? Then, she recalled how her papa would often tell her that if the Lord did anything, it was not without reason. 'Forgive me, Lord,' she murmured now, as she quietly closed the vast panelled doors, 'but I hope you know what you're doing!'

The next stop was Corporation Park, a place of great beauty, with a myriad of narrow footpaths and secluded places where a person could sit and lose themselves for as long as they liked. Emma loved this park, for it took her back to the days of her childhood when she and her papa enjoyed many a happy time together exploring the meandering walkways and feeding the ducks in the lake. Every Saturday,

Emma still always found a space in her drawstring purse to secrete a small bag of crumbs for that very purpose.

But first of all, Emma felt the urge to visit what had always been her favourite place in the park. This was the very highest point, where the gun turrets from the Crimean War were on display. Emma took the route along the main broad walkway, which would lead her there, via the tall glass-domed conservatories which housed all manner of beautiful plants. As she hurried along the rhododendron-lined walkways, where every now and then the long swaying tentacles of the many weeping willows dipped and played in the breeze, a soothing sense of peace and love came into Emma's heart. Now, rather than grieve for her losses, she gave thanks that at least she still had Manny – her very dear friend and confidante. And here she was, young and healthy, with her whole life ahead of her. Only once did a shadow cross Emma's heart – when she let herself think how empty life might be without Marlow Tanner by her side.

Climbing the last few steps, Emma realized just how long ago it had been since she had come this far. There they still were – the great long-barrelled guns from the Crimean War. Emma was not surprised to see people already strolling about. To her left there was a tall, willowy man with a flat cap and heavy boots, and by his side, a weary-looking woman. The woman was carrying a large hessian bag and wearing a long dark frock, covered with a grey shawl. This she pulled tight about her against the breeze, which cut like a knife across the hill-top. Since taking up her clerical duties at the mill, Emma had become aware of many things she hadn't known before, such as the fact that many unemployed and hard-up families were forced to find out-of-the-way hiding holes in the park, where they made themselves a shelter in which to sleep. She wondered whether that was the plight of this sorry-looking pair. If it was, she thought, they had such a proud and independent look about their faces, that it made her heart go out to them.

In the distance, Emma could hear the laughter of children and, stretching her neck as she approached the gun-barrels, she could vaguely distinguish five figures approaching. Smiling at the sight of the two smaller figures running and jumping ahead in the same way she herself had once done, Emma pulled herself up on to the cold, hard gun-barrel, all the while puffing and panting from the long upward climb. Once she was settled comfortably in a secure position on the slippery metal barrel, Emma straightened up to take in the view. It was a magnificent and awesome sight to behold. From here, she could see over almost the whole of Blackburn town, with its sea of graceful church spires, and, standing tall beside these, as many mill chimneys – the former sending prayers to Heaven, and the latter sending up black rancid smoke, which day after day settled over the houses to become an intricate part of the landscape. Yet, for all that, Emma saw a curious magic in Blackburn town, particularly on a busy day when it was filled with the hustle and bustle of horses and carts, bent, shawled figures, and flat-capped little men, all answering the summons of the mill siren, and all either hurrying to, or from, their weaving and spinning machines. How they talked and laughed, Emma thought, as though they hadn't a care in the world. They would exchange friendly greetings as they hurried towards those great formidable mills, as though they were on their way to make a fortune – their indomitable spirits belying the fact that their wages did little more than feed and clothe them, and maintain a distance between themselves and the workhouse.

From the better houses the clerks and the other more important business folk would emerge and, like her own papa, Emma remembered nostalgically, they presented a very different spectacle – all sporting handsome tail-coats, together with those familiar tall hats of black and sombre appearance and some carrying canes. Then, at a later hour still, the ladies would step out in their pretty flowered bonnets and rich taffeta skirts. And, constantly, making their own particular music over the jutting cobbles, the clip-clop of horses' hooves could be heard up and down the street as they pulled along the merchants' flat-waggons, brewers' drays and carriages of all manner and style – all going about their business and all most exciting to Emma.

Today was market day, and from her vantage point, Emma imagined she could see the grey flapping canopies which covered the stalls and hear the urgent and colourful shouts of waremongers. As she sat there, perched on the gun-barrel with the breeze numbing her face and pinching her ears, Emma gazed across Blackburn town and told herself that, in the whole of her life, she would never want to be anywhere else but here.

When the family of five strolled by, Emma thought what a lovely sight they made. There was Papa, impressively dressed in a dark suit, with a white silk scarf around his neck, and on his head a most expensive-looking tall hat. He had long side whiskers and a friendly smile, which he directed at Emma. His wife was also extremely well turned-out in a fine green velvet outfit, with a large sweeping bustle. The two older children, both boys, were smartly dressed in short, dark breeches, grey cloth caps and little fitted jackets. Emma could see by the way they constantly broke free from their parents to run and hide, that they were probably quite a handful. Holding onto the woman's hand was a little girl of about three years old; a pretty chubby-cheeked child with a serious face and regal step. As the family sauntered away, they reminded Emma of the Royal Family. The little girl in particular looked just like that picture in the paper of Queen Victoria's youngest child, Princess Beatrice.

Smiling to herself, Emma got down from her perched position, rubbing her hands against the cold and thinking it was time she started making her way back down. She would head for the lake and the ducks and spend a while there.

Emma was surprised to find herself the only one down at the lake. But then, she reminded herself, she was much earlier today on account of wanting to get away before Caleb Crowther might change his mind. Coming to where the railings finished and the grassy bank sloped gently down to the lake's edge, Emma stepped forward until the tips of her boots were almost touching the water. Then, throwing the crumbs as far out as she could, she watched with pleasure as the ducks sped forward, loudly quacking and nudging each other in order to be the first to grab them. Emma reflected on how peaceful it was here, and how soothing for a person's turbulent thoughts.

Not far away, there was another who was of a similar mind to Emma. After seeing to his sister's comfort that morning, Marlow Tanner had walked the mile or so which took him to Corporation Park. He felt a great need for peace and quiet, away from the incessant banter of Sal – who he thought must be the worst creature on God's earth when struck down and made virtually immobile – so that he might reflect on things. It was in Sal's nature to be obstinate and demanding, he knew, but never more so than since the accident. And, above all else, she insisted on constantly reminding him that there was only one thing to be got from giving your heart above your station – and that was grief. 'More grief than you could ever imagine!' she'd warned over and over. This morning, however, she had finally got under his skin. If he hadn't got away he might well have been tempted to dunk her in the canal, for he knew only too well the wisdom of her words.

'Come here, Jake!' he called now, as the panting dog strained hard on its lead. 'Ease up there!' But the dog did not like the rules which dictated that he must at all times be kept on a lead. He was hot and thirsty – and his eye had caught sight of the wide, shimmering lake, alive with noisy fluttering ducks.

Meanwhile, Emma was so captivated by the comical antics of the water fowl that she was totally unaware of the dog presently bounding up behind her – the great bull-mastiff had slipped his lead and was now full of mischief. The first she knew of it was when, with a great energetic bound, the dog launched itself towards the lake. The only obstacle between the dog and the water was Emma. With a thud the bull-mastiff careered into her shoulder sending her reeling off balance, and with a cry she flung out both hands, one into mid-air and the other to clutch hold of the railings. The dog landed heavily in the lake, sending both water and ducks in every direction – the ensuing noise rising like a crescendo into the hitherto still and quiet air. As the ducks fled, flapping their wings and sending up a volley of noise, Emma also yelled as she hung suspended by one hand from the railings, her feet and skirt-hem in the water, and her arm aching so much that any minute she was afraid she might let go. Emma was frantic as she believed the water here was considerably deep.

Suddenly, the dog's owner came rushing round the corner. 'Jake!' he was shouting. 'Get back here!' – every word accompanied by a threatening shake of the dog's lead. Emma saw him before he saw her, and when she realized who it was she began calling, 'Help! . . . Please help!' Whereupon, seeing her through the railings, he flung down the lead and raced towards the lake's edge where he immediately plunged into the water, sinking up to his knees as he waded to where Emma was hanging by her fingertips. Within a minute he had her by the waist and the next moment she was in his arms, being gently carried to the bank. When Emma saw that the water was not as deep and dangerous as she'd feared, and in fact came no higher than Marlow's knees, she looked into his concerned eyes with a smile. The smile quickly became a grin and then she began laughing. She felt such a fool as she realized what a comical spectacle she must have presented, and, what a comical sight the two of them must look now – with Marlow's dog yapping at their heels in a delighted frenzy, and the ducks quacking their disapproval from a safe distance.

When Marlow stumbled on to the bank, where he fell over with Emma still in his arms, they were both gripped by fits of laughter; and when the dog bounded from the water to shake itself vigorously, and in so doing drenched the pair of them, Marlow and Emma laughed even louder and clung to each other beneath the deluge of water that showered down.

It was at that moment that two other regular visitors to the park entered this uproarious scene. One was a shawled lady of some fifty years of age, slow of footstep and with slightly stooped shoulders beneath a sour, wizened face. The other was a small homely-looking fellow with sandy-coloured hair, and was none other than Gregory Denton. The disagreeable woman with her arm linked in his was Doreen Denton, his fearsome, widowed mother.

Gregory Denton was somewhat embarrassed to witness such untoward frolicking, although, for a brief moment, he envied the couple their obvious joy in each other. Coughing and quickening his step, he averted his gaze and began to change direction.

'Really! Upon my soul!' Doreen Denton gripped her son's arm as she forced him to a halt so that she might observe the scene more closely. 'Disgraceful!' she declared with a fierce scowl, 'I shall have words with the park attendant, you can be sure of that!' she told her acutely embarrassed son. 'What in Heaven's name is that young lady doing in the company of a ruffian like him? She looks to come from a decent family . . . while the fellow, well! He seems no better than a bargee!' She hoped to catch their attention with her loud tutting noises, so that she could give them both a piece of her mind.

Something in what his mother had said made Gregory Denton look back at the couple. On looking closer, he was horrified to see that they were no other than Miss Grady and Marlow Tanner! For a long, unbearable moment he refused to believe what was painfully obvious. Then, as the truth sank in, a black, suffocating jealousy arose in Gregory Denton's heart. He found himself unable to tear his wide, disbelieving eyes away from where Marlow had raised himself up on one elbow and, his laughter now replaced by a serious expression, was gazing down on Emma intensely. On seeing the way in which Marlow was looking at her, Emma also grew quiet. This shared moment of silence between them was spellbinding and, as Marlow's passionate gaze mingled with the wonder in Emma's soft eyes, it became one that they would both treasure forever. In her heart, Emma was afraid. Every corner of her body was trembling as she experienced sensations of excitement such as she had never known. She sensed that Marlow was going to kiss her, but still she made no move, for she was held helplessly in the same magic spell as Marlow. Now, as he lowered his head towards her, Emma's heart jumped and her hand reached up towards his face. When his mouth covered her open lips and his body leaned into hers, Emma thought there could never be anything more wonderful in the whole of her life.

Meanwhile, as Emma found herself moved by great joy and love as she lay in Marlow's arms, witnessing this scene Gregory Denton was immersed in the darkest, most crucifying mood, which swallowed his reasoning and suffocated the kindliness of his nature. As he quickly turned his stricken eyes away and led his mother from that place, a malicious plan of action was already forming in his affected mind. Once before he'd warned Caleb Crowther of Emma's involvement with the river-people, but because of his concern for Emma he had not followed it through when confronted by her furious uncle. Now, however, he would have no such reservations. For the first time in his uneventful life, Gregory Denton intended to put himself first – and bugger the consequences!

'No!' Emma's eyes were anxious as she looked into Marlow's surprised face. Whatever was she thinking of, to roll about in the grass and to conduct herself in a way that, to certain eyes, was no better than if she were a harlot! As she scrambled to her feet, Emma was both ashamed and frightened – ashamed of her own behaviour and, remembering how his back still carried the scars of another incident, desperately afraid for Marlow. Instinctively, she looked all about her, praying that no one had seen them. When she saw only two figures – a man and a woman in the distance – she gave a little prayer of thanks. Then she swung herself away from Marlow – who was still on his knees and looking up at her with a quizzical gaze – and, pausing only to call out in a troubled voice, 'Please! Stay away from me!' she clutched the cumbersome folds of her skirt in her hands, and, ignoring the wet discomfort of her boots, ran as though the devil himself was chasing her! With every step she took, Marlow's voice was in her ears, 'Emma! I love you. Wait . . . please wait!' But she paid no heed, only quickening her steps even more. In her trembling heart she prayed for forgiveness and help: forgiveness of the Lord for those feelings she had experienced in Marlow Tanner's arms when she'd craved much more than the feel of his mouth against hers, and when every instinct in her body had been that of a woman; and forgiveness for having so easily betrayed the promise given to her papa. Emma could feel herself slipping away from all she had been taught, and it frightened her. In her heart, even while she was running from him, Marlow Tanner made her feel warm and intoxicated, and he filled her with such a joy that it took all of her will-power to stop herself from turning round and going to fling herself into his arms. Emma doubted whether she would ever be able to get him out of her heart, especially when she didn't want to! Yet, she knew she must, and so she asked the Lord for the strength to do so. She also asked that Marlow might find the strength to put her out of his heart; for Emma knew that if she loved Marlow Tanner, it was no less than he loved her. And, for both of them, it was an impossible love – a love which, although born in Heaven, could carry them both to Hell!

# Chapter Five

Monday, 17 October 1860 was a fierce kind of day. It was a day of bitter cold winds and driving rain; a day when the sky stayed dark from morning till night and even the dogs took shelter. It was also a day which heralded a chain of events destined to bring about Emma's worst nightmare.

On the late evening of this particular day, two men stepped from a hansom cab in a back street of London town. Both were well-dressed and authoritative in their bearing. They had both been drinking and were full of high spirits, and had come to this area of Spitalfields to indulge their baser nature. The one who went by the name of Bartholomew Mysen was a man of law; he was tall and willowy with clean-shaven features. The other was a large, loose-limbed fellow, with dark hairy features and formidable blue eyes. He was also a man of the legal profession, who had a reputation for being a man of little mercy. His name – Caleb Crowther.

'Come on, Crowther . . . the night's almost spent!' reprimanded the tall, willowy man as his companion delayed in giving instructions to the cab-driver – these being that he should return for them on the morrow before the break of day.

'Have you got that?' Caleb Crowther demanded. When the fellow touched his cap and assured him that he certainly had, the fare was put into his palm and he was dismissed.

The two men immediately went into a large, red-bricked, seedy establishment. By their confident manner, it was obvious that this was not the first time they had frequented such a place. Inside, the subdued lighting made the surroundings appear gloomy. The grimy walls and threadbare carpets were effectively camouflaged by the deep, dark shadows and the plentiful, long frilled curtains.

In the distance the sounds of laughter, music and frolicking could be heard. Then, the air was cut silent by the sudden cessation of music. Presently, there came a man's voice announcing the evening's programme of entertainment, which was greeted by an uproar of shouting, clapping and stamping of feet.

'Looks like yer just in time, guv,' said the man at the desk, presenting a comical sight with his bald, shiny head, full face of whiskers and wide, spectacular, pink dickie-bow. 'I reckon they're about to start.' When neither Caleb Crowther nor his companion showed even the slightest appreciation of his comments, he gave a snigger, then a shrug of his shoulders, and when Caleb Crowther dipped into his waistcoat to spill a number of coins on to the counter, he grabbed them up and pointed to the double doors ahead. 'Yer knows yer way, guv!' he sneered, already preparing to sink back into his chair, and continue with his solitary game of cards.

On the other side of the double doors was a narrow walkway, beyond which was the heart of the club. There, numerous chairs, tables and people – mostly men – were squashed into the vast space. At the far end was a grand old stage, adorned with rich, red velvet curtains, and which was lit up by the footlights hidden in the recess along the front. Remaining in the dark private walkway, the two men watched and waited. On seeing them there, the portly proprietor made his way towards them, with the semblance of a smile on his face and one hand fidgeting about in his pocket, as if preparing to count the money which these two eminent figures represented.

The next moment, a great wave of shouting and cheering erupted as the music started up again and the dancers tapped their way on to the stage.

'Now, *there's* a sight to set your pulses racing, Crowther!' murmured Bartholomew, running the tip of his tongue over his lips and gently nudging his companion.

Caleb Crowther gave no answer but continued to move his narrow eyes along the line of chorus girls. When the proprietor made his presence known, by stating, 'Young an' fresh . . . *all* of 'em,' the two men nodded, all the while observing the scantily clad girls who were thrilling and exciting the audience with their provocative body movements and beckoning smiles.

Without either shifting his gaze or uttering a word, Caleb Crowther raised his cane and pointed it towards the far right of the stage. When, in a low cunning voice, the proprietor murmured in his ear, 'The redhead? . . . you mean the tall redhead?' he merely nodded, lowered his cane and gave a soft laugh as he turned to his companion saying, 'Come on, damn your eyes . . . there's a game waiting.'

'The little baggage third along,' the willowy fellow told the proprietor with a drunken giggle. 'The little blonde. Do you see the one?' he asked.

'I see,' confirmed the proprietor, with a knowing look from one man to the other, asking, 'I take it you want their company *after* the game?'

'Of course *after* the game!' Caleb Crowther intervened. 'Use your common sense, man!'

'Of course, yes, indeed!' came the hurried response. 'I'll see to it.' He held out one hand, and, when the tall, willowy fellow dropped a guinea into it, he bent his head forward, saying in a patronizing manner, 'Off you go then . . . room eight. You know where it is.'

In room eight the evening was spent in a serious mood, with a number of straight-faced, dedicated men seated round a table, each one with a fist full of cards and a wallet bulging with money – most of which rapidly found its way into the centre of the table, until the mound of bank bills there represented a small fortune.

As the night went on and the pile of money grew, each man furtively watched the others, wallets were emptied and flung down in anger, and the atmosphere became unbearably tense. Of all the devastated faces, there was none more so than Caleb Crowther's. Having lost more than most, and seeing no way to make restitution, he was obliged to bow out of the game, after which he sat in a dark corner downing glass after glass of whisky. Finally, in the small hours, when the game was eventually over and the players departed, he struggled to his feet, hardly able to walk across the room to where his companion, Bartholomew, was gleefully counting his handsome winnings.

'Leave it!' he said, in a slurred voice. 'Get the women!'

'They'll be along, Crowther . . . any minute now,' assured his companion, 'and you surely don't expect me to leave this money just lying about?' The very thought caused him to glance at Caleb Crowther with horror. He finished stuffing the bank notes into his coat pockets before reverently folding the coat and laying it over the back of a chair some safe distance away. 'You know how light-fingered these trollops are!' he reprimanded. 'Pluck the gold from your teeth, they would!'

Apart from the large oval table in the centre of the floor, and the chairs around it, there were five other items of furniture in the room – an ornate wash-stand containing a jug and bowl, a tall, ungainly clothes cupboard, a short, broad chest of drawers, and two narrow iron-framed beds, one either end of the room. As the girls were ushered into the room by the proprietor, Bartholomew grabbed the small blonde one and hurried her away to the farthest bed, the pair of them laughing and stumbling as they went, eagerly shedding their clothes along the way.

For a long moment, the tall red-haired girl stayed by the door, her round green eyes intent on Caleb Crowther's features. On seeing his unsteady gait and the manner in which he began to look her up and down, she asked cheekily, 'D'yer think yer can manage me, Toff? . . . Yer look to me as though it's all yer can do to stay awake!'

'You think so, do you?' murmured Caleb Crowther, a strange look on his face as he gestured for her to go to the bed. As he followed, the cries of pleasure coming from the other side of the room caused them both to look. The two figures thrashing away there were already naked, both in a frenzy of excitement, and both totally oblivious to the presence of anyone else. Like their gyrating bodies, their anguished and fevered groans rose and fell one into the other, the sight and sound of which enthused Caleb Crowther into hurrying toward the other bed where the red-haired girl stood waiting.

With his eyes looking directly into hers and without uttering a word, he lifted his hands and began fumbling at her clothes, firstly loosening the straps at her shoulders, then tugging at the tiny pearl buttons at her breast. The drink he had swallowed that evening made him more clumsy than usual, and when, after unsuccessfully attempting to undo the buttons, she began to softly laugh at him, he became agitated and the look in his eyes darkened with fury. With a low, rumbling growl, he clutched his fingers over the bodice of her dress and, leaning all his weight forward, he ripped the garment from top to bottom, afterwards wrenching it from her back and slinging it across the room. The girl was not shocked, nor was she afraid, for she had been subjected to such rough handling before. It was not in her nature to question such men – only to assure herself that they were here to make love, *not* to hurt or maim.

Now, when Caleb Crowther pushed her back on to the bed, she lay there impassively, looking up at him as he made hard and laborious work of undressing himself – all the while muttering and cursing – until, with a smile still on her lips, she stood up to help. Presently, they faced each other in their nakedness, all barriers between them gone, and in their eyes the look of hunger – his for the taste of her body, and hers for whatever money he might later see fit to leave her.

At first, as his fingers explored every inch of her body – touching first her ravishing red hair, then travelling from her neck to her nipples, where the light touch of his fingers lingered a moment before reaching down to where her thighs were warm and moist – there was a gentleness in his approach, almost a reverence. But then, when she also reached out to stroke and caress that most sensitive part of his body, he began to shiver and grow excited. Suddenly, he had his arms around her and was pulling her to him, moaning in ecstasy as her warm naked body merged with his. In a moment they were on the bed and he was bearing down on her with bull-strength.

It was then that Caleb Crowther was rendered useless by the drink he had consumed and, in spite of his repeated attempts, it became obvious to both himself and the girl that he was unable to satisfy either of them. With a contemptuous expression, she pushed him away from her, saying with a laugh, 'I'm buggered if you ain't the very first let-down I've ever had!' The effect that her cruel taunt had on Caleb Crowther was immediate. With a cry of 'Bloody whore!' he flung out a hand to grasp the back of her head, his fingers intertwined in her hair and his nails digging into her scalp. Even before she could cry out, he had formed his other hand into a fist, and with a cry of 'Trollop!' he swung it into her face with such force that he sent her reeling across the room towards the fireplace, where the coal was still glowing. As she fell against it, her arm was flung sideways to touch the searing-hot bars of the basket. With a cry of pain she snatched it away and, clambering to her knees, she looked up at Caleb Crowther with venom in her eyes. 'You bastard, you!' she uttered through clenched teeth, at the same time raising her hand to where the blood was gushing from her nose and from the deep gash along her cheekbone made by his ring.

'Get out,' came the instruction, 'before I forget altogether that I'm a gentleman!' He scooped up the torn dress and, with an angry flick of the wrist, sent it through the air towards her. Without delay, she collected the garment, held it over her nakedness and swiftly left the room.

Unaware that the two occupants of the other bed had ceased their activities to watch his treatment of the girl, Caleb Crowther stumbled to the table, from where he collected the last remaining bottle of booze. Then, throwing his grotesque and naked form on to the bed, he downed every last dreg of the fiery liquid. Soon after, he fell into a deep, restless stupor, every now and then flailing the air with his arms and constantly calling out two names – first Mary, then Emma. Only once did the name Thadius touch his lips, after which he was seized by a fit of uncontrollable trembling.

For a long while afterwards, Caleb Crowther's companion lay quite still on the other bed, his eyes narrow and wary as he studied Caleb Crowther's sleeping form. 'You really are a bastard, Crowther,' he murmured, giving a low laugh, 'but you'll get your come-uppance if you're not very careful.'

'What's that you say, darlin'?' came the sleepy voice beside him. 'Want some more do yer, duckie?' Whereupon he told her with a friendly laugh that she had worn him out. Then, throwing Caleb Crowther a scornful look, he flung his arm about the girl next to him, and the pair of them fell into an exhausted sleep.

With the dawn came a summons from the proprietor that the hansom cab was waiting outside. In no time at all, Caleb Crowther and his companion were out of their beds; washed in the warm water brought by their host and poured into the wash-stand, and were hurriedly on their way downstairs before the coming day might rise to light up the skies and expose them for the dregs they were.

At the door, Caleb Crowther felt the urge to glance back, and there he saw the tall, slender red-headed girl watching his every move. While he had slept, she had paced the floor, her swollen face a mass of pain, and in her heart the fervent desire to see the devil who'd done it fester in Hell! Pure hatred was in her eyes now as she glared at Caleb Crowther. Seeing the loathing she harboured for him, Caleb Crowther thought it thoroughly amusing. With a gentle laugh, he reached into the top pocket of his waistcoat, from where he withdrew a silver coin which he spun in her direction. 'For services rendered,' he told her with a cunning smile, which became a laugh when she plucked the coin from the threadbare carpet and threw it back at his feet.

'Your money's tainted darlin',' she said scornfully, 'like *you*! . . . And just as bloody useless!' At the last words, the smile slithered from Caleb Crowther's face. Ignoring the coin at his feet, he swung away and went smartly through the double doors to where the cab was waiting.

'Cor! Gerra bloody move on, mate!' urged the driver. 'The old horse is bleeding-well agitated . . . an' I'm bloody frozen!' He pulled his cape tighter about him and began blowing into his gloved hands, at the same time giving instructions to the handsome bay horse to 'be patient, yer old mare! Be patient!'

Once inside the cab, Caleb Crowther settled back into the buttoned leather seats, as Bartholomew gave the driver directions. 'Fourteen Bedford Square,' he called out, adding at Caleb Crowther's request, 'then on to King's Cross Station.'

Before the driver could urge the horse forward, three men appeared as if out of thin air; in fact they had been waiting for quite some time in a second carriage further down the street, and had observed the proceedings with particular interest. When one of the three dark-suited men took hold of the horse's reins, saying to the astonished driver, 'Just sit tight. None of this is your business, grandad!' he did exactly as he was told, for this was an area where crooks and villains thrived in every dark corner. Behind him, the driver could hear a scuffle and shouts of protest from the occupants of his cab, but he wisely kept his eyes looking directly ahead; even when he heard a heavy thud as the tall, willowy fellow was pulled from the cab to the pavement, he did not avert them. The other two dark-suited men had by now climbed into the cab, and placed themselves one either side of Caleb Crowther. When he began thrashing his arms about and threatening to call for assistance, the larger of the two men grabbed his arm, wrenching it behind his back until he cried out. The second man, finding it amusing, said in a mocking voice, 'Really Jack . . . you mustn't *hurt* Mr Crowther.' Then, throwing Caleb Crowther a menacing look, he continued, 'Not *yet* anyway. You know the boss likes folk to be given every opportunity to settle their debts. Now . . . if they don't *care* to settle their debts, well . . . they *deserve* to be hurt, don't they?' He prodded a sharp stiff finger into Caleb Crowther's fleshy stomach. 'It's well-known that Victor Sorensen has a kind heart. Wouldn't you agree?' he asked quietly, his eyes never leaving his victim's fearful face.

'Yes! Yes . . . you tell your boss I have every intention of settling my debts.' With this, Caleb Crowther drew up his shoulders in a futile attempt to regain his dignity. Then, looking from one of his assailants to the other, he told them in a more controlled voice, 'I've never let Mr Sorensen down, he knows that. It's just that, well, I have to step carefully with my brother-in-law not long gone. But, I have it all in hand . . . in fact, I have a meeting with the bank official this very week.'

'Is that so?' remarked the fellow seated on Caleb Crowther's right. 'Mr Sorensen heard about the responsibilities you inherited. Cash, too, we understand?'

'No! . . . no cash. Just two mills, and they're like a dead weight round my neck! I'd sell them tomorrow if I could.'

'Well now, the boss don't care which way you get the money. Just get it, Crowther – or there'll be more of a dead weight round your neck than the mills! Get my meaning, do you?' When Caleb Crowther nodded, he continued, 'You've got one week from today.' He prodded Caleb's stomach again, this time more viciously. 'Remember that, Crowther. One week!' Then he made a short sharp movement of his head, whereupon the other man released Caleb Crowther, before throwing open the cab door and stepping out into the road. His colleague did the same on the pavement side, after which he held the door open and, peering into the club doorway, where Bartholomew Mysen had retreated, he beckoned him forward. 'You were going somewhere, I believe,' he said in a smarmy voice, as the man came out of the shadows to climb with haste back into the cab . . . but, not before the dark-suited man had slipped a roll of notes into his fist and given him a knowing wink.

The journey was completed in silence. Only when Bartholomew was delivered to Bedford Square and was about to close the door behind him, did he warn Caleb Crowther, 'You don't mix with their sort, Crowther . . . not if you've got any sense. You're a bloody fool! For too long you've been sailing close to the wind. I'm telling you for your own good . . . get them off your back, man! Whatever it takes to free yourself of them, *do* it!' With that, he slammed the door shut and called up to the driver, 'Get him to King's Cross Station,' at the same time reaching up to hand him a generous fare. As he watched the cab pull away, he clicked his teeth and shook his head. 'You're a fool, Crowther,' he murmured, thinking how glad he was that it wasn't he who had fallen foul of the likes of Victor Sorensen, for he did not know of a man more evil than that one. This abominable fellow ran his own empire underground; every sordid and corrupt organization was under his control; yet he was so cunning a fiend that nothing could be traced back to him. He preyed on men like Caleb Crowther – weak, indulgent men, who took women and played the gambling dens as though their lives depended on it. Well, now it *did*, and the possible consequences made Bartholomew Mysen shiver in his shoes. He fingered the notes in his pocket, and reflected on his part in betraying Caleb Crowther. But he had few regrets, for, if he had refused, it was likely he would not have lived to see another day. Besides which, he had come to know the dark side of Caleb Crowther's character, and was repulsed by it.

The very same sentiments were ravaging Caleb Crowther's thoughts as the train carried him back to Blackburn. What he had told Sorensen's men was the truth. He had every intention of selling the mills, but his hands were tied, and the bank already held them as security against recent loans. He had little hope that his meeting on Friday would bring the results he wanted, for, on the last occasion, the bank had warned him that he was getting in over his head. That left only the trust fund which Thadius had left in his charge for Emma. It was this which played on his mind for the remainder of the journey, and the manner in which he might safely cheat her of it! His thoughts might have been less feverish if he had known how events in his absence had already presented such a possibility.

'I hate these damned meetings!' exploded Caleb Crowther, as he got up from the fireside chair to storm across the drawing-room towards the window. 'Little bloody men . . . with little ideas!'

'But it's *those* men who keep things going in your absence!' Agnes Crowther pointed out in a respectful tone, being still somewhat peeved that her husband had stayed over so long in London. 'Thadius was always insistent on these meetings, as you know. He thought them very necessary.'

At this point he might have made a caustic comment, but his glance was drawn through the casement window to where Emma was running from the house. At the sight of her, he became darkly silent, as all kinds of thoughts crossed his conniving mind.

Unaware that both Caleb Crowther's thoughts and his eyes were on her, Emma kept running. After the deluge of rain yesterday, the sun on her face was warm and the birds could be seen nestling in the tree tops. Today was one of those rare autumn days which held a semblance of spring, and now, as the daylight began to fade, Emma felt her heart lighter and closer to the past than she had for a long time. At this hour, when her duties at the mill were done and she had talked long and deep with Mrs Manfred, her thoughts invariably turned to the happy times she'd had with her papa.

Now, with Marlow's dear love alive in her heart and with

thoughts of him in her mind, Emma made towards the bottom of the hill, where, gathering up the folds of her skirt, she ran and ran until her chest became a tight band squeezing the life from her. Yet, with the effervescence of youth – and feeling the need to put as much space between herself and the Crowthers as possible – she kept on running, stumbling and scrambling ever upwards over the grassy slope which fronted the house.

Only when Emma had reached the very top of the hill did she stop to look back. She felt exhilarated and as free as the wind, which, up here, was strong enough to blow her about. Oh! The taste of freedom – it was wonderful! Here, she could touch the sky and vie with nature; here, there were no rules or regulations, no Caleb or Agnes Crowther to scowl at her and make her miserable; here, there was only her, the breeze, God's lovely creations and her own thoughts. Feeling inspired, Emma loosened her auburn hair from its confining ribbons so that it tumbled about her shoulders and spilled down her back to touch her waist. Then, she began running like the wind, flinging out her arms to the heavens as she laughed aloud. Exhausted, she sank to the grass where she lay prostrate, blissfully out of breath and staring up at the sky to follow the light curling clouds as they were shifted first this way, then that, by the heightening breeze.

After a while, those deeper, more serious thoughts which were never far away, reared up to darken Emma's mood. Drawing herself up into a sitting position, she fumbled about in the folds of her skirt until her fingers located the deep narrow pocket there. Dipping into it, she brought out the silver watch, so slim and small between her fingers and thumb, and so surprisingly warm to the touch that she could almost imagine it was only in this moment that her papa had entrusted it to her. Holding it to her ear, she thought how like a heartbeat was its rhythmic tick. Tenderly, she sprang open the rear to gaze at that minute lock of hair which lay curled up inside. Not daring to take it out for fear that the wind might snatch it away, she cupped the watch in one hand while with the other she lightly stroked her fingertip against the soft golden hair. Emma had hoped that by so doing, she might somehow feel closer to her mama. But she did not. Nor was she comforted, for a great tide of sadness washed over her and, feeling disillusioned, she closed the watch and returned it to the safety of her pocket. Wherever she went, Emma always carried the tiny watch, because, little though it was, it was all she had of her past.

Falling back into the long, waving stalks of grass, Emma closed her eyes and surrendered herself to a feeling of peace and nostalgia. In the eerie silence high up on this pinnacle, where nothing but the wind and birds disturbed the air and where little else mattered, Emma felt a curious sense of contentment. However, when pleasant recollections of Marlow began invading her thoughts, she deliberately shut them from her mind, rising quickly into a sitting position, as though in doing so she would be better able to defend herself against those things which were forbidden and dangerous.

Her gaze drawn downwards, Emma couldn't help but admire the house which, like it or not, was her home. It was said that Breckleton House had been in the Crowther family for many generations. Flanked either end by huge turreted edifices and decorated with spacious bay windows – which were arched at the top and framed by exquisitely carved mullions – it had the quaint appearance of a small castle. The main entrance was also arched, but it was of a grander, more imposing dimension, seeming more like the entrance to a church. The roof was tall and graceful, its elegant lines accentuated by the inclusion of numerous high-reaching, fluted chimneypots. Immediately behind, the majestic trees formed a natural and fitting backdrop.

Not for the first time, Emma wondered how truly indebted Caleb Crowther was to her papa, for if her papa had not been so generous, he would most certainly not be so well endowed. This grand dwelling would by now surely be in the possession of some other fortunate person. Her papa had never revealed the full extent of his assistance to her uncle, for such matters of finance were always considered to be the business of gentlemen, with no place in such affairs for women-folk. But Emma was no fool, and since her employment as clerk to Gregory Denton, she had learned much more of her papa's generosity to the Crowthers when, on the odd occasion, she had walked in on conversations between the warehousemen. Also, Gregory Denton himself was never averse to singing her papa's praises, often to the detriment of the Crowthers. However, of late he had been in an unusually sullen mood – since the weekend in fact. These past two days he had been going about with a dark, angry expression on his face, asking occasionally whether her uncle was sure to be back for the arranged meeting on Tuesday evening. She had told him she didn't know, and that was the truth. Caleb Crowther came and went, sometimes to attend his duties at the Quarter Sessions and sometimes to other affairs in the city of London. Whatever the reason for his absence though, Emma was thankful for it, and the longer the duration, the more she liked it. Thinking about it now, though, Emma was most curious as to why Mr Denton should be so eager to see Caleb Crowther, for she knew he had no particular liking for him.

As though summoned by her thoughts, Gregory Denton was even now stepping down from the carriage which had drawn up at the front door. Emma leaned forward and peered down, her hand over her eyes to shield them from the sun. Yes, it was Gregory Denton right enough and with him was a gentleman Emma recognized as Mr Wordsworth, the manager of the other Grady mill on Cicely Top. Emma watched as the two men disappeared through the front door while the driver went to the rear of the house for some of Cook's cherry cake. Then, drawing her shawl tight about her small frame, Emma leaned back into the grass, bending a long, ripe stalk towards her and chewing on its end. 'Come for a meeting, I expect,' she murmured to herself. 'Well, sooner them than me.' Feeling safe and secure hidden there in the curve of the earth, she closed her eyes. A gentle smile appeared on her attractive mouth as she recalled the antics of Sal Tanner; but, suddenly, Emma felt deeply sorry that so many things were against the friendship the two of them might have enjoyed. Sighing, she regretted how sad it was that because of her age and because of adverse circumstances, she was not in charge of her own destiny. Ah, but one day, she thought, maybe, one day. Yet, had Emma known how the evening would develop, her thoughts would not have been charged with such ambitious hope.

'So!' Caleb Crowther stood up from his desk, flung his two fists behind his back and locked them into one. 'We'll consider that to be the end of it for today.' He looked long and pointedly at the short, stocky fellow in the chequered waistcoat, before saying to him, 'Just one thing. Wordsworth . . . you're too eager on stockpiling raw material. Not necessary. Not necessary at all.'

'But . . . what with these rumours concerning the American shipments, I thought . . .'

'I'm not interested in such rumours . . . nor in what you think,' returned Caleb Crowther with a definite warning in his voice. 'Run off some of that stock, man. It's dead money, I tell you!' When the man nodded and scribbled something in his ledger, Caleb Crowther smiled with satisfaction. He then gave the same instruction to Gregory Denton, who had also increased his stock of raw material, in view of the accelerating and worrying developments in America. Now, with all due reports meticulously made, Caleb Crowther called the meeting to an end.

'Mr Crowther, sir . . . could I beg a few more minutes of your time?' asked Gregory Denton, feeling somewhat nervous, but determined to convey the unpleasant details of what he had seen with his own eyes that very Saturday in Corporation Park. 'It is *most* important,' he quickly added, on seeing Caleb Crowther's hesitation. 'A . . . personal matter . . . not regarding myself, you understand.' He glanced sideways to where Mr Wordsworth was paying sharp attention to this intriguing little development.

'You be off, Wordsworth,' instructed Caleb Crowther now. 'Thomas can take Denton home shortly.'

'Oh, there's no need for that,' assured the fellow, his curiosity heightened, 'I'll wait in the carriage. No trouble at all.' And, before anyone could raise an objection, he quickly departed from the room.

'Now then, Denton, what's on your mind?' demanded

Caleb Crowther, returning to seat himself behind the desk, while leaving the other man standing. 'Be quick with it, man. My time's precious!' If the truth were to be told, he was still suffering the effects of his trip to London. He kept his eyes fixed on Gregory Denton's pink features as, first in a nervous tone, then gradually growing in confidence, Gregory Denton relayed the whole sorry episode – his voice quivering with anxiety when he relayed how 'The fellow had Miss Grady in a disgustingly bold embrace . . . the two of them rolling about and laughing quite shamelessly!' That said, a heavy and frightening silence settled over the room, during which Gregory Denton fidgeted in a most agitated manner while Caleb Crowther sat deathly still, his head bent forward and his fingers tapping out a frantic rhythm on the desk-top.

'I'm convinced that Miss Grady played a *lesser* part in the dreadful incident!' Gregory Denton added lamely. He was very much afraid that he might well have gone too far in confiding the whole business and, suddenly, his only concern was that he should not be the cause of Miss Grady being cruelly punished. Oh Lord, he thought in a panic, if only I'd kept my mouth shut! He hated the jealousy which had driven him to do such a terrible thing! 'Mr Crowther,' he ventured again, 'I wouldn't want you to come down too hard on Miss Grady. After all, she is very young, and easily taken advantage of.' His voice was trembling, and, seeing how dark Caleb Crowther's countenance was, he would have given anything to turn the clock back.

Caleb Crowther was not unaware of the fellow's anxious state. Indeed, he thought any minute Denton would start blubbering like a baby. His first instincts on learning of his ward's latest and very serious misdemeanour was to administer the gravest punishment without delay – both to his wilful ward *and* to the bastard who had dared to encourage her! But now, confronted by this fellow Denton, whose motive was undeniably that of painful jealousy, a plan was already being devised in the back of his mind. One which just might get him off the hook, and rid him of Emma Grady into the bargain. For she was a constant reminder of things he would rather forget!

'Denton, my man . . . tell me . . .' As Caleb Crowther stood up to come round the desk, a cunning smile on his face and his two arms outstretched, the sight so terrified Gregory Denton that he took an involuntary step backwards. When the two sizeable fists fell on his shoulders in a fearsome grip, and those startling eyes drilled into his with the most evil smile, he began visibly trembling. 'Relax, my dear fellow,' urged Caleb Crowther now. 'Just tell me the truth. Have you a deal of affection for my ward, Miss Grady?' When Gregory Denton's mouth opened and closed without uttering a sound, he went on, 'Do you *love* her, you fool? . . . *Desire* her, eh? Do you?'

Gregory Denton was so taken aback that he found himself gaping open-mouthed into the other fellow's smiling face. What's he playing at? he thought. What trick is the devil up to?

'Come on, man!' Caleb Crowther told him in growing impatience. 'Any blind beggar can see you're sorely struck by the girl. Isn't that so?' he insisted, both his eyes and fists holding the victim fast.

Acutely aware of the warm breath which stank of stale booze fanning against his face, Gregory Denton's words came out in a rush. 'Well . . . I must admit I do find Miss

Grady . . . most attractive!' There! It was said. And, because
of the effort it had taken, he felt weak all over.

'Ah!' The word fell from Caleb Crowther's lips with a
smile. Patting both his hands several times against the
younger fellow's shoulders he said it again – this time
actually laughing out loud as he moved away. 'You and I
have a deal to talk over,' he said, seating himself behind the
desk and gesturing for Gregory Denton to occupy the seat
before it. With that done and each man eyeing the other, he
went on to question Gregory Denton at great length on issues
concerning his domestic arrangements, his relationship with
his old mater, and whether it was she who had discouraged
him from ever taking a wife. In answer to the first question,
Gregory Denton spoke with great pride of how he and his
mother still resided in the smart little house on Montague
Street, explaining how it had been in their family for some
years now.

'It's a well-dressed, cosy little dwelling, though I say so
myself,' he emphasized, not being able to resist puffing out
his wiry chest just a little. 'I've spent a lot of time and effort
on that little house in Montague Street,' he said.

He was a little more coy when coming to the business of
his never having taken a wife, but it was *not* because of his
demanding parent, he was quick to point out. 'Oh no . . .
indeed no!' He felt most hurt by such a suggestion. 'Although
I must be truthful and say that she is never the easiest person
to get on with. In fact, she can be quite a demon at times!' he
admitted. 'But, you see I've never met the right woman
whom I might take as a wife.'

'But you are attracted to Miss Grady, are you not?'
insisted Caleb Crowther.

141

'Tell lies and you'll make the Virgin Mary blush!' remonstrated the young man now, becoming bolder by the minute. 'Yes! Yes! I *am* very attracted to Miss Grady.' Then, made fearful by his own words, he swiftly added, 'Begging your pardon, sir!'

'Fine!' smiled Caleb Crowther, ignoring his employee's apology and leaning across the desk towards him. 'That's all I wanted to hear. Now then, Denton . . . how would you feel if I said I thought you to be a man worthy of my ward?' The younger man gave no reply, for he was so dumbstruck that all he could do was to prickle involuntarily from head to toe and continue staring in disbelief. Thoroughly enjoying the situation, Caleb Crowther went on, 'Miss Grady will be sixteen years of age in a few days' time. She'll be a woman, with a woman's needs.' Here, he paused to let the meaning sink in. 'We neither of us want her messing about with these lowly river-people.' Now, at the thought, his eyes grew darker. 'Scum! That's what they are . . . scum!' he murmured, seeming to be lost in a deep, distant mood.

'No, no, Mr Crowther, that would never do,' agreed Gregory Denton. 'Miss Grady is a fine and lovely creature, and she must be protected from such folk. Why! . . . Isn't that the very reason I spoke out this evening!' He began to feel pleased with himself.

'We're in agreement then!' Caleb Crowther was back in command. 'Tell me, Denton . . . what *is* your financial state? Do you have any money in addition to what you earn from me?'

'No, sir.'

'Then you would not refuse the sum of one thousand pounds if it were offered to you?'

'*A thousand pounds*, Mr Crowther? Why should anyone offer *me* such a grand sum?'

Caleb Crowther sat slowly back in his chair, his hard eyes fixed on Gregory Denton's astonished features, and a half smile on his mouth. For a long time – too long for Gregory Denton's comfort – he stayed thus, tapping his fingertips on the arm of the chair and eyeing the younger man with such intensity that Gregory Denton had to force himself to remain in his seat.

At length, the silence was brought to an abrupt end when Caleb Crowther sprang up from his chair to unlock a drawer in the desk. Taking from it a sheaf of documents, he began browsing through, until at length he snatched one out and put it face down before him. He explained to his patient employee, 'I have here a most vital piece of paper, and it concerns Miss Grady.' Pausing, he subjected the younger man to a most severe look. 'I rely on your word, Denton, because you have proved yourself to be a most truthworthy man. I want your word now, indeed, I *demand* it! Your bond that what I'm about to confide in you will never be repeated. *Never*, you understand. *Not even to Miss Grady herself.*'

'You have my word.'

'Excellent! Of course my ward is familiar with the general terms of her late father's will. But, it would be in bad taste, and most distressing, for you ever to discuss it with her. You *do* accept that?'

'Of course, of course! I do understand, Mr Crowther, sir. And I have given you my word,' declared Gregory Denton with a serious nod of his head.

Satisfied, Caleb Crowther continued, 'Thadius Grady provided well for Miss Grady, bequeathing her the very sum

I have just mentioned . . . one thousand pounds . . . to be paid over to her husband in the event of her marriage.' He watched as realization spread over Gregory Denton's face, amused to see a dark red blush suffuse the younger man's cheeks as he added, 'I can see that you understand my meaning.' Still smiling, he asked, 'So, Mr Denton, what is your answer?'

'My answer? Please, Mr Crowther, sir, am I to believe that you are . . . you are offering Miss Grady's hand to me, in *marriage*!' He dared not believe his own ears. He was convinced that he was imagining things. But, he was not, and in the next few minutes, no time was lost by Caleb Crowther in securing a short legal statement and a number of signatures from the trembling hand of the fortunate young man.

'These will ensure that, on the very day you are joined in wedlock to my ward, you will receive the sum due, as I've said . . . one thousand pounds.' His tone grew more serious, as did the look he now bestowed upon the fellow before him, as he continued, 'Mark me well though, Denton. If you're foolish and spendthrift enough to go through this legacy in a short time . . . you had better not come crying to me, for you'll not get one more farthing out of me! There'll be nothing more until my ward reaches her twenty-fifth year. You had better understand that from the outset.' When he was assured that 'no such thought would ever cross my mind', he shook the hand of Gregory Denton, who was, unknowingly, his saviour. Then, bidding him farewell, he said, 'Say nothing of this to anyone. *I* will inform the necessary people, after which you will be summoned to finalize the finer details . . . a date for the ceremony and so on.' As an afterthought he added, 'I'm placing a great responsibility in your hands,

Denton. A great and precious responsibility, for I am exceedingly fond of Miss Grady, as you no doubt already know.' Gregory Denton did *not* know, but he nevertheless gave an agreeable smile. The only thing he *did* know at that moment in time was that everything he'd dared to dream had come true! Momentarily, he wondered how Miss Grady might feel towards him, for of that he was unsure; yet he dared to hope she might nurture the same affection for him as he did for her.

Meanwhile, from her vantage point, Emma watched as the two men emerged from the house. Already, dusk was creeping over everything like a shroud, and the breeze had grown sharp and bitterly cold. Yet, Emma made no move. It fascinated her to see these two men together. It also aggravated her to witness the clear arrogance of one compared to the gentler nature of the other. Even from this distance, and in the gathering twilight, Emma thought how very easy it was to distinguish master from servant – the former being a large, ungainly yet formidable figure, seeming to avoid any physical contact whatsoever with the latter, who in turn appeared to bow and scrape in a totally subservient manner. It sorely irked Emma to see how Gregory Denton grovelled before her uncle, for she truly believed that, of the two men, Caleb Crowther was the lesser man.

As the carriage pulled away, Gregory Denton was still in a daze, his face warmly flushed as he marvelled at his unbelievable luck.

'By! . . . you look like the cat who got the cream, Denton!' observed Mr Wordsworth, with a laugh. 'Sommat *I* should know, is it?' he asked, hopefully. When there was no answer, his colleague seemingly completely unaware of his presence, he prodded him roughly, saying in a firmer voice, 'I say, Denton . . . what went on atwixt you and the big man, eh? Sommat *I* should be told, is it? Is it, eh?'

'No! No, indeed, Mr Wordsworth!' Gregory Denton assured him, in a greatly alarmed voice. 'Nothing at all that might concern you. It was . . . a personal matter, and one which Mr Crowther would prefer to be kept quiet . . . at least, for now,' he added with a secret smile. Oh, how excited he felt; so elated and exhilarated that he wanted to shout out from the roof-tops. But, he was also afraid: he felt as though he was walking on eggshells and at any minute the ground would give way beneath him. Mr Crowther had given instructions that he was to say *nothing* of his impending marriage to Miss Grady, and, he would not! For, even now he felt it to be such a delicate and unbelievable thing that he was mortally afraid it would crumble at the very first opportunity – and he dared not risk that! Whatever he was told to do, he would do it gladly; and, if keeping his mouth shut for the moment ensured that Miss Grady would soon be his very own, it was a small price to pay for such an honourable and wonderful thing. He admonished himself for dwelling too much on his forthcoming marriage, since the very idea made him tremble so violently that he felt positively ill. The prospect of telling his mother had the same effect!

Going back into his study, Caleb Crowther threw himself into the chair and stared down at the documents spread out across the desk. Picking up one in particular, which he had surreptitiously slipped between two others, he congratulated himself at having so cunningly concealed the *real* figure of Emma's inheritance – not one thousand pounds, as he had led that fool Denton to believe, but *six* thousand! The larger part was now *his*, and only a much smaller share would accompany Emma Grady to her marriage-bed.

Now, chuckling quietly to himself, he scanned the short statement which he had written in his own hand, and which the naïve and trusting young man had promptly signed. He experienced a deep satisfaction and a welcomed rush of relief, as he read:

I, Gregory Denton, having been accepted by Caleb Crowther as being suitable to join with his ward, Emma Grady, in wedlock, have been fully acquainted with the details of her inheritance. It agreed that, on the day of our marriage, the entire sum due – being £1,000 – will be entrusted to me, on Miss Grady's behalf, thereby complying with the terms of Thadius Grady's last will and testament.

When the younger man's signature had been added after his own, Caleb Crowther had held his breath. He had to admit a great deal of surprise when Gregory Denton's signature was so readily given, since this young fellow was, as a rule, very astute in matters of business. But then he was in love, was he not? And, Caleb Crowther knew only too well – from one particularly painful experience long ago – just how cruelly blinding and all-consuming fierce love can be!

Taking up his pen, he carefully added a loop to the bottom of the one following the pound sign, thereby making the figure read six thousand pounds. Then, putting the pen down, he leaned back in his chair and smiled a knowing smile. 'My thanks to you, Denton,' he murmured, 'though you're more kinds of a fool than I took you for! *This* is my insurance.' Collecting the papers together, he returned them to the drawer, afterwards locking it and slipping the key into his waistcoat pocket. There! Now it only remained for him to make arrangements to draw the money from the fund, and the rest would be child's play. It occurred to him that the sooner the wedding, the better. So, with this in mind, he went in search of his wife, finding her in the drawing-room, busy with her embroidery.

'Mr Denton was a long time going,' she remarked in a stiff voice, her eyes intent on the circle of tapestry, and her nimble fingers seeming to move with increased agitation at his sudden intrusion.

'Could you put down your work?' he asked, lifting apart the tails of his coat as he made a great fuss in seating himself opposite her. 'There are matters you will need to know, concerning both Gregory Denton and Emma.' At once she lowered her hands and lifted her gaze attentively. Seeing her ready, Caleb Crowther launched into a long and detailed explanation of his prolonged meeting with Gregory Denton; concealing, however, the matter of his own fraud and concluding with the words, 'So you see, my dear, there is much to be organized, as it would suit all purposes to have the thing over and done with as soon as possible. Already she appears to have taken an unhealthy liking to this unsavoury river-person. There must be a stop put to that . . . at once!'

As the news had begun to unfold, Agnes Crowther was visibly astonished that her husband had matched Emma with such a mouse as Gregory Denton – a fellow with pitifully small means of support, and who was socially inferior to themselves. Yet, she did not interrupt, since she thought

Caleb to be a shrewd man and an excellent judge of character. He would not have agreed to this betrothal lightly, or without good reason; of that she was certain. Then of course, there was this dreadful business of Emma's fascination with the river-people. Indeed, it was of great concern to her. Just think of the awful scandal which could erupt if this wild and wilful girl persisted in these disgraceful encounters! It was all too much for her – what with that shameful experience concerning Martha and her school!

'I can see that she *must* be married off as soon as it can be arranged,' she said now, with a great sigh of relief, 'but why Gregory Denton? Surely there must be someone more suitable, more *socially* acceptable?'

'Who else has expressed a desire to marry Emma?' he replied, before going on to answer his own question. 'No one, but the fellow concerned. Who else can bring her down a peg or two, and let her see the folly of taking for granted our fine big house and way of life?' Again, he quickly gave the answer. 'Only a modest man like Gregory Denton, with a modest manner of living, and the kind of simple virtues that might just teach her to be more thankful!' He made no mention of the main reason for his decision – that of embezzling Emma out of her inheritance.

'You're right, of course!' agreed Agnes Crowther, now caught up in the rush of events. 'There is much to be done, and I shall start at once.' After her initial surprise, she was positively enthusiastic. Emma Grady had been pampered for too long; and, perhaps she might even fit in better with a simple working-man's family. Yes, of course she would! But suddenly, it occurred to her that Emma would not be going to him empty-handed. 'Is the trust fund to be handed over?'

she asked quietly, not particularly liking the idea, but knowing it was unavoidable.

'But of course, my dear!' Caleb Crowther appeared suitably horrifed that she should even question such a thing. All the same, it would not do for his wife to dwell too much on this particular issue, so, putting on his most authoritative and judicial voice, he told her, 'I don't want you bothering your female head over such matters . . . nor discussing them with anyone, anyone at all! Your brother entrusted me to carry out his wishes, and I will do just that. As far as you are concerned, my dear, let that be an end to it. You may rest assured, it is all in hand.' When he was promptly informed that she was more than delighted to leave such matters in his capable hands, and that it was not her business to discuss such delicate and private issues as finance with a single person, he was much relieved. 'Be so kind as to fetch Emma to me straightaway,' he instructed.

Putting down her work, Agnes hurried from the room. At long last, she thought jubilantly, we'll be rid of the wretched girl, and the responsibility that goes with her! The trust endowed in her by Emma's papa, her own brother, touched her conscience only briefly.

High up on the hill, Emma had watched the carriage disappear out of sight, and now as the pinching cold began to make her teeth chatter and the light of day was swallowed into a greying sky, she thought about making her way back down. But she was loath to do so, for up here, surrounded by so much beauty and precious freedom, she was answerable to no one.

'Miss Grady!' The call came from down below and was carried by the breeze to where Emma was already on her feet. Looking down towards the house, she could see the familiar figure of Mrs Manfred waving her arms and shouting, 'Come down from there, come down!'

Waving in response, Emma was warmed by that familiar little figure, and, cupping her hands about her mouth, she shouted, 'All right, Manny . . . all right!' At once, she began to scramble down the slope with the same exuberance with which she had climbed it, laughingly slipping, sliding and tumbling until at length she came to the bottom, where Mrs Manfred was waiting with a look of frustration on her face.

'Just look at you!' she told Emma between a series of tutting noises. 'Covered in grass and bracken and looking less like a well brought-up young lady than I've ever seen!' She carried on tutting while she proceeded to brush Emma's dishevelled skirt most vigorously. Presently, looking Emma up and down, she seemed satisfied. Then, patting Emma's long auburn hair into a semblance of tidiness down her back and beginning to tut again, she asked, 'Where's your ribbon, child?' When Emma replied that it must have been lost on the way, she gave a great noisy sigh. 'Well, you do look more presentable now,' she said, 'so the ribbon won't matter.'

'Oh, Manny . . . why all the fuss?' Emma wanted to know. She was both intrigued and amused at Mrs Manfred's concern over her appearance. 'I'll go straight in, have a wash and change my clothes . . . will *that* satisfy you?' she laughed, throwing her arms about her good friend in a fearsome hug.

'*Listen* to me, Miss Grady.' She disentangled herself from Emma's arms, her voice falling to a more serious tone, as she cautioned, 'You're wanted. You're to go to the drawing-room right away.'

'What for? Who wants to see me?' Emma was puzzled and, racking her brains to find a reason why she should be summoned to the drawing-rom, her heart nearly stopped when she remembered a certain incident. But no! How could anyone know of what happened between her and Marlow in the park on Saturday? Calm yourself, Emma Grady, she told herself. Whatever it is, it *can't* be that, it's not possible! All the same, though, she couldn't stop her heart from beating fearfully.

'It's the master who wants to see you,' explained Mrs Manfred. 'Oh, child . . . what have you been up to now?'

She looked so distressed that Emma's heart went out to her. 'Now Manny, don't look so worried, darling. It'll be all right, you'll see,' she assured her, leaning forward to kiss the older woman's face. 'I don't *think* I've done anything so bad.' She lifted her hands to catch the strands of hair which had strayed over her shoulders; flicking them backwards, she then ran her hands over the top of her head and afterwards patted the bunched-up pleats of her voluminous skirt. 'Come on, Manny,' she said, starting forward, 'into the lion's den I go. Wish me luck!' Emma truly felt as though she *was* about to do battle, and the flippancy of her words belied that knot of fear inside her, which would not go away.

As she was soon to learn, Emma had every right to feel afraid. For what seemed to be a lifetime, she was made to stand before Caleb Crowther while he relayed a graphic account of what had taken place in Corporation Park between herself and 'this river-person by the name of Marlow Tanner'. When he had accused her of the incident itself, Emma had been mortified, but when he actually spoke out Marlow's name, her trembling heart fell like a dead weight inside her.

'Please, Uncle Caleb . . . it really *wasn't* what it might have seemed,' she began, only to be silenced when, coming to stand so close to her that she thought for a minute he intended to strike her, he said in a harsh voice, 'It is *exactly* what it seemed! I've told you before, Emma Grady . . . you have it in you to be a harlot! The lowest woman on the streets!'

'Am I to be punished then?' Emma was desolate at the prospect of being confined to her room yet again. But, more than that, she was afraid for Marlow. 'Please believe me, if anyone is to blame, it is me, *not* Marlow Tanner,' she pleaded.

'Do you think you don't deserve to be punished?' demanded Caleb Crowther. 'Do you think this river-trash should be allowed to get away with what he's done?' He paused, staring at Emma with deliberation, and waiting for her answer. When her eyes challenged his, he went on, 'I had a mind to flay the skin off his back, then to hand him over to the authorities . . . with a recommendation that he be shipped off to Australia on the next sailing!'

'You *can't*!' The thought was too much for Emma. 'He's innocent, I tell you. He did nothing to be treated so. Please, Uncle Caleb, leave him be, for none of it was his fault. His sister was crippled in the fire . . . she has no one but him.'

'Be quiet, damn you! Listen to what I have to say.' He was no fool. It was plain to him that she was in love with this Tanner fellow. Fate did seem to be handing him a most useful and rewarding set of cards. 'Arrangements have been made for your future. Should you see the sense in these arrangements, and go into them wholeheartedly with both your aunt's and my blessing, then you have my word that not only will you escape punishment but this fellow also will be let off with only a warning. But, a *severe* warning, on account of the nature of the incident. Of course, I can't allow him to continue in my employment!' he added.

Emma was puzzled. She was not in the least surprised that Caleb Crowther should terminate Marlow's employment at the Grady mill. But that would be of little consequence, she was sure, since there were other mills which would be only too pleased to employ someone of Marlow Tanner's hard-working breed. But why? *Why* would he be let off so lightly, when for just laughing with her on a previous occasion, the skin had been sliced from his shoulders? And what were these 'arrangements' to which her uncle referred? She dared to question him now on this subject. His immediate answer was to walk away and, with irritating slowness, to seat himself in the chair behind his desk – from where he continued to regard her with a quizzical and cunning expression. At length he said, 'You should thank Gregory Denton, for pleading with me on your behalf.'

'*Mr Denton*?' Emma could hardly believe her ears. Since when did Caleb Crowther listen to the likes of Gregory Denton? There was something strange here, thought Emma, but, for the life of her, she couldn't think what. 'Why? Why should he do such a thing?' she asked now.

'Because the fool thinks the world of you!' came the retort. 'Because he does not want to see you punished. Because he has asked for your hand in marriage. And I have agreed!' He grew increasingly irritated.

Emma was riveted to the spot. *Marriage*! She had been promised in marriage to Gregory Denton! For a moment, Emma couldn't fully comprehend the significance of her uncle's words; but when she did, they froze her heart and paralysed her tongue. She had been naïve enough to believe that she was not to be punished; when, in actual fact her uncle was exacting the very greatest punishment he had it in his power to do. He was ridding himself of her, and she was not in a position to defy him. Oh, she could make things difficult, by being obstinate and unwilling to see things his way; she could irritate and frustrate him. But that would only bring the full weight of his wrath down on both her and Marlow. Emma didn't care what *she* might endure, but the thought of Marlow being beaten and hounded was more than she could bear. Furthermore, she had no doubts about what Caleb Crowther threatened. If it became his intention to see Marlow Tanner transported to Australia as a convict, there would be no power on this earth to stop him. So, when he now put the question to her, 'You find Gregory Denton to be an amiable young fellow, do you not?' she answered truthfully that yes, she found him to be so.

'And you think him also a conscientious and industrious person, who would look upon marriage as a serious and pleasant state . . . where he would execute the duties of a husband to the very best of his ability?'

'I believe so.' Emma also believed that no matter what *she* thought, said or did, the outcome would be the same. If the price for Marlow's safety was to be her own freedom, then it was a small enough price to pay, for she had never really known freedom since coming to this house. And, in all truth, Emma wondered whether life with Gregory Denton might not actually be preferable to life here, beneath the iron rule of Caleb Crowther.

'Good!' Caleb Crowther got to his feet. 'I find the

arrangement altogether satisfactory. As from today, you will no longer attend your clerical duties. It would not appear proper. Your aunt will speak with you in due course, and Gregory Denton will shortly begin calling on you.' Making a dismissive gesture, he added, 'You may go!'

Emma did not need to be told twice, and hurriedly departed, her heart heavy with despair, and lightened only by her deep, abiding love for Marlow.

As she closed the door behind her, a small four-leaf clover fluttered from her shoulder. Stooping down to collect it into her hand, she marvelled at its simple beauty and striking deep green colour. As she gazed at it, she recalled Marlow's laughing words when he had plucked a four-leaf clover from the canal bank the very first time they had met. 'God's little secrets, these are,' he'd told her, 'meant to be lucky, too.' Smiling quietly, Emma closed her fingers around it, murmuring as she departed the room, 'Perhaps you'll bring me luck one day?'

Upstairs in the privacy of her bedroom, Emma folded the four-leaf clover into the case of the silver watch. As she did so, she could never have known how truly prophetic were her words.

# Chapter Six

It was New Year's Eve, the last day of 1860, and for many it was a time of rejoicing; but, as she prepared herself for the celebrations which even now were underway downstairs, Emma could find no real joy in her own heart. As the orchestral music filtered up the stairs to fill her room with its haunting melodies, Emma was moved and, as was her way, she tried to look on the bright side of things – realizing that, following her marriage on 14 January, she could turn her back on this house and on the Crowthers for ever! The thought cheered her so much that she found herself humming in tune to the music and gently swaying from side to side.

'Keep still, child!' ordered Mrs Manfred, who was growing more agitated by the minute. 'I'm blessed if I've ever come across such unruly hair as yours, in all my born days!' When Emma immediately sat still, saying, 'Sorry, Manny,' she continued her efforts to pin the wild auburn hair into a cluster on the crown of Emma's head. 'It's no use!' she declared after another frustrating moment. 'These pins are too delicate . . . I shall have to fetch a few of my own. Just you sit still!' she told Emma, before hurrying from the room. 'I'll not be a minute.'

No sooner had the amiable housekeeper departed the room, than there came a knock on the door and a quiet voice asking, 'Can I come in, Miss Grady?'

'Please don't,' Emma replied, turning on the dresser stool to look towards the half-closed door. 'I'm not ready yet, Mr Denton.'

'Will you be long then?' he asked, but before Emma could say anything, there came another voice, assuring the timid young man hovering at Emma's door, 'She'll be *twice* as long if you don't let me by, so I can finish her hair!' Much as she had tried to dislike Gregory Denton for taking away her darling Emma, Mrs Manfred found that she could not – although she would *never* take to the idea of Emma being wed so young. And not if she lived to be a hundred could she ever forgive Caleb Crowther for ridding himself of the girl in such a way. She still had her suspicions regarding the manner in which Emma's papa had departed this world, and now this whole hurried and unexpected business of Emma's betrothal to Gregory Denton had only increased her suspicions. Mrs Manfred had worked hard at convincing herself that her suspicions were groundless and were rooted in her dislike for the Crowthers. But that cold uneasy feeling remained with her. Caleb Crowther was a bad, heartless fiend, of that she had no doubts whatsoever, and his wife was little better. Right from the moment Emma told her the news and then wept on her shoulder, the belief that Caleb Crowther had first helped Thadius Grady meet his maker and then sacrificed young Emma to an ill-suited marriage – all in the name of greed – haunted her.

'I'm very sorry, Mrs Manfred,' muttered Gregory Denton, turning an uncomfortable shade of pink and stepping quickly away to hasten towards the stairway, 'only . . . I'm so looking forward to seeing her,' he explained.

'Of course you are,' Mrs Manfred declared with a warm smile. 'Be patient, young man. Miss Grady won't keep you waiting much longer, I promise.' When he gave a small nervous laugh and thanked her, she went into Emma's room, closed the door behind her and remarked to Emma, 'He's a nice enough fellow, I'm sure.'

Emma's response was a quiet smile and a thoughtful look. During the next few moments, as her hair was pulled this way and that, pinned up then loosened, and finally arranged such that the centre portion was pinned up with the outer curls falling naturally about her face, Emma resigned herself to take just one day at a time. That way she felt more able to face what lay ahead and more determined to try and make the very best of it. However, there was one particular event which was to take place on the morrow which she was positively dreading; she was due to meet, for the very first time, Gregory Denton's old mother, a woman who, according to talk below stairs, was a 'cantankerous and bloody-minded old tyrant!'

'Manny,' she asked now, looking into the mirror and anxiously gazing at the older woman, 'will it be just *awful*, meeting the infamous Mrs Denton?'

'Awful . . . nothing!' retorted Mrs Manfred, who in spite of her efforts to put Emma at ease with regard to the girl's forthcoming trial, suffered no illusions where the elderly woman was concerned; for, if there was anybody more spiteful and more demanding than that old bully, then Mrs Manfred had not heard of her. There were only two things that mattered to Gregory Denton's aged mother – her own comfort and the absolute attention and obedience of her only offspring. Her domineering nature regarding the latter was well known, and it would not be easy for Emma to success-fully fit into this strange and rigid set-up; nor would it be without a certain degree of pain and determination. But, Mrs Manfred was confident that Emma, who had known enough pain to help her cope, would prove a good match for that determined old woman. Mrs Manfred concealed a little smile, for she truly believed that, if this possessive parent meant to break Emma's will, she must expect to see sparks fly.

'I do so want us to get on,' Emma said, getting down from her seat and walking the few steps to the full-length mirror where she looked at her reflection, her expression still troubled by the thought of leaving one tyrant behind only possibly to be faced with another.

'Don't dwell on it, child,' remonstrated Mrs Manfred, coming to stand by Emma's left side. 'If she *does* start her old games, then you just stand up to her . . . like you often do with me!' she laughed. 'The old bugger'll soon learn to respect you.'

Emma was so astonished to hear Mrs Manfred using a swear word that she promptly forgot about the troublesome subject which had prompted such colourful language.

'There!' declared Mrs Manfred. 'For the first time in my life the old sod's got me swearing!' Whereupon Emma began chuckling, and soon they were both convulsed in laughter and holding on to each other when Emma pointed out, 'If she has that effect on *you*, Manny, whatever might become of *me*?'

\* \* \*

Two weeks before the New Year's Eve ball, Caleb Crowther had ordered his wife Agnes to accompany Emma into Manchester where they were to purchase a gown which 'will show how the girl has matured into a woman'. Emma suspected his intention was to show all who might have quietly thought her still a child, too young to be married, that she was in fact a woman, more mature than they had realized and ready for marriage. Finding a suitable gown had not been easy, since Emma was so slim and petite and the adult gowns so heavy and overwhelming. After Agnes Crowther had impatiently rejected several rather loud and fussy articles, a particular gown in a warmly attractive shade of burgundy was brought out. The skirt was not full and flouncy, but long and flowing, with a silky look; the hem was deeply scalloped and edged with fine black braiding; and the waist was tiny, and at the back was the merest suggestion of a bustle. When Emma slipped it on and came out for inspection, Agnes Crowther was visibly taken aback; for there before her stood not a young girl, but an incredibly beautiful woman, possessed of poise and graciousness.

Now, as Emma came down the stairs, every admiring pair of eyes were turned in her direction. Agnes Crowther's gaze was also drawn to her. As she followed Emma's every step, her narrowed eyes swept from the top of Emma's lovely hair, which shone the colour of polished chestnuts, to the straight delicate lines of her bare shoulders, which were enhanced by the small unfussy dropped sleeves. She looked the whole length of Emma's tiny and exquisitely formed figure, her young breasts rising from beneath the gown, and her small feet dressed in black button-over shoes to match the pretty frilled bag at her wrist. Agnes Crowther suffered such terrible pangs of envy as she gazed at her niece's beautiful face, with that perfectly generous mouth and those deep grey smiling eyes, and saw the natural and elegant way in which she moved. She saw Emma's papa's – her own brother's – qualities so evident in Emma's own proud, handsome features, and was so affected that she hurriedly averted her eyes, turning her head away and moving to where she need not gaze on her brother's child any longer. Instead, she looked at her own daughter, Martha, and tried, with extreme difficulty, not to draw comparisons.

'Oh, Emma!' Gregory Denton felt as though he had waited a lifetime, and all of that lifetime had been lived only for this moment, with Emma as the focal point of his every dream. As he took her hand and threaded it through his arm, there wasn't a prouder man alive on God's earth. 'You're the loveliest creature I've ever seen,' he murmured, leading a path through the dancers and into the centre of the floor where they might find a space. Having done so, he stopped and turned to face her. 'I do love you so,' he whispered above the music.

'I know you do,' Emma whispered back. It would have given her a lot of pleasure to be able to say 'And I love you,' but she could not, as there would be no truth in such a statement. However, she was fond of him, and gazing into his sincere eyes, which now looked on her with such warmth and shining adulation, Emma was deeply moved. 'You're such a good man, Gregory,' she told him with an affectionate half-smile. 'I pray I won't disappoint you. I do so want to make you a good wife.'

For a long, lingering moment, Gregory Denton continued to gaze at her, his eyes feasting on her gentle beauty and his face saturated with pleasure at her words. At length, he said quietly, 'Any man would be more than proud to have you for his wife, Emma. I know how lucky I am. And, if you don't love me now the way I love you, I feel you will . . . in time.' He stepped closer to murmur in her ear, 'I know it in my heart. You *will* come to feel as I do.'

But Emma thought not. She had already given her heart to Marlow Tanner. It had been given freely, and for ever. It did not matter that she might never see him again, for she was powerless in her love for him. His tall, strong image and those dark, brooding eyes, which simultaneously tortured and pleased her, were always in her heart and more alive with every life's beat – and, Emma knew, would remain with her for the rest of her life.

Telling herself that she mustn't think of him, not here, not now, Emma took to the floor with her partner and, for the remainder of the evening, she danced and smiled, she listened attentively to the meaningless chatter of others, and she gave to one and all the appearance of a young woman looking forward to her imminent marriage. She fooled everyone but those who knew better. She did not fool Caleb Crowther, who spent most of the evening huddled in a quiet corner with other industrialists, whose intense conversations covered everything from the rebellious attitude of the common worker to the persistent rumours regarding the unrest in North America.

Neither did Emma's forced gaiety fool Agnes Crowther and her daughter, Martha, who commented, 'How clever of Papa to hand over the burden of Emma to that peculiar little man. By all accounts he has a nasty and overbearing mother . . . who, no doubt, will curb Emma Grady's wilful ways at the first opportunity!'

'Really, Martha, that's a very strong and condemning attitude, if I may say so.' The speaker was a large, well-built fellow with quiet brown eyes, a military-type moustache and thick mop of hair – all of the same shade of brown. His skin was of an even deeper shade and, because of his seafaring interests, was leathery in texture. He and Martha had met when, during her recent holiday, she had accompanied her mother into Lancaster to purchase shoes and accessories for the New Year's Eve ball. With their shopping finished, they had begun to make their way across the busy main thorough-fare, when, through her own foolishness, Martha was almost trampled underfoot by a coach and four. It was the quick thinking of Silas Trent which had saved her. Afterwards, finding certain things in common, they had struck up a friendship which had later deepened into a manner of courtship. Both Caleb and Agnes Crowther heartily approved of the relationship. Agnes believed him to be a stabilizing influence on her daughter, and, at the age of twenty-four years, he made both a commanding and kindly figure. Also, in spite of Martha's many faults and plain appearance, he was obviously extremely fond of her. Caleb Crowther's reasons were two-fold and very different from those of his wife: one stemmed from the recent and shameful business regarding Martha's deceitful behaviour at her school; but much more importantly were his enquiries which revealed that Silas Trent was the only son of Marcus Trent – founder and sole owner of the highly lucrative Trent Shipping Line out of London and Liverpool. The Trent fleet of ships was most impressive, and from the execution of his duties as Justice of the Peace, Caleb Crowther recalled that, not only did the Trent fleet sail various other cargoes across the

Atlantic, but these ships were the foremost carriers of convicts to Australia. The company was a proud and success-ful one. Therefore, never being one to miss an opportunity, Caleb Crowther was seen to actively encourage the relationship between Martha and the young man Silas Trent. Yet, he was most careful not to confuse the character of this accomplished young man with that of the timid and sub-servient Gregory Denton: the latter was easily cheated, but Silas Trent was no fool, and had strong opinions of his own which he would express without hesitation.

'Martha . . . don't you think it would be proper to introduce me to your cousin?' Silas Trent's disapproval of Martha's spiteful remarks concerning Emma sharpened the tone of his voice. 'I should like to be allowed to form my own opinion of the young lady in question.' The smile on his face belied the frown in his voice. His smile deepened on seeing Martha pout in that familiar manner which he had become accustomed to – a bad habit which he intended to break at the first opportunity.

Agnes Crowther also had noticed her daughter's immature and sulky attitude, and at once she had stepped from Martha's side and was graciously assuring Silas Trent that 'Of course you must meet Emma.' She did not want this eligible young man to be left with the impression that Martha was churlish in her attitude towards Emma, nor that she possessed a spite-ful side to her nature. Quickly now, she made her way around the perimeter of the dance floor to where Emma was seated, waiting for Gregory to return with her glass of sarsaparilla.

From her place in the hallway, where she watched to see that all was going well, Mrs Manfred saw Agnes Crowther collect Emma from her chair. She saw how the woman ignored Emma's protests that Gregory would wonder about her disappearance, and she saw the two of them returning to where Martha waited with her rather large but good-natured young man. When Emma was introduced to Silas Trent and he, gallantly taking her hand to his lips, smiled down at her, it warmed Mrs Manfred's heart to witness the stony and petulant features of Martha Crowther as she looked on reluctantly and with some disgust. But it also hurt the dear woman to realize how this selfish and undeserving girl had secured for herself a strong and wealthy man, while her own lovely Emma had been fobbed off with second best as usual. Oh, it wasn't that Mrs Manfred had not come to like Gregory Denton, for she had, yes indeed. But, to her mind, Emma's going from the Crowthers to that old Denton woman, was akin to falling from the pan into the fire. She only prayed she might be proved to be wrong. But, somehow, she doubted it.

As Emma looked up into Silas Trent's kindly smiling eyes, something in their genuine honesty made her heart warm to him. She liked him instantly and she considered Martha to be very fortunate in having gained his affection. 'Martha's told me about you, Mr Trent,' she said with a smile, when in all truth she should have said that Martha had never stopped bragging about him and cruelly comparing him to poor, harmless Gregory. 'I'm very pleased to meet you at last.'

'And I you, Emma . . . if I may call you that?' When she gave a half-smile and nodded, he ventured, 'I wonder whether your intended might object to me dancing with you?'

For a moment Emma was quite taken aback. She could feel Martha's eyes glaring at her, daring her to accept. And she was not unaware of Agnes Crowther, standing rigidly, with her hands joined and pointing to Heaven. Probably praying to God that I'll fall through the floorboards and out of sight, mused Emma, with the desire to laugh aloud. She was also aware that Silas Trent still had hold of her hand and was waiting for her answer.

'Thank you, Mr Trent,' she said, 'I'd love to dance . . . I'm sure Gregory won't mind.' As he swept her on to the dance floor, Emma couldn't resist glancing back. As she expected, there stood Martha in her severe grey dress – which was adorned with a huge, unsightly bustle and frilled with broad white ribbon – with such a dark and furious scowl on her face that would surely be enough to curdle the cream! And there beside her, looking regal and splendid in a cream-coloured, extravagantly designed, voluminous gown, was Agnes Crowther, her familiar posture of prayer even more fiercely disciplined and her lips drawn in with such severity that her mouth had become a thin, taut line and the muscles in her neck stood out like tramlines.

'Now I can see where Martha gets her fits of petulance from,' remarked Silas Trent as he began with much enthusiasm, the steps of a foxtrot. 'Looks like I've got my work cut out when I take her for my wife,' he laughed. It was an easy, infectious laugh which enthused Emma to reply light-heartedly, 'I think I'd rather you than me, Mr Trent.' To which, and to the fury of the two Crowther women watching, they both burst out laughing.

In a quieter mood, Emma asked him, 'You love her very much, don't you?'

'I'm afraid so,' he replied, 'but I'm not blinded to her faults. But then we *all* have faults, do we not?' To which Emma replied that there was nothing surer.

When the dance was over and each about to return to their respective partners, Emma thanked him. 'Not at all!' he replied with a sweeping smile. 'I can't think when I've had so much fun!' But suddenly, the smile disappeared from his face and in its place was a tender concern. 'Emma . . . I know enough of your background to suspect that there may come a day when you need someone to turn to. I hope such a day never does come. But, if it does, I want you to consider me as a friend. Will you do that?'

For the second time since meeting him, Emma was deeply surprised by this man. But, there was something about him – an honesty, a compassion and truth – that prompted her without hesitation to say, 'Yes. To have you as a friend would be a fine thing.'

'Good!' he said, smiling down on her and slowly nodding his head back and forth. As she watched him striding back to the sulking Martha, Emma believed that the day when she had to run to him for help would never come. But Emma could not know that in the hard years to come, there would be occasions when Silas Trent proved to be both a friend and an invaluable tower of strength to her.

When the last guest had gone and Gregory had reluctantly said goodnight, Emma went to her room, took off her clothes, slipped into a nightgown and, after brushing out her long rich hair, climbed gratefully into bed. Yet, in spite of her tiredness, she felt strangely restless. There was something uniquely sad about seeing out the old year, she thought, and for her, it wasn't just a farewell to 1860, but to her life as she had come to know it. Soon, she would leave this house. She would be a wife and, one day, she must also mother Gregory Denton's children. For the moment the prospect was too daunting to dwell on at any length – especially when, in her deepest heart, Emma had prayed that it could be Marlow who was about to make her his wife, and Marlow's children whom she might bring into the world. But, however much she found herself wishing it, she knew that this could never be. She was wise enough to accept that.

'If you have any influence up there with the angels, Papa,' she murmured into the darkness, 'will you ask them to send a little good fortune down here? Help me to be a good wife to Gregory and see that his mother might grow fond of me?' Then, with all kinds of unsettling images and thoughts in her mind, Emma fell into a restless sleep.

The short sleep was feverish and fitful. In the early hours, Emma woke suddenly from her nightmares with a cry of alarm. Realizing that she was safely alone in her room and that the clawing monsters had remained behind in the realms of her frantic dream, she relaxed against the cold brass bars of the bed-head. With a grateful sigh, she brought up her hands to wipe from her face the sweat which stood out in small wet beads, clinging to her skin like early morning dew. Then, stretching out her arms and locking her slender fingers together behind her neck, she leaned back again and closed her eyes. 'You'd best shake your feathers, Emma Grady!' she reproached herself. 'Dreaming isn't for the likes of you!'

She found herself thinking of Martha, who at least had been given some say in choosing her man. The thought of Martha brought a wry little smile to Emma's face, and as she imagined her cousin with a brood of children she couldn't help herself from laughing out loud. She wondered for a fleeting moment whether, given the choice, she would prefer to swap places with her cousin Martha. The thought terrified Emma! No! She was who she was – Emma Grady, daughter of Thadius and Mary. She had some wonderful memories and she had Manny. If her lot now was not everything she might have wished for, then there were many more worse off than her.

In the face of such reasoning, Emma chided herself and decided that she must be grateful for every mercy, small or otherwise. After all, Gregory Denton was a good man, and he loved her. But, try as she might to console herself with this, Emma's heart could not wholly accept it, for the image living there was not of Gregory. Nor was that deep well of love she felt, meant for him. And, even though her memories of her beloved Marlow warmed her heart and gave her immeasurable pleasure, she yearned for more: she longed for those dark eyes to gaze on her and for those strong arms to hold her close. Emma knew she could never be truly happy without Marlow; she could never forget him. But she could – she must – learn to live without him.

Getting up from the bed, Emma crossed over to the window where she opened wide the curtains and looked out at the sky. Soon, the sun would rise and a new day begin. A new year, and, for her, the start of a whole new life. What would it be like, she wondered, with that deep anxiety which would not leave her.

Emma went across to the small circular table where she lit the oil lamp. Then, glancing at the small brass clock on the mantelpiece which told her it was almost five a.m., she realized that the day had already begun for her because it would be futile to return to her bed and try to sleep. There was no more sleep in her, not now. She grabbed a shawl from the back of the stand-chair, which she flung about her shoulders before going out of the room and down the stairs to the kitchen. Seeing that the fire had been well stacked the previous evening and was still giving out a cheery glow, Emma half filled the big blackened kettle with water and wedged it on top of the coals. When she thought it must be warmed, she took a cloth from the bar which fronted the big oven, and, wrapping it firmly round the kettle handle, she lifted it from the fire.

Quickly, she returned to her room, where she tipped the warm water into the large ceramic bowl on top of her dresser. Then, putting the kettle down in the cold fireplace, she opened the top drawer of the dresser and withdrew from it a face flannel and clean towel. From the second drawer, she collected a freshly laundered set of underclothes. After stripping off her nightgown, Emma took the soap from its stand beside the bowl and washed herself thoroughly all over. That done, she quickly dressed, brushed her hair into its ribbons, wrapped the long, fringed shawl about her, gathered up her small dark boots into one hand and went on tiptoe back down to the kitchen. There, she put on her boots, and going into Cook's larder she helped herself to a cup of milk, a muffin and a portion of Cook's special fruit jam. After heartily enjoying her early breakfast, she took the cup and plate to the sink, washed them under the tap and dried them, before returning them to the big pine dresser. Then, going to the great black fire-range, she scooped up a measure of coke from the brass scuttle and got the fire going more cheerfully. That done, she pulled up Cook's favourite deep, horse-hair armchair and curled up into it.

It was on the stroke of six a.m. that Cook came bumbling into her kitchen, a dumpy vision of clean, starched whiteness with her sleeves already rolled up ready to tackle the day ahead. 'Well, I never!' she called out, seeing Emma fast asleep in the chair, her face warmed to a fetching pink by the glow from the fire. 'The little rascal!'

Of a sudden, Emma was wide awake, giving her apologies and assuring Cook, 'I haven't interfered with anything, except I had a muffin and a drop of milk from the larder.'

'I should hope you ain't interfered with anything, young lady!' remonstrated Cook. 'You'd best take yerself off while I gets the breakfast underway. I can't be doing with you under me feet, and that's a fact!' She then began ranting about 'folks as wander around instead o' sleeping quiet in their beds'.

Thinking it best not to antagonize Cook any further, Emma decided she'd better either return to her room or go for a walk in the early morning air. She decided to go for a walk.

'And don't you go far, Miss Grady!' Cook shouted after her. 'Ye'll likely catch yer death o' cold out there. And breakfast'll be served within the hour!'

'Don't worry,' Emma told her. 'I won't go far.'

Once outside Emma drew her shawl more tightly about her. Cook was right, it was cold; but she was not deterred for, if anything, the cold morning air gave her a feeling of well-being. She stood for a while taking in deep revitalizing breaths, before exhaling slowly and watching with curious delight as her breath curled and danced in the still, crisp air.

As she began walking down the path which would take her across the meadow, round by the spinney and on to the banks of the canal, Emma was cheerily greeted by old Benjamin – the same ancient and bewhiskered old fellow who had been delivering the milk in his churns every morning since she and her papa had first come to this house. Seeing him reminded Emma of what Gregory had told her – that it was about this hour of the morning when the barges began their way along the canal towards Liverpool Docks, where they would be bright and early for their first cotton cargo of the day. It always amused Emma to see how much old Benjamin resembled his faithful horse, who was also ancient and bewhiskered. As it passed her by, the flat waggon rumbled and swayed, making its own kind of music. 'Good morning, Benjamin,' she replied with a bright smile, thinking it wouldn't be long before the other tradesmen were coming up the path, when the day would snowball into the busy pattern of life that went on, come what may.

There were always plenty of comings and goings to and from Breckleton House. And the day always started when most folks were still in bed. It crossed Emma's mind to compare how different life here must be from that of the residents along Montague Street in Blackburn town. Well, she reminded herself, she would know soon enough. And in just a short time she would also be brought face to face with the one they called 'the old tyrant'.

Reaching the canal bank, Emma recalled the last time she had found her way here and her heart ached. Such an innocent little adventure, she thought with both regret and pleasure, yet one which had inflamed Caleb Crowther enough to launch a spiteful and wicked attack on Marlow Tanner. Sitting for a while on the stump of a felled tree, Emma's attention was caught by the unmistakable snorting of a horse and that soft swishing of water which only a barge on the move could make. Gregory was right, she thought, the canal is already coming alive. Of a sudden, the big piebald cob was in sight, his neck straining hard as he towed the barge around the curve towards the spinney. Emma recognized the horse at once as belonging to the Tanner barge. Her every instinct told her to hurry away from that place as fast as she could; but her heart persuaded her to stay and watch as horse and barge went slowly by. Being some way back from the canal, and being partly hidden by the shrubbery, Emma thought she would not be easily seen.

Whether it was the bite of the morning air so near the water or whether it was the nearness of Marlow, Emma didn't know, but she found herself trembling more the closer the barge came. So much so that suddenly she was afraid. She must go! She must not stay here to torment herself so! Emma could not control the emotions which raged through her; emotions which brought with them their own kind of pain. Already she was on her feet, but even as she began to turn away, she saw Marlow standing tall and straight at the tiller, his dark, magnificent eyes stretching ahead to scour the water. What great delight the sight of him brought to Emma. Joy and a searing tide of love surged through her. Yet, she knew she must hurry away, for this love was not to be, and it could bring nothing but heartache for both of them. But she lingered too long...

'Emma!' He had seen her, and like the wind his anguished cry sailed the water towards her. But Emma did not look back. Instead, she ran faster and more blindly, until in her haste she was slipping and tumbling over the bracken beneath her feet – her heart racing with both fear and excitement, and the overhanging branches catching her face and hair as she fought her way through the spinney. In her determination to flee, Emma did not see the deep rabbit-hole ahead. When she ran headlong into it the heel of her boot caught fast, throwing her to the ground and knocking the breath out of her. She had heard Marlow pursuing her, and now, when he came upon her, Emma was frantic. 'Go away!' she told him. 'Please, leave me be.' For a moment he stood quite still as she began struggling to her feet. But then, with a cry of 'You can't send me away from you, Emma,' he came forward to catch her in his arms. As he rained kisses on her face and mouth, all of Emma's resolves melted away. She clung to him, kissing him back, and wanting him so much that it hurt.

'You love me! Tell me you love me, Emma!' he demanded, half laughing, half afraid as he pulled her to him and covered her mouth with such fierce demanding kisses that left her weak and vulnerable in his arms. Her response was every bit as passionate and eager as his own, until, somewhere in the distance, the sound of Sal Tanner's voice could be heard shouting, 'Marlow! Yer a bloody fool! That lass means nothin' but grief an' all kind o' trouble. I'm warnin' yer. If yer don't come back this very minute, I'm leavin' . . . I'm washin' me 'ands o' yer. D'yer 'ear me, Marlow Tanner?'

Marlow paid no heed, except to hold Emma even tighter and kiss her harder. But for Emma, Sal Tanner's warning was enough.

'Go back!' she told Marlow, snatching herself away. 'Your sister's right. I *will* bring you only grief.'

'Emma, do you love me? That's all I need to know,' he asked in a soft voice, holding her by the shoulders, his fiery dark eyes gazing pleadingly into hers. 'Just say you love me, and nothing else in the world matters.'

Emma gave her answer, though it stuck in her throat. 'No, I *don't* love you. I'm to be married in two weeks' time, you must know that.'

'Aye, I *do*! You're to be wed to Gregory Denton, or so they say. But you can't love the fellow . . . not when you love *me*, Emma, and you do love me, I know it. Don't try to hide that from me, Emma. Don't deny what we feel for each other.'

'You're wrong, Marlow. I do love Gregory, very much,' Emma lied. 'Caleb Crowther warned you away, didn't he?'

'He did.'

'Then do as he says. You must stay away, or you'll ruin us both.'

'Do you really want me to stay away?' Marlow asked now, his grip on her relaxing and his eyes filled with pain and disbelief. When, in a firm, quiet voice, Emma assured him that yes, that was what she wanted and he must forget her, he took away his hands, saying, in soft anger, 'There will *never* come the day when I forget you, Emma Grady. Nor when I stop loving you! But I'll not go against your word, don't fear!' Then he turned from her and disappeared into the spinney.

'That day will never come for me either, Marlow,' whispered Emma, as she watched him go, the tears running freely down her face, 'but it's for the best, believe me. Please believe me.' She cared not for what might happen to her, but Emma knew in her heart that should she go against Caleb Crowther's wishes, he would move heaven and earth to have Marlow transported to Australia as a convict. She sensed it, and was terrified by it.

\* \* \*

'Fools, the lot of them!' Caleb Crowther folded the newspaper into a tight rod before flinging it down on the table in disgust. 'They haven't got the slightest idea. Not the *slightest* idea!' He snatched up his napkin and viciously wiped each corner of his mouth. Of a sudden, he grabbed the newspaper again, opened it out and spread it before him. Then, peering down at it, he told his wife, 'I shall make it my business to have words with the editor about this.' He prodded his finger over and over again at the offending article, and Agnes Crowther became so curious that she leaned over the breakfast table in order to see more clearly. What she saw was a large cartoon, over which was a bold black caption which read, 'WHO ARE THE SLAVES?'

The cartoon showed a prosperous and surly-faced fellow standing on a barrel in the centre of the picture, his arms flung wide open – his left hand pointing to a family of dark slaves in the American South, and his right one pointing to a Lancashire cotton mill family. The former appeared to be well fed and clothed, with the child in its mother's arms positively chubby; while the Lancashire family were shabbily dressed and painfully undernourished. The man in the middle was drawing a comparison and concluding that of the two, it was the Lancashire cotton mill worker's family who seemed more subdued by slavery than did their dark-skinned counterparts.

'I pay my workers good money, and if they've got no more self-control than to breed like rabbits, then they deserve to starve!'

Seeing the look of utter disgust on his face, Emma wondered whether there was even one ounce of compassion

177

in Caleb Crowther's bitter heart. It was no wonder that of all the men previously employed by Thadius Grady, not one of them either liked or respected her uncle. That much she had learned during her time working alongside Gregory Denton, and it had come as no surprise to Emma. Indeed, she would have been surprised had it been otherwise.

'Emma, go along and get yourself ready. Mr Denton is due to collect you within the hour, is he not?'

'Yes, Aunt.' Emma excused herself from the breakfast table and was almost out of the room when Agnes Crowther instructed her, 'As Mrs Manfred is to accompany you, I would like a word with her first. Of course, I myself would be taking you,' here she made a small grimace and moved about in the chair, 'but I really haven't been feeling too well. Still, it is only a courtesy meeting between yourself and Mr Denton's mother. A necessary and dutiful one, however . . . since you will be moving in with her, in her own home. Yes indeed. Send Mrs Manfred to me straight away. I'll be in the drawing-room.' She turned her head to where Caleb Crowther was still brooding, his eyes scouring the page before him. 'That is all right, isn't it, dear?' she asked.

'Yes! Yes!' He did not look up, but he waved his hand with some impatience. 'Do as you think best. I intend to leave all this woman's business to you. As for myself, I must attend the courts at Manchester.' With that he pushed the newspaper aside and straightened his neck to peer at Emma, who was still waiting at the door. 'Be off with you, girl!' he told her. 'You have your instructions from your aunt. Inform the Manfred woman that she's wanted in the drawing-room.'

As he rose from his chair Emma nodded and, grateful to depart from their company, she excused herself again, and closed the door behind her. As she approached the stairs, Amy came rushing along, her cap askew and a look of apprehension on her face. In one hand she carried a dustpan and brush, in the other a large wooden tray.

'Oh, Miss Grady!' she cried. 'I shall get the full length of the mistress's tongue an' no mistake. I 'ad a bad night . . . a real bad 'un! An' I can't seem to catch up with me work no how!'

'Are you on your way to clear the breakfast table?' Emma asked, noticing how dishevelled Amy appeared and seeing that she was in such a state of agitation that she would probably end up by breaking every cup and plate on the table. When the frightened maid nodded in response, Emma continued in a kindly voice, at the same time putting a hand on the girl's shoulder to turn her back in the direction from which she had just come, 'Mrs Crowther is on her way to the drawing-room, and Mr Crowther is about to depart for the Manchester Assizes, so there's no need for you to panic. How about if you go and straighten your cap and calm yourself down? Mrs Crowther would not be too pleased to see you like this, now would she?'

'Ooh, you're right, Miss Grady,' the girl agreed, as she hurried away in the direction of the kitchen, 'an' she's been in such a sour mood lately. Oh, but Mrs Manfred will give me what for an' all, when she claps eyes on me!' said the little maid, shaking her head from side to side and growing more agitated by the minute. When Emma assured her that she herself was on her way to see Mrs Manfred to tell her to go immediately to the mistress in the drawing-room, the girl gave a great noisy sigh of relief. 'I'll be away an' tidy meself up, Miss Grady,' she said. 'Mek meself more presentable afore I come to do the breakfast things . . . oh, but I did 'ave a bad night, I'm telling yer . . . a *tirrible* night!' Then she scurried away, all the while muttering to herself, 'Be quick, Amy, be quick!'

Emma watched until the figure had gone from her sight. Amy's not much younger than me, she thought, and already she's learned to be afraid. Why! She's dictated to by more people than I am! The thought was a sobering one – as was the belief that the little maid was a true survivor and would come to no real harm. Emma hoped the very same could be applied to herself, because, in spite of her determined spirit, she could not rid herself of the feeling that there might well be rough times ahead.

Just over an hour later, Emma and Mrs Manfred emerged from the house. The older woman was dressed in a navy straw boater, dark dress and fitted calf-length coat which left the full hem of her skirt peeking out, while Emma looked lovely in a royal-blue full length coat over a paler blue dress. Her hair was brushed up and covered by a small plain bonnet of the same deep blue as her coat. She carried a black drawstring purse and wore black, small-heeled shoes with a cross-over bar at the ankle.

'How pretty you look, Miss Grady,' Mrs Manfred declared on first seeing her.

'By! Mrs Denton won't be able to resist you, Emma!' Gregory Denton remarked as he ushered both ladies into the carriage. Hiring this conveyance had set him right back on his savings, but he didn't begrudge it, for he intended to do everything in style to impress Emma, knowing, however, that his mother would never approve of such extravagance.

When the little party was safely aboard and comfortable, he gave the driver instructions to 'make for Montague Street, if you please'. Then he settled back in his seat opposite the two women. He gave Mrs Manfred a small nervous smile, and he looked at Emma, his face blushing a dark shade of pink at her very closeness, with the fawning eyes of a man either in great pain or extreme love – or both!

The carriage went from Breckleton to Blackburn by way of Preston New Road. The journey was not too long, only some four miles in all and, the main road being pleasantly free of traffic, it hardly seemed even that distance. Emma found herself under close and embarrassing scrutiny all the way. She could feel Gregory's eyes on her, and she knew that his adoring gaze had not left her face for an instant. Now and then, to reassure both Gregory and herself, she looked up to warmly smile at him. But this only seemed to make matters worse as, bit by bit, he edged forward in his seat, until, by the time they turned into the steep and cobbled Montague Street, he was clinging so precariously to the very edge of his seat that when the carriage swung in from Preston New Road, he slithered to the floor. For a long, excruciatingly embarrassing moment Gregory Denton seemed perfectly surprised to find himself on his knees before Mrs Manfred, with his right hand actually clutching the top of her leg.

When, completely taken aback, Mrs Manfred declared, 'Mr Denton! Do get up!' Emma was struck by the absurdity of it all and, in spite of her every effort not to, she collapsed into a fit of helpless laughter.

'Oh, Mrs Manfred, I do apologize!' Gregory Denton was mortified. But, for Emma, the whole incident was delightful. Somehow in laughing at poor Gregory, and in seeing the shocked, indignant expression on Mrs Manfred's face, she felt less nervous of the encounter she herself was about to endure. Surely the woman who gave birth to such a gentle and apologetic creature as Gregory couldn't possibly be the awful creature that people claimed she was. This thought gave Emma a great deal of comfort.

The carriage was brought to a halt and the passengers disembarked. Emma and Mrs Manfred waited while Gregory paid the driver and asked him to return to collect the ladies upon the hour.

Oh, Lord! thought Emma, as she stood before the gate, her gaze taking in how regimental and neat the small front garden was and how sparklingly bright the lace curtains were. There was no going back now!

In a moment, Gregory had inserted his key into the front door lock. Pushing the door open to reveal a long narrow corridor with an open stairway at the end and two doors along the right wall, he shepherded Emma and Mrs Manfred inside. He then closed the door, plunging them all into semi-darkness, since the only incoming light was through the half-circle of stained glass above the door.

Still Emma was determined not to feel too apprehensive and was succeeding in keeping herself calm until, with the best intentions in the world, Gregory said in a low, trembling voice into her ear, 'Emma, don't be nervous. And, please . . . do be careful not to upset her, because she can be *very* touchy.' Whereupon Emma's brave resolve instantly crumbled, leaving her so apprehensive that she was annoyed to discover herself actually trembling.

'It's cold in here, isn't it?' she asked, looking from one to the other for reassurance.

'You're right, dear,' Mrs Manfred quickly agreed, 'it is a bit chilly to the bones.'

'Yes, well . . . Mother can't abide it being too warm,' explained Gregory, propelling them towards the first door on the right, 'she says it meks a body soft to be too warm,' he finished lamely. Now, turning the brass door knob, he inched open the door saying, 'If you'll just mek yourself comfortable in here, I'll bring a pot of tea. Then, I'd best go upstairs and see whether she's ready to receive visitors.'

'Upstairs?' asked Emma with some surprise.

'Is your mother ill?' rejoined Mrs Manfred, feeling decidedly uncomfortable and wondering how in God's name would Emma fare in this house.

'Oh no! No, indeed, she's not *ill*,' replied Gregory, with a forced laugh, 'just a little off colour, I dare say. There are days when she doesn't set foot downstairs, you see, but, she's not ill, or bed ridden. Oh no!' He seemed most anxious that Emma especially should believe that. 'It's just, well . . . the old ones do have their funny little whims and fancies, don't they!'

Mrs Manfred merely nodded, thinking to herself how one of Mrs Denton's 'whims and fancies' was no doubt the pleasure she got from being waited on hand and foot by a doting son!

'It's all right, Gregory,' Emma felt the need to reassure him, for she could see how desperate he was that all should go well on this first meeting between his mother and his prospective wife. 'Mrs Manfred and I would love a cup of tea. Then you go and talk to your mother, like you said.' She cast an appealing glance in Mrs Manfred's direction. 'That's all right isn't it, Manny? We'll be content supping our tea until Mrs Denton's ready to receive us.' When back came the grudging reply, 'Yes, of course,' Gregory was visibly relieved, and a moment later had gone to put on the kettle. Emma would have much preferred to busy herself in making the tea, but she thought the offer might offend Gregory.

It was fifteen minutes later when Emma and Mrs Manfred were ushered up the enclosed and darkened stairs. On reaching the landing, Emma was reminded by the anxious Gregory, 'Remember, Emma, you mustn't be nervous. Her bark really is worse than her bite, you know.' The look on his face, and the pleading tone of his voice was enough to make Emma want to turn round and flee. But, bracing herself, she stiffened her back, brushed down her dress, patted her bonnet and, in a deliberate voice told him, 'I'm quite ready, Gregory, and not a bit nervous.' Oh, if only that were true, she thought, making sure that Mrs Manfred was not far behind as they all trooped alongside the polished carved ballustrade towards the main front room.

If Emma had been expecting to be confronted by some sort of ogre when she entered that bedroom, then she was *not* disappointed! The very first thing that struck her was the size of the room which was surprisingly large and, judging by its dimensions, must span the entire width of the house. Situated at the front and facing east, it was well positioned to enjoy the best of the early morning sunshine. To Emma, the room was in stark contrast to what she had already seen of the rest of the house, which was unpleasantly cramped and gloomy. But, even though the sun brightened it up, the huge and oppressive articles of furniture cast their own dark shadows, sadly negating the effect of the light coming through the wide bay windows.

To Emma's right, and taking up a greater part of the green distempered wall, was a long cumbersome chest of drawers, made in dark wood and some three feet deep from front to back. It contained six drawers, each with two enormous wooden knobs at either end. On top of the dresser was a solitary wooden-framed photograph of a man, woman and young boy standing between them. The humble-featured man had a long drooping moustache and his fair colouring was echoed in the face of the boy. The woman had a sour, impatient expression on her face and, by the way in which she thrust herself in front of the other two, she totally dominated the picture. Emma could see that the small boy was Gregory, and she assumed that the man and woman were his parents. He was later to confirm this and to tell Emma how the whole experience of having that picture taken had been not only a long, laborious and frightening procedure, but that it had cost his father no less than three days' takings in his butcher's shop. He remembered quite clearly though, how his parents had argued the issue, but, as always, his father had given in to his mother's insistence, and, ever since, the picture had pride of place on that dresser.

Along the wall to the left was a tall, broad wardrobe in the same dark wood and design as the dresser, and beside it stood an iron-legged washstand, the lower shelf of which was packed from end to end with all manner of toiletries. The centre of the floor was covered by a large, patterned rag-peg carpet, with the highly polished floorboards visible around the edges. To one side of the window was a small rush-seated stand-chair which held a bulbous circular snuff-tin and a brass candle-holder containing a half-used candle. Directly beneath the window was the largest bed Emma had ever seen. Made of brass, it was most decorative. It had two corner-posts at either end; halfway down each of these was a large petalled flower in fine beaten brass, each one touching another to form a garland right across. On the top of each post was a tall, ceramic, floral acorn, each one polished to a brilliant shine. The bedcover was of the same rag-peg design as the carpet which Emma now stood on, and, sitting bolt upright beneath it, with her back stiff, yet slightly stooped, was Doreen Denton – the formidable sight of whom turned Emma's stomach over in a series of somersaults. Physically, she was small and, with her pretty lace-coloured nightgown, tiny frilled white cap and large green-speckled eyes, at a distance she might have appeared to be no more than a child.

In truth, her presence was overpowering. Emma could feel her influence from every corner of the room. Then, when those large, all-seeing eyes came to rest their probing gaze on her, Emma wished herself a thousand miles away.

'Here!' The voice was thin yet charged with such authority that one dared not disobey. 'Don't stand dithering there! Come *here*.'

When the voice pierced the air, it also seemed to pierce something in Gregory Denton, for he was now fidgeting uncomfortably and nervously winding his hands together. 'Emma . . . she just wants to see you more closely,' he said softly, beginning to step forward, 'it's all right.'

'You were not asked to speak, Gregory!' came the sharp retort from the bed. 'Nor were you asked to stay. Kindly leave! And you can take that other woman with you.'

'But this is Mrs Manfred, Mother . . . the lady sent by Emma's aunt, to speak on her behalf,' he spluttered.

'Take her with you, I said. If she's here to speak on Miss

Grady's behalf, then there's no need, is there, for the young lady herself is here? She can speak on her own behalf. And, if this . . . Mrs Manfred is here to speak on behalf of Miss Grady's *aunt*, then I don't want to hear. If Mrs Crowther has something to say, or to ask, then she must come here and speak on her *own* behalf!' With this, she swung her eyes round to Mrs Manfred, asking, 'Unless of course the woman's struck down badly! Is that the case?' When Mrs Manfred gave the somewhat impatient and indignant answer that, yes, Mrs Crowther had been poorly on getting from her bed that very morning, there was a painfully long silence before, with a sharp clap of her hands, the older woman told her, 'I can't say as I altogether believe such a convenient excuse, but, very well . . . Take yourself downstairs with Gregory, and I'll let you know whether to come back up.' Before Mrs Manfred could voice the protest which was already registering on her face, Gregory Denton had moved forward to assure her quietly, 'It's best we do as she says. Emma's all right, Mrs Manfred. Please . . . let them get to know each other.'

When the door had closed behind them, Emma thought she hadn't felt so alone since her papa had been taken from her – except, of course, when she had forced herself to tell Marlow that they had no future together.

'Now then,' the voice piped up, 'fetch yourself closer.'

Emma was moved by the urge to take off her bonnet, and quickly doing so, she came forward to stand beside the bed. She was aware of her fingers nervously twisting the bonnet in her hands, and she could see the old lady watching with irritation; but, for the life of her, she couldn't keep still! Then, in a sharp angry voice, came the instruction to 'Put that blessed thing down!' But when Emma felt the bonnet being wrenched from her hand and flung on to the bed, her fighting spirit came to the fore. Bad-tempered old thing! she thought. I won't let you get the better of me, because I intend to start as I mean to go on. Reaching forward, she retrieved the bonnet, held it perfectly still in her hands, and, looking directly into that sour, wizened face, she said in a firm voice, 'I'm pleased to meet you, Mrs Denton.'

After curiously regarding Emma for a long time, the older woman's expression grew darker. 'I can't say I'm pleased to meet *you*!' She began looking Emma up and down, noting the blue outfit, of a kind not worn or afforded by the likes of folk round these quarters. She saw how Emma's rich auburn hair shone in the sunlight, and searching those strong and defiant eyes she saw how beautiful Emma was. Now she was even more suspicious than she had been when Gregory had first told her the news. Gregory, *her* Gregory, her unattractive son, whom she loathed to share with another woman. *Any* woman! Yet, there was something strange here. Something not quite right that she hadn't fathomed out. Now, she bluntly asked the questions which had presented themselves to her.

'What do *you* want with my lad? You, a young woman from a far better background, whose uncle is a man of the Law, and who should know better than to think you could fit in with the likes of us? What do you want with my Gregory, eh? Is there sommat *wrong* with you, that you're not telling?' Of a sudden, she was bolt upright in the bed, her eyes enormous and her hands thrown up in alarm. 'That's it!' she said with astonishment. 'You're with child! I'm right, aren't I, eh? You're with another man's child and the Justice thinks to rid himself of you . . . palm you on to my Gregory!' Her voice had risen with every word, until she was shrieking at the top of her voice. Before Emma could assure her that such suspicions were totally unfounded, the door had burst open to admit both Gregory and Mrs Manfred.

'What's all the shouting?' Gregory demanded. 'We could hear you downstairs!' One look at the woman in the bed told him she was indulging in one of her tantrums, and coming to put a protective arm about Emma's shoulders, he led her away towards the door and Mrs Manfred. When, in a high-pitched and hysterical voice, his mother told him, 'You're being *used*, you bloody fool! The girl's with child! Ask her! Go on! Let her deny it if she can!' he was stopped in his tracks. Bringing his gaze to Emma, he saw her smile and shake her head. It was enough.

'Emma is a good and lovely creature,' he told the agitated woman. 'I love her, and I'm deeply grateful that she's agreed to be my wife.'

'You're being *used*, I tell you!' insisted Doreen Denton, struggling to get from the bed. 'You'll not fetch her into *this* house, I say!'

Emma felt Gregory's hands fall from her shoulders. She watched as he slowly turned, went to the bed, and looking directly into his mother's eyes told her in a tone of voice which neither Doreen Denton nor Emma had heard him use before, 'Emma and I are to be wed in a fortnight's time, and I shall be bringing her here to live with me. But, only for as long as it takes for us to buy our own home. That's now my intention, and that's the way of things . . . whether you approve, or whether you don't.' When he had finished speaking, the silence in the room was painful to Emma. She might have stepped forward to diffuse the situation, but was stopped when Mrs Manfred's hand gripped her arm. Seeing the fire in Gregory's face, and having heard how lovingly and fiercely he had defended her, something warm stirred within her.

But Emma had also seen the venom in old Mrs Denton's eyes as the old woman had stared across the room at her. There had been such loathing in her voice hitherto, that when she now spoke in a completely different tone, Emma was totally shocked.

'It seems I've been too harsh on you, Miss Grady . . . Emma. If my son loves you enough to fight for you in such a way that I never would have believed, then you must be everything he says you are.' Now, she switched her attention to Mrs Manfred, who also was puzzled and surprised by this sudden change of attitude. 'Mrs . . . Manfred, isn't it?' When there came a nod of confirmation, she went on, 'Thank you for having the courtesy to come along. You can go back to Mrs Crowther and tell her that I am in full approval of the marriage between Miss Grady and my son. She will be made welcome in his house.'

'Oh, thank you, Mother!' Gregory bent to kiss the wizened cheek. 'Emma *is* everything I say. You'll see. You'll come to love her as I do.' He was greatly relieved to see the old woman's change of heart, and he believed above all else that his mother *would* come to bless the day when Emma came to live under this roof as his own darling wife. God had been good to him, and he would strive to be as loving and dutiful a husband, as he had always been a son.

Emma also was glad of Mrs Denton's change of heart. It had been so sudden and unexpected that it had at first worried her. But then she reasoned that the old woman must be prone to such swift changes of mood, for Gregory seemed to have accepted it and of course, he knew his mother better than *she* did. No doubt, in time she would get used to old Mrs Denton's ways – though, in all truth, she had not taken to her, and would never go out of her way to keep close company with the old woman.

As they climbed aboard the carriage for the journey back to Breckleton House, Emma began to think she was fortunate in finding such a champion as Gregory, who was kind and thoughtful in every way. And though there were many things she would change if given the chance, Emma was gradually coming to accept the deep and generous affection Gregory Denton had for her. She would make him as good a wife as she knew how – working at it that much harder because she knew she could never love him in the way she loved Marlow Tanner. Emma consoled herself with the belief that, because of her marriage to Gregory, Marlow would be safe. I *am* doing the right thing, she thought. But the deeper she thought, the more curious she became about the old feud between her papa and the river-people. There was something sinister about it, Emma knew – something ominous that rose like a phantom between her and Marlow. In marrying Gregory and removing Marlow from Caleb Crowther's antagonism, Emma trusted that this phantom would no longer haunt either her or Marlow. The thought gave her a small feeling of contentment.

*Too* trusting! Mrs Manfred thought, as she gave Emma a quiet sideways glance on their way back to Breckleton House. You're too trusting, Emma, my girl! But, you'll be all right, child . . . because I'll never be far away.

\* \* \*

Upstairs in the house on Montague Street, old Mrs Denton watched from the window as Gregory said goodbye to his darling Emma and her companion. She ached with bitterness when she saw the look on his face, so filled with love. She recalled the way he had stood up to her, defending that Grady creature with the ferocity of a tigress defending its cubs. She recollected his words which were etched on her heart: 'I shall be bringing her here to live . . . But, only for as long as it takes for us to buy our own home!' But she had cleverly put paid to *that* idea by her devious little display. It had been a damned hard thing to do, but she was determined. Nobody would ever take her son away from under this roof. There wasn't a soul alive who she would ever allow to part her from her darling Gregory – not even Emma Grady!

As Gregory waved the carriage out of sight, Doreen Denton murmured venomously through clenched teeth, 'So, Gregory, you think I'll come to love her, do you? *Never*! Not while there's a breath left in this old body of mine! Oh, but I'll do what needs to be done, to keep *you* here, where you belong.' She hurriedly climbed back into bed, contriving to look suitably exhausted for when her devoted son mounted the stairs to fetch her some refreshment.

There was something else niggling her also. She'd seen this Emma Grady before, she was sure of it. But where? Where? It would come to her – one of these days it would come to her.

# Chapter Seven

'Lord love an' save us, Marlow Tanner, will yer never go to bed?' Sal Tanner squeezed her way through the narrow doorway which led from her sleeping cabin into the living area. She had been suffering a restless night herself, but for very different reasons than those of her brother. Firstly, the sound of his footsteps pacing up and down with increasing agitation, had prevented her from falling easily into a slumber; then, when she had eventually managed to close her eyes, the wind had picked up into a mad frenzy – shifting and thrashing the barge about until she gave up all attempts at getting a good night's sleep. 'It's like the bloody divil's 'aving a party underneath us!' she complained with a shake of her tousled head.

'Aw, Sal . . . I'm sorry if I've upset your night's sleep,' Marlow apologized, coming to put his arms about her and leading her to the narrow seat which was fixed round the corner beside the small black stove. 'Sit yourself down here, and I'll fetch you a hot drink.' He was wonderfully patient as she laboriously made her way on slow faltering footsteps, for, since her accident, neither her leg nor her nerves had fully recovered. Still, she was in finer form than the week before, and Marlow knew she'd be in even better form as the weeks went by. Smiling to himself at her merry abuse of him now, Marlow eased her on to the seat. Then, going to the small bench beneath the porthole, he lifted the hinged lid and withdrew from it a thick grey blanket, which he wrapped tightly around his sister's ample form. Next he stoked up the stove with the small coke pieces from the nearby scuttle, and, seeing that the fire was going well, he went into the galley to fetch a small pan of water. By the time he had gone back into the galley and returned with two sizeable mugs, into which he'd spilled a good helping of tea, sugar and milk, the water was boiling. In another moment he was seated beside his sister, each of them warming their hands around the hot, comforting mugs, with their faithful dog, Jake, stretched out at their feet, indignant at having been disturbed from his night's sleep.

Pretending to sip the scalding-hot liquid, Sal gave her brother a crafty but concerned sideways look. God above, she thought, how tortured he looks. In all the time since their parents had been tragically taken from them, Sal could not remember ever seeing Marlow so badly troubled. And, oh she loved him so much that to see it now tore her apart. So deeply affected by his heartache was she, that Sal had to swallow several times in order to melt that great hard lump which was stuck in her throat, preventing the words she wanted to say from coming out. Even when she did manage to speak, the tears which were threatening to fall, trembled in her voice. 'Aw lad, will yer stop punishing yerself?' she asked. 'Can yer not see what it's doing to yer?'

At once, suddenly aware that Sal had been closely watching him, and anxious not to be questioned on matters too painful to discuss, Marlow's expression changed. When he turned his eyes to her, they were smiling, and the answer he gave was not the one he truly felt in his heart. 'The only thing wrong with me is a sister who will insist on reading the darkest things into the smallest upset!' he told her in a chastising voice.

'Oh, I see.' Sal Tanner knew that she'd subtly been told to mind her own business, however gently it had been put. 'Keep me long nose out? That's what yer telling me, ain't it, yer bugger?' she laughed, although the laugh lacked merriment. 'All right, fella-me-lad, I'll not mek matters worse by harping on at yer,' she conceded, unable to stop herself from adding, 'Aw but lad, it'll do yer no good to keep baying fer the moon, yer do know that, don't yer?' She waited for an answer, her troubled eyes never leaving his face.

'Don't worry, Sal.' Marlow put down his mug on the small round hearth, and giving a deep inner sigh, patted the back of his sister's hand, saying with a brighter smile, 'I may be *wanting* the moon . . . but I'd be a bloody fool to think I could ever *have* it! I know that, sweetheart. And it's only a matter of coming to terms with it.' With this, he put his arm around her and drew her near to him. They stayed like this for a while, Marlow concerned that he was causing his sister to fret about him, and Sal, although comforted by his embrace, was still disturbed because she had never seen her brother in such a quiet, distant mood. Yet, she knew Marlow to be an honourable and sensible man and it was these very qualities which she counted on now. For, however much he loved Emma Grady and longed for her to be his, Sal Tanner knew that Marlow would never pursue her once she had made her marriage vows to another man. And that day couldn't come quickly enough for Sal Tanner, because there was never more heartache caused than when two men craved the same woman, and she wanted only one.

In her heart, Sal gave thanks that Emma Grady had made her choice and promised herself to the Denton fellow; for Marlow was fooling himself in hoping that the likes of her would ever give her favours to a bargee. Indeed, Gregory Denton was not as high up as the Crowthers, but neither was he as low down as the mill-hands and bargees who worked beneath him. He evidently had both the seal of approval of Caleb Crowther and the devotion of Emma Grady. The thing was settled, and, as far as Sal Tanner was concerned, it had been settled the right way – though she would never be so callous as to declare such a thing out loud in Marlow's presence. But, in time he would come to see this for himself, she hoped. Until then, she must guard her tongue.

Of a sudden, Marlow stood up, saying in a cheerful voice, 'It's Saturday tomorrow. I've to ferry a cargo of fowl from Liverpool to Lancaster, so, what say if I take you round the market afterwards . . . I need a new stout pair of boots, and you can choose that curtain material you've been going on about these past weeks.' It was a deliberate ploy to change the subject, and also to compensate for his sister having been laid up in this cramped barge for such a long time, with little else to occupy her mind but *his* business.

'That'll be right grand!' Sal Tanner was at once enthused by the idea. 'Over four years them curtains 'ave been at them there winders . . . an' if I wash the buggers just once more, they'll end up in tatters!' Now, she was on her feet, tugging at the worn floral curtains and addressing Jake, who peered up with only half-awake, droopy eyes. 'Blue 'uns, I think,' she said, 'bright blue 'uns, wi'out flowers on.' She made her way back to the cabin, muttering to herself, and, just before disappearing through the narrow doorway, she turned to tell the bemused Marlow, 'Nothin' wi' *green* on! We don't want to upset the little folk. Well . . . unless there's some right grand material there, an' nothin' else ter choose from, eh? But if it's got any green in it at all . . . we must ask permission from the little people first. Oh, yes!' Even after she was out of sight, Marlow could hear his sister's voice, low and reverent, and he knew she was talking to the 'little people' – asking them whether she might be allowed to choose a material which had a *little* green in it.

Later, as he stood at the window in his own berth, from where he gazed out across the water, Marlow found himself smiling at Sal's fervent belief that the colour green was most precious to the 'little people', and that anyone using it, wearing it or keeping it without their permission, would be horribly punished. It was a peculiar belief of Sal's which went as far back as Marlow could remember. But Sal had always been that bit different from anybody else he'd ever known; eccentric some folks called her. Whatever her little quirks and fancies though, she had a heart of gold and she was all the family he had, and if anybody was ever to cause her harm, he'd tear them limb from limb!

Marlow was a man of deep loyalties and great passion. And now, as he watched the wind churning up the waters outside, he felt his own heart churning over and over with his memories of Emma. Sal was right, he thought, he might just as well be crying for the moon. He had heard from her own lips her declaration of love for Gregory Denton. Yet, Marlow would have laid down his life in the belief that it was he whom she really loved. Had he really been fooling himself when he'd seen that same look in her eyes that was in his own? When his mouth had covered hers and she had trembled in his arms, was he so wrong in feeling their hearts beat as one? Could a man be so misled and blinded by his own love that he should imagine such a thing? Dear God! How could he tell? What else could he be guided by if his own instincts proved him wrong? The more Marlow tortured himself for an answer, the more he realized that only Emma herself could confirm or deny what he felt in his heart; only she could raise or dash his hopes. But Emma had told him that she loved the man who would soon be her husband; she had begged him to leave her be; and Marlow knew that, however much it grieved him, he had to respect her wish. Nothing good ever came of a man forcing himself on a woman – particularly a woman so soon to be wed. Oh, but it was a hard thing to do! And even harder for Marlow was the thought of remaining in these parts once Emma had become Mrs Gregory Denton.

Of a sudden, Marlow thought he and Sal might sell off the barge and go to America – the land of opportunity they called it. But then he considered how Sal would react to such a proposition, and his hopes were dashed. Sal did not possess such a spirit of adventure as he. She was a home-loving soul who wanted no more than a fire with which to warm her outside, and a bottle of booze to warm her inside. They were both born and bred river-folk, but, whereas he would now be tempted to sail the seven seas, Sal would never leave the shores of old England, not for all the treasure in the world. Marlow knew this, and though it might curtail the boundaries of his own existence, he loved her nonetheless. He was bound by his love for the sister who had selflessly raised him. He was also bound, and even more deeply, by his hopeless love for Emma. He could no more suppress the love he felt for her than he could graciously accept her rejection of him – however much he might wish otherwise.

'I wish you were coming with me, Manny.' Emma lifted the hem of her wedding gown and, seeing that Mrs Manfred had gathered together her sewing paraphernalia, stepped down from the stool, at once beginning to feverishly strip the ivory silk gown from her body as though its very touch was unbearable to her skin.

'Stuff and nonsense, Miss Grady!' declared Mrs Manfred, easing her aching back into the chair and frowning as Emma carelessly flung the expensive wedding gown over the bed. 'Don't be so rough with that dress!' she chided, at the same time dropping her sewing basket to the floor and adding in a weary tone, 'Twice they've had the blessed thing back, and *still* they can't get it to sit right on you, child! I did tell Mrs Crowther that it would save time and money to let *me* make the alterations in the first place.' She blew out her cheeks in exasperation. 'And here we are . . . the very evening afore your wedding, and it's all rush and push!' She scraped the straying locks from her face and seemed to visibly sag.

'That gown will *never* feel right,' Emma interrupted. Then, having put on her nightgown, she came to sit cross-legged at the older woman's feet. 'It isn't the dress, Manny . . . it's *me!*' she said in a quiet, forlorn voice.

'Come here, child,' said Mrs Manfred, holding out her arms as Emma gratefully leaned into them. 'Tell me what's playing so heavy on your mind. This past week you've seemed to be miles away.'

'I sometimes wish I *was* miles away,' replied Emma, feeling cheered by Mrs Manfred's comforting presence, but growing more and more dismayed by the fact that from tomorrow, when she left this house as Gregory Denton's wife, these long intimate talks with this darling woman could never again be taken for granted. 'Oh, Manny!' she said now, her eyes sorrowful as they looked up to that kindly face. 'I shall miss you so very much.'

'Away with you, Miss Grady!' came the retort. 'You'll be that busy as Mrs Denton . . . what with being a wife and running a house, together with making new friends and afore long, looking forward to being with child.' Here, she smiled warmly and gave Emma an extra tight hug. 'Well . . . there'll be little time left for missing anybody, I can tell you!' She became nostalgic as she thought of times long gone, of a husband she had lost, of the children she never had, and her eyes grew misty. 'Be happy, child,' she said softly, stroking the girl's hair, 'you must try to be happy.'

Emma wondered about Mrs Manfred's past, for it was something the dear lady had always been reluctant to discuss. Yet, seeing how deeply affected she seemed, Emma felt obliged to ask, 'Were *you* happy, Manny . . . with your husband? Were you very much in love on the day of your wedding?'

'Bless you, of course not!' came the surprised reply. 'It was a rare thing for a lass to be in love with the man she married. Often, she had little say in who it was to be . . . very much the same as you. Circumstances prevailed and convenience was more important than whether or not the two loved each other. Oh, but I can tell you, Miss Grady, that you do grow to love a man over the years.' With this she paused and gazed into Emma's uplifted eyes with deliberation. When she spoke again, her voice was soft but serious. 'Tomorrow you'll stand in God's church and you'll be asked to give yourself to the man who stands beside you. When you make your vows, it can't be just your voice that speaks . . . it must also come from the heart. There will only be room in your heart for one man – and that man *must* be your husband. From the moment you give those vows, you give yourself also, *all* of yourself, mind and body, to Gregory Denton.' Cupping Emma's small troubled face between the palms of her hands, she asked meaningfully, 'You do know what I'm saying, child, don't you?'

Emma was left in no doubt as to what Mrs Manfred was saying. What she was telling her was that she must put Marlow Tanner out of her heart for ever! She was stressing the purity of the marriage vows Emma was shortly to take, and the total commitment they demanded. Mrs Manfred was warning Emma, but Emma could also sense the older woman's fear. Yet, she need not be afraid, thought Emma, for hadn't she herself gone over it all again and again these past weeks? Hadn't she tormented herself and questioned the rapid sequence of events which were taking her along at such frightening speed that she could hardly catch her breath? Didn't she know how serious, and demanding, and final were the vows which she would utter in that church tomorrow, before God and before Gregory? And wasn't she all too painfully aware of how, in that moment, she would be called on to ban all thoughts of Marlow Tanner from her mind? Never again must she think of him; never again must she indulge herself in her memories of that splendid, radiant smile which lit up her heart as nothing else could; never again must she close her eyes and listen to the soft murmur of his voice which caused her heart to tremble so. Those dark, laughing eyes and the feel of his strong arms about her . . . that wonderful, exquisite sensation when his mouth had covered her own in a kiss which had spread its pleasure throughout every corner of her being. These things would all be forbidden her. In their place would be Gregory, a kind and gentle man who, Emma knew, loved her perhaps in a way she would never deserve. But she would *try* with all her heart.

Emma said as much now to Mrs Manfred, before asking in a shy, quiet voice, 'How am I to behave . . . as his wife, Manny?' So acutely embarrassed was Emma by her own question, that she withdrew her gaze from the older woman's face and rested it on the floor.

Mrs Manfred's answer was given with great love, and tempered by an awareness of Emma's innocence in such matters. 'Behave as he wants you to. Behave sensibly and don't be afraid, for I'm sure Gregory won't hurt you, child. When he speaks softly to you, just listen quietly and know that he loves you. When you see his nakedness and he takes you in his arms, comfort yourself with the fact that he will be gentle . . . for Gregory Denton seems to be a tender-hearted fellow. And when he makes love to you, think on pleasant things . . . fill your heart with gladness, and it won't seem as terrible as you anticipate.'

Without lifting her face, which by now was suffused with a burning pinkness, Emma murmured her thanks, adding, 'I'll try to remember everything you've told me, Manny.'

But, in her heart, she was still terrified of the ordeal to come. Unable to stop herself, she contemplated the fact that, if it was Marlow's bed she was going to, the prospect would not seem anywhere near as harrowing!

The day of Emma's wedding might have been a day in the middle of summer rather than January, for it was warm and filled with sunshine. The little church was packed as Emma came up the aisle to the resounding music of the organ. Everyone agreed that, in her lovely silk ivory gown, with a simple spray of yellow rosebuds in her hands, she was the most beautiful bride they had ever seen. On this splendid occasion, her rich, burnished hair was swept into clutches of ringlets either side of her head, secured by delicate mother-of-pearl combs.

As she knelt before the altar, Emma turned to look into Gregory's face. What she saw were the proud eyes of a man who adored her, and she felt ashamed that, on first waking that very morning, her thoughts had been drawn not to Gregory, but to Marlow Tanner. For his part, what Gregory saw as he looked deep into Emma's magnificent grey eyes, was a host of emotions which greatly moved him. He saw her fear, and prayed that it was not fear of him; he saw trust and compassion; he believed he saw the glimmer of love – but it seemed a sad kind of love, for there was pain in Emma's eyes, not joy. There was kindness also, and such strength that it made him tremble inside. Yet, in spite of all this and of the all-consuming love he felt for Emma, Gregory Denton was afraid. From the first moment Emma had been promised to him, he had been afraid – afraid he might lose her. Now, even while he heard her speak the marriage vows, he was mortally afraid that she might never love him in the way he loved her. He was afraid of the change she would find in her way of life, and he knew it would be difficult for Emma to adjust. Yet, for all his fears, Gregory Denton had hope – hope for their future together, and hope for Emma's lasting affection.

In the celebrations which followed, Breckleton House echoed to the sound of music and dancing. Throughout the evening, a wide variety of guests mingled in and out of the rooms; some were business acquaintances of Caleb Crowther, dressed in dark formal wear; others belonged to Agnes Crowther's social circle, and were serious-faced and full of meaningless talk; and there were those known only to Martha and her intended, colourful in dress and loud of voice, and all of whom constantly pecked Emma on the face and forgot her name!

Emma was pleased to spend a few quiet moments in the company of Silas Trent, who took the opportunity to remind her, 'Don't forget, Emma. If ever you need a friend . . .' Whereupon she thanked him once more and assured him that she would not forget, but that, 'I am now in the hands of a good man, and doubt that I'll ever need to take you up on your kind offer.'

Three times Emma made a gentle approach to old Mrs Denton, and three times she was made to feel so uncomfortable that she tactfully gave up the effort.

It was some way past nine p.m. when Emma saw Caleb Crowther leading Gregory into the study. Ten minutes later they both emerged, seeming pleased with themselves and crossing the room in opposite directions – the older man to rejoin his cronies, and the younger to firstly join his mother, and then to hurriedly make his way towards Emma. Emma, meanwhile, had observed how stony-faced her mother-in-law appeared during the few exchanged words with her attentive son.

When Gregory told Emma, 'Please make your goodbyes, Emma, for it's time we left,' Emma's heart sank. This was the moment she had been dreading – when they must depart for that little house on Montague Street where the presence of old Mrs Denton brooded in every dark corner. Emma lost count of the number of times Gregory had apologized for the fact that 'I had it in mind to take you to Scarborough for a week, but, what with my duties at work and Mother being in such delicate health, well . . . I know you understand, Emma.' Emma understood all right. She understood that, on this occasion, at least, she was not of paramount importance in her new husband's life – first came his work, then came his elderly mother and *then* came his wife. Emma understood and, for the first time, she saw the imperfections in Gregory's love for her. Yet, she weighed that up against the imperfections in her love for him, and believed that it was *she*, not he, who had need to apologize.

When the word was given that the newly-weds were about to leave, well-wishers came from all sides.

'Good fortune,' said one.

'May you be blessed with many children,' said another.

'I don't suppose we shall have occasion to see each other often,' remarked Martha, with her arm linked boldly in that of Silas Trent's, and a cunning look on her face.

'Quite!' rejoined Agnes Crowther, whose hands were stiffly joined and pointed to Paradise.

The sentiments of Emma's aunt and cousin were echoed by Caleb Crowther's remark, 'Emma is a married woman now, and all responsibility for her has gone from this house.' Then, addressing himself not to Emma, but to her husband, he continued, 'Thomas has instructions to deliver your wife's belongings to your house first thing in the morning. I believe Mrs Manfred has the matter in hand.' Giving a sly look and lowering his voice, he surreptitiously patted Gregory Denton's jacket above his waistcoat pocket. 'You have the most important item right there. Be frugal with it, Denton . . . for it was hard earned!' When Gregory nodded and made the observation, 'I know how careful Thadius Grady was, and I shall be equally careful with what he has entrusted to me, Mr Crowther, sir,' Emma knew at once that they were discussing the marriage fund left by her papa, and which she suspected, like her, must now be the responsibility of her husband. The knowledge that she was no longer under the jurisdiction of Caleb Crowther gave her a curious feeling of satisfaction and a sense of freedom – but the latter was cruelly curtailed when Gregory remarked, 'Come along, Emma. It's been a long, exhausting day for Mother, and she's ready for her bed.'

Before Emma climbed into the carriage, she clung to Mrs Manfred, who on impulse had thrown her arms around her. 'Oh, Manny!' she murmured, in a quiet voice unheard by anyone else. 'Pray for me, eh?'

When the older woman held her at arm's length to say in an equally soft voice, 'Emma Grady, your strength is in yourself! I'll just pray that you use it well,' there were tears in her eyes, and in Emma's also.

'You will come and see me, won't you, Manny?' Emma

felt the need for that reassurance.

'You see if I don't!' came the retort in a choking voice. 'You just see if I don't!'

When a third voice interrupted, saying, 'Of course you'll be welcome at my house, Mrs . . . Manfred. But please don't forget that it is *my* house, and that your own duties as far as Emma's concerned, are at an end. She is, after all, answerable to my son now,' both Mrs Manfred and Emma abruptly looked up at the carriage where old Mrs Denton was leaning forward on the edge of her seat. The conniving smile on her face was not pleasant, and nor was her voice as she instructed Emma, 'It's time we went, young lady! Afore the cold gets into my poor old bones.'

The big mantelpiece clock struck eleven, and Emma wondered who was more loath to climb the dark narrow stairway to bed. Certainly the thought gave her little comfort, and neither Gregory nor old Mrs Denton seemed prepared to make a move.

On returning to the house on Montague Street, the elderly woman had made a great fuss about folks wasting good money on fancies and fripperies, but then, 'folks such as the Crowthers are partial to showing off and making fine displays!' With that said, she had taken off her cloak and bonnet, which she promptly handed to Emma with the curt instruction, 'Put the bonnet carefully on to the peg. And make sure that you drape my cloak *inside out* . . . it keeps the dust from settling on the outer material.' From the hallway, where she took care to do exactly as she was told for fear of alienating old Mrs Denton any further, Emma could hear the conversation now taking place in the back parlour. First she heard Gregory's voice pointing out to his mother how late the hour was, and did she not think it was time he helped her up to her bed? Then came the surly reply that it was not for *him* to say when she should go to her bed! And, what was more, she should like him to prepare her a hot drink, which 'might well help me to sleep all the better, and keep me unawares of what's going on in the dark under my own roof!'

Hurrying back down the passage and into the parlour, Emma pleaded with Gregory, who was already on his way into the adjoining scullery, 'Let *me* do it, Gregory . . . please?' Of a sudden she would have done *anything* to escape the scathing eyes which constantly sought her out, and, if the truth be told, she resented Gregory being used in such a way.

'Why, thank you, Emma.' Gregory was obviously delighted. 'Come on then, I'll show you how Mother likes her drink made up.'

'You'll do no such thing!' Old Mrs Denton had grabbed her walking-stick from its resting place beside the fire-range, and was hitting it on the floor with increasing agitation. 'I want nobody else messing with my drink . . . nor my food, neither! You see to it, Gregory,' she said in an authoritative voice, 'same as you've *always* done. Or I shall simply go without!'

'But I'd *enjoy* preparing your drink, Mrs Denton,' Emma intervened, her sympathy for Gregory tempered by his obvious inability to stand up to this spoilt and vindictive old sourpuss.

At Emma's protest, old Mrs Denton gave out a gasp, then followed a choking cough. Quickly recovering, she fixed Emma with narrowed eyes, and in a low voice said, 'When I speak to Gregory, I expect *him* to reply. You being his wife does not give you the right to interrupt a conversation between mother and son.' Pausing, she glanced from Emma to Gregory, who seemed to be about to defend Emma. Seeing this, she immediately bestowed on Emma a begrudging half-smile, saying in a more friendly manner, 'You are young and you have a lot to learn about your duties as a wife. The first thing you need to learn is that your husband's word is law. Please remember that.' She began struggling to her feet, and, in a pitiful voice, pleaded with Gregory, 'See me to my bed, son. I feel faint after a most tiring day. I don't want a drink now, because if I ever tried to swallow it, I think I might be ill.'

As Gregory lit a new candle from the sideboard, cupped his hand beneath his mother's elbow, and led her from the room, neither of them looked back at Emma, who had seated herself on the horse-hair stand-chair by the scullery door. She sat with her head dejectedly bent forward, her thoughts in turmoil. When, a moment later, she heard Gregory's footsteps hurrying down the stairs towards her, she put her head in her hands and shut her eyes tight. 'Oh, Manny!' she whispered, 'I pray I'll remember everything you told me.'

So many things rushed through Emma's mind as Gregory led her by candle-light, so tenderly, up the stairs and into the bedroom which was to be theirs. It was a good deal smaller than old Mrs Denton's, and was situated directly at the top of the stairs. From its long, narrow windows, the flag-stoned yard could be seen and the mill chimneys stretching out beyond. The furniture was of the same dark wood and practical design as the rest of the furniture throughout the house. Beneath the window stood a sturdy squat chest of drawers with a dark-framed mirror standing on top of it, together with two glass containers and a small crucifix on a stand. Either side of this chest of drawers was a rush-seated chair. Fitted into the alcove on one side of the floral-tiled fireplace was a deep, handsome wardrobe with shiny brass handles. In the other alcove was a smaller, more dainty wardrobe of exactly the same pattern, but with a fancy scalloped pelmet above.

As they entered the room, Emma caught sight of the bed itself. Her first impression was that it was immense. Indeed, standing close to it, she found that it almost reached up to her chest. For Emma, the tall, panelled ends resembled the confines of a coffin – this image being reinforced by the raised laurel leaves and sprigs of lilies carved in every deep, dark panel. The eiderdown was clearly woven from home-made patchwork, with each piece in the most ghastly of colours. The thought crossed Emma's mind whether old Mrs Denton had deliberately chosen such a cover in the hope that it would make Emma as sick as she herself professed to be! If Emma had been brought into this bedroom under different circumstances, she might have seen the funny side of it. But, as it was, the forbidding atmosphere of the room and that hideous eiderdown, only served to make her feel even more nervous than she already was.

As though sensing her fear, Gregory put the candle-stick down on to the chest of drawers, then, touching her shoulder lightly, smiled at her with gentleness. Bending to kiss her softly on the forehead, he murmured, 'Emma! Emma!' all the while letting his hand slide slowly down her back. 'If only you knew how long and how often I've dared to dream of this night.' For a moment longer he gazed into her eyes and, in spite of the knot of fear inside her, Emma could feel the warmth of his love spilling from his gaze to wrap softly about her, and her heart was filled with gratitude when he said in a quiet voice, 'I'll leave you alone a while, Emma . . . I'm going downstairs to make sure the house is secured.' Emma had seen for herself just how meticulously Gregory had bolted all the doors and checked the windows downstairs and knew that, being the good and considerate person he was, he was giving her the opportunity to undress away from his eyes. In a quiet voice, she thanked him.

By the time Gregory returned to the bedroom, Emma had taken off her dress, petticoats and undergarments and having laid them over one of the chairs, she had taken the white cotton nightgown from the valise, which Thomas had brought to the house the previous day. Then, with every limb shivering – more from fear than cold – she had climbed into that great bed and slithered down into its icy interior as far as she possibly could. When Gregory came into the room, holding another candlestick, only Emma's frightened eyes could be seen, peering apprehensively from the bed into the shadows where he stood.

The sight seemed to amuse him as, giving a soft laugh, he said affectionately, 'What a child you do seem, Emma.' But Emma wondered how he could make so light of the situation when to her it was a most traumatic and nerve-wracking experience.

Gregory sensed Emma's nervousness as she shyly watched him, and the smile slid from his face to be replaced by a deeply serious expression. His eyes, which still held Emma's fearful gaze, seemed to darken until, in the candle-light, they appeared almost black.

For Emma the tension was unbearable as he continued to gaze at her in that most unsettling manner. He blew out the candle in his hand and placed it beside the still-lighted one on the chest of drawers. Making no effort to blow this one out, he proceeded to undress with slow and fumbling movements. Emma was completely mesmerized by the gradual unveiling of Gregory's body, and was unable to avert her eyes despite her deeper instincts which told her to. Witnessing Gregory's awkwardness, she was comforted by the realization that he too was nervous about the ordeal which awaited them.

Silhouetted in the candle-light with the shadows moving all about him, Gregory stood for a moment in his nakedness. Still Emma could not avert her eyes; she noticed how slim he was; how narrow and well-proportioned his shoulders were – almost like a woman's, she thought with surprise. But when he turned slightly to round the foot of the bed and approach her, Emma saw how naïve she had been! Quickly, and with all of her fears cruelly returned, she looked away. But the image of this man exposed in a way she had never known, would not leave her. As he slid into the bed beside her, Emma was still afraid and trembling; but she also shivered with a murmuring of excitement which surprised her.

As his warm nakedness touched her, Emma tried hard not to cry out. When he murmured softly in her ear, 'I do love you so, Emma,' she began to melt inside. And when he began kissing her hair, then her neck, and roving his hand towards her breast, Emma tried desperately to recall Manny's words, 'When he makes love to you, Emma, think on pleasant things.' Emma tried to do this now. She thought about flowers and little creatures, about sunny days and rippling brooks; and, as her thoughts dwelt on these things, they conjured up memories of other, happier days in the past when she laughed out loud and felt joy in her heart.

Before Emma could deny it, there he was – Marlow! With his dark, handsome features and laughing eyes he looked just as he had on their first meeting when he had been stripped to the waist, resembling a bronzed god. She could hear his voice, murmuring softly of love. But, no, it wasn't *his* voice! It was that of her husband. They weren't Marlow's gentle fingers which caressed her breast – they were Gregory's. The kisses being rained on her face and body were indeed gentle and loving, but they weren't fired with a passion intense enough to light her own. They weren't fervent or teasing enough. They didn't demand that which, deep within her, was waiting to be stirred. The voice whispering in her ear wasn't evocative and trembling, nor was it filled with that excitement and animation which would lift her out of herself. The body which pushed against hers didn't awaken that within her which cried out to be released and fulfilled. In that instant of realization, Emma hid something precious deep within her that she knew she could never share with Gregory; she could share it with only one man . . .

'I won't hurt you, Emma,' murmured Gregory's voice in her ear, 'but you must help me . . . please.' It was with a small shock that Emma realized that this was *his* first time also. Of a sudden, she was confused and more afraid than ever. The only thing she could do was to remember Mrs Manfred's words, and to do as she was asked. She felt him lift his body over hers, and she lay passively as, with a gentle touch, he parted her legs and roved the tips of his fingers over her inner thighs, and she waited tremulously while he positioned himself above her. Then, as he began to lower his body, he murmured over and over how lovely she was, until, his voice breaking with excitement and the beads of sweat dropping from his face on to Emma, he thrust himself into her again and again with mounting frenzy. His heady cries were rapid and filled first with anguish, then with mounting rapture. Emma cried also – but not from joy, nor pleasure. Her tears were quiet, bitter tears, and her feelings were only of disappointment and pain.

With a small, suffocated climactic scream, he gripped his arms so tightly about her that she could hardly breathe, and, like a pent-up dam, he burst inside her, all the while whimpering and moaning and telling her he loved her. But there was no such response from Emma, for she felt no love for him in her heavy heart. She felt nothing but sharp, searing pain and disillusionment. Whatever warm feelings she had begun to have for this man who was her husband, had been driven away in terror, like a small, frightened creature who feared for its life and who nothing on God's earth could ever persuade to come out into the open again. Emma would fulfil her wifely duties, as was her station, but beyond that, God help her, there was nothing more she could ever give.

As the dawn broke, the clouds burst open, spilling out a deluge of rain to splatter the pavements and drive against the windows with a vengeance. For a long time, Emma lay awake listening to the rain's patter as it fell on the roof, playing merry music on the tiles. One of her favourite feelings was lying in bed, cosy and warm, while outside the rain poured down and washed the windows, and then ran speeding into the overflowing gutters. She had always derived great comfort out of knowing that while outside the world became cold and drenched, she was warm and safe within. But that had been in the days when she had her papa and Manny close by, when there had been happiness in her heart and a sense of adventure in her soul. Now, there were only long, endless days stretching before her, when she must learn the ways and duties of a wife and, whatever illusions had been shattered on her wedding night, to please her husband and to bear his children.

In the half-light, a smile crept across Emma's mouth as she thought of the idea of children. No doubt carrying and giving birth to a child would be as degrading and painful as the conception of it. Oh, but at the end of it all there would be a reward in the form of a tiny and wonderful babe, warm and real, with a heart which would love her as its mama. That much at least she could look forward to; and she would, for it was a joyous and natural thing to want a child in your arms – a new-born child of your own flesh and blood whose life was so intimately bound up with your own. Emma wondered now whether that life was already starting deep inside her body. If it was, she would welcome it, but, she prayed to the Lord that if he saw fit to bless her with a child, he would never let her use it in the same way Gregory's mother used him.

Emma now turned her head to glance at Gregory, whose tousled hair touched her shoulder; and, looking at that boyish face, she thought how much kinder life might have been to him also. For, she could not be all he might have desired in a wife – any more than his domineering mother could be all he might have been blessed with for a parent. Still, she thought, there isn't a single soul in this world who doesn't have a cross of some sort to bear, and, as long as the good Lord sees fit to bless us with the strength to carry it, there's little else we can ask for. With that small comfort in her heart, and warm thoughts of motherhood, Emma went gently back to sleep.

If Emma was determined to rid herself of the memory of her first unhappy night under this roof, there was another who preferred to dwell on it, and to let the memory fester until it ate at her very reasoning. In that dark hour when Doreen Denton had lain in her bed listening to her son's cries of ecstasy as he had taken his new virgin wife to himself, there had fused in her heart a wickedness and a deeper hatred of Emma than even she could have envisaged. Doreen Denton wanted her son's wife out of this house now more than ever; so much so that in her fevered mind little else mattered. Emma Grady was an intruder. She would *always* be an intruder, and, like all intruders she must be routed at the first opportunity.

As a rule, Sunday in the Denton household followed a hard and fast routine which had not varied for nigh on thirty-five years – since Gregory Denton's father had brought his new bride to the house on Montague Street. On the stroke of eight a.m., when the sound of church bells resounded over the length and breadth of Blackburn town, the worshippers would tumble from their houses, answering the summons of the Lord with the same automatic response with which they answered the summons of the mill whistle. One of the first doors to open was always that of the Denton house, when, looking respectably sober and devout, the family would follow the well-trod path up the hill and into the church.

In earlier years, there had been only Doreen Denton and her husband; then along came Gregory, making the number up to three. After Mr Denton's demise, the number had reverted back to two. Doreen Denton had never once trod that particular path alone, and she had grown used to having a man by her side. Now the number had become three again, but it gave her no comfort, and she would have no part of it. So, for the first time in many years, the church bells rang out and the door of the Denton household remained firmly shut.

'Fetch me my rosary, and I shall talk to the Lord in my own way,' came the command from the bedroom, whereupon Gregory hurried about, fussing until she was left to 'talk to the Lord' in privacy, with the door firmly shut and both Gregory and Emma left in no doubt as to how dreadfully ill she felt.

For Emma, the day began as a long and tedious ordeal, with old Mrs Denton constantly banging the floor with her walking-stick, and Gregory fetching and carrying until Emma thought he would fall down from sheer exhaustion. Emma also kept herself busy. She took up the coconut matting and the big rag-peg carpet from the hearth, taking them out into the backyard where she beat the dust from them. Then, after cleaning the oilcloth floors, she polished the furniture, washed the breakfast things brought down from Mrs Denton's room, and cleaned and tidied the upstairs room which was hers and Gregory's. With that done, she then collected the kindling wood from the cellar, and watched most carefully as Gregory stuffed newspaper and wood into the fire-grate before lighting it with a match and quickly forming a pyramid over it with the smaller pieces of coke taken from the scuttle.

As he worked, he took great care to explain the procedure in meticulous detail to the attendant Emma. For her part, she was surprised to find herself somewhat ignorant of such matters; she had seen the scullery maid make a fire often enough, and thought it an easy thing to do. Certainly, she would make it her own foremost task from now on.

'There'll be little need for *you* ever to make the fire, Emma,' Gregory told her as he held a sheet of newspaper over the open fire-grate to create a pulling draught up the chimney. When the small brown scorch which appeared in the centre began to spread right over the page, he swiftly drew it away and crumpled it into the coal-scuttle.

'But I won't mind at all,' replied Emma, who would be thankful for *any* little job that might keep her from under Doreen Denton's feet.

But before Gregory could comment any further, another voice interrupted, 'The fire is *Gregory's* job! I'll thank you not to interfere with the smooth running of this household, Emma Grady. With a little help from Tilly Watson next door, we've managed admirably these many years, and I see no call to bring about a change now.'

Emma bit her tongue though she was sorely tempted to make a scathing comment as Doreen Denton made her way slowly across the room, her white frilly cap pulled low on her wrinkled brow, her full dark skirt squeaking and swishing as she went, and her brass-capped walking-stick making a soft thudding sound against the floor.

Quietly incensed by what he suspected was a deliberate mistake on his mother's part in addressing Emma with the surname of Grady and not with the name he had given her, Gregory said in an unusually firm voice, 'There *has* been a change brought about in this house recently though, Mother. You referred to Emma just now as Emma *Grady*. You remember . . . she is Emma *Denton* now, *Mrs* Denton, like yourself.' His words pierced the air like daggers, and each one seemed to make the uneasy silence beneath that much more intense.

Sensing that there was more fire to Gregory's character than she'd previously thought, Emma watched as the older woman sat stiff and stooped in the chair, her eyes staring hard into the crackling flames of the fire, her mouth a tight, thin gash in the angry redness of her face, and her jaw muscles working in a fury. She straightened herself up, the thin gnarled fingers of her right hand gripping the handle of her walking-stick so tightly that the blood had completely drained from them, and the other fist resting on her lap, clenching and unclenching like the muscles of her jaw bone.

Despite her pretence at making Emma welcome here, Gregory's words had unleashed her acute dislike of what she considered to be the cuckoo in her nest. When she spoke, it was with a viciousness which shocked Emma to her roots. If she had any hopes at all about this woman coming to accept her in this house, they were utterly dashed with these words, which were spoken to Gregory, but so obviously intended for Emma. 'Don't you dare speak to me of our good name! The good and respectable name of Denton . . . a name which I have been proud to carry these many years. A name given to me by a man of upright and faultless character, and who I prayed you might one day live up to!' Not for a moment did she remove her cold, condemning stare from Gregory's face, and, because of the desolate look which was wrought on it by the onslaught of her words, all of Emma's sympathy rose towards that poor, cowardly fellow who was her husband. But it was not finished yet, as old Mrs Denton poured scorn upon scorn – belittling his efforts as a son, and condemning his new status as a husband. Finally, exhausted by her own tirade, she gave out a cry, let her cane fall to the floor, and, dropping her head between her hands, she began sobbing as though her heart would break, muttering through her crocodile tears, 'You don't want me any more, do you? I'm old and weary . . . and you're tired of me. She'll be the same, I know. She'll want rid of me soon . . . out of my own house.'

Never having come across such a situation before, Emma was at a loss as to what to do. Gregory came to her and, putting his arms around her shoulders, murmured, 'Emma, will you busy yourself in the front parlour while I talk to her. Don't worry.'

At that same moment, old Mrs Denton looked up to see why her doting son had not come to put his arms about her like he'd always done before. When she saw that instead his arms were wrapped around Emma and the two of them appeared to be about to depart the room, she was incensed. Getting to her feet, she shouted, 'I heard you! Last night, I heard the pair of you . . . like animals! Filthy animals!'

The outburst shocked and shamed Emma. But it was the last straw for Gregory, who almost flung Emma to one side as he burst from her to confront his mother. 'That's enough!' he told her. 'You've gone too far!'

'Too far, eh? It's *you* that's gone too far. Fool that you are, you don't know what you've taken on.' Now her tone became less severe as she cajoled. 'Oh, son . . . think what you've done. We're not moneyed folk, and while you might keep two of us on a manager's wage, you'll never keep three. And what if she gets with child?'

To her astonishment, Gregory was not fooled by her change of manner, nor was he placated. 'If Emma gets with child, we'll manage well enough, for she didn't come to this house a beggar!' Here, he thrust his hand inside the jacket pocket of his best Sunday suit, and drawing out the long bulky package given to him by Caleb Crowther, he brandished it under her nose. 'Emma brought a handsome sum to this household . . . more money than you or I have ever seen! I thought you might accept Emma with more grace, but I see you never will! But, thanks to Emma's money, we can make our own plans . . . for we're neither of us welcome under *this* roof, that's clear enough!'

For a long time afterwards, Emma thought that something in Doreen Denton's face should have warned her and Gregory of what was to follow. But, when it happened, it came so quickly that they were both taken completely unaware.

On her son's defiant words, Doreen Denton reached herself up to meet his face and, fixing him steadily beneath a terrifying look, she said, 'So! Your trollop came here with her fancy money, did she? Well, we can do without *her*, and we can bloody well do without her money!' In a swift movement which belied the stiffness of her bones, she thrust out her arm and grasping the package from Gregory's fingers, she flung it into the farthest reaches of the fire where, in a matter of seconds, it was engulfed by the flames.

As both Emma and Gregory surged forward with the intention of grabbing the poker with which to salvage the blackened package, Doreen Denton pushed herself in front of the fire, grappling with Gregory as he fought desperately to remove her. When, with a triumphant look, she shouted, 'You're too late!' Emma saw that it was true, and her heart sank within her.

In that same moment, Doreen Denton's cry of victory became a cry of terror as the fringe of her shawl was caught by the flames and the back of her hair began smouldering. In a panic, she began screaming and thrashing at herself, and the more she panicked, the harder it was for Gregory and Emma to snatch the burning shawl from her and to stamp it out on the floor. Quickly, Emma threw off her own shawl and smothered it over Doreen Denton's hair and shoulders, and though she had been saved from serious burns by the swift action of her son and Emma, it was plain that the old lady was badly shocked and in a state of hysteria.

Outside, Thomas was about to knock on the door when he heard the dreadful commotion. Finding the door unlocked, as it always was during the day, he rushed inside to find Gregory stooping over the chair in which sat his mother, her face a ghastly colour and every inch of her trembling. 'It's all right, Mother,' he was telling her, one arm holding her tight and the other raised to his forehead as he wiped his hand backwards and forwards across it in a state of great agitation. Emma meanwhile had rushed to the scullery, where she was hurriedly filling the saucepan with water – her first thought being that a hot, strong brew of tea might help to calm Doreen Denton's shattered nerves.

No sooner had Thomas poked his head round the parlour door to ask Emma, 'Is everything all right, Mrs Denton? . . . I've fetched your belongings,' than Gregory had pounced on him, saying, 'Stay with my wife and mother. There's been an accident . . . I'm going for the doctor!'

As Gregory sped away up the passage towards the front door, Thomas returned to the room, where his eyes were immediately drawn to the bent, shivering figure hunched in the chair; he was terrified by her low, whimpering cries and the wide stare which wandered round the room looking at nothing in particular. 'Lord above!' he exclaimed in a quiet voice. 'What's happened, Mrs Denton?'

Having neither the time nor the inclination to stop and explain, Emma swiftly recruited Thomas to watch over the pan of water while she gave whatever comfort she could to Doreen Denton.

In no time at all, Gregory returned with Doctor Harrison, whose home was situated just over the Preston New Road in one of the big houses. Within a matter of minutes, he had examined old Mrs Denton, pronouncing, 'She's a very fortunate woman indeed. And it's due to your quick action that she's not badly hurt.' Sweeping his small, bright eyes from one to the other, he added for Emma's benefit, 'Take heart, Mrs Denton. All I can say is that your mother-in-law can thank her lucky stars that she was not alone in the house when it happened.' This led Emma to suspect that Gregory had not told the full tale, for had she been alone in the house, there would have been no argument, and consequently no accident! Pride and shame kept her from mentioning the money. As Gregory's wife, it was not for her to draw attention to such private and domestic matters, and she instinctively felt he would not thank her for doing so.

As Emma watched the doctor and Gregory assist the badly shocked patient up the stairs, she found herself trembling also. What had taken place in this house today was something she wouldn't forget in a hurry. But, in spite of the awful things that had been said, and regardless of how spiteful old Mrs Denton had proved to be, Emma couldn't help but feel some compassion towards her, for her son was all she'd got and she felt herself being replaced by someone else in his affections. But the money! Oh, what a tragic thing to have happened, because, without that, she and Gregory were really trapped here. Still, Emma wouldn't lose hope; they'd have to stay until the old lady had recovered, she knew that, but perhaps later they could find a house to rent.

Before he left, Thomas cheered Emma up with the news that Mrs Manfred intended calling on her Monday week. 'After you've had time to find your feet, so to speak,' he added with a forlorn look, thinking that, as far as he could see, she had been knocked right *off* her feet.

Shortly after the doctor had gone, with instructions for Emma to 'Just keep her quiet and follow the procedure I've written down for your husband. She's not injured at all . . . but she is in a deep state of shock. I'll be back first thing tomorrow,' Gregory sat with his head in his hands, staring at the floor and saying again and again, 'God forgive me, Emma. I could have caused her terrible injuries . . . even . . .' His voice broke and dropping his head lower, he began quietly crying. Watching him, Emma wondered who was in a deeper state of shock – Gregory or his mother!

Coming to kneel before him, Emma said comfortingly, 'You can't blame yourself, Gregory. She *will* be all right . . . didn't the doctor tell you so?' When he nodded his head and reached out to take her hand in his, Emma realized that fate had thrown her into a situation where, of the three of them, *she* must be the strongest.

If it was a day of revelations for Emma, it was also a day of reckoning, for, on this day, Doreen Denton took to her bed and was never again seen out of it alive – except on one occasion, which was to have far-reaching and disastrous consequences.

# Chapter Eight

'Oh yes, Manny, I'm more content than I ever was at Breckleton House.' Emma leaned over to place the wooden tray on to the sidetable. Lifting the china teapot, she poured tea into one of the pretty floral cups, and then handed it by the saucer to Mrs Manfred, who graciously accepted both milk and sugar together with a root biscuit from the small plate. Emma collected her own cup and saucer, before seating herself on the opposite side of the fire, directly facing the familiar little figure, who so often visited on her time off to keep Emma company.

'I have to be honest,' Mrs Manfred said, 'I never believed in all my born days that you'd fit comfortably into this household.' As she spoke, she examined the delicate bone china tea service, thinking how even Mrs Crowther had no finer.

Emma considered the other woman's words and she recognized some truth in them, for hadn't she herself believed the very same at first? And if she were to be honest, wasn't there *still* a semblance of truth in Manny's observation? Her reply, however, betrayed none of these inner thoughts as she said, 'I count my blessings, Manny. I have a comfortable home, and a good husband.'

Emma might have added 'loving' husband, but somehow she couldn't bring herself to say it; not because it wasn't true, for it *was* – Gregory positively doted on her – but because Emma's idea of love was not the same as Gregory's. He smothered her with his affections, and what took place in the bedroom at night gave her no pleasure; indeed, without exception, it was a humiliating and painful ordeal for her, and she thanked God that, though it was always frenzied, it was over very quickly.

'It does my old heart good to know that you're content and looking much stronger since your illness.'

'Oh, you mustn't worry about me, Manny. I'm a survivor, you know that!' Emma said with a small laugh. Then she added more seriously, 'I don't miss the Crowthers, *ever*. But I do miss having you around all the time.' There had been many occasions since she had come to Montague Street – particularly during the two endless weeks when she had been confined to her bed because of a vicious chill – when Emma had sorely needed a shoulder to cry on, usually because of old Mrs Denton's spiteful tongue and constant condemnation of her. All of this had come to a head when the old woman had flung the breakfast tray, which Emma had fastidiously prepared, across the room with the warning, 'If you ever dare to step one foot in my room again, I'll not be responsible for my actions!' Emma had wondered at the time what form the threat would come in: would she throw herself out of the window, or cut her wrist on a teacup, or perhaps make a dive for Emma's throat. In the ensuing weeks, Emma became convinced that she meant the latter!

Even Gregory could not persuade his bedridden mother to be more amiable towards Emma. So, at an extra cost of one shilling and sixpence a week, he assigned Tilly Watson to attend his mother under Emma's instruction. Since the young woman from next door had been employed for the previous two years to carry out the more menial tasks in the Denton household, the arrangement was a simple one. Tilly Watson was a bright young thing whom Emma had grown quite fond of, and her year-old son, Joey, had become the highlight of Emma's day. However, Emma knew virtually nothing about Tilly's husband, for he worked long hours as a weaver and according to both Gregory *and* Tilly, he had a very quick temper. Emma had not made his acquaintance, nor did she particularly want to.

Emma asked after Cook and other members of the Crowther household, with the notable exception of the Crowthers them-selves. But Mrs Manfred couldn't resist telling how Martha had suddenly turned up on the doorstep just two days before, 'in a dreadful state, and calling Mr Trent all the names under the sun!'

Emma was astonished. 'But they've only been married four months!' she said. However, she was not surprised when Mrs Manfred explained how Martha was still spoilt and selfish.

'Being married hasn't altered her one jot. I'll tell you what, though . . . she's met her match in that husband of hers, for he seems untouched by her sulky manner.'

'A good thing too, if you ask me,' declared Emma, thinking what a handful Martha was, and sure that her cousin would never grow up. 'But what made her come running home from Liverpool, Manny?'

Mrs Manfred gave a low snort of disgust and, leaning forward, she lowered her eyes, saying, 'She's with child.'

Straightening herself up and adopting a thoroughly disdainful look, she added, 'It's only just been confirmed. When the news was given her, it seems that her husband had a sailing commitment which he had to honour and which would take him away for the better part of two months. Well, of course, he was delighted at Mrs Trent's news – she didn't deny that to Mrs Crowther – and he spared no expense in ensuring her comfort and well-being till his return. But she would settle for nothing less than his abandoning his contractual obligation and staying with her. Well, of course, since his father's demise, Mr Trent has a great responsibility on his shoulders, as Mr Crowther pointed out to Mrs Trent with a deal of impatience.' Mrs Manfred leaned forward once again to look Emma in the eye and say more intimately, 'In fact, he told her in no uncertain terms that she was a married woman now, and neither he nor her mama would be seen to be interfering in private affairs of matrimony. Well, he as much as showed her the door . . . "Your place is in your own home, waiting for your husband, and looking forward to the arrival of your child," he told her. And, I do believe that if it hadn't been for his own imminent departure on a tour of the Assizes, and Mrs Crowther's fawning attitude to her daughter, Mrs Trent would straightaway have been sent packing!'

'And what of Silas Trent?' asked Emma. 'Had he already set sail for foreign parts?'

'Well, no. Just as Mr Crowther was ready to depart, Mrs Trent's husband turned up. There was a private discussion in the study, after which I was informed that Mrs Trent would be staying at Breckleton House for the duration of her husband's absence. Oh, Mr Trent was very attentive towards her, and was seen to kiss her goodbye before he left.' Here, Mrs Manfred clicked and tutted disapprovingly. 'A blind man could see how he worships the ground she walks on. Oh, but she is a mardy and sulky madam. Lord only knows what kind of parent she'll be for the coming child!' Mrs Manfred suddenly realized how she had let her tongue run away with her. On seeing Emma's crestfallen face, she put her cup and saucer down on the table, saying in a forlorn voice, 'Oh, child, forgive me for prattling on so.' She reached forward to pat Emma's hand, asking in a low voice, 'Have you still no sign of being with child?'

Deliberately lightening her expression into a smile, Emma shook her head. 'Afraid not, Manny,' she replied, cleverly disguising her growing disappointment that, in spite of almost five months of marriage and Gregory's insatiable sexual appetite, she had not yet conceived a child. She dreamt longingly of holding her own new-born babe in her arms, but as the months passed and there was still no sign, she had begun to feel less and less of a woman. She also knew that, despite his assurances to the contrary, Gregory had come to believe that she might be lacking in some way. In fact, once Emma had recovered from her illness, he had arranged for all their bedroom furniture to be taken up the flight of stairs to the large attic bedroom. Emma was in no doubt as to his reasons why: he obviously felt as keenly distressed as she did at the thought of old Mrs Denton lying awake at night, listening to every word and noise they made. She was glad to have moved to the upper bedroom, but it disillusioned her to see how Gregory had already started stripping their old room, with the intention of turning it into a nursery.

'Now, you mustn't fret, child.' Mrs Manfred was not fooled by Emma's disarming smile. She thought to herself that, while the Martha Crowthers of this world could never live up to motherhood, Emma was of such a warm, loving nature that she would cherish a child and bring fulfilment to them both. 'It'll happen . . . in its own good time, it *will* happen, you mark my words.'

'I know, Manny,' murmured Emma, 'I know.' After which, a silence ensued as they each sat staring deep into the fire's dancing flames.

Looking around the room, Mrs Manfred couldn't help thinking what a remarkable difference Emma's delightful and bright presence had made to his house, and to this room in particular. On that very first occasion when they had made their courtesy call to meet old Mrs Denton, there had been a most forbidding and unwelcome atmosphere in this very room. Yet now, it positively glowed with warmth . . . reflecting Emma's enchanting personality, thought Mrs Manfred. But then, maybe it was not very different after all, and perhaps it was just the fact that she was close to Emma herself, that brought such comfort and delight to Mrs Manfred.

The room itself had not changed physically. The walls were still a murky cream colour and the curtains the same flock-tapestry ones. The furniture was in exactly the same place – a low, polished wood sideboard spanned the length of one wall; there was a small circular table in the far corner, which was covered with a lace cloth that draped down to the brown patterned carpet, and on which was a silver five-stem candelabra that had been a wedding present to Gregory's parents; two deep, black, horse-hair armchairs sat either

231

side of the fireplace, and a small, square side-table stood beside the larger of the two chairs. Standing pride of place in the centre of the room was a huge round table, covered in a frilled green-cord tablecloth and surrounded by four long-back chairs finished in rich tapestry. Both the quality of the oak furniture and the ornaments dotted about gave a feeling of decayed grandeur – almost like the old lady herself, mused Mrs Manfred.

'Coo-ee!' The call came from the front door and immediately following it came the slim, beshawled figure of a young woman, with painfully thin features, bright blue eyes, and a chubby child in her arms. The child's thick fair hair was identical in texture to the woman's and, like hers, was short and curly about his face. The child was bare-headed, while she had on a small white cap with a gathered and frilly brim which flopped on to her neck and forehead. 'It's only me,' she said, coming into the room, 'only Tilly.' Then, catching sight of Emma's visitor who was by now a familiar figure to Tilly, she added, 'Oh, hello Mrs Manfred, I'd no idea you were here.' At once, she pulled out a chair from the table and fell wearily into it, lowering the child on to the floor where, for a while, he stood on unsteady legs, clinging to her skirt. 'I ain't stopped all day,' she said, looking first at Mrs Manfred, then at Emma. 'I woke up with the urge to clean the house from top to bottom, once the man had gone off to work.' She leaned back in the chair and laughed out loud. 'It was the very same when I was carrying Joey here,' she explained. 'I'd like to bet a tanner that there's another on the way.' She opened her shawl and patted her stomach. 'I can tell. I feel different in here.'

Emma was not in the mood to discuss whether Tilly was

or wasn't likely to be with child. So instead she asked, 'Would you like a cup of tea, Tilly?'

'No thank you, luv. Seeing as how it's nearly time for the duchess's tray,' she replied, pulling a face and jerking a thumb up towards the ceiling. 'I'd best set about giving her a wash first eh? Y'know what a pain she can be if I'm late making a start.' Giving a loud shiver, she exclaimed, 'By! It's that nippy in the air this morning . . . you wouldn't think we were well into June.'

Emma was always conscientiously aware of her duties regarding old Mrs Denton and even now the big old kettle was happily spitting out its bubbling contents on to the burning coals. In no time at all, Emma had removed the kettle to the kitchen where she mixed both hot and cold water into a large bowl; then making sure it was comfortable to the touch, she collected soap and flannel from a drawer in the small pine dresser. She put these into a draw-string bag which she threaded over her wrist. Then, taking care to avoid the area where the child was playing, she went through the parlour and up the stairs. At the top of the stairs, she put the bowl and toiletries against the wall on the landing. As she turned to descend the stairs, her eyes glanced towards the closed door of Mrs Denton's room. She paused for a moment, wondering whether the old lady was asleep or awake and whether, just once more, she might go into the room and make a determined effort to befriend her. It was something which Emma often thought about, for she couldn't easily accept things as they were. When she tentatively made her way forward along the landing, she was abruptly stopped in her tracks by the loud shriek which came from the room.

'Go away! I don't want you anywhere near me, Emma Grady! I know that's you skulking about out there.'

Feeling both angry and belittled, Emma hurried down to the scullery, deliberately averting her gaze from the two watching women who must have heard old Mrs Denton's cry. Having quickly refilled the kettle, Emma brought it back into the parlour and wedged it firmly on to the coals in the fire. Then, thankful for the discreet silence, she gave her full attention to the child, who eagerly clambered into her arms when she reached down to enfold him.

'Right, then,' said Tilly, getting to her feet, 'I'd best get on with it eh? Fresh towel in her chest-drawer as usual, is there luv?' she asked. Upon Emma's affirmative nod, she said, 'Y'know, you don't *have* to take the bowl upstairs, luv. Though I expect you like to feel you're doing your bit for the old duchess, eh? . . . in spite of her surly ways.' She knew Emma would have preferred to look after the old biddy herself, but that Doreen Denton would have none of it, oh dear me no! Still, it earned Tilly an extra one and sixpence a week, so she didn't want to complain.

Long after both Tilly Watson and Mrs Manfred had departed, Emma sat ruminating on the way of things. She had meant what she'd said to Mrs Manfred – she *was* more content than she'd been for a very long time. It wasn't a hard thing to be, she mused, once you had the commonsense to accept that the things you *really* want in life are not always the ones you get. There was much that Emma would have chosen to be different; but choice was a luxury reserved only for a few. So, she had come to terms with her disappointments; she had learned how to push disturbing thoughts of Marlow to the back of her mind; and she had hardened her heart to the callous attitude of old Mrs Denton. Emma had also resigned herself to the frequent and insensitive night-time advances of a man she could never love and who, in the light of day, was gentle and selfless. It was almost as though the grasping, thoughtless man who climbed on top of her at night was someone totally different from the man who tenderly pecked her on the cheek when he left for work and seemed to live only for the hour when he came home to her again. Emma wondered whether all men were like that. It was all a revelation to her, and not a very pleasant one at that.

'That was wholesome, Emma.' Gregory Denton picked up his napkin and dabbed at each side of his mouth. 'I do believe you make the best rabbit pie in the whole of Lancashire.' Stretching up, he patted the flat of his hands on his stomach, gave a groan of satisfaction and, pushing back his chair, got to his feet. In a moment he had rounded the table to where Emma had already started clearing away the plates and, coming up behind her, he placed his hands on her shoulders. Then, bending his head into her neck, he kissed it with the utmost tenderness. 'Never a day passes,' he murmured, 'that I don't know how lucky a man I am.'

He then spent a few minutes standing with his back to the fire, contentedly smoking his clay pipe but seeming to Emma restless in his manner. As a rule, once he had eaten his fill of the meal she prepared so well – thanks to the guidance of Mrs Manfred over these past months – he would chatter incessantly about many things: what could have been if only her money had not been so wantonly destroyed; the price all three of them were now paying for it; and how, in spite of it all, he supposed they were content enough. Then he would go on at great length about his fervent desire for a child and of how, when the child *did* arrive, as surely it must, then please God that it be a son. He also talked with great pride about his work, exaggerating the praises bestowed on him by Caleb Crowther when the figures showed a good return and making small of any condemnation that might have come his way from the same source.

On this Friday night, however, he was unusually quiet and Emma sensed that something was wrong. So, after Gregory had brought down his mother's tray and Emma had finished the washing-up, she sat herself in the armchair facing him across the fireplace. Taking up her sewing, she glanced at him and, seeing that he was leaning forward in his chair with his head dropped in his hands and his eyes trance-like as they gazed at the glowing coals, she asked quietly, 'Are you ill, Gregory?'

At once, his full attention was on her. 'No, of course I'm not ill, Emma.'

'But there *is* something wrong, isn't there?' Emma was sure of it.

'No, no . . . nothing at all for you to worry your lovely head about.' He made no mention of the rumours which had assailed him from two sides these past days. On the one hand there was talk concerning Emma's own uncle, Caleb Crowther, who, or so it was said, was deep in debt to the bank and the two Grady mills had been used as collateral against that debt. Then there was talk that both Arkwright's Mill and two of the smaller ones along the wharf had gone on drastic short-time due to a glut on the market. In addition to all that, the unrest in America had accelerated beyond all their fears.

Like many whose livelihood depended entirely on the cotton industry, Gregory Denton sensed an avalanche developing over his head and what struck the fear of God into him was the knowledge that he was powerless to prevent it.

Being unable to draw her husband into any kind of conversation, Emma concentrated on her sewing. She was not ignorant of the way things were going in the industry, for as the child of Thadius Grady she had grown up to understand its fluctuating moods. Nor was she blind to the newspaper articles that followed developments in certain areas of America and which indirectly controlled the well-being of Lancastrian folk. Abraham Lincoln had assumed office some three months ago, in March. A month previous to that, the Southern Confederacy had been constituted, and, only six weeks ago, in the month of April, Fort Sumpter was captured by the Confederates. Emma had read every report with the realization that a civil war between the North and South of America was no longer a threat – it was a reality. But, even now, many believed it would have few repercussions, if any, in Lancashire itself.

Emma had persisted in looking on the bright side, for she knew only too well how Gregory had been building a healthy stockpile of raw cotton despite Caleb Crowther's belief that such a measure was unnecessary. Emma sensed that matters of work and security greatly troubled Gregory. She also knew that whatever she might say, he would derive no comfort from her words, for he was the sort of man who saw every problem as being one which he alone could solve. Although Emma admired him for this, she would have preferred it if he could at least talk these matters over with her and respect her opinion. But he could not. His paramount intention was to protect Emma at all costs from troublesome responsibilities, the consequence of which was only to make Emma feel that she was the most troublesome of his responsibilities.

Later, after Gregory had said goodnight to his mother before going to their own bedroom, he lost no time in climbing into bed beside her and Emma discovered that, while his appetite for conversation had waned, the same could not be said of his lustful appetite for her body. She had grown used to the precise manner in which he satisfied himself, for it never varied. Nor did it awake any response in her. If anything, it had become a tiresome and uncomfortable experience which left her feeling only relief when it was over. In absolute silence, he would lean himself up on one elbow, with his face nudging hers and his hand feverishly pulling up her nightgown. When it was up about her waist and his hand had found her thighs, he would begin to frantically explore that which he most coveted. Then, making a low, smothered cry, he would hoist his naked body above hers and, roughly prising open her legs and thrusting himself into her, he would make no more than six feverish strokes, all the while smothering her face with his mouth, before collapsing with a groan on top of her. Emma often thought that she got more pleasure from washing up the dishes!

'Things are going from bad to worse, Marlow lad. What shall we do?' Sal Tanner had been gazing at the ripples in the water made by the small stones which Marlow occasionally skimmed across its surface. Shifting herself about on the big upturned crate which they both now shared on the wharf, and trying to capture his downcast, thoughtful gaze with her round, violet eyes, she repeated, 'Marlow, lad . . . I said things are going from bad to worse!'

'I know, Sal,' he murmured, keeping his troubled gaze on the water, 'I know.' He leaned down to throw into the water the small handful of pebbles which he'd scraped into a pile with the edge of his boot. Then, stretching his back, he ran his hands through his long dark locks which had fallen about his face on stooping. 'It's a sorry state of affairs, Sal,' he said, dropping one hand to affectionately stroke the dog which was sitting to attention by his side. 'Yet there's folk much worse off than we are, and that's a fact.' Sighing noisily, he got to his feet and began walking along the wharf to where the barge was moored. The dog trotted close to his heels and Sal hurried along by his side trying to keep up with his long, determined strides, and the more she hurried, the more prominent the limp she'd sustained from her accident became.

'Folks worse off than us!' she snorted. 'Well, if that's so, where are they?' she demanded. 'You tell me that!'

As she shook her fist in the air, Marlow wrapped his fingers around it and brought them both to a halt. When he looked down at her with serious eyes which seemed even darker than usual because of his anger, Sal wished she'd learn to keep her mouth shut.

'I don't *need* to tell you, Sal,' he told her, 'you know well enough. You've seen them . . . in the soup queues. And you've seen the boarded-up houses where folks have been thrown out because they can't pay the rent. We at least have some work, and we have a roof over our heads.' Releasing her hand, he turned from the direction in which they had been going, 'I'll be back before dark,' he said in a quiet voice, and with a click of his fingers he signalled for the dog to follow him as he departed at an impatient pace.

'Where yer going?' shouted Sal, following him a short way, but slowing down as the distance between them grew even wider. ''Tain't my bloody fault if 'Merica goes to war! 'Tain't my fault if folks is hungry! I have ter count us bloody pennies an' all, y'know, since the work's dried up. Marlow! Come back here, yer bugger!' But he had already gone from her sight. Crashing her two fists against her sides, she hung her head low and headed home, muttering, 'Yer a windbag, Sal Tanner . . . a bloody windbag!'

An hour later, Marlow had climbed to the highest point in Corporation Park where, seated on the turret of a Crimean War gun – the very spot to which Emma had been drawn when deeply troubled – his eyes scoured everything below. The long winding shape of Montague Street was just visible and it was here that his gaze lingered for a seemingly endless time. Emma lived down that street, he knew. He didn't know which house it was, but it was no secret among the mill-hands at Grady's that Gregory Denton resided in the better-class part of Montague Street. 'Oh, Emma,' he whispered now, his heart simultaneously heavy and joyous by the memory of her and by the feel of her name on his lips. 'Emma, Emma,' he repeated, pulling his brown cord jacket tighter about him and thrusting his hands into his pockets out of reach of the biting October air. Though the wanton wind whistled frantically across the hill top, screeching gleefully as it sliced into everything vulnerable, Marlow hardly felt it as he was warmed by tender thoughts of Emma. Yes, she was wed to another, but he still loved her. Yes, she had told him that he had no part in her life now and never would have, but there wasn't a single waking moment when he didn't crave her with every fibre of his being. A man might have many women; he might know tender loving times with each of those women, and he might profess to love them. But in every man's life, there is just one very special woman who reaches so deep inside him that she becomes a living part of his very existence; just one woman with whom he could spend the rest of his life and never regret a single heartbeat of it. For Marlow, that woman was Emma. That was the simple truth and the knowledge that she belonged to another only made his love that more tragic.

So much had happened in the nine months since Emma's marriage. It was said that, despite old Mrs Denton's impossible character, Emma was happy enough. He was glad of that, but he was also devastated that Emma had not found it in her heart to return the love he felt for her. So often of late, with Emma growing ever distant, the thought of a new life in foreign parts had become more prominent. Now, in these hard times – when American ports were blockaded and cotton shipments stopped, and when the industry was grinding to a halt and hundreds of thousands were struggling to survive because of it – Marlow consoled himself with the knowledge that at least one of the Grady mills was still working; the one managed by Emma's husband. He thanked God that she was secure, yet, in the same breath, he prayed that relief might come to others who were not so fortunate.

After a while, the wind subsided and the air grew colder. Dusk began gathering and still Marlow made no move, until even the dog at his feet grew weary. When he felt the dog's warm nose nuzzling into his hand, he looked down to see how miserable his four-legged friend was. Reaching down to laughingly rough-up the flat, smooth coat which felt cold to the touch, he said, 'Aw, sorry, old thing,' at once getting to his feet and fishing out the leather lead from his jacket pocket. 'Let's away home, eh? See what Sal's conjured up for tea.'

'I don't *want* tea!' Gregory Denton pushed away his plate, got to his feet and stormed from the table to stand facing the fire, his two hands resting on the mantelpiece and the fiercest look on his face Emma had ever seen there. 'Don't question everything I say!' he told her in a harsh voice. 'When I say I want no bloody tea, I mean exactly that!'

Thinking her best course of action was to clear the table and depart to the scullery, Emma lost no time in doing just that. For the rest of the evening she busied herself doing this and that, while Gregory silently brooded. He brooded late into the night; he brooded as they climbed the stairs to bed; and when they lay side by side in the darkened room, he remained lost in a deep dark mood, until, with a mumbled 'Goodnight, Emma', he turned away from her. But, even then he would not sleep and for a long time afterwards he turned and fidgeted, more restless and disturbed than Emma had ever known him. From her very first meeting with him, when she was a child by her papa's side, Emma had known how devoted he was to his work. It was only now, however, seeing him in such despair at possibly losing it, that she realized how passionately obsessed he was with the means of his livelihood. All of his tireless efforts, all his enthusiasm and that particular fierce pride which only a man could feel towards his work, Gregory Denton had channelled into his responsibility and duties at the Grady Mill. He had carved himself a coveted place in the running of things. He was highly respected and answerable to only one earthly authority above him; and, having achieved such esteem, he was now fearful of having it all snatched away. Every day he saw it happening up and down Lancashire as the stranglehold which America had on an entire industry many miles from its battlefields, was squeezed tighter and tighter until the cries of hunger and deprivation were beginning to be heard from every corner.

Emma was also conscious of the dreadful consequences the cotton starvation could reap on the people of Lancashire and in Blackburn particularly because of its concentrated investment in this industry. She wondered where it would all end. Yet, although the signs were alarming, Emma convinced herself that reason would prevail and things were never as bad as they might seem. She did her best to persuade Gregory of this, but for her pains she was dismissed with the comment, 'You're only just seventeen, Emma. What can you possibly know of such manly matters!' At which point he would grow even more agitated, and she wisely withdrew.

Some four weeks later, in the month of November 1861, Emma's peace of mind was further disrupted. It was on a Thursday evening, after Gregory had brought down his mother's dinner tray. 'God!' he shouted, crashing the tray down on to the table and bringing Emma hurrying from the scullery. 'Will that bloody woman *never* let up?'

'Your *mother*?' Emma couldn't hide her astonishment at hearing Gregory refer to old Mrs Denton in that way. As a rule, he went out of his way to defend her.

'It's this article in the *Standard*,' he said, collecting the folded newspaper from the tray. 'I knew I shouldn't have let her see it, but she can be fiercely demanding when she has a mind!' He opened out the newspaper at a certain page and peered at it, a deep frown etching itself into his brow as he did so.

Emma knew at once which article her husband was referring to, for she had also been disturbed by it. It reported on how the newly elected Mayor of Blackburn, Mr R.H. Hutchinson, had anticipated that great distress and trouble would manifest itself in the coming winter. To this end, it had been agreed that the sum of two hundred pounds would be set aside for distribution to the growing number of needy by the clergy and ministers of the town. But, meanwhile, a meeting of the textile manufacturers had resulted in the drastic step of closing down even more establishments, the consequence of which was to throw an even greater number of operatives into the ever-increasing ranks of the unemployed. Not a man was safe in his work and though Emma's heart bled for those families already living in fear, she also felt desperately concerned for her husband. Gregory Denton was a changed man. Whereas he had once gone to work of a morning with a spring in his step and a warm kiss for Emma, he now left without a word of farewell and with his face gravely serious. His stooped figure went down the street as though he was approaching the hangman rather than his place of work.

In all of this, Emma had to admit a sneaking admiration for the way in which Caleb Crowther had managed to keep the Wharf Mill functioning when so many others were going under. Time and time again, Mrs Manfred had assured Emma of her uncle's grim determination to keep open that particular avenue of income. 'I can tell you this, Emma,' she said, 'he's so determined not to lose that revenue, that at times . . . well, he seems like a desperate man.' She had shaken her head, adding, 'Almost as though he's driven by the same fear as drives the lesser mortals like us. Still and all, whatever his reasons for fighting like a madman against closing down the Wharf Mill, if he's looking after his own interests then it must follow that he's looking after yours, eh?' Emma had replied how she realized that one day her papa's concerns would be passed on to her and she was aware in these hard times what an uphill struggle it must be to keep the looms turning, but, her greatest concern at the moment was for Gregory's sanity, in the light of his ever-changing moods.

On the last Monday in November, when she had seen Gregory out as usual and Tilly Watson had returned home after attending to old Mrs Denton, Emma had an early-morning visitor.

'Manny!' she cried on opening the door. 'What a lovely surprise!'

'Hello, child,' said Mrs Manfred, placing a swift kiss on Emma's face. 'Mrs Crowther asked that I fetch a few urgent articles from the shops, on account of her having invited a number of ladies to a social gathering this after-noon . . . where they might discuss matters which mean absolutely nothing to anyone at all!' Emma smiled, for it was clear that Mrs Manfred's opinion of the Crowthers was still as low as it had ever been. 'I took the opportunity to leave the tram early, so I could call in on you.' With that said, she expertly gathered her skirt into her hands just enough to lift the hem above the step of the door, and then swept past Emma and down the passage. By the time Emma reached the parlour, the homely little woman was already seated and warming herself by the cheery fire. As Emma came into the room, she was asked in a quiet tone to, 'Come and sit near me, child.'

'Are you all right, Manny?' asked Emma, being somewhat perturbed by the serious expression which greeted her. 'Is everything all right at the Crowthers'?' Of a sudden, and in spite of the way she had been treated by Martha Crowther in the past, Emma was fearful that something terrible might have happened regarding Martha's pregnancy. When she was assured that both Martha and her mama enjoyed an excellent state of health, Emma asked, 'Then what's troubling you, Manny?' As she spoke, she seated herself in the armchair directly facing the older woman and not for a moment did her worried eyes leave Mrs Manfred's face.

'I'm afraid it's bad news.' She reached out a hand as though to touch Emma in comfort, but the distance between them was too great and instead her hand lay fidgeting in her lap, screwing and unscrewing the taffeta folds in great agitation. 'Yesterday evening, Mr Crowther met with a number of other manufacturers at Breckleton House. Twice I was instructed to personally take in refreshments. On the first occasion the intense discussions fell to a hush on my entry.' She screwed her mouth into a tight pucker, as though making an effort to stifle those words which might tumble from it.

'Manny . . . please!' Emma had already sensed that Caleb Crowther's meeting might indirectly affect her, otherwise, why was Mrs Manfred so concerned to inform her of it?

'When I went in the second time, the discussion had

reached the pitch of a heated argument, and I was hardly noticed at all. Oh, look child, I overheard a statement made by Mr Crowther.'

'What was it, Manny?'

'The Wharf Mill. He's closing it down, and he intends to inform Gregory of his intentions this very day.' There, it was said! But she felt no better for being the bearer of such unwelcome news.

For a while, Emma was struck silent, her thoughts churning over and over in a flurry. He's closing it down, she told herself, yet hadn't she seen it coming? It had to come because, the way things were, there was no alternative. Gregory had seen it coming also and now, this very day, his worst nightmare would be realized.

'He'll take it badly, won't he, child? Although, by all accounts and thanks to your papa's foresight regarding yourself, you'll fare better than most. He must think on that.'

Emma was aware that Caleb Crowther had made sure it was common knowledge how he had handed over 'a sizeable dowry' on the marriage of his ward. Old Mrs Denton's disposal of it was known only in this house and Emma preferred it to stay that way.

'He'll be devastated by the closure, Manny,' she replied, 'and I'm at a loss to know how I can help him over it.'

They sat in deep thought: Mrs Manfred secretly even more disturbed by Caleb Crowther's crippling debts to the bank, which, although common knowledge below stairs, Mrs Crowther was totally and blissfully ignorant about; and Emma thinking how shattered Gregory would be on hearing Caleb Crowther's plans.

'Oh, Manny, do you think I should go to him?' she asked

now, feeling the greatest sympathy for him. 'Do you think I ought to be there when he's told?' The thought of being in the same room as her uncle made Emma's stomach turn. But she would be there if it might help Gregory.

'No. You mustn't even think of it, Emma!' declared the older woman, with a hint of compassion in her voice. 'It will be enough for him to cope with, child, without you being there to witness it all.' Rising from her chair, she went to where Emma sat quite still and unsure as to what to do next. 'Just be here when he gets home. He'll tell you in his own good time,' she advised, and Emma knew she was right.

After she had seen her dear, concerned friend out of the house, Emma closed the door and made her way down the passage. As she reached the parlour door, she heard a loud insistent knocking from upstairs and old Mrs Denton's voice calling out, 'Who's that? Who've you been entertaining in my son's absence, you little baggage!' When the knocking grew even louder, seeming to bounce off the walls and shake the house, Emma pressed her hands to her ears and went into the scullery where the noise was not so terrible. For what seemed like ages, she leaned against the cold windowpane, staring out into the flagstoned yard and wondering what kind of mood her husband might be in when he came home that night.

At half-past six the meal of steak pudding and roast potatoes was ready. The kettle was boiling on the range and the table was laid. In its centre was a lighted candle which, together with the glow from the fire, made a warm, cosy atmosphere ready to lift the night chill from Gregory's bones, while Emma waited to lift the spirit in his heart.

By half-past eight, the meal was ruined, the kettle almost

dry and the candle-light flickering dangerously low. Several times, Emma had gone out into the cold night but there was no sign of Gregory. When old Mrs Denton began her persistent knocking and demanding her dinner at the top reaches of her voice, Emma took the remainder of the Sunday pork-roast from beneath the mesh cover in the larder and slicing four helpings of it, she made a plate of sandwiches and a pot of tea. These she put on a tray, then, feeling both frustrated and angry, she threw caution to the wind and climbed the stairs to her mother-in-law's room – every step taken to the increasing volume of that witch-like shriek, which first demanded the whereabouts of its meal, then launched into a vicious attack on both the son who neglected her and Emma Grady who was 'a trollop in fancy clothes'.

When, undaunted, Emma flung open the bedroom door, never once bringing her eyes to gaze on the source of that harsh, abusive voice, she was subjected to the vilest verbal attack she could ever have imagined, which finished with the demand, 'GET OUT OF MY ROOM!' A series of strangled cries followed which, to anyone else might suggest that the old lady was breathing her last, but which only told Emma that the crafty article was using every means at her disposal to rid herself of her unwelcome intruder. Emma acted as swiftly as possible, for she had no intention of staying in this room for one minute longer than was necessary. After placing the tray on the chair beside the bed, she went quickly from the room, breathing a sigh of relief as she closed the door behind her – just as the heavy brass bed-knob came hurtling through the air, to thud into the door with such force that it split the upper panel from top to bottom.

Downstairs, in the long silence which ensued, Emma

thought that old Mrs Denton must be tucking into the sandwiches. 'You old bugger!' she said under her breath, feeling both indignant and amused at the old lady's artfulness. Only once did Emma suspect that the silence might be ominous, but then she reminded herself of such games previously played by old Mrs Denton for her son's punishment. 'God doesn't want you yet,' Emma told her through the ceiling. 'You're too much of a handful!'

The mantelpiece clock struck nine and there was still no sign of Gregory. When, of a sudden, the knocking and abusive shouts began emanating from upstairs once again, Emma thought she'd go mad! Frantic, she threw her cloak about her shoulders and ran next door to Tilly Watson's house.

'Well o' course I'll come and keep an eye on the old 'un,' Tilly said on Emma's request. 'The bairn's not got a wink of sleep in him, an' my old fellow's gone off to one of them blessed meetings in the Thwaites pub near the Wharf.' On learning that Emma intended to go out in search of her husband who had been given bad news concerning his own livelihood, she added, 'I'll bet my last farthing that you'll find him in the pub along the Wharf an' all!' She added one more thing as Emma went on her way; it was a warning. 'You watch yourself down that Wharf at this time of night, luv. There's all manner of curious creatures roaming the streets in the dark hours!' That said, she gave a loud shiver, pulled the bairn into her shawl, wrapped the shawl tighter about her slim figure and disappeared into the Denton household, slamming the door shut with such panic that the sound echoed after Emma as she hurried away down Montague Street. Another sound rent the quiet evening also.

It was the same banshee wail which had haunted Emma all day. 'Who's that? Who's banging the door? Answer me, you harlot!' rang out the offensive tones of Emma's mother-in-law.

Not certain whether Gregory might come home via Preston New Road or King Street, Emma made the decision to walk up King Street, along by Ainsworth Street and onto Eanam Wharf that way. If her uncle's news had hit him harder than even she imagined, Emma believed it might just be possible that he *had* sought refuge in a public house. Such a thing would be quite contradictory to Gregory's nature, Emma knew, but he had changed so much of late and had become so unpredictable that Emma thought Tilly Watson might just be right. At least, it was something to bear in mind.

Going straight to the Grady Mill along the Wharf, Emma noticed that there were no lights on at all – save for the cheery red glow from the night-watchman's brazier. ''Ow do, miss,' he called out, rubbing his hands together over the fire, before doffing his cap as Emma drew nearer. 'By, yer a brave 'un to be out on such a cold night, lass,' he said through a large, toothless mouth. Then, on seeing that Emma was not the usual type of female to be seen loitering in the shadows along the Wharf, he added in a more serious voice, ''Tain't a safe place round these parts after dark, lass. Yon pubs won't be long afore they turn out, then there'll be drunks and ruffians stalking about. Best be off 'ome, miss . . . where it's safe.'

Emma thanked him for his concern, assuring him that she had no intention of staying out longer than was necessary. As she talked with the old fellow, she took off her mittens and warmed her frozen hands. 'But I'm looking for my husband,' she explained, while replacing her warmed mittens, fastening her bonnet tighter and drawing the cloak more snugly round her shoulders. 'You might know him . . . his name is Mr Gregory Denton, and he's the manager of this mill.' She inclined her head towards the big iron gates behind him.

'Oh aye!' came the reply. 'I knows Mr Denton right enough. But I ain't seen 'im, miss.' Here, he frowned hard and, rubbing his gloved fingers behind his ear as though scratching away a bothersome irritation, he went on, 'That's a shame about the closure, eh? . . . A right bloody shame! D'yer know, miss, there were folks as could a sworn by Mr Crowther keepin' it open. But, like I telled 'em . . . when times is bad, we *all* on us get dragged into it! It don't matter if yer a rich powerful fella, or a broken down-and-out, 'cause if yer can't sell the goods, yer gets no brass. And if yer gets no brass . . . well, like I say, the world stops turnin' an' we're *all* on us affected.' He fell silent, slowly shaking his head from side to side and dropping it lower and lower until Emma could no longer see his face.

'Goodnight,' she said, hurrying away and wondering where to look next. The old night-watchman gave no reply, but shook his head all the more.

Coming out on to Penny Street, Emma paused beneath the gas lamp on the corner. She reached into the neck of her dress and withdrew the tiny, delicate watch that had been given to her by her papa. Then, holding it carefully between her finger and thumb, she raised it to the flickering light to see that the time was half-past nine. The public house which Tilly had referred to was further along Penny Street and so Emma immediately began making her way there.

'Hello, darlin' . . . looking for company, are you?' The voice came out of one of the darkened doorways, causing Emma to hurriedly look away and quicken her footsteps towards the bright windows of the public house, where the accordion music wafted into the night air and the merry sound of singing voices promised a safer haven.

Not daring to set foot in such a place, Emma stood on tiptoe in order to look through the windows. Her vision was impaired by the frosted pattern on the glass and the large words which read 'Public Bar' on the first window and 'Snug' on the second. Peering through a small corner below, where there was an area of clear glass, Emma's view was still frustrated by the thick smoke screen and the wall of bodies inside. 'Where are you, Gregory?' she muttered through frozen lips, pressing her nose harder against the windowpane. Suddenly a cackle of laughter erupted from within and as Emma peered through the haze in search of her husband, the unmistakable figure of Sal Tanner rose before her. The next moment, the laughing figure was hoisted on to one of the tables by a bevy of reaching, grasping hands. The music took on a more urgent note and the hands all began clapping as Sal Tanner executed a frenzied dance – showing her pink, grinning gums at one end and her pink, dimpled thighs at the other. The whole spectacle was that much more comical because of Sal's pronounced limp, which had the effect of throwing her off balance in a most peculiar yet rhythmic manner.

Dropping from her tiptoes, Emma moved away from the window to lean back against the wall, the cold air seeming to have penetrated every inch of her body. She knew the time must by now be approaching ten o'clock and some deeper instinct made her suspect that Gregory might have come to harm. 'He would *never* stay out till this hour without telling me where he was,' she muttered to herself, a part of her feeling desperate enough to go into the public house where she could at least satisfy herself as to whether or not he was there. Yet, there was an even greater urge within her to run from that place, and to get home safely. Before Emma could decide what to do for the best, the decision was abruptly taken out of her hands.

'Bloody hell! Look at this, lads! We've got the buggers queuing up at the door for us, eh?' If the voice was gruff, its owner was even more so. The burly, unshaven fellow all but fell out of the pub doorway on to the spying Emma who, on hearing the loud and drunken revellers emerge, had tried to wedge herself behind the large concrete mullion which surrounded the entrance. Unfortunately, she was quickly spotted by this burly fellow who, though he appeared to have the weight and size of an elephant, possessed the small beady eyes of a shrew. As his hand pounced on her shoulder and drew her out, Emma vehemently protested. At the sound of her voice, another of the group lurched forward to look at her. Emma was shocked to see who it was. 'Gregory!' she cried, shaking herself free from the big fellow's grasp and rushing forward. Her first sensation at seeing him was utter relief; her first thought was to get him home as quickly as possible. To this end, she began looking up and down the street for a carriage. 'I've been searching everywhere for you!' she told him, preparing to take his arm. As she smiled up at him, he stared down at her, a drunken frown on his face.

'See that, fellas?' shouted another of the group. 'His little wifey's come ter find 'im!' There followed tumultuous laughter and taunts of 'Aw! Did thi mammy lose yer, eh? The little woman wants ter tuck 'im in his little bed!'

'Shut it, you fools!' Not only were the men taken aback by Gregory Denton's acid tone, but so was Emma! Now he turned on her, and as he bent to deliver his instructions, the stench of booze on his breath was so powerful that it turned her stomach. 'Get off home!' he told her. 'I don't want you here . . . I don't need you to come looking for me like I was a bloody kid!' He gave a cruel laugh, saying, 'Oh, but happen you look on me as a kid, because you ain't got any of your *own*, eh?' His voice fell to a whisper, so low that only Emma could hear it and so vicious that it made her heart tremble. 'Oh, but it ain't been for want of trying. Oh no! But you see . . . I'm no good as a man, am I? If I was, then you'd have been with child *months* ago! I ain't got the ability to make a bairn. And I ain't got the ability to keep my work. I'm no good either way. I'm useless, d'you see?' He lifted his hands to her shoulders and, to the delight of his cronies, he began shaking her.

'Stop it!' Emma was mortified by his words. But now she was even more determined to get him home, because to leave him in such a drunken state with such low company, was more abhorrent to her than was his verbal attack, which in her heart she knew was the drink talking. Emma had been horrified to discover that the very sentiments which had been going through her mind regarding their childless state, had been torturing her husband even more. He had been thinking it was due to his inadequacies as a man, while Emma had been equally convinced that it was her fault.

'Are yer coming with us, or are yer running off home like a good little lad?' Once again, the other men fell into uproarious laughter, whereupon Gregory shook Emma all the harder. 'I've told you,' he said, 'I don't need you following me, making me look even less of a bloody man! Take yourself off home.' That said, he turned to fall in with the others as they made their way along Penny Street to the next ale-house, all stumbling about in the same witless but merry state – all except one, for Gregory Denton was a bitter and sorry man, who saw the drink not as a friend, but as a means of forgetting his own shortcomings.

'I'm not going home without you!' Emma called out, pursuing them down the street. 'I won't!' Somehow, she felt responsible for him. Maybe it was because of the guilt she always carried for not being able to love him in the way a woman *should* love her husband.

Hearing Emma's cry, Gregory Denton came to a halt, turned sharply and, encouraged by the other revellers, came hurrying back towards her on fast, angry footsteps. At first, Emma was delighted because she thought he had decided to accompany her home after all. But on seeing how swiftly he came towards her and, as he drew nearer, realizing the thunderous expression on his usually kindly face, she halted in her tracks. As he came to within arms reach of her and the street lamp bathed his face in its trembling yellow glow, Emma was actually frightened to see the fury on Gregory's features. 'Will you not be bloody told!' he snapped, at the same time bringing the flat of his hand hard against her head with such a spiteful swing that it sent her reeling towards the wall. 'Now! Perhaps you'll do as I say!' he told her through clenched teeth and whereupon, hardly glancing back at her, he rejoined the others to quickly disappear down Penny Street, into Eanam and out of sight.

Dazed from the force of the blow to her head and desperately trying to stem the flow of blood from her nose, Emma leaned on the wall for support. Her thoughts were in turmoil and her heart was in shock. She would never have believed it possible that drink could change a man so much. Yet, as she recalled Gregory's every word, his every mood over these past weeks, Emma realized that it wasn't simply the drink that had changed him, it was fear, and, because she herself had known that same destructive emotion, she could perhaps understand at least a little of what he was going through. But whether she could *forgive* him for his treatment of her this night was something else. For now, however, she must make her way back to Montague Street, and leave Gregory to come home when he was ready.

Emma dabbed the blood-stained handkerchief to her face and seeing that the flow of blood had stopped, she found a corner in the cotton square with which she scrubbed her face clean. She then straightened the bonnet which had been knocked askew and, with her head throbbing painfully, she emerged on to the kerb from where she cast her gaze up and down the street. I must find a carriage, she thought, beginning to walk along the narrow pavement. Feeling as ill as she did, Emma was sure she could not make the long trek back to Montague Street on foot. Furthermore, the night was pitch-dark and dismal, and Emma was mindful of the danger she could be in at this hour of the night and in this particular area. As she walked along, only once did her thoughts stray to forbidden territory, and that was when she felt briefly tempted to turn the corner into Eanam Wharf, where she suspected Marlow's barge might be moored. Quickly, and with a rush of guilt, she dismissed these thoughts, but, in doing so, she felt only sadness in her heart.

As Emma came towards the top of Penny Street, she was relieved to see a number of carriages crossing Ainsworth Street and beyond that the street lamps seemed brighter. But she was still a long way off yet and here, between one public house and the next, it was uncomfortably dark. Alarmed, she quickened her footsteps, at the same time becoming aware of the resounding tap-tap of her boot-heels, which rent the night air with a disturbing echo.

Emma was so intent on escaping the dark area of Penny Street that she did not hear the footsteps which crept stealthily up behind her. The moment they were on her, it was too late! Emma felt herself being swung round and even as she opened her mouth to scream, a hand was clapped roughly over her face, smothering the sound and striking a greater fear into Emma's heart than she had ever known before. She was propelled harshly against the wall and in the brief glimpse she caught of her attacker's face as he thrust her away from the glow of the gas lamp, Emma was horrified to see that it was the same unshaven burly fellow who had been in Gregory's company earlier and who had got such satisfaction out of the humiliation she'd been made to suffer.

'Oh what a little beauty you are!' he murmured in a low trembling voice as he pinned her against the wall with one hand, keeping her mouth covered with the other and bending his coarse face to brush against her neck. The more Emma struggled, the more excited he became by it, and the harder she pummelled at him with her small clenched fists, the more it amused him. ''E's a fool, your man,' he muttered in a drunken breath, 'but if 'e don't want yer . . . I do!' Now, using the brute strength of his enormous body to pin her fast against the wall, he raised the hand which had been holding her and, with spiteful force, ripped the bonnet from her head and threw it contemptuously away, afterwards grabbing at the coil of hair so beautifully curled into the nape of Emma's slender neck. When her hair came tumbling freely about her shoulders, he began stroking it and frenziedly thrusting himself against her body, all the while moaning and clutching at her clothes as if he were about to tear every shred from her back. 'I won't hurt yer,' he murmured, wiping his open mouth up and down her neck until Emma feared she would die or lose her senses and be even more at his mercy. As it was, the hand across her face desperately impaired her breathing and she was growing weaker by the second. She had to get free. She *must* get free! But how? Oh, dear God, how?

The moment came when, in his feverish excitement, the burly fellow relaxed his hold on her in order to take down his trousers. Though he still had her pinned fast with his chest and shoulders, Emma saw her chance and she took it. Summoning every remaining ounce of strength within her, she quickly twisted away, at the same time sinking her teeth into his shoulder. When with a growl he grabbed at her, a swift and furious struggle followed, during which his nails scored deep and bloody grooves down her neck and as she fled with her heart in her mouth, he whipped the cloak from her back before pursuing her relentlessly along the shadowy lamp-lit streets and across towards Eanam Wharf. Whatever Emma's misgivings about contacting Marlow, she had no choice now but to seek his help, for her assailant appeared to have been sobered by a more driving appetite, and his determined strides as he came after her were both longer and faster than her own.

'Dear God, help me!' she prayed, as, racked by pain and feeling her strength ebbing, her steps began to falter. As she rounded the corner into Eanam Wharf and saw the lights from two lone barges along the water, Emma's heart almost collapsed with relief. 'Marlow! Marlow!' she shouted repeatedly, fearful that he might not hear her cry. By now, her heart was pounding and feeling like a lead weight inside her. Her legs felt like rubber beneath her and the cold had bitten so deeply in through her dress, that every inch of her body was numb.

When there was no rush of help from either of the barges, Emma grew frantic, stumbling towards them, calling out Marlow's name and tears streaming down her face, blinding her.

Emma could hear her pursuer coming ever closer, until, in a minute he was on her and the two of them were struggling dangerously close to the water's edge.

'Yer bloody wildcat!' the burly fellow shouted as he caught hold of her. 'But that's 'ow I likes my women!' he chuckled. When Emma bit him hard on the hand, his triumphant cry turned to one of pain and anger. 'Sod yer eyes!' he yelled, slapping her about the face and shoulders. 'Ye'll not get the best o' me!'

In that moment when she began to lose consciousness, feeling that on this night she would surely die, Emma heard a dog frantically barking. She saw a running figure launch itself through the air towards her attacker and when the burly fellow saw it too, Emma felt herself being thrown aside as the two became locked in combat. When she lost her footing and the icy-cold water sucked her into its dark, quiet embrace, the last words on Emma's lips were a desperate prayer.

'Oh, Emma! Emma sweetheart . . . thank God!' Marlow's voice reached Emma through a haze, where, for a long, strangely peaceful time, she had felt as though she was floating – neither asleep nor awake, and not wanting to be either. Only when he slid his arms about her body and pressed her close to him, did she realize that the nightmare was over. She was alive! She was safe in the arms of the man she loved. For just a fleeting moment, nothing else mattered, and the rush of overwhelming happiness to her heart was more than Emma could bear.

'Marlow,' she murmured, the tears rolling down her face but her great love for him alive and burning bright in her eyes. But, suddenly, as everything became clear again in Emma's mind, the pain returned to her eyes. 'I must get home!' she told him, stiffening in his arms and drawing away.

When he spoke, Marlow's voice had also changed. It was not the soft endearing tone it had been; it was now quiet and sad, yet still filled with love and aching to utter those words which were so deeply etched on his heart. Instead, however, he chided her gently, 'What in God's name were you doing wandering about the Wharf this time of night?'

Softly, and not without some shame, Emma explained how Gregory had not come home and how she'd gone in search of him. She then described the sequence of events which followed.

'I heard that Crowther was having to close down,' replied Marlow in a serious voice. 'I can't say anybody's all that surprised, what with the way things are.' Here, he sat up stiff and straight as he went on angrily, 'All the same, that's no excuse for Denton to take it out on you! I ought to lift the bloody head from his shoulders!' He punched one clenched fist into the open palm of his other hand. 'You could have been killed because of him!'

'No, Marlow.' Emma could see he was so agitated that he was ready then and there to search out her husband. 'It's as much my fault as his. Just let me get home.' She began to draw herself up in the bunk, but the effort was great and seemed to charge her every limb with agony.

'Easy does it,' Marlow said. 'You've had too much of a rough and tumble to start gadding about afore you're properly rested.' Gently, he cupped his hands on her shoulders in order to ease her back against the pillow. It was when his rough, warm hands touched her bare flesh that Emma realized with horror that she was naked. Marlow was quick to see the alarm in her eyes as she tugged the over-blanket up, until all that could be seen above it were her two startled grey eyes.

'I'm sorry, Emma,' he said, his gaze growing darker the longer it fed on her beauty, 'you fell into the canal . . . though I don't suppose you remember.' Emma did. 'When I fished you out, you put the fear of God in me. Oh, Emma!' He paused, as though remembering it was too terrible. 'I thought you were drowned, Emma. God help me! There was nobody else to strip away your wet things. Sal's on one of her jaunts and won't likely be back till daylight.'

Still clutching the over-blanket beneath her chin, Emma self-consciously lowered her eyes from the dark intensity of his gaze, because, despite her desire to get away from here as quickly as possible, the warmth and unashamed passion in those troubled eyes together with the mere nearness of Marlow and the way every part of her being trembled at the wonderful intimacy of this moment, created a fearful struggle inside Emma, so that she secretly prayed that this precious moment could go on forever. There was so much she wanted to say to him, so many heartfelt words she would have liked to confide to him. But something even stronger, an ingrained sense of right and wrong, prevented her. Instead, she asked, 'And the man who chased me?'

At this, Marlow leaned backwards to rest his weight on the palms of his hands and, laughing aloud, he told her, 'The bigger they are, the more cowardly. Me and my old friend here,' he dropped a hand to stroke the dog's head, 'we saw the bugger off. One crunching blow from me, and a bite up the rear end from "fangs" here . . . well, he went up that Wharf like something demented!'

Picturing the whole scene, Emma burst into laughter. 'I'm glad!' she said. Then, more seriously, 'Oh, but Marlow, there can never be a way for me to thank you enough!'

'I just thank God I was there,' replied Marlow, rising from the edge of the bunk. 'Your clothes should be dry by now. I'll get them. But it's two o'clock of a morning, and I must insist on seeing you safely to your door.' His expression became more serious, as he added in a quieter voice, 'There are things I need to say to your husband as well.' When Emma pleaded with him to leave Gregory to her, he merely looked deeply into her uplifted eyes, saying, 'We shall see!'

When he returned with her clothes over his arm, the sight of Emma lying with her slender shoulders now exposed and her long chestnut tresses falling gently over them, caused such a storm in Marlow that he was moved to hitherto unknown depths of emotion. 'Oh, Emma! My darling Emma!' he murmured. Without taking his eyes off her, he draped the clothes over a chair and coming to kneel beside the bunk, he told her with tenderness, 'You said just now that there could never be a way for you to thank me. There *is*, Emma. One way.'

'Don't, Marlow.' Emma was afraid of the feelings he was creating in her, disturbing, glorious feelings which took her breath away. Involuntarily, she reached out her hand from beneath the bedclothes and, when he grasped it tight within both of his fists, she made no move to withdraw it. In fact, she thought there had never been anyone in her life as dear to her as Marlow. Not even her papa, for that was a very different kind of love.

'I'm making arrangements to leave England,' he said quietly. 'I've talked it over long and deep with Sal. She won't come with me, so I'll send for her just as soon as ever I can. But you, Emma! Oh, you *must* come with me! Please, Emma . . . say you will?' The fear that she would refuse dulled the light in his eyes and the tension within him betrayed itself in the fierceness of his grip on Emma's small fist.

For a long, agonizing moment, the silence between them was unbearable. Emma desperately wanted to go with him. Indeed, she craved for nothing else and the thought of him leaving these shores and that she might never see him again, filled her lonely heart with dread. How she longed to cry out, 'Oh, yes, Marlow! Take me with you!' But she thought of her husband and the distress he was already suffering; she reached deep inside herself, down through the years, over every moral lesson she had learned from good people – from her papa, from Manny – and in her heart she could find only one answer. When she gave it, it broke her spirit to see how Marlow's head bowed low, and in a crushed voice he said, 'How will I live without you, Emma?'

'In the same way I must live without you,' she murmured, raising her hand to his dark, tousled head.

'No!' he exclaimed, clasping his hands about her shoulders. 'I won't *let* you refuse me!' With a small, stifled cry, he had her in his arms, kissing her hair, the deep scratches along her neck, all the while murmuring his love and creating chaos in Emma's overburdened heart.

'Don't Marlow . . . don't!' she cried, grabbing the blanket around her and struggling from the bunk. 'It's no good, you *know* that!' She was now crying as she fumbled helplessly with her clothes.

'I love you, Emma,' he said, coming to stand before her and, with his fingers, raising her face to look up at him. What he saw in her eyes tore him in two. 'Come with me, sweetheart,' he said again, his magnificent dark eyes willing her to say yes. 'Please . . . come with me.'

Emma became still, her gentle sobbing filling the air and seeming to bring it alive all about them, like the softest heartbeat. She spoke not a word, not even when his hands began to gently stroke her hair. Instead, she lifted her arms and entwined them around his neck, letting the blanket slither to the floor, showing him what was really in her heart and how very much he meant to her.

As he bent towards her, his mouth eager to taste hers and his hands following the curves of her nakedness, Emma was helpless to resist the urges of her heart. As he gathered her up into his arms and laid her tenderly on the bed, such a wave of warm and wonderful emotions raged through Emma that she was left trembling from head to toe. When, in a moment, Marlow was stripped naked, she thought she had never seen anything so beautiful as his strong, magnificent body; the upper part was broad and warmed by the sun and his entire physique was sculptured to manly perfection by the laborious means of his livelihood. Yet, though he was muscular and of splendid appearance, Emma sensed a great tenderness and beauty of heart about Marlow Tanner. She also sensed his enveloping love and need for her, as strong and compelling as hers was for him.

'I love you in such a way that there are no words to tell it,' Marlow told her now in the softest murmur, as he knelt by the bed and gazed into her eyes.

Emma was so choked with emotion that she was unable to say anything, although her answer was there in her heart. Instead, she reached out her fingers to touch his shoulder and when he came to lay beside her, the whole of her being shuddered with pleasure at the warm shock of his nakedness. He began kissing her in such a way that made her cry out. His soft, moist lips took the taut nipple of her breast into his mouth, sending shockwaves into every corner of her body. Now he was seeking out those sensual areas of pleasure which Gregory had never found, and Emma was transported into rapturous and burning emotions, the like of which she had never known.

Marlow had lived and loved many times, as all healthy young bargees did. But with Emma it was different. She was that someone special; the one he had searched for; the only woman he would ever truly love. Yet, even now as he held her in his arms as intimately as any man might hold a woman, he knew that it was to be short-lived. How could he have this woman? How could he keep her for ever? His heart cried out and as he took Emma's soft yielding body into his, his desire was such that he craved not just her body, but her heart and soul as well. Dear God in Heaven, *must* he let her go? How could he bring himself to part from her, for she meant more to him than his own life.

In Marlow's arms, Emma found Paradise. Time and time again, she gave herself to him and together they blossomed with the beauty and pleasure which neither had found in any other's arms. Like two enchanted dancers, they clung to each other and moved and weaved in and around each other's bodies, finding ultimate pleasure and exquisite pain in the ecstasy which bound them together and which neither wanted to ever end.

But the beauty and wonder which held them fast was not merely physical. It was beyond that, for their very souls were merged. And when, at last, she lay quiet and exhausted in her lover's strong, protecting arms, Emma thought she had never felt so much at peace in the whole of her life. When Marlow found her softly crying, he laughed kindly, saying, 'Have I made you so unhappy, my darling?'

Emma wiped her eyes and smiled up at him. 'I love you so very much,' she said softly. It was a painful thing to say, for soon she would have to go – back to her life and her husband. Never again would she know such precious moments as she had experienced on this night. This had been their farewell, for she could not expect him to stay and neither could she go with him. Soon, Marlow would be far away and she might never see him again. This was her night – hers and Marlow's – and they must be forever thankful that it had given them a memory to last a lifetime. May God forgive them both.

Yet for all those guilty feelings which now plagued Emma, one persistent question tore at her heart: how could something as beautiful as she and Marlow shared be so terribly wrong?

# Chapter Nine

Emma was pregnant! Night and day she had tormented herself with the knowledge that the child growing inside her had not been conceived in wedlock with her husband, but in a night of shame with Marlow Tanner. Yet, despite being beside herself with fear, Emma would not have missed a single exhilarating moment in Marlow's strong and loving arms. She had loved him ever since their very first meeting and throughout the endless time in between, he had never been far from her mind or her heart. During that last wonderful meeting, they had shared such tenderness, such harmony of body and spirit, such deep need for each other and such glorious love, that Emma knew she would never in the whole of her life experience its like again.

Now, on this cold February morning, Emma crept out from beside Gregory's sleeping form. Going across the room on tiptoe, she collected her slippers, took up the long fringed shawl from across the back of the chair and, wrapping it about her small, shivering shoulders, she grasped her long chestnut hair in one hand, drew it from beneath the shawl, and flicked it back so that it fell freely and magnificently down her back. As she silently left the room, which was already being penetrated by the growing daylight, Emma took care not to make any noise, for she had no wish to disturb either her husband or her mother-in-law – at least not yet. She felt the need for a moment or two on her own before the house was properly awake.

Downstairs, Emma put on her slippers and quickly opened the curtains, but the light was not yet sufficient to brighten the parlour, so she took a match from the tray on the sideboard, struck it alight and put the flickering flame to the candlewick. Lifting the brass candle-holder and moving towards the fireplace, she placed it up on the mantelpiece. Then, she set about emptying the dead ashes from the grate and making a small fire. When she saw it crackling cheerfully, she filled the kettle and wedged it into the coals. Already, the day ahead seemed that much brighter, for Emma thought there was nothing more peaceful than sitting in a quiet room, watching the spitting, dancing flames of a coalfire and sipping a cup of tea held snugly between one's hands. Times like this were becoming increasingly rare. On the odd occasion when she was fortunate enough to steal such precious moments for herself, Emma would use them to the full, contemplating what the future might hold.

Having prepared her cup with a small helping of tea, Emma placed it in the hearth and, while the kettle boiled, she wandered to the sideboard where she peered into the mirror, looking at herself intently, once again astonished at how she had changed in the year since coming to live in this house as Gregory's wife. The small elfin structure of her face had not changed, for her cheekbones were still high and prominent, her forehead still wide and her mouth set full and rich above a firm rounded chin. Her thick chestnut hair fell, as always, from a centre parting into a rich wavy pattern which spilled over her shoulders and way down her back; but now, it was very much longer. None of these features had changed too much – although they were perhaps more pronounced and more mature. But her eyes! Those magnificent grey eyes – which, in moments of stress or pensive mood, were streaked with black, making them darker and more mysterious – had changed above all her other features. In their peaceful beauty, they appeared even more brilliant as her emotions were cleverly hidden beneath. In anger, the emotions would surface, striking astonishment in the beholder; the greyness would darken to ebony and their beauty seem fathomless. Through her eyes, Emma saw and felt everything. They were the filter of her soul, the mirror of all she suffered and, at the height of their splendour, they had the power to hold a person mesmerized. Yet, they had also become secretly scared and at times, the light in them would grow dim as Emma's deepest emotions and most-treasured memories surfaced.

'Oh, Emma Denton!' she now reproached the image in the mirror. 'You had your time with Marlow . . . you both clutched at what small happiness you could and it was a memory to cherish for ever. But now . . . oh, now Emma, your secret will find a way out. In a short time, your condition will surely become evident to all and Gregory will know that the child couldn't possibly be his!' The thought made her tremble. Gregory was no fool. Even before she had become pregnant by Marlow, her husband's urges to take her to himself in their marital bed had greatly diminished. Since being deprived of work, he seemed at times to be so altered in personality that he frightened her. Emma was now haunted by how he would react when he knew that the wife, who seemed destined not to bear *his* child, was pregnant by another man.

Emma shivered loudly as she turned her attention to brewing the tea. There was no escaping the fact that Gregory would know soon and, in all truth, she would rather confess the whole thing than wait for the horror of it to suddenly dawn on him. But how could she tell him? Dear God above, she thought fearfully, how can I bring myself to tell him such a thing! Yet, however daunting the prospect seemed, Emma told herself that she had no alternative. Of late, the child had begun to move inside her and, though it warmed her heart to feel Marlow's flesh and blood mingling with her own, it also struck the fear of God in her!

'Why the hell didn't you wake me?' It was eight a.m. when Gregory rushed into the parlour, his braces dangling over his hips, and his chin bristling with sandy-coloured hair-stubble. 'I must be on that quarry site bright and early if I'm to make a good impression.' Quickly he dashed about, dressing, shaving, washing and rushing down the eggs and bacon which Emma had prepared. 'Get me a shilling or two from the jar,' he told Emma between mouthfuls. 'There's the tram fare . . . and, like as not I'll need something for a bite to eat, because if I get work I'll start right away.' Emma was pleased to see him so enthusiastic. It was said that the work in the quarries was hard and demanding, but it was the only prospect which had come up these past weeks. As she took two silver shillings from the earthenware jar in the cupboard, Emma gave thanks that they were still better off than most folk. With the small amount of money carefully put by when Gregory was in work, together with the proceeds from her various bits of jewellery, they were not yet in danger of starving.

Emma often asked herself what she would do if circumstances *were* ever to become that desperate. Two things she knew for certain: she would *never* go cap in hand to the Crowthers – nor would Gregory ever allow such a thing – neither would she ever pawn the little watch entrusted to her by her papa. Indeed, as though to put it out of the way of temptation altogether, Emma had slit a tiny pocket in the inner collar of one of her best boots. She had wedged the delicate watch inside and there it had remained. So small and inconspicuous was it, that its presence went undetected even when she wore the boots to church on Sundays. In fact, if Emma didn't now and again take a private peep at it, she might never even know it was there.

At the door, Gregory snatched his coat from its hook, shrugged himself impatiently into it and, without even a backward glance at Emma, he said, 'I pray to God he finds me a man's work on this day!' As she closed the door after him and the freezing February morning, Emma prayed also. 'If he gets work,' she murmured, 'he'll get his purpose back, and life might become that much easier.' She daren't also ask the Lord for an easy way to tell Gregory of the child. Not now, for she remembered Mrs Manfred's teaching that, if she dared to ask for too much, she might end up with nothing.

Quickly, before old Mrs Denton started banging her stick on the floor and shaking the ceiling, Emma cleared away the breakfast things and refilled the kettle. While the water was heating, she tiptoed back upstairs and brought down her undergarments, petticoat and a full-skirted soft green dress of serviceable cotton, which had a high white collar, fluted hem and bib front. She also brought her dark stockings and lace-up black shoes with small square heels. When the water was boiled, she filled the bowl from the scullery, stripped herself naked and, in the warm glow from the fireplace, she washed from top to toe. It alarmed Emma to see how evident the rise of her abdomen was becoming and, there and then, she decided that come what may, she must confess all to Gregory within the next few days – placing herself and her unborn child at his mercy. It was not a pleasant thought and, having decided on the only course of action left open to her, she put it deliberately out of her mind.

No sooner was Emma washed, dressed and ready to face another day, than the rhythmic, insistent banging began, accompanied by the loud harsh voice of old Mrs Denton. Emma was thankful when, as though summoned, Tilly Watson called through the letter-box just as the mantelpiece clock struck half-past eight.

'By!' she exclaimed as Emma let her in. 'It's bloody freezing! I've left the lad in bed a while, 'cause he was deep in the land of slumber and it seemed a pity to disturb him.' Inclining her head sideways, she cocked a cheeky grin towards the source of the increasing volume of noise coming from above. The sight of the small brass candelabra swinging to the tune of old Mrs Denton's stick upon the floor, set her off in a peal of laughter. 'Old sod!' she cried above the racket. 'She's got more strength than all the rest of us put together.'

Emma also couldn't help but laugh. 'That's true,' she agreed, 'and I believe she'll be the death of us too . . . if we let her.'

\* \* \*

'It'll be the death of me!' wailed Agnes Crowther, one hand gripping the frilly lace handkerchief with which she dabbed at her puffy eyes and the other clutching her daughter's arm, as though without the support of it she might fall in a faint at her husband's feet.

'Nonsense, woman!' Caleb Crowther cried, impatiently shunting his clenched fist back and forth along the mantelpiece. Clearly made more agitated by his wife's reaction to what he had just told her, he stared hard at his daughter, Martha, saying in a clipped tone, 'Leave us! Leave the room!'

'I'd rather stay with Mama, if you don't mind,' came the pertinent reply. 'It's all come as such a shock to her.'

'I told you to leave!' Caleb Crowther thundered, looking impatiently at his wife when she began shaking and crying anew. 'As a matter of fact, Martha, please take your son and return to your *own* home! I understand your husband is due back any day. *He* is your concern – not us! I'll thank you to remember that this is *my* house. You have been made welcome here many times since your marriage. Not once, when your husband has seen fit to sail the seven seas, have you been turned away by either myself or your mama.' Here, his expression darkened and, coming forward a pace or two, he looked her straight in the eye. 'Now . . . I'm asking you to leave. Please do so, at once!'

One look at her papa's twitching features warned Martha Crowther to do exactly as she was instructed. Removing her hard round eyes from his face, she gave a kindlier look to her mama, kissed her on the forehead and said, 'If you need me, please send Thomas and I'll be here straightaway.'

'She won't need you,' Caleb Crowther interrupted and

275

when, without further argument, Martha flounced from the room, he gave a small, unpleasant smile. Then, taking his wife by the arm, he led her to a nearby chair where, with small ceremony, he sat her in it. 'The plain fact is, my dear, we must preserve what funds we still have. I'm sure you . . . like myself . . . have no wish to leave Breckleton House. But unless we budget very carefully, there may well be no alternative.'

'Oh, dear me!' Agnes Crowther wrapped the fine lace handkerchief round the tip of her nose and blew delicately into it. 'How will I ever manage without a housekeeper? And with only one maid?' She found the prospect horrifying.

'Come now, woman.' He began to grow impatient at her whining. 'You'll still have Cook, and with a maid to see to all the menial tasks, it won't really be that bad!'

'But the housekeeper. Oh, I just wouldn't know where to start.' It seemed there was no consoling her. 'I know the mills are closed, Caleb, and perhaps I have been a little too extravagant at times, but I *will* try. I really will!'

'You'll do more than try, my dear,' he told her with a surly look. 'In fact, you won't get a *farthing* from me before I've seen for myself exactly where it is going.'

'Is all this frugality really necessary? Aren't you panicking just a little?' Uppermost in her mind were the cruel, humiliating things people would say.

But, Caleb Crowther was not prepared to discuss the matter any further. He could have pointed out that the bank had foreclosed on the mills. He could have explained how even Breckleton House itself might be in danger if they did not immediately, and drastically, cut down on expenditure. And, not by any stretch of the imagination, could he see the financial returns from his judicial office as being sufficient to keep either a full stable or a full staff – certainly not if he was to continue enjoying life's other little pleasures. Things were desperate! *He* was desperate! And, though in one or two low moments he had briefly thought about how he had squandered Thadius Grady's legacy to Emma, Caleb Crowther's pity and regret was reserved only for his own fate. It was *his* well-being that was ever paramount in his mind – not Emma's, not even his own wife's. It was his own escape from the walls of deprivation which were closing in on him, more and more, that concerned him most.

Even in the midst of his selfishness and greed and his determined fight for survival, Caleb Crowther knew that the day of reckoning with Emma would come eventually, for, even though he hated to admit it, the woman had spirit. She was still young, but she had a strong character. The day would come when she would expect him to hand over that which Thadius had left to her. If he remembered rightly, that particular day of reckoning would come on her twenty-fifth birthday.

Here, Caleb Crowther chuckled. 'Hhm,' he told himself, 'by that time every penny due her will be long gone.' And, he thought, with the grace of either God or the devil, so would she! Who knows what dreadful *accident* might befall a young woman before she reaches her twenty-fifth birthday.

The thought gave him a great deal of pleasure as he turned it over and over in his mind. The more he dwelt on it, the more his evil smile deepened, until, feeling benevolent towards his weeping wife, he said, 'If it will help, you may keep Martha here with you for a further week or so while I'm away about my legal duties. She can perhaps give you a hand about the place, once Mrs Manfred and the upstairs maid have departed.' If he thought that might cheer her he was mistaken, for his wife suddenly got to her feet and in a sullen mood she told him, '*You'll* be all right! Staying in the best inns and being waited on hand and foot! Really, Caleb, you have no idea how difficult it will be here without Mrs Manfred!'

'Then you must learn to cope, my dear,' came the stiff reply, 'for I intend to terminate her employment this very evening.' Turning his back on her, he instructed curtly, 'Be so kind as to send her in on your way out.'

'But where will you *go*, Manny?' Emma called from the scullery. She was horrified at her old friend's bad news. It had hardly occurred to her that the present hard times, which had befallen so many of Lancashire's working population, could ever seriously affect those who seemed too high up for the present tide of need to lap about their ankles. Even in the face of Mrs Manfred's news this evening, Emma was convinced that her dismissal had less to do with any financial hardship on Caleb Crowther's part and more to do with his dislike of her. He had never made any secret of that dislike and, when Emma put it to her now, Mrs Manfred made it quite clear that the feeling between her and Caleb Crowther was mutual.

'He's not a good man,' she told Emma, pausing for a while as her mind was beset by images which would not go away. Images of Emma's papa, lying in his sick-bed and crying out to hold his beloved child. Images of the way in which he had departed this world – with his cries suddenly stifled and Caleb Crowther standing over the bed with the most evil look on his face that she had ever witnessed. 'No, he was never a good man and it may be that he has good reason to hate me.' Dropping her voice to a whisper, she added, 'Or, even to *fear* me!'

'What was that, Manny?' Emma came rushing in from the scullery with a tray of sandwiches and a pot of tea. She had not quite heard that last remark and half expected it to be repeated. When it was not, she put the tray down on the sideboard and passed her visitor a freshly brewed, and much welcomed, cup of tea. 'Help yourself to sandwiches, Manny,' she said, the concern she felt at the older woman's predicament still evident in her voice. 'Oh, Manny, if only I could have you here . . . to stay with us.' But Emma knew only too well that neither Gregory nor his mother would ever condone such a thing.

'Not at all, child!' Mrs Manfred was at once alerted to Emma's distress. 'I have my plans already made,' she said with a kindly smile, 'and Mr Crowther gave me four weeks' severance pay. If you ask me, the owners are also finding this depression most uncomfortable . . . though they'll allus have a guinea or two tucked away, no doubt. Even Mr Trent has had to sell off a number of his ships. Apparently, he's been hit bad, what with the blockades on American ports. It's the transportation of convicts to Australia that keeps his business from floundering, so they say. It's all a sorry state of affairs, and no mistake! But I have a lot to be grateful for, child, when I think of the soup queues, the bulging pawnshops and the faces of starvation and misery I've seen.'

'Oh I know, Manny, I know.' Emma had also witnessed these things. 'But where will you go? Oh Manny, I couldn't bear it if I never saw you again!' Through all the bad times,

Manny had been like a rock of support to Emma and the thought that she might be gone from her for good was too painful for Emma to contemplate.

'I shall travel down south, to Luton,' she told Emma. 'You remember, I have an older sister there?' When Emma nodded, vaguely recalling Mrs Manfred's mention of such a relative, the older woman continued, 'But I shan't stay, oh no! We're very fond of each other, d'you see . . . but we've never been the sort to live in each other's pockets. No, I shall likely stay a week or two, then I'll make my way back to settle in these parts. There's allus plenty of work for women who don't mind a bit of skivvying and I've done enough of that in my time. Happen I'll secure a position in one of the bigger places along Preston New Road or up by the park. We shall see.' While she had been talking, Mrs Manfred had grown increasingly aware of how pale and troubled Emma looked. Somehow, she wasn't convinced that it was altogether her own predicament that was at issue here. She ventured to ask, 'There's something else on your mind, child, isn't there?'

Ever since Mrs Manfred had arrived, Emma had been deeply tempted to confide in her the secret she was carrying. In fact, although Emma was as certain as she could be that she was with child, she knew very little of these things and would have welcomed Mrs Manfred's advice. But, when she had seen that she wasn't the only one with problems, she hadn't the heart to pour out her troubles. 'What makes you ask that?' she queried her caring friend now.

'Oh, child, I've known you since you were this high.' She lifted her hand to signify a height no more than three feet. 'D'you think I don't know when there's something preying on your mind?' She brought her hand up to pat Emma's knee and with her soft, devoted eyes bathing Emma's face, she coaxed, 'You'll have to tell me, y'know, because I won't go until you do.' When Emma made no reply and just dropped her eyes to the floor, Mrs Manfred said nothing. Instead, she let her gaze wander over Emma's countenance more closely. She saw the pinched white face full of anxiety; she saw how Emma's hitherto small breasts appeared somewhat fuller beneath the bib of her dress; she noticed that Emma's waist was not as reed-thin as it had been and there was a gentle rise beginning to show below it, which perhaps only a woman might perceive. Yet if, as Mrs Manfred suspected, Emma was at long last with child, why should it make her so unhappy? She could have sworn it was what Emma wanted. All the same, she mustn't force matters, because no good ever came of such a thing. If Emma wanted her to know, she'd confide in her in her own good time. What she did say, however, as she patted Emma's hand more vigorously, was, 'If you'd rather I didn't pry, then of course I won't. But, there's an old adage that a troubled shared is a trouble halved. And if you need me, I'll never be that far away from you.' Her voice was soft and her homely face a great comfort to Emma, who lifted her eyes to meet her old friend's anxious gaze as she went on, 'I mean it. Whatever it is that worries you so, well, it can't really be so bad now, can it, eh?'

For a long time there was such a deep, undisturbed silence between them that Mrs Manfred suspected Emma might not have heard a word she'd said. Presently, she got up from the chair. 'I'll just take the tray out for you,' she told Emma, thinking it might be best to potter about and give Emma a few quiet moments to herself. But she was worried, very worried, and did not really want to abandon Emma in such a strange, quiet mood.

'No, Manny! Please . . . sit down.' Emma had made up her mind. She would tell Manny everything, for who else could she turn to?

Without a word, the older woman resumed her seat and, before her resolve disappeared, Emma told her everything. She explained how things between her and Gregory had gone from bad to worse since he'd lost his work. She spoke of her deep abiding love for Marlow and of how she had kept a great distance between them, remaining as dutiful and loyal to her husband as any wife could be. She told of how he'd grown cold and distant, blaming himself for their childless state and for the loss of his livelihood, and of how he had turned to drink in his most depressed moments. She explained the impossibility of ever creating a relationship with his mother who 'hates me beyond reason, Manny'. And, finally, with the tears by now falling helplessly down her face, Emma gave an account of the night when Gregory hadn't come home. She held nothing back and, in a whisper, she finished, 'I'm sure I'm with child, Manny. Not Gregory's child . . . but Marlow's.'

'Lord above!' Mrs Manfred was shocked at the series of events just related to her, but even as the seriousness of the situation dawned on her, her only thoughts were for Emma. The very idea of condemnation never even entered her mind. 'Does Gregory suspect?' was her first question.

'I don't think so, Manny . . . not yet.' But Emma knew it was only a matter of time.

'And Marlow?'

Emma wiped the tears from her face with the back of her

hand, her voice firm and determined as she replied, 'Marlow doesn't know. And he never will. He's gone.'

'Gone where?'

'Sailed away to foreign parts.' Now, fully composed and feeling better having confided her secret worries to another person, Emma continued, 'Gregory has to be told the truth, Manny. You see, when he discovers that I'm with child he'll *know* it isn't his. For a long time now . . . since before Marlow and I . . . well, you see, Manny . . . Gregory didn't . . . he . . .' Emma couldn't go on.

'All right, child. It's all right. I understand.' Mrs Manfred leaned forward and lifting both of Emma's small hands into her own, she quietly agreed. 'You're right. There is no other way as far as I can see, but to put yourself and the unborn child at your husband's mercy. Oh, but Gregory's a good kind man, even in spite of his present distress. You told me earlier that he'd gone off to look for work in the quarries. Well, he's not back yet, is he?' she said optimistically, glancing up at the clock and pointing out to Emma that, as it was already well into the day and he hadn't returned, that might just mean that he'd been successful. 'You'll see. Come tea-time, he'll breeze in through that door with a smile on his face and secure work at last!' She prayed it was so, for it would take a special man to accept not only that his wife had sought refuge in another man's arms, but that she was also carrying that man's child; and he wouldn't even be able to get the satisfaction of leathering the fellow concerned, because by now he was in a far-off country.

In her heart, Emma wasn't convinced by Mrs Manfred's words, though she knew that the darling woman meant well. And, even though she had already decided that Gregory would have to be told, it wasn't a prospect she was looking forward to. Mrs Manfred didn't know how wrong she was about Gregory. Oh yes, he *had* been a 'good and kind man', but that was so long ago now that Emma could barely remember it. These days he was morose and silent. He was unloving and bitter, for he had lost all that he revered most: he had lost his work, his dignity and, above all, his belief in himself as a man – and it was that in particular which made Emma most fearful of his reaction to her confession. Just thinking how she might even begin to tell him left Emma trembling, so much so that she said now, 'Perhaps it might be better if I'd done as Marlow wanted, and gone with him!'

'Never!' The mere suggestion of compounding what she believed to be a sin of the worst kind, was unthinkable to a woman of Mrs Manfred's strict moral beliefs and, much as she adored Emma, she was convinced that there was only *one* course of action. 'How can you even think of such a thing, child?' she demanded. 'What you two did was wrong enough, without seeking to make matters worse!'

There was little left to say; it was now just a matter of confessing to Gregory. At Emma's request, Mrs Manfred agreed to stay over for one night. 'But this is purely between you and your husband, and, of course, he must agree to my staying. There's an early train out on the morrow and, once matters are resolved between you and Gregory, I'll be on my way.' Her fondness for Emma shone in her small brown eyes, as she assured her, 'I'm only staying just so you know I'm near. Beyond that, it's really no business of anyone's but yours and Gregory's.' She did not want to intrude in their private affairs, but, when Emma had asked her to delay her departure until the morrow, how could she refuse her?

'Thank you, Manny.' Emma was grateful all the same. What she had to do wouldn't be such a lonely thing with Manny so close by. 'I can't make your sleeping arrangements too comfortable, though,' she apologized, 'because the back bedroom still hasn't got a bed in it. I think there's a small spare bed in the loft, so perhaps when Gregory comes in . . .'

'You'll neither of you put yourself out for me!' interrupted Mrs Manfred. 'I'll be quite cosy snuggled up in this here armchair, afront of a small cheery fire.' As Emma began to protest, she put up a halting hand. 'That's settled!' she said. 'I've put up with far worse in my time!' When Emma smiled, she smiled back and soon they were both laughing. To Emma, it felt wonderful. Thank God for friends such as Manny.

At five p.m. Tilly Watson came round to see old Mrs Denton, leaving Emma and her visitor to enjoy her little lad's antics. First of all she took up a tray prepared by Emma and then she carried up the bowl and toiletries with which to wash the old woman. 'I've never known such fuss in all me born days!' she cried in exasperation when, finally, she brought down the soiled linen. 'She gets more and more cantankerous! It took me ten full minutes to get her to use that blessed bedpan. She's more of a baby than that little fellow there!'

'I don't know what she'd do without you, Tilly,' Emma said affectionately, 'she doesn't deserve you.'

'Aye, well, I get paid for me troubles,' came the twinkling reminder, 'though if your fellow don't get work soon, happen even *that* won't go on, eh?'

Emma smiled, saying, 'Well, she won't let anybody else within an inch of her, Tilly, so I don't know what would happen in that event.' All the same, thought Emma, Tilly wasn't far from the truth.

On her way out, Tilly remarked in an intimate manner, 'Between you and me, that old fox has a big tin box underneath her bed, and she screams blue murder if I even touch it with me toe. I wouldn't mind betting it's stuffed full o' banknotes!' Whereupon they all laughed, but none of them would have been surprised to discover that Tilly was right! Mrs Manfred believed it to be of small consequence, since Emma was secure financially because of her marriage settlement and Emma gave her no reason to think otherwise. Emma wondered whether Gregory suspected old Mrs Denton might be hiding a sizeable nest-egg. Still, they were not desperate yet and whatever old Mrs Denton had or didn't have, she considered to be none of her business.

On the stroke of six, Gregory burst in through the door, his face brighter than Emma had seen it in a long time and he actually rushed forward to grab her by the waist and swing her round. 'They took me on!' he shouted jubilantly. 'The buggers took me on!'

'Oh, Gregory!' Emma was overjoyed at his good news. 'That's wonderful!' The thought that perhaps her ordeal might not prove to be as fearful as she'd anticipated, fleetingly crossed her mind. Oh, but there was time enough for that later, when he had washed and eaten and they were in the privacy of their bedroom. Somehow, the knowledge that Mrs Manfred would be downstairs made Emma feel much braver and this seemed the perfect moment to raise that particular matter. 'Gregory,' she said, adjusting her dress which, in his exuberance, Gregory had made uncomfortably tight across her middle, 'Manny's come to visit.'

'Oh, goodness!' He followed Emma's smiling eyes to where Mrs Manfred sat. 'Forgive me,' he said, going towards her, 'I didn't even see you there.' Mrs Manfred told him that her employment with the Crowthers had been terminated, and he offered his sympathy. 'Oh, I'm really sorry to hear that, Mrs Manfred,' he said, with such polite and genuine concern that Mrs Manfred wondered how Emma could possibly describe him as a changed man. In fact, when Emma explained how she had invited Manny to stay the night and delay her departure until the morning, he made no objection whatsoever. 'There's a narrow bed up in the loft,' he said, 'I'll bring it down and set it together in the back bedroom before I go out.'

'Before you go out?' Emma was already on her way to collect his meal from the oven, when his words pulled her up short.

'It's grand, Emma,' he said, seeming to her more like his old self than he'd been for a long time. 'Look at that! He pointed first to the clay on his boots, then to the clay beneath his fingernails. 'I've got work again! Work! I can hold my head up alongside *any* man, at long last. I feel proud . . . proud to be fetching home a wage!'

'But you're surely not going out without a hot meal inside you?'

'My stomach's that excited, it would just churn over at the sight of any food. No! I shall get myself washed and changed, give the old 'un the good news, get that narrow bed down . . . then I'm off to spread a bit of cheer and hope in the alehouse. I've been drowning my sorrows far too long, Emma, now, I've some celebrating to do!'

In less than an hour, he was gone. He didn't kiss Emma

goodbye in the manner of old, before hard times had come on them; neither did he walk out with a surly face and without a word, as he had done of late. Instead, he smiled, waved his hand and, before he turned away from Emma at the door, leaned forward to murmur in her ear, 'It seems our luck is changing, eh? Happen other things will fall into place as well. We shall see . . . we shall see. Expect me home afore eleven.' Emma was left in no doubt as to what he meant, though, before such intimate relationships could be resumed, he must be made aware of the situation. If there was any kind of a choice, Emma would have taken it, but there was not, and the issue must be faced head on. It was the only way.

'I'm surprised he'd choose to go off drinking,' remarked Mrs Manfred with concern in her voice. 'I never took him to be a drinking man . . . though I can understand how he turned to it in his worst hours. Still an' all, I should have thought he'd want to celebrate his good news here, in his own home, with you.'

Before Emma could voice her own concern and as though she had heard Mrs Manfred's words, another voice pierced the air as that dreaded rhythmic knocking began to shake the ceiling. 'If my lad's gotten a taste for the drinking, Emma Grady, it's on account of *you* . . . you'll pay for your sins, you'll see! The Lord punishes the wicked in his own way!'

Being used to such abuse, Emma paid no attention, but Mrs Manfred was appalled. 'For two pins I'd go up there and give her a piece of my mind! she declared, her face uplifted and her eyes glittering. 'You let her get away with too much, my girl!'

Seeing her old friend seething with indignation and listening to that voice from above still screaming out its vile abuse, Emma couldn't help seeing the humorous side of things. 'Oh, Manny!' she laughed. 'Do you really think I dare let the two of you at each other's throats? Like as not, you'd have the whole street out!' Whereupon, the stiffness in her old friend's face melted away and the homely features began crinkling into a smile. It only took Emma to begin gently giggling and the two of them collapsed into fits of laughter.

'Oh, ssh, child!' came the broken warning, as Mrs Manfred composed herself. 'Or she'll be down them blessed stairs and laying that stick of hers about both our shoulders!'

Smothering the laughter which insisted on bubbling up inside her at the comical image presented by Mrs Manfred's words, Emma promptly offered to brew up a fresh pot of tea. Then she asked, 'Perhaps you'll cast an expert eye over my sewing, Manny, and tell me where I'm going wrong?' Emma despaired of ever being truly able to master the art. In fact, since her marriage to Gregory, Emma had had many regrets regarding her limited experience in domestic matters, for every new task she had to learn seemed like a milestone which, without Mrs Manfred's constant help, she would never achieve.

'Of course, child. It'll be grand, eh? You and me aside o' the fire and spending a cosy evening together,' came the smiling remark. 'I can't think of anything more lovely.' And Emma agreed – unless it was an evening spent in Marlow's adoring arms!

When eleven o'clock came and went, Mrs Manfred made the announcement that, try as she might, 'I just can't stay awake another minute.' Emma lit her a candle and led the way upstairs to the back bedroom. 'Sleep tight, Manny,' she said, lighting the dresser-candle from her own and feeling the bed sheets to ensure they were not damp to the touch.

At the door, she turned to receive a peck on the cheek and the warning, 'I don't know if it is wise to tell Gregory the way of things . . . not at such a late hour and when he's only just returned from a public bar.'

The very same thought had occurred to Emma. 'Don't worry, Manny,' she said with a wry smile, 'bad news can always wait. At least till morning.' After which she went quietly back downstairs, tidied away the crockery, washed up, put a little more coke on the fire and settled down in the chair to wait.

When the clock struck midnight and still there was no sign of Gregory, Emma told herself she might just as well go upstairs to bed. 'Like as not he's gone off to some fellow's house, till the early hours,' she murmured into the half-darkness. Anyway, she decided, there was nothing to be gained by staying down in the parlour. So, placing the mesh guard in front of the fire, she took up the candlestick from the sideboard, clutched a handful of skirt to lift up the hem of her dress and slowly, all the while listening for footsteps at the door, she mounted the stairs.

Judging by the loud and rhythmic breathing sounds as she passed first Mrs Manfred's room, then old Mrs Denton's, it seemed they were both deep in slumber. As she closed her own bedroom door behind her, there was a strange and eerie moment when Emma felt utterly alone in the world. So real did it seem that, for a while, she felt panic-stricken and began trembling. But, reminding herself that this upper room was always chilly, Emma shrugged her shoulders, put the candle down on the stool and started to undress.

Of a sudden, there was a scuffling and rattling at the front door, with the sound of Gregory's voice rising muffled through the letter-box. 'Open the door, yer buggers. I've lost my key!'

Quickly, Emma flung her shawl about her shoulders and was halfway down the first short flight of stairs when the sound of the front door being flung open to crash loudly against the passage wall rocked the house. 'The buggers were in my pocket all the time!' came Gregory's jubilant shout and it sounded even stranger from drink than Emma could ever remember.

'Who's that? Gregory! Where's my son?' Emma winced as old Mrs Denton's angry voice sailed through the house.

'It's all right,' she called out, 'it's nothing to worry about. Go back to sleep.'

'Who are *you* to tell *me* what to do, you little trollop!' came the indignant retort. 'Where's Gregory? Gregory!' she called even more loudly.

As Emma carried on down the stairs and along the landing, the back bedroom door opened and a tumbled grey head peered out. 'Is everything all right, child?' asked Mrs Manfred.

'Yes, it's only Gregory . . . thought he'd lost his front door key,' replied Emma in a whisper. 'Goodnight, Manny. You'd best get back to sleep if you want to be up bright and early,' she reminded her.

'All right, lass. Goodnight, God bless.' As she disappeared back into her room, Mrs Manfred's thoughts were troubled. She'd had no idea what Emma had to put up with, and, although it went against everything in her upbringing, she half wished that Marlow *had* taken Emma with him. There was a bad situation here. But, deep down, Mrs Manfred believed that Emma would cope. She'll make the best of a bad job, she told herself, the lass always does.

From the top of the stairs, Emma peered down, holding the candle out at arm's length. 'Are you all right, Gregory?' she asked in a loud whisper.

'Course I'm all right, sweetheart.' He began stumbling up the stairs. 'Never felt better in all my life! There were two other fellows tekken on at the quarries today. By! We've done some bloody celebrating!'

'I can see that.' Emma hated to see a man so affected by drink. 'Be quiet as you come up. You've wakened your mother.' She wondered how in God's name he'd be fit to go to work the following day. It was likely he'd end up losing the job which was the very cause for his celebration.

'Don't you worry about the old bugger!' came the retort, as he fell up the last few steps. 'I'll have a word with her.' As he mounted the top tread and came on to the landing, he grabbed hold of Emma to stop himself from reeling backwards down the stairs. 'I think I'm drunk,' he chuckled, his breath fanning out over Emma's face and turning her stomach. 'Hey, look at you, you little vixen!' he said with delight, on seeing that Emma had removed her dress and beneath the shawl her shoulders were bare. 'Oho! Waiting for me, were you?' he asked, roving his hand over her upper arm and leaning forward as though he might kiss her. 'You be a good girl and get the bed warm, eh?' he said with a sly wink. 'I'll just look in on the old 'un . . . see she gets off to sleep, eh?'

Without a word, Emma turned to leave him groping along

the landing towards old Mrs Denton's room. The touch of his hand on her naked skin had seemed somehow revolting to her. She would go to bed, feign sleep and hope to God that her drunken husband would be so exhausted by the time he got into bed, that the idea so evidently uppermost in his mind would come to nothing!

Lying in the dark, Emma heard every sound Gregory made, his movements so exaggerated and clumsy that they drove all tiredness from her, replacing it with such nervous panic that her heart seemed to be turning somersaults of its own accord. As he lumbered into the room, it became apparent to Emma that since that glorious night spent in Marlow's arms, when the child now moving inside her was created, no other being but herself had cast eyes on her nakedness. Somehow, despite the fact that she had a husband, it seemed right to Emma that this was so. The thought of Gregory ogling her and exploring her body with his own caused such turmoil within her. Yet, she was his wife and, as such, must be prepared to yield to his demands.

'Awake are you, my beauty?' came the slurred voice into the half-darkness. 'Waiting for me, are you, you little vixen?' Emma gave no indication that she was still awake. She made no move, nor uttered even the slightest sound. Instead, she lay quite still, her eyes tightly shut and a little prayer in her heart that Gregory would be so exhausted from his evening of revelry that he would fall fast asleep the minute he tumbled into bed beside her. For what seemed a lifetime, Emma could hear him falling about and chuckling, as time and time again he made the effort to undress. 'Buggered if I ain't too drunk to stand up!' he kept saying, as he crashed first on to the bed, then on to the floor. Emma could hear him hopping about on one leg and when, curious in spite of herself, she opened one eye, it was to catch a glimpse of him in the long wardrobe mirror with one leg bent in the air, his hand making desperate grabs to yank the trousers from it, and all the while performing a comical tap dance, which looked all the more fascinating in the eerie flickering candle-light. 'Told me off, she did!' he now complained to Emma's back. 'My old mater! Said I was drunk and should be ashamed!' Suddenly his trousers were jubilantly snatched into the air, followed by his belt and braces, shirt and undergarments. 'I told her straight, Emma! I told the old bugger I'd give her cause to be proud of me. Oh aye! You wait till I present you with a grandson, I told her! Me an' my little woman – we'll do it this very night. I've got work, and I feel it in my blood that, between us, we'll make a grandson for her tonight!'

When he slid into bed beside her, his hands coveting her neck, her shoulders, her hair, Emma felt herself shrink from him. When the warm nakedness of his body pressed itself into her back and his face leaned forward to touch her own, Emma thought she would die. God help her, but she couldn't let him invade her body! Not now, with Marlow's seed warm within her; not *ever*, her heart growing cold as his fingers began pulling up her nightgown. 'Come on, Emma,' he coaxed in a whisper which seemed to have suddenly sobered by his desperate need of her. 'It's been so very long . . . I'm sorry. Oh, but I want you now. I need you so badly that I can hardly breathe!' Feeling her resistance, his demands grew more urgent and when he roughly gripped her thigh in order to swing her round towards him, he quickly sensed the stiffening of her body. 'Stop that!' he growled, his tone marbled with both astonishment and anger. 'Your husband has need of you and by God, he'll have you!' He spat the words in her ear, at the same time beginning to straddle her crouched body. In that split second, Emma looked up and, seeing his naked body towering above her, she made a desperate scramble to get out from beneath him.

'What the hell's the matter with you?' Gregory lashed out with his right arm, intending to pin Emma to the bed. But she would not be held! In the ensuing frantic struggle, she managed to escape his clutches, but not before he had ripped the nightgown from her back. From the far side of the room where she had run to escape his searching eyes, Emma stood transfixed, ashamed that both Manny and old Mrs Denton must by now be listening to every word which passed from this room. As Gregory came towards her in slow, deliberate steps, holding the candle flame out at arm's length and a look of terrible confusion on his face, Emma averted her eyes. He stopped within only two or three paces of her. She felt his colourless eyes scrutinizing every inch of her nakedness. She heard the gasp of incredulity which, to Emma's trembling heart, seemed to infuse the very air with terror.

When the cry came, it was like a roar of thunder, yet it was transfused with the threat of tears. 'Christ Almighty! *You're with child, Emma*!' Now, he was on her, so close that the heat from the candle flame seared into her skin as he held it near her face. When he asked her, in a suspicious voice, 'Is it mine? . . . can it be?' and she lowered her gaze to the floor, he had his answer. 'Whose bastard is it, then, eh?' He was shaking her to and fro, not caring that each time her head was banged hard against the wall. '*Whose* bastard, I asked?' The shock of his discovery showed on his twisted face as, flinging her away from him with contempt, he went on drunken, unsteady legs to the dresser, put down the candle and began frenziedly pulling on his clothes as though his very life depended on it. 'You think you'll not tell me who it was, do you?' he scorned. 'Well, you'll do better than that, because you'll bloody well *take* me to the swine! He'll not touch another man's wife again, I'll be bound. And, as for you, you *are* a trollop! A harlot . . . just as my mother warned me!' In Gregory Denton's eyes there was no worse sin to be committed than that which Emma had committed against him! Having put on his shirt and trousers, he grabbed Emma's pile of clothes and, flinging them at her, yelled, 'Get dressed!'

Never having seen any man in such a fury – not even Caleb Crowther – and feeling all the more intimidated because it was Gregory, her own husband, Emma was mortified. But, even so, she did not wish to leave this room on a fool's errand. She frantically scrambled for her best course of action. Should she put on her clothes and make some futile trek into the streets with him, where the cold night air might temper his fury and give her the opportunity to reason with him? Or would her best move be to dress, but to go no further than the downstairs parlour, where she might have the chance to explain and talk more calmly. Or might she fare better by refusing to budge from this room until he had listened to what she had to say. Oh, but dear God, what *could* she say, other than to confirm what his instincts told him already – that the child was not his, but another man's and that that man was the bargee, Marlow Tanner. No! That was the one thing she would never reveal. Whatever else she might confess to, Emma would not betray or defile the exquisite memories of that night, of Marlow's fathomless, undying love for her and of her own for him. She would hold close those wonderful memories and treasure them in her heart for always – whatever the consequences!

'There's no point in discussing anything, until you can listen *calmly* to what I must tell you.' Emma's voice was quiet and controlled, belying the tightening knot in her stomach and the uncomfortable fluttering of her heart.

The sound of her voice cutting the air with such dignity seemed only to infuriate Gregory Denton further. 'I will not tell you again,' he said through clenched teeth as he bent to lace up his boots. 'What! . . . I've half a mind to flay you alive here and now. Get dressed and cover up your sins! Or, so help me, I'll do it for you!'

When, in defiance, Emma made no move other than to take the shawl from a nearby chair and wrap it about her shivering body, he seemed like a man demented. 'So you're *proud* of your sins, are you? Proud that you're nothing but a cheap trollop, eh?' He rushed towards her, his work boots making a peculiar sound across the floor and his face pinched with rage and filled with loathing as it thrust itself into Emma's. '*Proud* is it?' he demanded, gripping hold of Emma and propelling her violently towards the door. 'Well, then . . . why not show the whole world, eh?'

Unable to fight his manic strength, Emma felt herself being pulled across the room and through the door. Out on the landing she was dragged from one bedroom door to the other as he yelled at the top of his voice. 'We've a harlot here, who's *proud* of it! Come and see, why don't you?' Whereupon the back bedroom door was opened wide and through it emerged the homely figure of Mrs Manfred. Attired only in the long white nightgown taken earlier from her portmanteau and with her hair, which was usually rolled neatly up, hanging just as tidily about her shoulders, she had a look of both consternation and disgust on her round, honest face.

'Take hold of yourself, Mr Denton!' she told him, coming forward to place the lighted candle on the landing windowsill, her eyes as hard and condemning as her voice. 'If Mrs Denton has little to be proud of, then *you* have even less! Take your hands off her this instant!'

'No, Manny . . . go back to your bed, please!' pleaded Emma, for she had seen the rising anger in her friend's face and she knew of old that Manny's sharp tongue would get her into deep trouble. 'I'm all right, believe me.' She was not afraid of Gregory now. Ashamed yes and also regretful that she had not found the courage to face the whole issue many weeks before when she'd first suspected her condition. But she now felt indignant that Gregory should humiliate her so in front of others, for if he had been half a man, he would have found the courage to discuss the situation more rationally. Instead, he had chosen to use it as a means to belittle her even further and to subsequently demonstrate his total lack of compassion and tolerance. In this illuminating moment, Emma saw Gregory for what he really was and she did not like what she saw. She herself had a great deal to answer for, that was true enough; she had no reason to be 'proud', as he had claimed – but then, neither had he! No! Emma wasn't ashamed, nor was she afraid. She was angry! Angry enough to turn on him now, first with her fists, then with her teeth, sinking them into his arm, and finally with her feet, when he attempted to knock her off balance against the balustrade.

'You little cow!' he screamed as the blood trickled down his arm.

'Leave her be, I tell you . . . leave her be!' Now Mrs Manfred dashed to help and all hell was let loose.

Of a sudden, old Mrs Denton's door flung open, revealing a face as dark as thunder and eyes alive with hatred. Standing there, silhouetted in the glow from the candle on her dresser, she made a fearsome sight. Over her cream cotton nightgown a fringed brown shawl was flung, crocheted by her own hands when they had been more nimble. Enormous in size, it reached down to touch her bare, gnarled feet and to tangle itself in the crooked walking-stick upon which she now leaned so heavily. Her nightcap was at a peculiar angle, covering one ear, and her surprisingly long grey hair protruded from beneath in wild tangled clusters before falling about her stiff bony shoulders in such disarray that it gave her a witch-like appearance. Her eyes were slitted and venomous as they took in the scene before her. 'I *knew* it!' she hissed, letting her weight slump on to the door-jamb as she viciously thrashed the air with her stick. 'I know what you've been up to, Emma Grady! My son might only just have found out, but I've known all along what you are! Who gave you the right to fetch your cheap, loud-mouthed friends into this house? Who, eh . . . tell me that!' But her voice fell on deaf ears, only adding to the noise and confusion as the struggle between the two figures – one intending to harm Emma while the other tried to save her – grew even more frantic.

Meanwhile, outside, Tilly Watson was terrified that there was a murder being committed. 'For God's sake, open this door!' she yelled through the letter-box. 'Else I swear I'll fetch a constable!' When there was no acknowledgment and the shouting grew even more fierce, her husband pushed her aside and, peering through the letter-box, he was so alarmed to see Gregory frantically struggling with the two women, that, giving no further warning, he ran like the wind to seek out an officer of the law, telling his wife as he went, 'There's madness goin' on in there, Tilly. Stay well away till the constable comes!' As he ran, it crossed his mind that, unless he acted swiftly, some poor unfortunate would go hurtling down those stairs and end up with a broken back. He thought again on what he'd seen and judging by the way that aggressive older woman was grappling with Mr Denton, his instincts told him it would likely be his neighbour who came off worst! As for young Mrs Denton, well, she seemed more *against* her husband than *with* him! By God, it was a right do!

Tugged and torn between the two equally determined forces, Emma was also terrified that someone would be badly hurt. On the one hand Mrs Manfred was like a tigress protecting her cub, while on the other, Gregory was beside himself with inconsolable fury, made all the more terrible by drink. It was when Gregory lashed out with the intent of stripping the shawl from Emma's otherwise-naked body that the inevitable happened. At the very moment when the enraged Mrs Manfred struck out to prevent his arm from grasping the shawl, Emma twisted from the vice-like grip of his other fist, which had seized her and pinned her fast to him. Without Emma's body to hold him balanced against the older woman's feverish attack, he stumbled backwards and, with a cry which struck a chill deep in Emma's exhausted heart, he hurtled down the steep, narrow stairs, to land crumpled and misshapen at the bottom.

For what seemed a lifetime, not a sound could be heard: not the slightest movement disturbed the eerie silence. Until a few moments later, the odd shuffling of old Mrs Denton's bare feet penetrated the unnatural quietness as she slowly took herself from her bedroom door to the balustrade. From there, she stared down at the tragic figure which was barely visible in the shadowy passage below. At once the silence was broken with her low pitiful sobbing, which, to Emma's shocked spirit, was terrible to hear. Amidst it all, Emma ran swiftly down the stairs to where Gregory lay unmoving. Bending close to him, she began murmuring his name and looking into his face. When his wide, shocked eyes stared back at her unseeing, Emma's hand flew up to stifle the cry in her throat and, her heart torn with anguish, she turned to look at Mrs Manfred who seemed frozen to the spot. In a broken voice she said in a loud whisper, 'Oh, Manny! . . . he's dead. Gregory's dead!' Whereupon Mrs Manfred visibly sagged and seemed close to collapse.

'Murderers! It were you . . . the *both* of you! You killed him . . . pushed him down the stairs! Murderers!' Old Mrs Denton fell forward across the balustrade, her eyes going from Mrs Manfred to Emma and her voice at such a pitch that, within minutes, there wasn't a soul along Montague Street who hadn't been roused from their beds. On and on she went, growing more and more hysterical. When the sound of the constable's whistle outside rose above her shrieking, she went into a spasm, her every limb shaking so violently that the stick in her hand played a sinister tune against the balustrade and her grief-stricken wails became like the sound of muted laughter.

Suddenly, the door was burst open. The constable stretched out his arms in order to keep the crowd back. What he heard behind him was Tilly Watson's husband telling one and all 'The buggers 'ave done for him! We saw it! . . . me an' Tilly, we saw the poor sod struggling for his life!' What the constable saw by the flickering light of the candle which brightly burned on the landing windowsill, was Emma kneeling ashen-faced and terror-struck beside the still figure of her husband. Above her, on the landing, was the figure of Mrs Manfred, flattened back against the wall, on the verge of collapse, her eyes closed and, clutched tightly in her hand, a torn remnant of Gregory Denton's shirt sleeve. Some further way along the landing, old Mrs Denton was slumped over the balustrade like a rag-doll, her eyes fixed on the still and twisted figure of her precious son. Over and over in a small shocked voice she accused Emma, 'You killed my lad! The both of you . . . you murdered him.' And, going by what he had been told by those who had seen the fracas through the letter-box, together with what his own eyes told him now, the constable's first instincts were to totally agree with what that frail old woman was saying. However, when he moved down the passageway and saw Emma's tragic eyes looking up at him, he could find nothing there to convince him that she had a wicked heart. Still, he had a duty to perform, where instincts and feelings did very little to influence the outcome.

When the constable took hold of Emma's arm, saying in a kindly but firm voice, 'Come along now. Let's get you decently dressed,' Emma felt numb, but not from the biting cold which took her breath away and made the pores on her skin stand out; she was numbed by all that had taken place and by the tragedy which she had witnessed with her own eyes. Emma prayed that it was all some terrible nightmare from which she would soon wake up; but deep in her heart she knew it was not.

Some time later, when the house on Montague Street had seen more visitors and officialdom in a few hours than it had seen in many years, an uneasy quietness descended upon it. The constable had secured all the details of what was construed to have taken place. Tilly Watson and her husband gave their excited and colourful account; old Mrs Denton gave her version in the greatest detail, laying the blame with renewed vigour on Mrs Manfred and Emma. Now, after she had helped Emma to dress in her best clothes and boots before delivering her, along with Mrs Manfred, to the waiting officers, Tilly Watson had only old Mrs Denton to contend with.

'My lad . . . they murdered my poor lad!' was all the old woman could murmur from the depths of her bed – her voice, like her shocked heart, growing weaker with every breath.

'That'll be for the Judge to decide,' Tilly Watson reminded her. Although, if the truth were to be told, she thought, there was little hope that the Judge's verdict would be any different to that of old Mrs Denton's because, much as she liked Emma and Mrs Manfred, there was a powerful case against them – including what she herself had seen with her very own eyes. However, if the question was put to her, she would have to say that, in her opinion, it was *not* Emma's hand that actually pushed Mr Denton, but that of Mrs Manfred.

Of a sudden, Tilly was struck by the unearthly quiet in the room and, looking down on old Mrs Denton's grey, silent features and wide-open eyes, she was riveted to the spot.

'Lord, love us!' she said in a thick whisper, making the sign of the cross several times on herself. 'Looks like the old bugger's followed her lad!' Quickly, she examined the old woman more closely and seeing that she had indeed left this world, a crafty look came over Tilly's face. Turning her head stealthily from side to side to ensure there was no one else present in the room, she gingerly picked up the old woman's wrist between her finger and thumb and lifted the arm which had been hanging from the bed towards the floor. Laying it over the eiderdown in reverent fashion, she looked about the room once more. Then, stooping so that she might easily stretch her hand under the bed, she began feverishly rummaging about.

'Got it!' Tilly gave out a little cry of triumph as her groping fingers clutched the square cold box. In her excitement, she was almost flat on the floor, both arms reaching beneath the bed to secure the hard metal object.

Tilly Watson's guilty heart was beating furiously as she eased her reward towards her, but it almost stopped completely when old Mrs Denton's arm slid from the eiderdown, to come tumbling on to her thieving neck like a tap from the devil! 'Jesus, Mary and Joseph!' Tilly screamed at the top of her voice, scrambling to her feet and grasping the cash box to her chest, just as the two officials from below came crashing into the room.

'You gave us the fright of our lives,' said one.

'What's up?' demanded the other, taking out his notebook and pencil.

Tilly had to think quickly. Gave *them* a fright, she told herself. 'Tweren't *nothing* to what that old sod did to me! With swift and dexterous hands, she pulled her shawl over the cash box, saying with a feigned look of regret, 'The old lady's gone, I'm afeared. Sudden like it was . . . gave me a real turn, I'm telling you!' She hurried out of the room before they had the opportunity to detain her. 'I'd best away and get help for the laying-out of the body, afore the bones begin to stiffen.'

Thankful that she had been allowed to leave the house straightaway, Tilly didn't stop until she'd safely closed her own front door behind her. 'I'm sorry for thieving your valuables, old Ma Denton,' she murmured, 'but you'll not be wanting 'em where you've gone and me an' mine have more need of this 'ere box!' Of a sudden, a startling thought entered her head. With both the old lady and her son gone, the cash box would next go to Emma. But not if Emma were never to come home again, she thought wickedly. Not if she was hanged for murder! A cunning and avaricious look washed over Tilly Watson's hitherto homely face. 'I'm sorry, Emma,' she whispered into the night, 'but, now I come to think on it more clearly, I swear it was your hand that sent poor Mr Denton to his maker. Oh yes, I saw what I saw and I'm duty bound to explain it in the very manner in which it all happened!' Whereupon, she crept into the darkened front parlour, making sure she did not disturb her husband in the back room, hid her treasure and hurried back to have quiet words with the officials next door. She must be quite sure they'd got her story right. There was time enough for the old one to be properly laid out – that was none too urgent. But what she had to tell the officials, well now, the sooner that was done, the better!

# Part Two

## *June 1862*
## Hearts of Stone

Beset me with trials
Or test my heart
And make my spirit lowly,
But I will grow stronger
Wherever the wind may blow me.
                                    *J.C.*

# Chapter Ten

'You get yer bloody 'ands off my arse, ye randy sod! Else I'll 'ave the law on yer!' From somewhere beneath the street grime and layers of holey clothing, Sal Tanner's weather-worn and wrinkled face expressed indignation at being so crudely manhandled. Her booted feet lashed out at the officer who had come up from behind the marauding trouble-makers, to thrust her out of harm's way.

'Now then old Sal,' he told her firmly, 'if you're locked up again, they'll likely seal up the door for good and all!' He took her by the scruff of her neck and as he propelled her from the black heart of the mob, his voice was kindly but threatening. 'Be off with you, Sal Tanner. Afore I'm tempted to run you in along with the rest of them!'

'Go on then, why don't yer?' she demanded, fighting and struggling in his determined grip.

'Because I know you're not here to cause real trouble, you old bugger! D'you think I don't know that you're just here to take advantage, whilst folks is looking the other way? Do as I say, and be off . . . else I'll turn you in for the pickpocket you fancy yourself to be, you silly old bugger!'

'I ain't pickin' *anybody's* pockets!' Sal was defiant,

though she knew well enough now that she'd been tumbled. When he contemptuously threw her to the kerbside, saying with a laugh, 'And as for being "randy", well now, that *might* be the case. But if I wanted to touch anybody's arse, Sal Tanner, it wouldn't be yours, I can tell you! I'd be a bloody fool to risk catching the pox from the likes o' you, wouldn't I, eh?' Sal knew when to leave well enough alone. As the constable turned to assist his fellow officers in trying to bring the ensuing crisis under control, Sal ambled away to where she might find better pickings – thinking there could well be a free gill o' beer going begging at one or other of the alehouses round the market square, never mind that the last time she'd gone into such a place for a gill and a card game, the result had been to reduce her to living like a beggar and sleeping in the cobbled alleys. 'Sod 'em all!' she muttered now, as she scurried away into the descending darkness, jingling the few coppers she'd swiped from a few back pockets. ''Appen I can catch another game, where I might win back me barge an' all me belongings! 'Cause if I *don't*, our Marlow'll likely skin me alive when 'e finds out what tricks I've been up to while 'e's across the seas!'

The scene which Sal Tanner had left behind was a bad one. Feelings of despair amongst a minority of the unemployed had erupted in a mutinous revolt. The cause of it had been the arrest and consequent imprisonment of a number of unfortunates who had been caught poaching. Following the harsh results of the hearing, an angry demonstration had ensued, which moved down King Street, causing much damage to property. From there, many of the marauders marched on to Pleasington Hall, smashing the windows, while others proceeded to the Town Hall and caused further aggravation. A meeting of magistrates was eventually called, the Riot Act read and special constables sworn in. In addition, a troop of soldiers was brought from Preston to quell what at first appeared to be the brewing of a long and bloody siege. As it turned out, hostilities quickly ceased and peace was sensibly restored. For many nights afterwards, however, talk of the commotion filled the alehouses and parlours, as ordinary, law-abiding folk condemned such behaviour, although they were themselves desperate for food and warmth, and still despairing of ever finding work. The community of Blackburn was shaken to its roots, and those in authority took a dim and serious view of what had taken place.

Caleb Crowther was more condemning than most. His opinion of the working-class was that they should all be either flogged to within an inch of their lives or hanged from the tallest gibbet! When, at a late hour on this particular night, after peace had been restored, he emerged from Blackburn Railway Station in search of a carriage to take him home, it did not improve his irritation and fatigue after a long journey from London, to find a ragged and drunken tramp besieging him for 'a copper or two for a poor unfortunate, if yer please?' Being in a sourer mood than usual, he cracked his walking-cane about the shoulders of the ragged creature. 'Out of my way!' he snarled. 'Unless you want to feel the weight of the *law* on your shoulders into the bargain!'

Locating a carriage, he climbed smartly into it – leaving Sal Tanner raising a bottle to his departure. 'May the divil keep yer company, yer miserable old bugger!' she called after him, taking a hefty swig of the colourless spirit and heartily chortling as she set off drunkenly to the back alleys which were her home. 'May the divil tek all yer fancy bloody folk, an' drown the lot of 'em!' she told a passing constable, tripping away at a faster pace when he paused to eye her more closely. From a safe distance she turned to inform him, 'The buggers are allus up to sommat! Allus whispering an' causing trouble fer some poor sod or other! Drown 'em all!' Shouting defiantly as the constable began making his way towards her, she repeated, 'Drown 'em all, I say!' Then, as he came too close for comfort, she tossed her head and ran off, stumbling and laughing as her legs gave way beneath her.

The constable watched her out of sight. Then, smiling to himself, he went on his way. 'Poor old bugger,' he said with sympathy. Everyone knew the story of how Sal Tanner had come to ruin since her brother had sailed away. She was a familiar sight, haunting the streets of Blackburn like a lost soul. Ah well, perhaps one of these days her brother would make his way back; there was nobody else who could handle Sal Tanner – and nobody else who could save her!

Meanwhile, in the carriage, with only the clip-clop of the horses' hooves to disturb his thoughts, Caleb Crowther reflected on the reason for his journey to London. Bartholomew Mysen was not an easy man to do business with. He had become stiff-necked and unapproachable since his appointment to Circuit Judge. At this point in his thoughts, Caleb Crowther smiled to himself as he softly murmured, 'If you don't want your sins to find you out, then you should be more careful, Mysen.' It pleased him to have succeeded in the errand which had taken him so urgently to seek out his colleague of old. As he himself was not to sit in judgment at the trial of Emma Grady as was, then who better to be acquainted with the necessary facts than the man in whose hands her future would lie? Facts which might also affect the future of the learned Judge himself! Facts which told of past indiscretions in the brothel houses and gambling dens. Facts which, if made public, could topple a fellow from the pinnacle of his career in the time it took to wink an eye! Indeed, there might well be repercussions for others who also shared those indiscretions, but, somehow, Caleb Crowther's instincts had been correct when they told him that Bartholomew Mysen would do anything rather than risk losing his own income and new-found status in society.

As to the facts regarding Emma Grady and her accomplice . . . well now, wasn't there more than enough evidence to show how they had deliberately murdered that poor young man? Wasn't it obvious how Emma Grady herself was the ringleader? And didn't the pair of them show such evil and cunning that warranted nothing less than to be publicly hanged! The fact that Emma Grady was with child and as such could not be hanged was no great stumbling-block, as had been painstakingly pointed out to the reluctant Bartholomew Mysen by his unwelcome visitor. By the time her trial came to court and the sentence called upon, Emma Grady would have delivered her brat into the world. There were institutions enough to see to such a burden on society.

Caleb Crowther's paramount objective was to ensure that Emma Grady be swiftly despatched from the face of the earth. That would conveniently rid him of his three greatest problems: his need to explain to her what had become of her legacy; his own nagging conscience; and his innate and desperate fear that, should she live, Emma might well discover certain things about the past which should be left forever buried, out of harm's way! Then, there was Mrs

Manfred, whose loyalties were steadfastly with Emma and her papa, and the very same woman who had seen more than she had revealed of Thadius Grady's death and of his own unholy part in it! He'd never been really sure how much she had actually seen, but had suffered tormenting nightmares that she must surely have witnessed something! However, he was now satisfied that both of them would be dealt with forthwith and would no longer represent any kind of threat to him. Persuading his legal colleague had not been easy, but, when it came right down to it, a fellow must look out for his own survival. There was no doubt that when Emma Grady and her companion were brought before the Courts in two days' time, they would each get their just rewards. It mattered not that they were probably innocent of all charges against them, only that here was a prime opportunity to be rid of them once and for all!

Only once did Caleb Crowther's thoughts touch on a much deeper issue. No one alive, apart from himself, knew that Emma was *his* daughter! His and Mary Grady's, got during an illicit affair behind Thadius's back. Oh, if only that was the *single* dark secret from the past, he thought now. If only that was all, he might rest easier in his sleep!

'Emma Denton, you have been found guilty of a serious crime. Whilst in the company of another, you behaved in such a way that contributed to the death of your own husband.' Judge Mysen's voice echoed across the courtroom like the strokes of a hammer on Emma's heart. Only now, after what seemed an eternity in these Lancaster assizes, did she raise her eyes to look into the face of Judge Mysen. She had told the truth of what happened on that fateful night some months previously, but her words had fallen on unbelieving ears; to them the more sensational accounts of others had seemed more credible. With every word now spoken, Emma could see the gallows looming up before her and her trembling heart was overwhelmed with fear. However, she was determined not to betray her terror; she would not let her spirit become cowardly at this late hour. Her love for Marlow and her cherished memories of him had been a great source of comfort and strength to her throughout. Her regrets were many, but, if she had the power to change anything, it would be only one thing; for her deepest regret was the injustice which would now be inflicted on the innocent inside her. Her heart ached when she thought of how that helpless little being, who was conceived in such joy and love, would be taken along with her to the gallows and there its beating heart would be stilled with her own. But Emma was prepared, and when the moment came, she would offer up a special prayer for her and Marlow's defenceless unborn child.

Although Emma gazed steadfastly at Judge Mysen's serious face, her thoughts were far away, constantly churning and always concerned for others rather than for herself. As he gave out his declaration, Bartholomew Mysen found himself deeply moved by Emma's calm strength and by the tragic innocence in those sad eyes which looked at him with such disarming directness. In his deliberations he was cruelly torn between the fate of this young woman who was so close to being a mother, and his own future, which rested on the sentences he passed here this day. He was not unaware of those who had sat in the gallery throughout this trial, in particular the man he had come to so despise; a man who, with other members of his family, had followed every detail with the utmost interest. Now, as he spoke, he could feel Caleb Crowther's eyes feasting on him, urging him to deliver the ultimate penalty on the two women who stood before him. 'Hang them!' he had been warned. 'Or face the consequences!'

Bartholomew Mysen was under no illusions regarding the treacherous character of the man with whom he had once foolishly haunted the fleshpots of London. Yet, how could he live with his own conscience if he was to send Emma Denton to the gallows? The older woman, in his eyes, had been more damned by the evidence put before him and he believed, in all truth, that she was indeed the guilty party. He, like others, was not entirely convinced that the younger woman's intentions had been truly malicious. Indeed, he himself had been half persuaded that initially, it was *she* who was being attacked. However, the verdict had been returned and he was now called upon to pass sentence. In a final effort to calm the dictates of his own conscience, as well as appeasing the demands of Caleb Crowther, he made his decision. There was one other option still open to him, which, though coming to a close, had not yet outlived its usefulness. In his eyes, it was as good as a sentence to the gallows. In latter years, such harsh sentences had been reserved mostly for males, but, as in cases such as this, there were always exceptions.

While her fate was being decided, Emma remained calm. In her heart, she softly asked that the Lord look upon his children with mercy and that dear Mrs Manfred, who had become so ill and pale, should be spared.

'And so, Emma Denton,' Judge Mysen's stern voice infiltrated Emma's thoughts once more, 'in view of these things, and taking into account both your tender years and advanced state of pregnancy, this court will show a measure of mercy.' Emma's heart was suddenly filled with hope, yet, not daring to anticipate her freedom, she held her breath and waited. But her hopes were not to be realized and, as the voice continued to reverberate around the courtroom, she had to grip the rail before her desperately tight, or all of her strength and resolve might have fled, and the black tide which ebbed about her senses would swallow her up.

'It is therefore ordered and adjudged by this court that you, Emma Denton, of the parish of Blackburn in Lancashire, be transported upon the seas, to such place as Her Majesty Queen Victoria, by the advice of Her Privy Council, shall think fit to direct and appoint, for the term of no less than ten years.'

Emma was devastated! She was *not* to be set free. She had escaped the gallows, yes, but only to be discharged from the beloved land of her birth and sent over some vast, terrifying ocean, to the edge of the world! All this time she had kept her strength, she had made herself hope against hope that justice would be done by both her and her unborn child. She had prayed as never before and she had tried so very hard not to be afraid. Yet, now, she *was* afraid! More than that, she was terrified, in awe of the unknown and in despair of what might become of her and the little one.

Of a sudden, Emma's fears were further charged as the court reacted to the sentence passed upon her, some people being in full agreement with it, and others – Caleb Crowther in particular – loudly condemning it to be a 'travesty of justice!' and 'too lenient by far!' Then, the court became quiet once again as they all awaited the sentence about to be imposed on the other defendant. When it was duly passed in echoing sombre tones, Emma's heart collapsed within her and she gave out a cry of anguish. If she had thought her own punishment to be harsh, then Mrs Manfred's must have come straight from Hell. Dear God above, it *couldn't* be! Her darling innocent Manny was to be committed to the gallows! Manny was to be hanged! The words echoed over and over in Emma's distorted and desperate thoughts. 'No, it can't be!' she heard her own voice cry out. She saw the shock and disbelief on her dear friend's face and when, suddenly, the child within her grew so agitated that the pains shot through her body like many knives, Emma felt her strength ebb away. She saw the peering eyes of strangers on her as the room spun into itself, until the darkness swamped her senses and she sank silently to the ground.

# Chapter Eleven

The laughter echoed from bow to stern of the coal-barge as wily Sal Tanner merrily hoisted up her ragged skirt and danced a jig on the spot. 'While their eyeballs is glued ter them there gallows,' she told one and all, 'we'll lighten their pockets an' be away, afore the buggers know what's hit 'em!' Her words were greeted by rapturous applause and raucous laughter, followed by a burst of accordion music and a great deal of ale-supping. After which the women got to their feet and entertained their menfolk with a tap of heels and vulgar show of legs.

'By! They're a motley crew and no mistake!' The bargeman stretched his neck from his place at the tiller and, casting his merry eyes over the live cargo which had made itself comfortable in amongst the mounds of black, shining coal, he laughed out loud, saying to the round, jolly woman by his side, 'I must a' been all kinds of a fool to give in to that lot, eh?'

'Away with yer, our Jack!' declared his wife, playfully nudging him in the ribs. 'They might look like the worst villains abroad, but they're harmless enough. Yer did right in giving them a ride ter Lancaster, 'cause they're no different from anybody else when it comes to attending a hanging.' She nudged him again and laughed out loud. 'But there's many a one as'll find their purses gone when this lot departs the scene!' Whereupon, the two of them laughed all the louder and shook their heads as they began tapping their own feet to the rhythm of the melody coming up from the hold.

Outside in the square, the gibbet was being put in place, and though the event was not scheduled to happen until early the following day, the crowds were already beginning to gather and jostle one another for the most advantageous position.

From her cramped and tiny cell, which was shared by others who awaited transportation, Emma could hear the outer hammering noises which told her that Mrs Manfred's time was growing ever nearer. She felt strange and disloyal that there was no sadness in her heart; no anger, no bitterness and no prayer for Mrs Manfred. She felt nothing but a cold, numb emptiness within her. And, in these past long hours, when she had lost all sense of time, Emma had come to realize that even the child inside her was still and silent.

When she and Mrs Manfred had first been incarcerated some long, endless weeks before, Emma had made several pleas that both her own and Mrs Manfred's plight should be brought to her uncle, Caleb Crowther's, personal attention. When the reply came back that Caleb Crowther and his family no longer considered Emma Denton to be in any way related to them, nor did they intend to intervene on behalf of either of the two unfortunates who had so callously caused the untimely death of another, Emma's heart had bled more for the child and Mrs Manfred than for herself. Now, there was nothing. She wasn't even fearful of the unknown journey which awaited her and, may God forgive her, she also appeared to be losing her faith. Her comforting belief in the good Lord had sustained her throughout, but now, because some deep, awful instinct told her that the small, helpless life within her was fast fading, so too was her faith. Emma had always possessed both the strength and compassion to forgive her enemies, but, if that tiny life created by her and Marlow was to be cruelly wasted, then how could she find it in her heart to forgive such a thing?

Now, Emma's thoughts were overturned as the other prisoners began to make a racket at the approach of a particularly formidable female warden. 'Watch out, 'ere it comes!' said one in a loud whisper. 'Aye,' rejoined another, ''appen the bugger's come ter march us *all* ter the gallows!'

'Enough of that, you lot!' rapped the officer as she thrust the great key into the lock. 'Back away from the door, I tell you . . . unless you want swilling down like the pigs you are!' As a second warden, a great hulk of a man, stood by with a bucket of ice-cold water, the first one beckoned to Emma, calling out her surname and instructing, 'Get out here. There's someone wants to see you!'

Astonished that she should be the one singled out, Emma threaded her way forward through those around her. When, harshly, she was pulled through the door to face the warden, it was to be told, 'Your partner in crime has been given permission to say her goodbyes.' She reached out a stiff arm and propelled Emma along the corridor, adding, 'If it was up to me, she'd not have her way, I can tell you. But this new governor's not yet had time to toughen up. He's too gullible by half, but he'll learn soon enough if I know anything!' Emma hoped not, for in a place such as this it surely wasn't a bad thing for the governor to show a measure of compassion. As for herself, some little corner of her being had lighted up with the thought that she was being taken to see her beloved friend. Maybe God was listening after all.

When the door to the cell was opened and Emma saw that dear, familiar face watching for her to appear, she was unable to put one foot before the other. Even when Mrs Manfred called out her name she stood rooted to the spot. Of a sudden, she felt engulfed by such pain and emotion that all she could do was to gaze at the older woman, tears tumbling down her face and her arms reaching out towards her.

'Oh, my darling child!' Suddenly they were in each other's embrace, clinging tightly to each other, and so filled with emotion that neither could speak. Presently, Emma felt herself being gently held out at arm's length, while Mrs Manfred gazed at her with great concern. 'Oh, child, look at you,' she murmured, the shock at seeing Emma so emaciated evident on her face. 'Why, you're nothing but skin and bone!'

'I'm fine, Manny,' Emma protested, not having seen the sorry spectacle she now presented and caring even less. 'But *you*, oh, Manny, I'm so afraid for you. And it's all my fault . . . if only I hadn't asked you to stay that night.' Emma thought that if she was given the grace to live a lifetime, she could never forgive herself for what Mrs Manfred must be going through.

'You must not blame yourself, my darling, for you have brought me nothing but joy in all the time I've known you.' When Emma looked up to see those generous, round eyes looking so softly at her, she was amazed at the peace and beauty there. There were tears also, but they were not self-pitying tears, nor were they tears of anger or bitterness. As those bright, friendly eyes roved over her, Emma felt ashamed.

'I'm not afraid, child,' Mrs Manfred said tenderly, thinking how if she *was* afraid, then it was for Emma and not for herself, because in all honesty she had come to accept the blame for Mr Denton's death. She looked long and softly at Emma's ragged countenance and her old heart was moved by it. Though heavy with child, Emma was painfully thin – her cheekbones jutting out from that small, pixie face and those expressive grey eyes deep and large with the pain she had endured. The dress on her back was nothing like the fine gown she had been wearing when they had escorted her from Montague Street; it had been replaced by a plain, ill-fitting brown dress with scooped neck, loose sleeves and limp skirt which was torn and dishevelled at the hem. Oh, there was nothing so despicable as those who took advantage of their authority to strip away anything of value which was the property of those left helplessly in their charge. However, the boots which peeped from beneath were Emma's own, which unknown to anyone but Emma, still carried her mama's tiny and precious watch secreted within the ankle-lining. But the biggest shock of all was seeing how Emma's long, magnificent chestnut hair had been savaged from her head, the remnants of which were left at various jagged and unruly lengths.

When Emma was asked, 'Will you pray with me, child?' she had to ask herself how could she possibly do such a thing when, in her heart, she had already begun to reject the very idea that there was a God. As a child and throughout her youth, Emma had been taught to love, respect and fear that special, magnanimous idol who watched over all those lesser creatures below. Now, when his help and mercy was sorely needed, where was he? How could she pray to a God who would let the child die within her and who would allow the innocent life of Mrs Manfred to be taken also?

'Please, child.' The older woman had sensed the struggle going on in Emma's mind and meant to resolve it in the right way. 'I need you to pray with me.'

As they knelt down together, to join their voices in quiet prayer, Emma felt her spirit returning and her heart growing stronger. Once more, a kind of comfort crept in to give her hope and when, as she embraced Manny in a final farewell, she was astonished to feel the child within her surge and struggle, Emma asked forgiveness for the doubts which had torn her in two.

Emma listened attentively as Mrs Manfred quietly advised her, 'When you get to those far-off shores, don't be afraid. Be careful not to antagonize those who hold the key to your freedom. Work hard, keep your mind busy and the years will swiftly pass. When the day comes that your life is returned to you, use it well. Cherish it, and never forget the things you were taught. Will you promise me that, child?' she asked now and, before she was returned to her own cell, Emma gave the promise with all her heart. It grieved her to learn how even Manny's only relative, her sister in Luton, had turned her back when she had been most needed. But Emma was greatly moved by the courage Mrs Manfred had shown in the shadow of the gallows. Both touched and shamed by it, she had cried, 'I'll never forget you,' as she wept in Mrs Manfred's comforting arms. Nor would she. For Manny had come to be a part of her that she would carry forever.

* * *

In the silent early hours of the morning, Emma got up from her crouched position on the floor to tiptoe over towards the metal grill which sliced the growing daylight into grotesque shadows on the wall. Through the window she could hear the soft thud of hurrying footsteps outside, yet she could see nothing, for the window was too high.

''Ere, climb aback o' me, darlin'.' The whisper bathed Emma's ear, and the touch of a hand on her shoulder was a gentle one. Emma recognized the girl as Nelly, a Cockney waif not much younger than herself. Since being made an orphan by tuberculosis which had taken most of her family, she had wandered from her East London beginnings to tramp the length and breadth of England in search of a better life. Circumstances had driven her to stealing, which in turn had landed her with the same fate as Emma. Together they were banished from the shores of their beloved and familiar homeland, to set sail under guard for some distant and unknown destination. Yet both were strong of heart and they had found a small measure of consolation in each other.

Emma had liked Nelly on first sight. She smiled warmly as she looked on that rather large and coarse face, the features of which seemed peculiarly exaggerated – the nose was too spread across, the chin jutted out a shade too much and the dark eyes were so round and large that they seemed almost bulbous as they stared fondly at Emma. Yet, for all this, there was an aura of such warmth and compassion about her as appeared almost beautiful, and to Emma, Nelly had become a shining example of great fortitude. In turn, with her stalwart and quiet strength of character, Emma gave Nelly a great deal of hope and comfort. In the short time since they had been thrown together, these two young women had forged a friendship which, in the years to follow, would help them to face many terrible adversities.

'Bless you, Nelly, I can't use you in that way.' Emma smiled affectionately at Nelly's suggestion. When Emma considered how undernourished and weak Nelly was, and she so heavy with child, the very idea of doing what Nelly instructed was unthinkable. Yet, it was a wonderful gesture and Emma was deeply grateful. She gazed fondly at those large ungainly features, noticing how the girl's blue dress was so tattered that she had been allowed to keep it; even the plain brown shoes on her feet had lost their laces somewhere along the way; and the dingy brown scarf knotted at her throat was riddled with tiny round holes, as though the moths or lice had found it to be a tasteful feast.

When, with a plea in her voice, Nelly protested, 'It's all right, Emma, you'll be light as a feather and I've a broad enough back to lift you up to the window,' Emma reached out a hand to stroke the girl's untidy brown hair and gently laughed when it sprang back up again as if it had a mind of its own.

'Happen there are things going on outside that window that neither of us ought to see,' she told her quietly, whereupon one of the louder, bolder women nearby, offered her own opinion.

'That's right enough, young 'un,' she said, 'gallows ain't a pretty sight – not for us to see an' even worse for them as is set upon it! Keep yer head down an' thank yer lucky stars it ain't you as is walking up them wooden stairs this morning!' Suddenly there was a loud, excited roar from some way off. 'They've seen their first sight of her!' the woman called out.

'The crowd's on their feet!' At this, every other prisoner in the cell got to their feet, a look of fearful anticipation on each one's face and an ear cocked so as not to miss a sound.

Making the sign of the cross, Emma sank to the ground where she sat small and still against the cold damp wall, a fervent prayer issuing from her lips in a whisper. 'Forgive me Lord, if I've doubted you, but Manny is so good, and her punishment shamefully unjust. Please, Lord, help her now and take her innocent soul to your arms.' Emma pictured her beloved friend in the smallest, most familiar detail. She recalled being comforted by that darling woman; she remembered her unceasing kindness and her steadfast love; she thought about the wise and wonderful words which dear Mrs Manfred had often spoken to her; and her heart ached with both regret and bitterness at the way in which the life of such a wonderful woman had to end.

'I'm afeared, Emma, gal,' said Nelly, coming to sit beside her, 'afeared that the buggers can string a body up so easily!'

'You mustn't be afraid, Nelly,' Emma told her, reaching out an arm and drawing the trembling girl towards her. 'Manny isn't afraid, and we must learn from her example.' However, when the crowd outside fell ominously silent, Emma also began to tremble; and when a great, tumultuous roar erupted, followed by loud, hearty clapping, she clung to the other girl for reassurance with the same desperate fear as that frightened creature clung to her. Manny's ordeal is over, thought Emma, while mine is only just beginning. Suddenly, the child inside her grew restless, thrashing and protesting at being so long incarcerated. 'Be patient, little one,' Emma reassured it, but thinking how she felt equally desperate. The idea of attempting to escape had crossed her mind more than once, but Emma knew the futility of that because, even if the officers' vigilance was relaxed somewhere along the way, she was so heavy with child that before she'd gone half a dozen steps, they'd be on her. Furthermore, it was likely she'd be severely flogged and further restricted for her pains. Yet it filled Emma with despair to think how her unborn child would simply be swapping one prison for another.

After a day of acute discomfort and cold, when the prisoners were roughly disturbed several times for one reason or another, Emma found herself being roused from a restless sleep in the still-dark early hours.

'Come on you lot! The waggon's arrived!' yelled the voice of an officer, as he threw open the cell door. 'File out one at a time, and don't get clever, 'cause we're ready for any o' your tricks!' He waved his cat-o'-nine-tails in the air, his face suffused with pleasure at the thought of laying it across some of their backs.

Emma followed the others, shuffling out with Nelly ever close by her side. Already made uncomfortable with her every bone aching from the cramp and cold, Emma prayed that the child inside her might be still for a while, for it seemed unusually agitated and the spasms of pain in her abdomen had become increasingly difficult to bear without crying out. Emma's anxiety must have shown on her face because, in the lowest and most urgent whisper, Nelly's voice sounded in her ear. 'Hold on, darlin' – it ain't the right time yet.'

But however desperately Emma tried to contain the upheaval taking place inside her, nature dictated that the child was ready to be born. Outside by the main gate, as Emma and Nelly were pushed towards the cage-topped waggon where a number of prisoners, whose journey had begun some time before, were already squashed inside, Emma felt her ankle being roughly grasped and shackled to Nelly by means of a heavy iron. It was as they were then propelled forward that Emma was racked with such a searing pain that it brought her to the cobbled ground and, try as she might, she could not find the strength to pull herself up again.

'On your feet!' With the officer's cry came the sting of leather across Emma's unprotected shoulders.

'Leave her be – *please*. Don't be so bleedin' heartless!' pleaded Nelly as he raised his arm again. 'She's giving birth, can't you see that?' Whereupon there came a volley of protest from the rest of the prisoners. After safely and swiftly securing the others inside the waggon, the older of the two officers stepped forward to look down on Emma's small, writhing figure. 'You!' he addressed Nelly, who was still held fast to Emma by the shackles on their ankles. 'Do you know what to do?'

'Yes!' lied Nelly, anxious that she and Emma should not be separated.

'Get on with it, then! We've a long way to go and a ship to board! A few minutes, that's all – then you'll both be flung in the waggon to do the best you can along the journey!'

Some twenty minutes later, the still-dark air was rent with Nelly's jubilant cry of 'It's a girl!' A cheer promptly went up from those in the waggon. 'Oh, Emma! She's beautiful!' Nelly said, as she followed the procedure which she'd seen her own mother follow after giving birth to a lusty-lunged boy. That babe had yelled the minute it appeared and Nelly was concerned when Emma's newborn made neither sound nor movement.

Numb with cold and weakened by loss of blood, Emma held out her arms to take the child which Nelly had wrapped in a piece of muslin torn from her own petticoat. When she saw the rich dark hair that was the very same as Marlow's, a warm happiness spread though Emma's heart and, holding the small bundle close to her breast, she cried bitter-sweet tears and gave thanks that the child had been delivered. 'Oh Nelly, she's got the look of Marlow.' Emma was half-laughing, half-crying as she ran her finger along the small, still face. But, suddenly, her deeper instincts were aroused as she realized how still the child was and that it had not yet cried out.

'Come on! We've lingered too long! In the waggon with you!' The officer had come to the end of his patience.

But Emma took no notice of his gruff instruction. Instead she asked the other girl in a fearful tone, 'Why isn't she moving, Nelly? Why won't she cry?' When, leaning forward, Nelly examined the child and, seeing the worst, murmured, 'I'm sorry, Emma. It was too much of an ordeal for the little 'un,' Emma's heart froze inside her. 'No!' she protested, hugging the small bundle tighter and pushing Nelly away. 'Leave me be! My baby's all right, I tell you!' Fearing that the shock would be too much for Emma in the face of what she had already endured, Nelly looked appealingly at the waiting officer, shaking her head and drawing his attention to the child in Emma's arms.

'No, I tell you!' Emma had caught the look which passed between them and she clung desperately to the defenceless infant that was hers and Marlow's, all the while fighting off the weakness which threatened to rob her of her senses.

'In the waggon, the pair of you! The brat's dead as ever

I've seen. Leave it!' ordered the officer, the compassion which Nelly had hoped to see never materializing.

Afraid that he might snatch the child from her arms, Emma began struggling to get up and when Nelly gave a helping hand, she took it gratefully. Yet, neither were prepared when the officer lost patience altogether, raised his leg, put his booted foot square on Emma's back and sent her sprawling towards the waggon, with Nelly stumbling also and the child rolling from Emma's arms across the cobbles and into the gutter, where it came to rest, silent and still.

Struggling to get to her feet, yet not having the strength left in her, Emma's frantic cries echoed into the darkness. Quickly, Nelly half-pushed, half-carried her into the waggon, both of them urged on by the prisoners there who, despite their renowned hardness of heart, were deeply moved by Emma's plight. But, being streetwise and familiar with the rudiments of self-survival, each and every one knew, as did Nelly, that the sooner Emma was whisked away from that poor lifeless little creature, the sooner she would mend.

Of a sudden, the cage doors were slammed shut and bolted. Both officers clambered up next to the driver, one of them cracking a horse-whip into the air above the geldings and causing them to jerk forward. 'Move away, man!' he instructed the driver. 'Move away!'

Behind him, the prisoners fell quiet, Nelly softly cried and Emma's haunted eyes remained transfixed on the spot where that tragic little bundle lay, until, like her, it became engulfed by the darkness.

As the waggon trundled away, only Nelly saw the shadow as it appeared beneath the solitary gas-lamp at the prison gates. The stooped, beshawled figure came out of nowhere, creeping along on unsteady legs made even more unsteady by the small limp which caused it to dip in a peculiar manner. At its heels was a great, thick-set and fearsome-looking dog that ran ahead and began sniffing Emma's blood which still bathed the child. The shawled figure called out to the dog and hurried to the spot where it began pawing the ground. Then, as the waggon lurched its way round the bend in the cobbled road, the pair were lost to sight – but not before Nelly heard a sound to make her ears prick. There was no mistaking that thin, distant wail which only a newborn could make – that demanding, persistent cry which seemed to tell the world, 'I was warm and now I'm cold. I was safe and now I'm afraid.'

Of a sudden, Emma was stirring, for she had also heard something. 'My baby!' she cried, pulling herself round so that she could see behind. But the streets were dark and strange and she saw nothing to console her.

As she gazed at Emma's weak and sorry countenance, Nelly was afraid that her new-found friend would be taken from her all too soon. 'No, Emma,' she said in a comforting voice. 'Your baby is gone. You must think of yourself now, darlin'.' She made no mention of what she'd heard, nor did she give Emma the smallest hope that her daughter might be alive. To do such a thing would only make the hard years to come that much longer and more difficult to bear. It was better for Emma to go on thinking the child had gone forever, because what she didn't know couldn't cause her any pain.

Emma felt herself raised to a sitting position as Nelly's strong arms cradled her close. But Emma could not be consoled and, despite her strong character and normally resilient nature, in her aching heart she cared not whether she lived or died.

'Well, I'm buggered! What we got 'ere then, Jake, eh?' Sal Tanner peered down through bloodshot eyes acquired from a night of revelry following the occasion of a hanging; and bending closer to see what it was that the dog was frantically licking, she suddenly sprang back, startled by the piercing cry which even took the dog unawares. 'It's a young 'un!' she cried, kicking the excited animal aside and stooping nearer to take another look. 'It bloody well is, Jake,' she said in an astonished voice, 'it *is* a young 'un!' She looked furtively about, sensing it might be a trap of some kind – a temptation put there as an excuse to clap her in irons. When she saw nothing to alarm her, she bent to pick the infant up, saying in a softer tone, 'Who d'yer belong to, eh? What in God's name are yer doing lying in the street in the cold, eh?' As she drew the muslin cloth round the tiny thrashing child, her foot kicked the boot which Emma had lost in her struggles and the tiny bright silver watch that had been secreted there spilled out, its dainty facets sparkling in the light from the street lamp.

'What's this, eh?' Holding the child securely in one arm, Sal reached down with the other and picked up the watch. 'Well, I'm buggered!' she cackled. 'It's a time-piece – an' worth a bob or two, I'll be bound!' Turning it over and over in her fingers, she was surprised when the back sprang open to reveal something tucked inside. At once, she crossed to the street lamp and, standing in the yellow stuttering light, she juggled with the bundle in her arms so that she could dip a finger and thumb into the small cavity of the watch. When its contents were laid reverently in the palm of her hand, she was at once struck by the four-leaf clover, so lovingly put there by Emma and now shining a brighter green in the garish circle of light from above. 'By! See that?' Sal asked the dog, who was busy sniffing and licking at the child's muslin shawl. 'D'yer see how bright an' green it shines, eh? Now that's a sure sign if ever I saw one.' She now looked from the clover to the fretful child and back again. ''Tis the *little people* as belongs this bairn! Oho! . . . I 'ad half a mind ter leave the wretched bundle where I found it, for I don't know what to do wi' no infant, do I, eh? What do ol' Sal Tanner know of fotching up an infant, eh?' She gazed once again at the rich green colour of the four-leaf clover and then, with round, fascinated eyes, she examined the dark hair and pleasing face of Emma and Marlow's child, indeed her own kith and kin if only she'd known it. 'Yer a pretty little thing an' all,' she said in a gentle voice, 'but what sort are yer, eh?' Here she peeked into the muslin shawl. 'A lass! It's a little lass,' she told the dog, 'sent to me by the little people, to watch o'er.' Raising her face to the dark sky above, she said more loudly, 'I'll do me duty, yer can depend on that. Ol' Sal won't let yer down.' As she reverently returned the clover to its place, the tiny lock of hair which had been with it was taken by a small gust of wind. Sal paid it no mind, for she was concerned only that the infant and the clover were safe. 'C'mon, Jake,' she told the dog, 'this little lass is 'ungry. There ain't nothing in *my* withered old tits ter satisfy it . . . so we'll mek our way back ter Blackburn and Derwent Street. Hildy Barker's not long lost a young 'un, and there'll 'appen be enough milk there ter keep this bundle thrivin' eh? That's if it can keep breathin' long enough to mek the journey back!'

Sal Tanner made a strange but agreeable sight as she moved away up the street, her small limp causing her now and then to give a little skip, the child still crying in her arms, the great bull-mastiff lolloping along beside her, and she holding a long, detailed conversation with the 'little people'. But, strange sight though it was, how it would have gladdened Emma's heart to have seen it.

# Chapter Twelve

On the fourth day of January 1863, Emma was disembarked, along with some two hundred and fifty other prisoners, at the mouth of the Swan River in the port of Fremantle, Western Australia – some thousands of miles and vast oceans between her and her beloved homeland. It was the first time the prisoners had set foot on land since boarding the ship in England; during the short stopover in Singapore they had been confined below decks. Now, the sun was so brilliant it was blinding, and the heat so intense that it sapped what little strength they had left. But, after the dark, cramped conditions they had endured the air smelled fresh and sweet and the big, open landscape gave a strange sense of freedom.

The long and arduous sea voyage was over. For Emma, it had been a terrifying experience, every detail of which would remain with her forever – from that first moment when she had seen the towering ship rising out of the murky waters in Langston Harbour, England, to this equally daunting moment as they were filed out like cattle, creating a dishevelled spectacle for those curious few who had come to watch, those whose duty it was to contain them and the privileged few who were given first choice of convict labour.

'Keep your fingers crossed that we'll be kept together,' Emma now told the girl by her side. For as long as she lived, Emma would never forget what a true and steadfast friend Nelly had been. During those first few weeks of their journey, when Emma had lain close to death's door, Nelly had never been far away. Emma remembered another who had also shown kindness and concern when she had been at her lowest ebb. She had been both embarrassed and relieved to find the voyage was being made in Silas Trent's vessel, and he was on board. He had persuaded the captain to allow Emma the company and support of her friend, Nelly, when she needed it most; and when Emma was eventually discharged from the sick-bay, he kept a constant eye on their well-being, though he was more careful not to show undue favouritism lest it should alienate Emma and her friend from the other prisoners.

The daily routine was the same for all. The cooks were usually the very first prisoners to show themselves, usually at the early hour of five-thirty. While they were up-top preparing the first rations of the day, the prisoners below deck would stow away their hammocks before washing. Then came the surgeon's sick round, followed by the issue of the daily ration of water and biscuits. At eight a.m. breakfast was served, usually consisting of a basin of gruel, a mug of cocoa and a few ounces of biscuits; at noon, dinner comprised of soup, salt beef or pork and a further helping of biscuits; at about five-thirty p.m., half a pint of tea and four ounces of biscuit were provided for supper. Each prisoner was allowed three quarts of water daily. There were religious services and assembly of school if needed. At eight o'clock the prisoners were sent back down below to the forward of the bulkhead, where space was severely limited and the air

rank and stale. Prisoners' berths were ranged in two con-
tinuous rows, above and below, against the hull, with a
walkway down the centre.

For Emma this was the worst time of all. The air was
stifling with so many bodies crammed in such a confined
space, and there was the constant, dreadful fear that any
minute they would all suffocate for want of air. Yet, if the
night brought its nightmares, so too did the long, trying hours
of the day. Security was formidable, with hatchways enclosed
by stout iron bars and barricades across the entire width of
the ship on deck, behind the main mast. A guard of grim-
faced soldiers with guns ready remained wary night and day;
loaded cannons were aimed forward, with other equally
fearsome weapons kept close by. A sight to sober not only
the prisoners, but all present on the voyage.

Severe punishments were inflicted for various crimes on
board. Emma remembered one in particular with great horror,
when a woman prisoner – known to be a 'seasoned lag' by
many of the others – was caught stealing another prisoner's
ration. For her troubles, she was dragged away screaming, to
be incarcerated in what was referred to as the 'Black Box',
which was a dark and narrow cell erected under the forecastle.
She was kept there for eight days, after which she emerged a
broken, nervous wreck.

'They're coming, gal!' Emma was alerted back to the
present situation by Nelly's loud whisper and, looking up,
she saw two grim-faced men approaching, with an armed
soldier either side and the figure of Silas Trent to their left.
Some short way behind them was another group of people –
one of which was a surly-faced woman of authoritative
bearing.

As Emma kept her eyes on the approaching party, they drew to a halt at the beginning of the line of prisoners, with quiet consultations taking place between the soldier in charge and various members of the civilian group. Much pointing and nodding of heads followed, before the one in charge was approached by Silas Trent.

Having taken off his hat some minutes earlier, he now smartly replaced it as, concluding his furtive discussion with the soldier in charge – during which Emma could have sworn she saw money changing hands between himself and the soldier – he now beckoned to two men to accompany himself and the man in charge. Together, all four came down the line at a fast, purposeful pace, coming to a halt directly opposite Emma. So shaken by it was Nelly, that she took an involuntary step backward, until Emma looked encouragingly at her, so that with a shameful face, she came back into line to stand shoulder to shoulder with Emma.

'Emma Denton?' the soldier in charge addressed her, continuing when she answered affirmatively, 'Your services have been assigned. Mr Trent here will explain the formalities and due procedure, after which you'll report to the authorities at the dock exit.'

When Emma appeared unsure as to what all this meant, Silas Trent smiled at her, saying in a reassuring voice, 'You've been assigned well, Emma . . . to assist at the trading post. They're good people and you won't be ill-treated.'

'And Nelly?' Emma was concerned that Nelly should be equally 'well assigned'.

After a moment's hesitation, Silas Trent gave the soldier in charge a sly look. 'I'm sure there's work enough at the trading post for both of them, wouldn't you say?' he asked, surreptitiously fingering his coat above the pocket where his wallet was kept.

'All right by me,' agreed the soldier, immediately casting his eyes towards the other two men – the older of whom was near fifty, round and jolly looking, while the younger one, with his blue eyes and unruly fair hair seemed to Emma to be of a decidedly arrogant disposition.

Both men nodded in agreement, the older one knowing he would be paid well – and anyway *two* healthy young girls would take the weight of the more laborious tasks off his back, what with his wife having fallen to bad health lately – and the other, Foster Thomas – Roland Thomas's son – in favour of having two healthy young girls about but for very different reasons! Life had become somewhat tedious of late and handsome girls the like of that one called Emma Denton were few and far between.

As Emma was led away, she gave thanks for people such as her friend, Nelly, and the caring Silas Trent, who had promised not to discuss her fate with Martha. Yet, even with what would appear to be a fair start in this strange and awesome new land, she wondered what might become of her. Through her mind raged distorted and painful images of all that had gone before, the loss of all those who were most precious – first Marlow, then Mrs Manfred, and finally hers and Marlow's precious little daughter.

No matter how desperately Emma tried to put these unbearable memories behind her, she could not. How could she ever forget that wonderful night when she and Marlow had lain in each other's arms? How could she not dream of his laughing black eyes, whose cherished gaze echoed the love in her own heart? Where was Marlow now, she thought. Where was he? And the babe? Oh, dear God, how often had she thought of that dear little creature, whose colouring was so like Marlow's and whose delicate life was so mercilessly denied?

Emma thought the world to be a cold, cruel place. Who could blame her, she wondered, for keeping those treasured memories alive if it meant her heart was warmed and revived? Of a sudden, she recalled Mrs Manfred's last words to her: 'When you get to those far-off shores, Emma, don't be afraid. Be careful not to antagonize those who would hold the key to your freedom. Work hard, keep your mind busy and the years will swiftly pass. When the day comes that your life is returned to you, use it well, Emma. Cherish it, and never forget the things you were taught. Will you promise me that, Emma?'

Under her breath, Emma murmured, 'I promise, Manny . . . with all my heart.' And as she gave this final promise to her dear friend, she made another one to herself. Her day of freedom *would* come and when it did, she would make every endeavour to return to the land of her birth. For there, she had old scores to settle, and an undying love to salvage. If only the Lord would keep her safe until then.

'I'm buggered if we ain't landed on us feet!' came Nelly's excited whisper. 'We've been placed well, and we've got each other. Oh, Emma gal! I reckon we're gonna be all right after all!'

As Emma smiled at her and took her hand to squeeze it in a gesture of friendship, she made the comment, 'We *will* be all right, Nelly. Take heart. Something tells me the good Lord will watch out for us after all.'